What Happened That Night

Sheila O'Flanagan

What Happened That Night

REVIEW

First published in Great Britain in 2017
by HEADLINE REVIEW
An imprint of HEADLINE PUBLISHING GROUP

1

Cataloguing in Publication Data is available from the British Library

ISBN 978 1 4722 3534 3 (Hardback)
ISBN 978 1 4722 3533 6 (Trade Paperback)

Typeset in ITC Galliard Std by Palimpsest Book Production Limited,
Falkirk, Stirlingshire

Printed and bound in Great Britain by Clays Ltd, St Ives plc

Headline's policy is to use papers that are natural, renewable and recyclable products
and made from wood grown in well-managed forests and other controlled sources.
The logging and manufacturing processes are expected to conform to the
environmental regulations of the country of origin.

HEADLINE PUBLISHING GROUP
An Hachette UK Company
Carmelite House
50 Victoria Embankment
London EC4Y 0DZ

www.headline.co.uk
www.hachette.co.uk

In memory of Carole Blake (1946–2016), lover of books, shoes and big jewellery, who took me on as a client and changed my life for ever.

Bey
Now

From her position behind the stage of the reception room, Bey Fitzpatrick could see but not be seen. She was hidden from view by the silk banners that had been erected earlier that day, while the careful placing of the lights around the room meant that she was standing in a pool of shadow. As the hum of conversation increased, her attention was fixed on the women in their colourful dresses and sparkling jewellery. Like vibrant birds of paradise, they laughed and chattered as they accepted canapés and glasses of champagne from silver trays borne by expert servers. Bey had a sudden recollection that it was the male birds of paradise who possessed the colourful plumage, not the females. But tonight the women shone and glittered while the men played second fiddle in their tuxedos and white shirts.

The background music was lost in the hubbub of voices and bursts of excited laughter. The guests were eagerly anticipating the launch of the exclusive Ice Dragon jewellery collection, which would be unveiled later in the evening. It included three unique necklaces made from white gold and set with diamonds as well as either rubies, sapphires or emeralds. Each necklace cost a six-figure sum. And each one, Bey knew, was truly exceptional, a piece that anyone would treasure.

She felt a flutter of anxiety as she scanned the crowd. She recognised some faces from the gossip pages of magazines or newspapers. There were a number of TV personalities. A famous singer. A prominent politician. And lots of business people. Every person in the room had been invited because they had already bought top-of-the-range jewellery from Warren's, the jewellery store. Not all of them could afford an Ice Dragon necklace, but each guest was flattered to have received an invitation to the launch. The atmosphere was filled with happy anticipation.

It's a make-believe world. The memory of his words echoed in her ears. *We only ever see people when they're rich and happy.*

He'd laughed, and so had she.

It had been a lifetime ago.

When things were different.

When she hadn't known half the things she knew now.

She shivered even though the room was warm. She was standing near the mullioned window and she could suddenly feel the chill of the night air through the clear glass. She glanced outside and caught her breath. Huge snowflakes were falling lazily from the heavy sky, turning the garden outside the ancient listed building into a carpet of white. The flakes landed on the window in a lattice of interlocking crystals that glittered as brightly as the diamonds inside the room.

There was a spider's web at the corner of the window pane, silvery white beneath the feather-light snow. She felt her mind shift into another time and place as she remembered a different night of snow and ice twenty years earlier, and a different spider's web. She remembered how she'd stared at it, willing it to stay unbroken, telling herself that she wouldn't be caught if it remained intact. She was suddenly there again, terrified to move, hoping that the mist of her breath wouldn't give her away, or that the beating of her heart couldn't be heard in the stillness of the night.

She felt the hand on her shoulder and she almost screamed out loud.

Then the lights went out.

Lola
Then

Chapter 1

Diamond: a transparent, extremely hard, precious stone

Lola Fitzpatrick always had a choice to make on Friday after-noons: to stay for the weekend in the flat she shared with three other girls in Dublin, or to spend the days at the family farm instead. Left to her own devices, the choice was simple. Dublin was far more exciting and vibrant than a weekend at the farm could ever be, and at least one of her flatmates was sure to be around and ready to socialise. On the other hand, Cloghdrom was home. But returning there was like taking a step back in time. Socialising was limited to drinks in one of the local pubs (excluding McCloskey's, which was only ever frequented by elderly farmers), or enduring what was still called a 'hop' at the GAA clubhouse – scratched records played beneath a disco ball by Baz Hogan, who fancied himself as a DJ. From Lola's point of view, Cloghdrom hadn't even made it out of the 1950s, let alone reached the 80s; the general assumption of the inhabitants was that their sons would inherit the farm while their daughters would marry other farmers.

'It's like *Pride and Prejudice* without the gorgeousness of

Pemberley,' she complained to her older sister Gretta. 'The men get the assets and we wait to be married off.'

Gretta laughed at her mutinous tones and told her that marrying a local lad wasn't the worst thing that could happen. She had to say that, Lola would reply; hadn't she been engaged to Mossy McCloskey (eldest son of the pub owner) practically since the day she'd left school? Which was fine for Gretta, who loved being part of the community and who never wanted to leave. Fine, too, for their older brother Milo, who was already married and working on the farm. But not fine for her, the youngest daughter, whose ambitions were very different, despite the fact that she could break a man's heart with a single glance from her vivid blue eyes and a toss of her luxurious dark hair.

Getting the job at the Passport Office in Dublin and moving into a flat with three other girls had been the start of a life that didn't depend on the weather and milk quotas and the happiness of the herd. It was a life where her opinion mattered, and having a drink with someone of the opposite sex didn't have everyone talking about their upcoming nuptials five minutes later. She hated having to interrupt it to go back to the old one, no matter that she did sometimes miss her family and the constant aroma of her mother's home-made bread wafting around the kitchen.

She was thinking about Eilis's home-made bread as she walked down Grafton Street during her lunch hour that warm Friday afternoon. She knew there was very little food in the flat – shopping was done on a need-to-get basis, and most times the girls raided the kitty and nipped out to the Spar around the corner for essentials. Lola herself had eaten out every night that week, although that was giving it a gloss it didn't deserve, she acknowledged; most times she'd just gone for pizza after a few drinks with the people from work. But she liked making plans at the last minute and having the kind of options that living in a city offered, even if she was pretty much broke after every weekend.

If nothing else, going home would save her a few bob and she could afford the dress she'd seen in Dunnes earlier, she mused as she strolled along Duke Lane. Though not being able to afford a dress in an inexpensive chain store said a lot about her current financial state. She knew she needed to cut back a little. She knew she was living beyond her means. But it was hard not to when her salary was basic and opportunities for fun were constantly knocking on her door. It would be different when she got promoted. She'd have money to spare then. Meantime, she was keeping her fingers crossed that her application for the next grade up in the Civil Service would be successful. Despite her love of late nights, she was a conscientious worker, and she felt she deserved her promotion. She'd been a clerical officer in the Passport Office for nearly four years. It was about time she started moving up the career ladder.

She stopped suddenly, her thoughts interrupted as her attention was caught by the sparkling diamonds in the window of Warren's the Jewellers. Warren's was an iconic store in Dublin and Lola knew a little of its history. It had been founded in the 1950s by Richard Warren, a watchmaker who realised that Dubliners wanted more than just utilitarian timepieces. He'd expanded to include jewellery that wasn't generally available in the city at the time, and established a reputation for good quality at reasonable prices. Over the years, and after his marriage to a Northern Irish beauty named

Adele Pendleton, the store had gone increasingly upmarket, until it relocated from its original premises near O'Connell Street to the current shop off Dublin's most exclusive shopping street. Although Warren's carried a variety of jewellery, it was most famous for the Adele collections, each named for a flower as well as for the founder's wife.

Lola gazed at the glitter of the all-diamond Snowdrops and wondered if she'd ever be able to afford anything as remotely beautiful as an Adele piece. Even in Cloghdrom they'd heard of Warren's – Betty Munroe, the wife of the creamery owner, had an entire Adele Rose set, which she wore to the farm festival every year. 'The money's in processing, not producing,' Lola had heard her father mutter to her mother during the last festival she'd gone to. 'I can't afford to buy anything like that for you.'

His words had stuck in Lola's mind and had influenced her decision to move to Dublin. She wanted to be the woman who owned beautiful jewellery, not the woman who stared at it from afar. And she wanted to be the woman who could buy it for herself, not someone who had to rely on a boyfriend or husband to give it to her. Every so often she would deliberately walk past Warren's so that she could look in the window and remind herself why she was here. To make money. To be a success. To prove that a woman didn't have to be married to have a good life. To be herself.

'Why don't you try it on?'

She jumped as she heard the voice behind her. A man had approached the shop from the other end of the lane and was now standing at the recessed doorway. He was tall, tanned and fair haired, and his electric-blue eyes were filled with humour.

'It would be lovely,' she said, 'but a waste of time. There isn't a hope in hell I could ever afford it.'

'No charge for trying, though,' he said.

'I doubt the owners would be happy with people loading themselves up with their jewellery just for the fun of it.'

'I'm sure the owners would be delighted to see one of their creations on someone as beautiful as you.'

Lola looked at him in surprise. No man had ever complimented her in quite that way before. The nearest a man in Cloghdrom had come to acknowledging her looks was to tell her she was a bit of all right. As for Dublin, most of the so-called compliments she'd received in the last few years centred around wondering if she was as good in bed as she looked out of it.

'Honestly,' he said. 'That set would look stunning on you.'

'It'd be false pretences.' She gave him a rueful smile. 'I'm so broke right now, a bread roll is the absolute limit of my budget.'

He laughed. 'The bread roll situation is one thing, certainly. Maybe we can deal with that separately. But the problem with fine jewellery is that often the most beautiful women can't afford it. So it's hanging around the crêpey necks of older women who can. And not that they don't look great, but they couldn't hold a candle to you.'

'All the same,' she said, still taken aback by his confident appraisal of her looks, 'I won't go in.'

'Pity. I would've liked to have seen it on you. I'm sure my dad would too.'

She looked at him in confusion.

'I'm Philip Warren,' he said.

She looked at the name above the shop before turning back to him.

'You own it?' she gasped.

'Not personally,' he clarified. 'It's our family business, but it'll be mine one day.'

'Wow,' she said.

'So it would be really cool if you came in and tried on the set.'

She hesitated.

'Take a chance?'

It was those words that decided her. She believed in taking chances. She'd said so to her parents the day she'd left Cloghdrom.

She nodded and followed him inside.

The shop was more opulent than she could have imagined. The pile of the mink-coloured carpet was so deep that she was afraid her high-heeled shoes would ruin it, and she walked cautiously after him, conscious of the indentations she was leaving in her wake. Instead of long counters, there was a polished walnut desk in one corner, in front of which were placed two chairs upholstered in purple velvet. There were three glass displays on the floor of the store, as well as others in the window.

A tall, elegant woman wearing a ruby pendant and an Adele Rose ring nodded at Philip, who smiled at her.

'Hi, Lorraine. Is Dad in the office?'

She shook her head. 'He's still at lunch with Arjan van Heerden,' she said.

'Has he bought the stones?' asked Philip.

'And how would I know that?' asked Lorraine. 'He doesn't tell me the backroom business. I'm merely the sales assistant.'

Philip laughed. 'Oh, Lorraine! You know we couldn't even open the door to the shop without you. It's a pity he isn't here,' he added. 'I wanted him to see the Snowdrop range on . . .' He turned to Lola. 'I'm so sorry. I was too dazzled by you to ask your name.'

'Lola,' she said. 'Lola Fitzpatrick.'

'I wanted Dad to see Lola modelling the Snowdrop,' he said. 'Don't you think it would look gorgeous on her?'

Lorraine looked at Lola critically, dismissing her inexpensive trousers and blouse but taking in her flawless complexion, her dark curls and her deep-blue eyes.

'Yes.' She nodded. 'It would suit her very well.'

'So let's have a look.'

'I'm not sure . . .' Lola was aching to try on the Snowdrop set, but she felt completely out of her depth.

'You'll love it,' Philip assured her.

Lorraine took the jewellery from the window display. Then she approached Lola and fastened the diamond necklace around her neck, taking time to arrange it exactly. She did the same with the bracelet on her wrist. Finally she slid the Adele Snowdrop ring onto the third finger of her right hand and stood back to admire her handiwork.

'Stunning,' said Philip.

'Amazing,' agreed Lorraine.

Lola turned to look at herself in the mirror. The girl who looked back at her was a different Lola. The flashing brilliance of the diamonds made her skin seem smoother, her hair darker, her eyes a more vibrant blue. She was the Lola Fitzpatrick she had always wanted to be. The Lola Fitzpatrick who deserved chances and who would grab those chances with both hands. She felt a wave of confidence engulf her as she moved and sparkled beneath the halogen lights.

'Didn't I tell you?' Philip looked at Lorraine in satisfaction. 'She's a Warren's girl, that's for sure.'

'You have your father's eye,' said Lorraine.

'She's the kind of girl we want buying our jewellery,' Philip said. 'Young and beautiful and . . . and modern.'

Lorraine, who was in her forties, raised one of her delicately shaped eyebrows.

'Of course you're modern too,' said Philip quickly. 'But you're different, Lorraine. You're a grown-up. Lola is . . .'

'Young,' echoed Lorraine.

'Exactly. And she's the person we want to be selling to.'

'Maybe I am.' Lola finally looked away from her reflection. 'And maybe I can be a customer one day. But right now I couldn't even afford the clasp of the necklace, let alone the whole thing.' She sighed as she slipped the ring from her finger and placed it on one of the glass displays while Lorraine undid the necklace and bracelet. 'Thank you for letting me try them on. It was amazing. But I'd better be going.'

'You can't rush away,' said Philip. 'We haven't discussed your bread roll yet.'

'I'm due back at work.' Lola looked at her watch and gave a little shriek. 'In exactly two minutes. I've got to go.' She hurried to the door and opened it.

'Wait!' called Philip. 'Where do you work? Will I see you again?'

But Lola didn't answer. She was already running up the road.

She clattered into the office and looked around anxiously for Irene, the staff officer generally known as Dot because of her complete lack of interest in any excuses for lateness and insistence that all staff were at their desks on the dot.

'She was asking for you a minute ago.' Pat Burke looked up from the passport she was working on. 'I told her you were dealing with someone from the general public.'

'Did she believe you?' Lola was still anxious.

'Of course,' said Pat.

Lola smiled. Pat was one of the clerical assistants who worked on temporary contracts with the Passport Office to cover the busy summer period. She'd started working there after the death of her husband a few years previously, and although she was still on a temporary contract, she worked eight months of the year and was far more experienced than Irene or Lola. Being older than most of the staff, Pat wasn't intimidated by Irene, and as she knew more about the running of the office than the more senior woman did, Irene relied on her whenever there were problems. Pat, who privately thought that Lola was one of the hardest-working people there, was also very supportive of her because she never tried to take advantage of her temporary status as some of the other girls sometimes did.

'Where were you?' she asked. 'You're never late.'

Lola sat down at her desk and picked up one of the passport application forms so that she'd appear busy when Irene returned. But she smiled at Pat as she related her lunchtime experience.

'Warren's!' Pat was impressed. 'I've always wanted a piece of jewellery from there. I love those Adele rings.'

'The Snowdrop was utterly gorgeous,' said Lola. 'The minute I put it on I felt like I could do anything. It was amazing.'

Pat stretched her hands out in front of her. Her significantly more modest engagement ring twinkled in the light.

'My husband always said that he'd get me one for our silver wedding anniversary,' she said. 'It would have been next year.'

'I'm sorry,' said Lola. 'I shouldn't have . . .'

'Oh, don't be.' Pat shook her head. 'He'd never have been able to afford it either. Those rings are seriously expensive.'

'I know. There were no prices.'

'So are you going to see him again?' asked Pat. 'Or was this just a business thing?'

'It was the weirdest experience of my life,' said Lola. 'And the only way I'd ever see him again is by standing outside Warren's looking hopeful. Which, quite honestly, would be a kind of creepy thing to do.' And then, as she saw Irene walking into the office, she bent her head over the application form and said no more about it.

Chapter 2

Iridescence: an optical phenomenon in which the hue of the stone changes according to the angle from which it is viewed

Philip Warren couldn't get Lola Fitzpatrick out of his head. He knew many pretty and attractive girls, but Lola was different. She hadn't been overawed by him like so many young women of his acquaintance were. Which was understandable – they all knew he was a Warren and it mattered to them. It had been refreshing to meet someone who didn't, and then to take her breath away by bringing her into the shop and insisting on her trying on the diamonds. He was annoyed at himself for not getting her number before she'd rushed away. Still, Dublin was a small city and she clearly worked nearby. He was pretty sure he'd see her again, especially now that he'd be on the lookout for her. With a bit of luck she'd stop outside the shop window and he'd get the opportunity to buy her a bread roll. And more.

The door to the office opened and his father walked in. Philip knew at once that he was in a good mood.

'Things go well with Arjan?' he asked.

Richard nodded. He opened his attaché case and took out

a brifka, an envelope containing a selection of loose diamonds, which he spilled out onto the desk in front of them.

'They're good.' Philip nodded as he picked one or two up and studied them. 'Really good.'

'I think they'll work well in the set for Mrs McBride,' said Richard.

Emily McBride was the wife of a leading industrialist, and her husband wanted something bespoke for her fiftieth birthday later in the year. David Hayes, Warren's designer, had already come up with some designs that Noel McBride approved of, so it had been a question of sourcing the appropriate stones, which Richard now hoped he'd done.

'It's going to be one of the most expensive pieces we've ever made,' he said.

'I was thinking about that,' said Philip, 'and wondering about our future lines.'

'Oh?' Richard scooped the diamonds back into the brifka.

'There was a girl in here today,' said Philip. 'She was young and gorgeous and she tried on the Snowdrop. It looked absolutely amazing on her.'

'The Snowdrop looks amazing on everyone,' said his father.

'True,' agreed Philip. 'But Lola made it come alive.'

Richard looked at him speculatively.

'So . . .?'

'So I was thinking we should be targeting young, beautiful women with our stuff,' said Philip. 'At the moment we're selling to matronly old dears who can afford sky-high prices. Or at least whose husbands can afford them. But we should be thinking of the future and women like Lola now. We should be getting them into our stores.'

'Does this girl have a rich father? Or a rich husband?'

'No,' said Philip. 'But she talked about owning an Adele piece some day. Wouldn't it be lovely if we had a range that was affordable enough for women to treat themselves sooner?'

'No, it wouldn't,' said Richard. 'We're exclusive. If everyone could afford a Warren's piece, then we wouldn't be exclusive any more. Besides, women don't buy jewellery for themselves. They get it from their husbands.'

'That's a very old-fashioned outlook.'

'It's true, though.'

'At the moment. But—'

'Are you thinking with your heart or your head?' Richard interrupted him. 'Or has this Lola person interested an entirely different part of your anatomy?'

Philip snorted but said nothing as he went to the upstairs office. All the same, he was still thinking about Lola Fitzpatrick when they shut up shop a few hours later. She was unforgettable.

Richard mentioned the conversation to Adele that evening, adding that their son's eagerness to extend their range seemed to be based on wanting the young woman who'd come into the store to be able to wear Warren jewellery.

'Who was she?' demanded Adele. 'Do we know her?'

Richard shook his head. 'I talked to Lorraine afterwards,' he said. 'Apparently she's noticed her looking in the window before.'

'Casing the joint?' Adele's eyes widened.

'I didn't mean it like that.' Richard laughed. 'Lorraine said she seemed to be an ordinary young girl. It was Philip who encouraged her to try on the jewellery.'

'He can be so idiotic at times,' said Adele.

'He'll inherit the business one day.'

'And when he does, he'll need a sensible wife beside him,' Adele said. 'Not some flibbertigibbet who could lead him down the wrong path like my own father. I suppose she was pretty.'

'Gorgeous, Lorraine said.'

Adele groaned. 'He's a sucker for a pretty face,' she said. 'And he has a habit of falling for totally unsuitable girls.'

'He usually extricates himself in the end,' remarked Richard. 'You don't have to worry that every man will do what your dad did, Adele. I haven't bankrupted the business and run off with my secretary, have I? I don't even have a secretary!'

'No.' She smiled at him. 'I chose well with you, Richard. You're a good man and I love you. But we have to look out for Philip. Peter, too. We're an established family with a successful business. We don't want money-grabbers riding on our coat-tails.'

Richard knew he could do nothing to sway Adele from her belief that young girls were always trying to seduce wealthy men in the way her father had been seduced years before. Tobias Pendleton had been the chairman of a medium-sized manufacturing company when he ran off with his secretary, a pretty woman nearly twenty years his junior. He'd siphoned money from the company accounts before his departure, and as a result the business was declared bankrupt shortly afterwards. Adele and her mother had been left virtually penniless. Lucia Pendleton had died the following year and Adele always insisted it was from a broken heart. Although she remained angry with her father, whom she never saw again, most of her ire was directed at Sophie, his secretary, who, she insisted, had thrown herself at him regardless of the fact that he was a married man.

Richard knew that she'd never lost her bitterness over it. So he simply remarked that he was sure Philip would forget about the girl in the shop quickly enough.

'Let's hope so,' said Adele. 'Because he's the future of Warren's and we can't afford for him to make a spectacular mistake.'

She wouldn't have been happy to know that Philip couldn't stop thinking about Lola, even though he hadn't seen her again since the day she'd come into the shop. He'd been totally smitten by her arresting beauty and her charming self-consciousness about trying on the Snowdrop range. He'd seen her light up when she was wearing it, the sparkle in her blue eyes matching the sparkle of the gems, and he'd decided there and then that he was going to sleep with her. And even though it was annoying that she'd run off on him, it was refreshing too. No girl had ever left him without leaving him her number before. He had to find her and he had to have her.

He was confident that he would, eventually.

After all, he was a Warren, and the Warrens always got what they wanted.

No matter what.

Chapter 3

Pearl: a hard, lustrous stone formed within the shell of a pearl oyster

'Is it the handsome man or the fabulous diamonds you're thinking of?' Lola's best friend Shirley asked the question a few days later while they were having a drink together in their local pub in Rathmines. 'You've been moony ever since you told me about him.'

Lola chuckled. 'Philip Warren is a total hunk,' she conceded, 'but it's that gorgeous necklace I can't get out of my head. Though I have to admit that a man with ready access to it might be worth getting to know. I felt like a million dollars wearing it.'

'It probably *costs* a million dollars.' Shirley grinned.

'I keep wondering how much it was all worth,' admitted Lola. 'I'm pretty sure I was wearing more than my annual salary around my neck.'

'More than both our salaries,' said Shirley. 'Being a librarian doesn't exactly put you in the diamond-buying bracket either.'

'I wonder what would've happened if I'd legged it out of

the store and down the street while I was wearing them,' said Lola.

'I doubt you'd have got past the door,' Shirley said. 'I bet they have all sorts of security.'

'I didn't see any, but I guess so,' said Lola. 'It's a totally different world, you know. The carpet, the display counters, the desk – there wasn't a cash register to be seen. I kept asking myself how people actually pay for the stuff.'

'Not with cash, obviously,' Shirley said. 'I mean, you'd hardly hand over thousands in used fivers, would you?'

Lola laughed. 'Unlike the mart.'

Shirley laughed too. Shirley's father was also a farmer in Cloghdrom, where the business of buying and selling cattle was generally conducted in cash. And, added Lola, in surroundings a million miles away from the plush carpets at Warren's.

'But seriously,' said Shirley, after they'd stopped picturing an auction of cows covered in diamonds, 'did you fancy him as well as the diamonds?'

'Oh yes,' agreed Lola. 'But I'm not in Dublin for the men, Shirley. I'm here for my career.'

'I think it's good that you have your priorities right,' Shirley said. 'All the same, marrying into Warren's could be a career move too. Certainly it's an entirely different kettle of fish to marrying a lad from Cloghdrom. It'd be like hitting the jackpot.'

'I don't see getting married to anyone as a career move,' protested Lola. 'Besides, you're jumping the gun. He didn't even ask me out.'

'Draping you in diamonds is a good sign.'

'He doesn't have my number and he doesn't know where I work,' said Lola.

'But you know exactly where *he* works,' Shirley pointed out. 'So you could be a modern, liberal woman and do the asking instead.'

'If I wanted to,' agreed Lola.

'Exactly.'

Lola smiled and didn't reply. But she couldn't help remembering how she'd looked with the Snowdrop necklace glittering around her throat.

And she liked the picture.

She went to Cloghdrom the following weekend and didn't think about Philip Warren or the Snowdrop necklace. Nor did she think about him when she returned to Dublin, as the busy season had kicked in and people were queuing down the street to get their passports in time for their holidays.

'Why they always leave it till the last minute I'll never know,' she said to Pat as she worked on yet another urgent set of documents.

'Worse are the idiots who think it's funny to fill out the form saying their sex is "yes please".' Pat sighed and put the third one she'd received that day to one side. 'Don't they realise it's going to be sent straight back to them?' She looked at her watch and then at Lola. 'Are you going on your lunch break?'

'Yes, but I won't be long because I have my interview this afternoon.'

'Of course.' Pat nodded. 'You look good.'

Lola was wearing a slim-fitting navy dress with a white collar and pearl buttons down the bodice. She wanted to give the impression of someone who was serious about her job and ready for promotion, but her nerves had been jangling all day and the only reason she was going out of the office for lunch was to take her mind off things for an hour.

She picked up her bag and left the building, passing the queue of hopeful holidaymakers. She strolled towards Grafton Street, where the flower sellers were doing a brisk business with their brightly coloured bunches of sunflowers and freesias. A couple of buskers were playing classical guitar music outside the St Stephen's Green centre, and she paused for a while to listen. She loved Dublin like this – warm, vibrant and buzzing, and full of people. She knew she'd never go back to Cloghdrom to live, even though some of her friends wanted to return. For Lola it had become a place to visit, even if she would always consider the farmhouse to be home.

Eventually she began to walk back towards the red-brick building. She made her usual turn along Duke Lane without thinking. She didn't want to stop in front of Warren's in case Philip Warren spotted her and got the wrong idea – yes, he was attractive, but as she'd told Shirley, she wasn't looking for a man right now. All the same, she couldn't help slowing down again as she passed. They'd changed the display and replaced the Snowdrop range with the Adele Bluebell, a mixture of dark blue sapphires and clear white diamonds. Behind the display she could see Lorraine talking to a male customer. As Lola watched, Lorraine showed him to a seat in front of the walnut desk, and placed a jewellery box on it. Lola couldn't see what was inside, but the man seemed pleased, because he was nodding his head enthusiastically. Lorraine started to wrap the box in purple paper.

Lola turned away and continued towards the office. As she was about to cross Molesworth Street, she heard her name being called. She swung around.

'I saw you outside the shop,' said Philip Warren a little breathlessly. 'I was at the upstairs window. I called out but you didn't hear me. Then you started walking away and I had to sprint to catch up with you.'

'Why did you want to catch up with me?' she asked.

'Because you ran off like Cinderella at the ball last time,' said Philip. 'We didn't have a chance to talk.'

'We don't have a chance this time either.' The pedestrian lights changed and she began to cross. Philip stayed beside her. 'I'm in a hurry.'

'Oh, come on,' he said. 'You can't run away again.'

'I'm not running away. I have to go back to work.'

'Who are these slave drivers?' he demanded.

She pointed to the queue still outside the Passport Office. 'Busiest time of the year.'

'What time do you finish?'

'Five,' she said. 'Unless I'm doing overtime.'

'And are you?'

'Tonight I am.'

'In that case, would you like to meet for a drink tomorrow? Or we could go for something to eat. Where d'you live? I can pick you up.'

Lola was a strong, independent woman who was hoping to be promoted. But even strong, independent women could be flattered by men chasing after them. Besides, he was nice. And much better looking than anyone she'd ever gone out with before.

She took a piece of paper from her bag and scribbled the flat's address on it.

'Seven o'clock?' he said.

'OK.'

28

'It's a date.' He smiled at her. 'Sure you don't have time for a coffee now?'

'My lunch hour is over. I really have got to go.' She pushed open the door to the Passport Office, but before she stepped inside, she stopped and glanced back at him. 'See you tomorrow.'

'See you.' He beamed at her and then strode away as Lola raced up the stairs to her interview.

The following evening, she sat on the end of her bed and did her make-up while Shirley watched her.

'It's very romantic,' she said. 'Him running after you like that. Cinderella-like, in fact.'

'That's what he said.' Lola swept silver-grey eyeshadow across her lids.

'So he's romantic too.'

'But I'm not,' said Lola. 'I don't do that mushy stuff.'

'Of course you do. All women are romantic at heart.'

'I don't want to be romantic. I don't want to sacrifice everything for love. If I did, I would've married Gus McCabe and stayed in Cloghdrom.'

'Oh, Lord God, poor old Gus. He was so besotted with you.'

'I was seventeen and he asked me to marry him!' Lola shook her head. 'And then he was affronted because I said no.'

'He's married to Ailish Grogan now.'

'So he is.'

'I met her the last time I went home,' said Shirley. 'I told you she was pregnant, didn't I?'

Lola shuddered. 'Poor girl.'

'I'm sure she's happy,' said Shirley.

29

'Well, I'll be happy when I'm a hard-hitting career woman.'

'In the Passport Office?' Shirley grinned.

'It's a start.'

'When will you hear about the promotion?'

'They take weeks to decide.' Lola took her mascara out of her make-up bag and began to apply it. 'When I'm in charge, it'll be much quicker.'

'If I was given the choice of being an executive officer in the Civil Service or the wife of a stonkingly rich jewellery magnate, I know which I'd choose,' remarked Shirley.

This time it was Lola who grinned.

'We're just going on a date,' she said. 'And even if his family is well off, he mightn't have a bean himself.'

'I'm telling you, he's a catch,' said Shirley. 'You'd be mad to let him slip through your fingers.'

'We're probably just going for a burger and chips,' Lola said. 'It's hardly a lifetime of diamonds and rubies.'

'But it's a start,' said Shirley as she ran down the stairs to answer the doorbell.

Philip had arrived in a green Volkswagen, which he parked directly outside the flat. Lola had never gone out with anyone who had his own car before and she couldn't help being impressed.

'I thought we'd go to the movies and then have something to eat afterwards,' he said after he'd given her a peck on the cheek and opened the passenger door for her. 'Does that sound all right?'

'Sure, absolutely,' said Lola.

'Seat belt,' said Philip as he turned on the ignition. 'Clunk click.'

'Oh. Right.' Lola pulled it across her. The family car in Cloghdrom was too ancient to have seat belts fitted. Philip's still had a new car smell.

'It's my dad's,' he admitted. 'But he allows me to use it sometimes.'

'Do you live with your parents?' she asked.

'Yes. I suppose that seems strange to someone who lives away from home.'

'Not really.' She shrugged. 'I had to get a flat to work in Dublin. I guess if I'd stayed in Cloghdrom, I'd still be at home too.' Then she laughed. 'That's the main reason I left.'

'Didn't you like it?'

'It's a small town,' she said. 'With a small-town feel. I wanted something more.'

'I'm afraid I've never heard of it,' he admitted.

'Unless you're from it, you wouldn't.' She grinned. 'It has two streets, two shops, four pubs and a hotel near the lake.'

'And do you live in the town itself?'

'Nobody lives in the town,' she said. 'It's farming country.'

'So you have a farm?'

She nodded.

'I've never gone out with a farmer's daughter before.'

'I've never gone out with anyone who borrowed his dad's car myself. Though I did get a lift on a tractor a few times.'

Philip laughed. So did she.

Suddenly she was glad she'd accepted his invitation. A career was all very well, but a girl had to have fun too.

And she was looking forward to a bit of fun with Philip Warren.

*   *   *

She sniffed surreptitiously at the end of *Dirty Dancing*, which was the movie he'd chosen.

'A little bit soppier than I'd expected,' he admitted as they left the cinema. 'But not bad. Did you enjoy it?'

She nodded.

They walked hand in hand along O'Connell Street to the car park. Philip talked about Warren's, a subject Lola was happy to hear more about. She also enjoyed his stories about working in the shop and the various customers he met, who sounded a lot more glamorous than the people she had to deal with at the Passport Office.

When he dropped her back to the flat, she thanked him and told him there was no point in asking him in – the lights were on, which meant that at least one of the girls was home.

'I don't mind,' said Philip. 'I like meeting people.'

Lola hesitated. She'd enjoyed her date with Philip but she wasn't sure she wanted him to meet her friends yet. She wasn't convinced she was ready for him to be part of her life. But he was smiling at her expectantly and so she led him up the stairs and unlocked the door. Shirley and Fidelma, one of her other flatmates, were there, along with a collection of friends and acquaintances. Lola made a face at the sight of the empty beer bottles and crisp packets on the table, as well as the overflowing ashtray on the mantelpiece.

'Hey, come and join us!' cried Shirley. 'There's room for a few more.'

'I don't know if . . .' Lola turned to Philip.

'Thanks.' He took a bottle of Harp from her and helped himself to some crisps.

'One for you, Lo-Lo?' asked Shirley.

She took the bottle. Philip clinked his against hers. He gave her a smile and then he kissed her.

Right there in front of everybody. Which was very flattering, Lola conceded as she broke away from him. Nevertheless, even if he was a great catch, she still wasn't ready to be caught.

Philip Warren's confidence and sense of entitlement was both exhilarating and annoying, Lola decided after she'd gone out with him a few times. He was decisive and determined, and aways quite certain of getting his own way. He told her where they were going on their dates rather than asking her what she'd like to do, but even though it irritated her at times, she had to admit that he always brought her to places she liked, and it seemed to matter to him that she was having a good time. She loved that he wasn't overawed by waiters, or even by proper restaurants, so unlike the cheap and cheerful bistros she was used to. There was something grown up and sophisticated about him, and he made her feel grown up and sophisticated too.

When she finally went to bed with him, he was skilled and thoughtful in a way she hadn't experienced either. For starters, he was the one who provided the condoms (always a tricky prospect in 1980s Ireland), and he never failed to ask her if he was giving her pleasure, if she was happy, if it was as good for her as it was for him.

It would be easy to fall head over heels in love with him, she thought. And easy to think that he was someone she'd want in her life forever. But he hadn't yet told her he loved her. And she wasn't at all sure she wanted to hear him say so either.

Chapter 4

Bruting: the initial shaping of a rough gemstone

Although she had no official position in the business, Richard Warren kept Adele up to date with everything that was going on. In his mind she was as much a part of its success as him. Not just because she gave her name to their most beautiful jewellery range, but because before their marriage she'd worked as an accounts clerk and in the early years had given him lots of advice about cash flow and balance sheets. He'd been surprised when he first met her that she'd been working at all – it seemed to him that she came from a class of girl who wouldn't have considered having a job – but when she told him the story of her father's betrayal, he realised that it had been an economic necessity for her. She told him she'd chosen to work in accounts so that no man would ever be able to pull the wool over her eyes.

'I wouldn't dream of even trying,' Richard had said. 'I'll never cheat on you or lie to you, Adele. You can trust me forever.'

There was something about him that inspired trust. And she hadn't regretted marrying him for an instant. She enjoyed

34

her role as the matriarch of the family and she always wanted to know what was going on. She looked forward to the details of Richard's trips to London or Amsterdam or Basle. But on his return from the most recent trip, she was less interested in the jewellery he'd seen than any conversations he might have had with Philip while they were away.

'Did he talk to you about his new girlfriend at all?' she asked. 'I'm getting quite concerned about this relationship, Richard. I've never known him so besotted. He's out with her again tonight.'

'We didn't have time for that sort of conversation,' replied Richard. 'We were busy at Hatton Garden, and then of course we had dinner with Peter and we were discussing the Warren accounts and how he'll take them over when he finally qualifies.'

Adele sniffed in exasperation. What was it with men, she asked herself, that they didn't talk about people, only about things? Not that talking about the future of Warren's wasn't important, but she'd have thought Philip's girlfriend would at least get a mention over the course of three days, especially when his younger brother, Peter, was part of the conversation too.

'Neither of us have met this Lola yet,' she said. 'And when we ask about her, all he says is that she's the prettiest girl in the world. Anyone can be taken in by a pretty face, but we know nothing about her or her background.'

'I'm sure she's a perfectly nice girl,' said Richard. 'Anyhow, it's nothing to do with us. He's an adult, and he's not a fool.'

Adele decided not to say that she thought all men were fools at heart. Even her beloved Richard could do foolish things depending on the circumstances. It was her job to save the men in her family from themselves, even if they didn't know it.

Her concerns about Lola continued unabated, especially as Philip contrived to ignore all her hints about bringing her home to meet them. Eventually she had to come out with a straight request that he bring her to dinner one evening.

'She wants to meet me?' Lola looked at him in astonishment when he told her. 'Why?'

'We're a couple. It's only natural she'd want to see you sooner or later.'

'Well, yes, we're a couple but we haven't been going out together that long,' said Lola. 'It seems a bit soon.'

'You have to come,' said Philip. 'Mum wants you to and so do I.'

His tone told her that there was to be no argument, and so she said nothing more. But when she spoke to Shirley about it later, she complained that it was more a command than a request.

'I don't see what your problem with meeting them is,' Shirley said 'You're seeing him almost every day as it is.'

'That's because he keeps turning up at the Passport Office and taking me to lunch,' said Lola.

'And that doesn't mean it's serious?' demanded Shirley. 'Plus, you're at it like rabbits.'

Lola blushed. 'We're not! And even if we were, that's just having a good time. It still doesn't mean anything.'

'It would in Cloghdrom,' said Shirley.

'But we're not in Cloghdrom,' Lola pointed out.

'So what is it about the rich, handsome, eligible hunk that you're not sure about?' asked Shirley.

'He thinks he knows better than me about everything,' said Lola after a moment's consideration. 'He thinks my job isn't important. If I say I'm too busy for lunch or working late and can't see him, he gets ratty with me. And even though he's good in bed, he sort of knows he is.'

Shirley roared with laughter. 'All men think they know best,' she reminded her friend. 'And your job isn't very important no matter how much you'd like it to be. As for the bed thing – what wouldn't I give for some guy who knew what he was doing instead of treating the whole thing like a game of pin the tail on the donkey.'

'Shirley!'

'I'm simply saying that if you're holding out for someone better, you'll have a very long wait,' said Shirley. 'You need to remember which side your bread is buttered.'

'I know. I know.' Lola couldn't help laughing. 'I realise how lucky I am. I just want to do other things too, that's all.'

'You're punching above your weight with Philip Warren,' Shirley advised. 'Don't let it all slip away for some nebulous dream. A girl from Cloghdrom is never going to do any better than a man with ready access to diamonds.'

Shirley had a point, thought Lola as she got into her narrow single bed that night. And yet it was hard not to dream about a future in which she was the star and had access to jewellery herself, not merely as somebody's wife.

The day before she was due to go to the Warrens' for dinner, the results of the interviews were announced. Lola ripped her envelope open with great excitement and read the contents. When she saw the words 'not successful on this occasion', her eyes brimmed with tears and she rushed to the ladies'.

'Tough luck,' said Pat when she returned to her desk, her eyes red and her mascara slightly smudged. 'Don't worry, you're young, there'll be other chances.'

'This was my chance.' Lola sniffed. 'The last time I applied, I didn't get it because I'd only just joined. I was OK with that. But now – have you seen the people who did? Fred O'Malley and Kenny Redmond?' She glanced across the room to where Kenny was high-fiving one of his colleagues. 'He nearly issued a passport to someone who sent in a baptismal cert instead of a birth cert last month. I've never done anything as stupid as that. Yet he's promoted and I'm not?'

'You should talk to Irene,' said Pat. 'She might be able to tell you why.'

When Lola approached the staff officer, Irene said that the interview panel had felt Lola was still a little young and inexperienced.

'I'm nearly twenty-three!' cried Lola. 'I've been working here for ages.'

'Most of the newly promoted executive officers have been in the service considerably longer than you,' said Irene. 'I hear you're upset that Kenny Redmond was promoted ahead of you. But he's one of the very experienced people, Lola. He's nearly thirty. It's only fair he gets his promotion now.'

Lola stood up and walked away.

She was afraid of what she might say.

Philip was hugely sympathetic. He put his arms around her and hugged her and told her that the Civil Service didn't know a good thing when it was right in front of their noses, and that she was the brightest, smartest person he knew. He said they didn't deserve her. That she could do better than them. That she was far too lovely to waste her time with people who didn't know any better. She relaxed into his hold and allowed him to comfort her, and thought to herself that perhaps everyone was right. That all her talk of a career was just nonsense, and that the best thing in her life was Philip Warren and she'd be lucky to have a future with him.

If he ever asked her to share it.

She was still upset about the promotion when she arrived at the Warrens' house the following evening. Philip had offered to pick her up from the flat, but she'd told him she'd rather make her own way. She was regretting that decision as she walked up the steps to the impressive detached house, because she was suddenly gripped by a wave of anxiety at the thought of meeting his parents. It would have been nice to have him standing beside her, telling her again that she was lovely and clever and the most wonderful girl in the world.

'So,' Adele Warren said as she opened the door and ushered her inside, 'you're the young lady who's charmed my son. I'm interested to find out everything there is to know about you.'

Adele's words immediately intimidated Lola, as did the older woman's immaculate style. She was wearing a maroon suit, cream blouse and high-heeled shoes, as well as the entire Snowdrop collection. The set looked magnificent on her, the diamonds sparkling fiercely against her still youthful skin. Her spun-gold hair was pulled back into a neat chignon and secured by a jewelled comb. Lola wondered if the diamonds in that were real too.

Lola herself wore her interview dress, which was the most demure item of clothing she possessed. She wished she had kick-ass stones like Adele's to give her confidence an added boost. And then she thought dismally that she'd have been brimming with confidence if she'd got the promotion.

She stayed silent as she followed Adele into the living room. Philip and his father were standing either side of the enormous marble fireplace, and after Lola had been introduced to Richard, Philip waved her to a floral-patterned sofa, where he sat beside her. Lola crossed her legs at the ankles as the nuns in her convent school had taught her to do. When Richard asked her what she'd like to drink, she asked for a sparkling water, even though she was thinking that her preferred choice of Bacardi and Coke might have steadied her nerves better. She told herself that it was ridiculous to be overawed by Philip's parents, but she couldn't help feeling as though she was back in front of the interview panel again.

'I believe you've worn them already.' Adele raised an eyebrow as she looked at the girl sitting opposite her.

'I'm sorry?'

'The Snowdrops,' said Adele. 'You were staring at them.'

'I . . . um, yes.'

'And you liked them?'

'Who wouldn't?' said Lola. 'They're beautiful.'

Adele's expression softened a little. 'Of course they are,' she said. 'All fine jewellery should be beautiful. Every Warren's piece certainly is.'

'I plan to buy myself some once I'm successful,' Lola told her. 'As a reward.'

'I see.' Adele looked at her intently. 'And what form will this success take?'

'Getting promoted, of course,' Lola replied. 'I want to get to the top grade in the Civil Service. I want to be a principal officer. Or maybe even the secretary of a department. The secretary isn't someone who takes phone calls and types,' she added hastily. 'It's the person in charge. Usually a man. They've had the better opportunities in the past. But hopefully not in the future.'

'Unfortunately Lola missed out on promotion yesterday,' said Philip. 'But if she stays with them, she'll definitely get it soon. I'm not sure about secretary of a department, though,' he added with a grin as he turned to her. 'That might be shooting for the moon a little.'

'Indeed,' said Adele. 'Where are you from originally, Lola? Who are your people?'

Lola cleared her throat, but her mouth was suddenly dry and she took a large gulp of her water, which made her cough. It was Philip who stepped in with the answer, telling them about the farm at Cloghdrom.

'A dairy farm?' Adele was completely out of her depth.

'Yes. It's not a big herd, but they're great producers,' said Lola. 'They're a Jersey cross-breed.'

Adele blinked.

'Cross-breeds are generally more profitable,' added Lola.

'Is *your* farm profitable?' asked Richard. 'I always thought farms only survived because of handouts.'

'We don't get handouts,' said Lola. 'We get some government grants; nearly every farmer does. But my dad works very hard.'

'Ah. Grants. So that's what they're called these days.' Adele shrugged and brought the discussion on farming to an abrupt close by telling them that dinner was ready.

The dining room was at the back of the house, with large French doors leading to a long garden. In the centre, an oval rosewood table set with a full complement of cutlery and napkins gleamed beneath the lights. Lola wondered if this was the way dinner was served at the Warrens' every day. Then she told herself she was being stupid. The extravagance was for her. Philip's mother wanted to make an impression. Not that she needed to try. Lola was more than impressed already.

But as she took her seat at the table, it suddenly struck her that Adele wasn't trying to impress her at all. She was simply showing her how different Philip's life was to hers. How far apart they were. How much better it was to be a Warren than a Fitzpatrick.

Not good enough twice in a week, thought Lola. I'm not half as smart as I thought I was after all.

When Lola saw that Adele had decided to serve snails as a starter, she knew that a gauntlet had been thrown down. She glanced across the table at Philip, but he was buttering a roll and didn't see the expression on her face.

'I'm sorry.' She studied the small bowl of stuffed shells Adele had placed in front of her. 'I can't eat these.'

'I thought they'd be a treat for you,' said Adele.

'Snails? A treat?' Lola was flabbergasted.

'They are, you know,' said Adele. 'You grew up on a farm, Lola. You should be able to eat anything.'

'Snails aren't high on the list of farm produce,' Lola said. 'I've no problem with a sirloin steak or a pork chop. Or chicken or lamb. But we don't do snails.'

42

'Have you tried them before?' asked Adele.

Lola shook her head.

'In that case you're saying no based on emotion, not logic. Taste one. If you don't like it, you needn't finish it.'

Lola took a deep breath. She'd been challenged and she hated passing on a challenge. But she had a sinking feeling that the snails would defeat her.

'If you'd prefer, I can do you a mixed salad,' Adele said.

'But snails are actually quite nice,' said Philip. 'Mum cooks them in garlic butter. And they're easy to get out of their shells. Look. I'll show you.' He picked up the tongs beside his plate, gripped a shell with it and speared the meat with the fork provided.

'Why didn't you mention the garlic before?' Lola smiled brightly. 'I love garlic.' Copying Philip, she gripped a shell, fished out the snail, closed her eyes and popped it into her mouth. She swallowed it whole.

'Well?' Both Philip and Adele spoke at the same time.

Honesty or not? wondered Lola. And does it matter?

'Very . . . garlicky.' She speared a second snail and swallowed that too. When she'd finished the bowl in front of her, she used some of the crusty bread to mop up the garlic butter.

'Well done.' It was Richard who nodded approvingly when she'd finished. 'You should never refuse food without tasting it. Who knows what culinary delights you might miss.'

If that's a culinary delight, I'm a principal officer, thought Lola as she buttered another slice of bread and vowed that she'd never eat another snail in her life.

Although she no longer felt in the slightest bit hungry, Lola finished the salmon fillet that Adele had cooked for the main

43

course without comment. Philip's mother had chosen cheese rather than a sweet dessert, and Lola took a small triangle of Brie, steadfastly ignoring the Cashel Blue and some of the other, smellier pieces. As they ate, Adele peppered her with questions about the farm.

'So your brother will take over from your father?' she said.

'Of course,' said Lola. 'Like my dad took over from my grandfather.'

'The same as Warren's,' said Philip. 'My grandfather, my father and then me.'

'It's not exactly the same,' said Adele. 'One's a farm, the other a family heritage.'

'The farm *is* our family's heritage,' Lola told her.

'Although we've built up the business from nothing,' said Adele, 'whereas you've always had the land.'

'But it's a family concern,' conceded Richard. 'And in that way we're a little bit alike.'

Lola smiled gratefully at him. It was clear that Richard was happy to take a back seat to his wife, but also that he helped to soften her harder edges.

'The big difference is that we don't get government hand-outs,' Adele observed. 'Which is what they are even if you prefer to call them grants.'

'They're necessary!' Although Lola's interest in farm management was limited, she certainly wasn't going to have her family rubbished by the Warrens. 'You'd be eating nothing but snails if it wasn't for farmers. And farming is a seven-day-a-week job.'

'So is running a business like Warren's,' said Philip. 'And you've got to remember that we're dealing in really expensive gemstones.'

44

'Some of our cows cost as much as your stones,' retorted Lola.

All three Warrens laughed at this.

'I hardly think you can compare Clover the cow with the Adele Rose.' Adele wiped her eyes with the corner of her napkin as she spoke. 'Do you have any idea how much pink diamonds cost?'

Lola shook her head.

'A lot more than a cow, I promise.' Philip was still laughing.

He wasn't on her side, thought Lola in surprise. He thought he was better than her too.

Richard began to lecture her about fancy diamonds, which apparently was the term for coloured gems, and when he mentioned how much some of them were worth, she was astonished. When all was said and done, they were still simply bits of stone, she thought. Or, as she'd now learned, carbon.

'I don't know if I'd like a coloured diamond,' she said when Richard had finished. 'People might think it was something else. And if you'd spent all that money, you'd hate it if someone thought it was only glass.'

'Nobody would think the Adele Rose was glass,' his wife assured her.

'I'll keep it in mind when I can afford to buy one,' said Lola.

'Or when someone buys one for you,' said Philip.

'I'm not sure Lola knows people who could afford Warren jewellery,' Adele said.

Lola's eyes narrowed as she looked at the older woman. It was clear that Adele wanted to put her in her place, but for the life of her she couldn't understand why. She didn't need to be shown that the Warrens were richer and more successful than the Fitzpatricks. She knew that already.

Richard broke the sudden silence, this time talking about the origins of the shop and how hard his own father had worked to build it up. He was a good storyteller, thought Lola, and the history of Warren's was an interesting one. But the evening hadn't been particularly enjoyable and she was eager to leave.

Eventually, after finishing her coffee, she told them she had to go.

'It was very nice meeting you,' she lied to Adele.

'You too,' lied Adele in return.

'It was a delicious meal.'

'I told you you'd like the snails.'

'Oh, I didn't really.' Lola was tired of being nice. 'But the garlic butter was good.'

'Perhaps it was unfair of me to offer them to you,' conceded Adele. 'You clearly would have been more comfortable with something like chicken.'

'We raise our own chickens at home,' said Lola. 'We wring their necks too. I learned to do it at a very young age. Well, goodbye, Mrs Warren.'

'Goodbye,' said Adele.

As she walked out of the door, with Philip beside her, Lola could hear the sound of Richard's laughter following them to the street.

She went to Cloghdrom the following weekend, without Philip.

Her mother, knowing that Lola hadn't got the promotion she wanted, wrapped her arms around her, hugged her close and told her not to worry, that it would happen one day. Lola allowed herself to be comforted, even though she was getting tired of people talking about 'one day' when she'd wanted one day to be now. But it was good to be among people who loved her and only cared for her best interests, even if she didn't always agree with them. And it was nice to know that the food wouldn't be a challenge.

Over dinner, she told them about her evening with the Warrens.

'Snails!' Gretta shuddered. 'How did you even swallow them?'

'With great difficulty,' admitted Lola.

'You must really love him to put even one of them in your mouth,' her sister said.

'He's lucky I'm still going out with him after that evening,' said Lola. 'Although he'd probably say I'm the lucky one.'

'Bring him here,' said Eilis. 'I'll show him what proper food is. And it's time we met him in any case.'

'Just because he brought me to meet his parents doesn't mean I have to bring him to meet you,' said Lola.

'If you've got to the meeting-the-mammy stage . . .' Gretta winked at her while her parents exchanged glances.

'Oh, please!'

'Is there a reason you won't bring him?' asked Eilis. 'Are we not good enough?'

'Of course you are.' Lola's voice was fierce. 'You're worth a million of those stuck-up Warrens. You wouldn't dream of making him feel uncomfortable like Adele Warren did to me.'

Eilis frowned. 'Does she think *you're* not good enough?'

'I don't think she'd think anyone was good enough,' said Lola.

'The cheek of her.' Eilis's face was red.

'Don't worry about it,' said Lola.

'I'm not having anyone looking down on my family!' Eilis was still fuming.

'And I'm not having the old bat look down on me either,' Lola assured her. 'I can't see myself being asked there again anyhow.'

'But if you and Philip are going steady . . .' Eilis didn't finish the sentence.

And Lola didn't say anything at all.

Chapter 5

Blemish: a scratch or mark on the surface of a stone

Philip and his father went to Basle the following week. Lola was glad about that because it gave her more time to think.

She hadn't spoken to him much about the dinner afterwards. His comments as he'd brought her home were that she'd stood up well to his mother and he was proud of her. She'd remarked that she hadn't thought it was meant to be a test, and he'd laughed and said that meeting Adele for the first time was always a test of sorts, but that she was a sweetheart when you got to know her. Lola didn't say that she hadn't the slightest desire to get to know his mother, or that 'sweetheart' was the last word she'd ever apply to her.

'Are you looking forward to him being back?' asked Shirley the night before he returned. 'If Sean didn't call me for a week, I'd be devastated.'

Sean was Shirley's new boyfriend. They'd been seeing each other for the past month and Shirley claimed to be head-over-heels about him, although as that was her default setting for new relationships, it didn't mean much.

'Yes, I am,' said Lola. 'I've missed him.'

'Jeez, Lo-Lo, you don't sound entirely convinced. I thought you were madly in love with him. Don't tell me that after a few days apart you've changed your mind.'

'It's hard not to love him,' said Lola. 'He's handsome, he's fun, he treats me really well. OK, so he's a bit arrogant, but why wouldn't he be, he's way better than me. It's just . . . I sometimes wonder if I love him enough.'

'Enough for what?' demanded Shirley.

'Enough for a lifetime,' replied Lola. 'Though given that he hasn't made any commitment, it's beside the point, isn't it?'

'I could learn to love a man like Philip for a lifetime,' said Shirley.

'D'you fancy him yourself?' Lola was startled.

'Who wouldn't?' asked Shirley. 'And you're stone mad if he asks you and you say no. He's a far cry from Gus McCabe, after all.'

Philip called the following day and asked Lola to meet him at the shop. She was happy to hear his voice again, and as soon as she'd finished work, she rushed into the ladies' to get ready.

'Hot date?' asked Irene as she pushed open the door and saw Lola applying carmine-red lipstick.

'Meeting my boyfriend,' said Lola.

'You young ones have a great life.' Irene ran a brush through her wiry hair. 'There was none of this gallivanting off with fellas when I was your age.'

Lola wasn't sure how old Irene actually was, but she guessed she was around the same age as her mother. However, while Eilis was good humoured and liked to see the brighter side of life, Irene seemed to moan and pick fault with everything.

Would I end up like her if I stayed here? Lola wondered suddenly. A sad old crone who's never got higher than staff officer and can't find joy in anything? Would I forget how to have fun? She watched surreptitiously as Irene dabbed a floral-scented perfume on her wrists, then replaced the bottle in her handbag and snapped it closed.

'Enjoy your evening,' said Irene. 'Remember to respect yourself and don't do anything you'd be ashamed of in the light of day.'

With that final comment, she turned on her heel and walked out. Lola dissolved into a fit of laughter. In a million years she wouldn't become Irene McBride. Even if she never got promoted and spent the rest of her career in the Passport Office, she wouldn't turn into such a sourpuss. She rearranged her hair, added still more colour to her lips and sprayed herself liberally with Anaïs Anaïs.

She arrived at Warren's shortly before it closed. Lorraine was just completing the sale of an Omega watch to a customer. She nodded at Lola and told her that Philip would be down shortly. Then she boxed the watch, placed it carefully in a Warren's bag and handed it to the man sitting at the desk in front of her. As the customer left the shop, Philip opened the internal door and walked in.

Whenever she saw him, Lola felt a certain thrill. Philip Warren knew what he wanted from life, and how he was going to get it. He didn't have to worry about undeserving people being promoted ahead of him. He was part of a dynasty-in-the-making and he knew it. He would be successful because he was born for success. He would have a good life because people like the Warrens knew how to live well. And his wife would have a good life too.

'How was your day?' he asked, as Lorraine put on her jacket, said goodbye and turned the sign on the door to 'Closed'.

'So-so. Irene was a real pain.' Lola made a face as she recalled the staff officer's stern words when she'd heard Lola taking a personal phone call. Then, amid another fit of laughter, she repeated what the older woman had said about respecting herself.

'She's jealous,' said Philip. 'She knows she could never be as gorgeous as you.'

'You're such a charmer.' Lola grinned as she moved closer to him.

He kissed her and she let herself enjoy the moment, thinking that he was right, that Irene *was* jealous, that being a staff officer in the Passport Office certainly couldn't measure up to being in the arms of a handsome man in the middle of a jewellery shop. And thinking that Shirley was right too; she'd never meet anyone better than him.

'Before we do anything else,' Philip whispered, 'there was something I wanted to say to you.'

'Oh?'

'I thought about you a lot while I was in Basle,' he said. 'I really missed you. Did you miss me?'

'Of course I did.'

He put his hands on her shoulders and turned her so that she could see herself in the full-length mirror. 'We go well together. Look.'

Her pretty red skirt and yellow top complemented her

olive complexion and the mass of dark hair that tumbled to her shoulders. The sweep of black mascara emphasised her long, curling lashes, and her red lipstick highlighted her rosebud mouth. Her high-heeled shoes made her legs look longer. Standing behind her, and a head taller than her, Philip's fair good looks made an attractive contrast.

'We're a good couple,' he whispered into her ear. 'A really good couple. And I like us together.'

'So do I,' said Lola.

'And that's why . . .' He turned her towards him and she gasped as he suddenly went down on one knee. 'That's why I'm asking you to marry me.'

No matter what she'd said to Shirley, she'd imagined this moment already. She'd thought about how she'd react, what she might say, how she might feel. But the feelings she had now were completely different to anything she'd imagined. Because, she realised, deep down she'd never really expected him to want to marry her. She'd never expected to have to answer the question. She hadn't been good enough for his parents. She'd thought that maybe she wasn't good enough for him either.

He reached into the pocket of his suit and took out a Warren's box, which he handed to her.

'Open it,' he said.

She lifted the lid. A round-cut solitaire diamond set in a white gold ring sparkled at her from inside. It was the most beautiful ring she'd ever seen. Except for the Snowdrop, of course. But he couldn't possibly afford a Snowdrop, even if he was a Warren. They were worth thousands. Besides, this . . . she continued to look at it wordlessly . . . this was utterly magnificent.

'Let me.'

He took it out of the box and slid it onto her finger.

'It's a half-carat internally flawless diamond,' he said. 'Warren's has the exclusive rights to these rings. Only our customers can buy them, so it's practically unique.'

'It's stunning.' She could hardly speak.

'Just like you,' he said. 'I knew I had to have you from the moment I first saw you. You're as perfect as that stone.'

She was mesmerised by the cut and clarity of the ring. She'd never been given anything like it in her life before.

'We'll be great together,' he continued. 'One day the shop will be mine and we'll be like my mum and dad, a partnership. I'll look after the shop, you'll look after our home, but we'll both look after the heritage that is Warren's.'

Lola pictured herself in a house like his. She imagined herself wearing Adele's elegant clothes and her collection of magnificent jewellery. And she thought about sitting at her desk at the Passport Office, her beautiful new engagement ring on her finger. She thought of how confident she'd feel knowing that she was wearing something that Irene herself couldn't afford. She imagined the staff officer muttering that in her day girls didn't get such magnificent engagement rings.

'I want us to spend the rest of our lives together,' said Philip. 'I know you're the right girl for me.'

The ring felt perfect on Lola's finger. As though it had been specially made for it. And just as she had when she'd tried on the Snowdrop jewellery, she felt a surge of confidence in simply wearing it. It marked her out as a woman who'd been chosen. And a woman who'd been chosen by a man who could afford beautiful things.

Philip moved away from her and went into the office. He

returned a moment later with a bottle of Veuve Clicquot and two champagne glasses.

'You've totally taken me by surprise,' she said as he put the bottle on the display counter.

'That was the idea.'

She looked at the ring again. She imagined being married to Philip. Being part of the Warren family. Being Adele's daughter-in-law. She thought about the future she'd always wanted and visualised two paths stretching in front of her. One of them led to the security of being Philip's wife, even if it came with a helping of Adele's dislike. Philip had assured her that his mother was all right when you got to know her, and there was no reason to doubt him. Adele was no different to the mothers of Cloghdrom. None of them thought the girls were good enough for their precious sons. It was an Irish mammy thing. Lola could get around her eventually.

The other path was less clear. Promotion at work, eventually. A move to a different department. Moving slowly up the career ladder, trying to get past people whose turn would always be ahead of her. But maybe achieving that. On her own. Because of her own hard work. Not because she was married to someone.

She tilted her hand so that the diamonds in the ring exploded into a rainbow of colours.

She'd never have a chance like this again.

She'd told Shirley she wasn't sure she loved him enough. But how did anyone know how much they loved anyone? And even if you were a hundred per cent sure, it could still go wrong. It would be crazy to say no to someone she cared about simply because she had a few insubstantial doubts.

Philip was opening the bottle of champagne. He'd clearly

decided that she was going to say yes. Or that she'd said yes already. Had she? Had she said it without even thinking, as soon as he'd put the ring on her finger? Because no matter what doubts she might have, she was flattered that a man like Philip Warren wanted to marry a farmer's daughter from Cloghdrom. His proposal had been far more impressive than Gus McCabe's mumbled suggestion while they were standing by the farm gate. She remembered saying no to Gus. She couldn't remember saying anything at all to Philip.

The cork made a quiet pop. He was good at opening champagne bottles, thought Lola. He hadn't spilled a drop. It was stupid to have doubts. Stupid to think for a minute that there'd be anyone better in her life than a man who loved her. A man who'd just given her the most extravagant ring she'd ever own. A man who could produce a bottle of champagne to celebrate his proposal. She did love him. She really did.

'I . . .'

'What?' He filled one of the glasses and handed it to her. She placed it on the nearest display counter, then smiled anxiously at him.

'I'm overwhelmed,' she said.

He laughed. 'It's always good to make a gesture when you're asking someone to marry you,' he said. 'After all, it's a day we'll remember for the rest of our lives.'

Taking a step on this path would mean changing her life forever. And why wouldn't she change it? What was so great about it the way it was?

'But I need to think,' she said.

'What?' This time his tone was one of astonishment.

'I wasn't expecting this. Not now.'

'How could you not have been expecting it?' asked Philip. 'I brought you to meet my parents, for heaven's sake.'

'I thought that was because your mother kept asking.'

'Partly,' he agreed. 'But I wouldn't have brought you at all if I hadn't been sure of you. And you were great that night, Lola. It made me realise that you're the right girl for me.'

'The thing is . . .' she looked at the engagement ring again, and then at him, 'I'm not sure I'm ready for it.'

'Every girl is ready for a Warren's engagement ring,' said Philip.

'Ready for being married,' Lola told him.

'We won't be getting married straight away,' said Philip. 'You'll have time to do all the things that girls need to do. And there'll be lots of organising. Dresses and flowers and all that sort of stuff. I understand that. Don't worry.'

'I meant *being* married, not *getting* married,' said Lola. 'I'm not sure I'm ready for that.'

'What's to be ready for?' asked Philip. 'We're good together. You know we are.'

'Good together and being married are two different things.'

'OK, now you're being a bit annoying.' He put down the bottle of champagne. 'What's the matter with you, Lola?'

'Like I said, I need time to think, that's all.'

'But what is there to think about? I love you. You love me. We've been sleeping together. What more do you need to convince you?'

She couldn't tell him she wasn't sure if she loved him enough. That would sound ridiculous. And hurtful. She didn't want to hurt him.

'It's my job,' she said. 'I'm really busy right now, and—'

'You've got to be joking!' His tone was one of disbelief. 'You're putting your bloody bottom-of-the-rung job ahead of marrying me?'

'No. Not exactly. I mean, the job is part of it, and then—'

'It's Mum, isn't it?' he said. 'She's always difficult at first, but you managed just fine with her. Which shows how right you are for me. Together we can do anything. Don't worry about her.'

'I'm not,' said Lola. 'This is nothing to do with your mother. It's about how I feel.'

'How you feel!' he exclaimed. 'Haven't you shown me how you feel already? We're good in bed, Lola. That proves how you feel.'

'It proves we're good in bed,' she said. 'But—'

'I'm making a one-time offer.' His voice hardened. 'I'm not playing silly buggers about this. I could have anyone but I've chosen you. You should be honoured.'

'I am. I am. I just—'

Suddenly he began opening the display counters, taking out handfuls of Adele jewellery. Lola stared at him as he heaped them in front of her, a glittering pile of diamonds, emeralds, rubies and sapphires.

'Put them on,' he said.

'What?'

'Put them on,' he repeated.

'All of them?' She looked at the jumble of necklaces and bracelets as well as the rings and earrings he'd also taken out.

'Humour me.'

'Philip . . .'

'Put the damn things on!' he cried.

She picked up the Adele Zinnia, an emerald pendant

surrounded by diamonds, and with trembling fingers fastened it around her neck. She followed it with the Rose necklace, then put the Snowdrop bracelet on her wrist and replaced her own cheap earrings with the Adele Bluebells – a pair of small, perfectly round sapphires. She slid the Zinnia, Snowdrop and Bluebell rings onto her fingers, alongside the engagement ring she hadn't yet taken off.

'You see.' Philip took her by the shoulders and stood her in front of the mirror again. 'You were born to wear them, Lola.'

She was a sparkling rainbow of colour. The gems seemed to pulsate in the light, becoming part of her, bringing an exotic air to her dark prettiness.

'You're the perfect person to be the new Mrs Warren,' he said. 'You light up the jewels as much as they light you up. But the thing is, Lola, I want to know now. Because this isn't something you need to think about. You either want to marry me or you don't.'

'I'm so sorry,' she said. She began to remove the jewellery, beginning with the diamond engagement ring, which she handed to him. 'I don't deserve you or this.'

'Were you just trying to make a fool out of me? The country girl traps the city slicker? Was that your plan all along?'

'Of course not!' she cried. 'Don't be stupid.'

'I'm not the stupid one here.' He pulled her towards him abruptly and brought his lips down on hers.

'Philip!' She wriggled free of him, banging her mouth on his chin in the process and biting her own lip so that it started to bleed. She wiped the blood away and unfastened the Rose necklace with shaking hands. 'What d'you think you're doing?'

'Well it seems to me that you're quite happy to make love to me without feeling a thing,' he said. 'So I thought I'd get what I was due.'

She dropped the necklace on the display counter and stepped back from him, her hair tangled around her face and falling into her eyes.

'Don't be like this,' she said. 'You're scaring me.'

'Good.'

'Philip, this isn't the way we are,' she said. 'It's not the way you want to be either.'

'How do you know?' he demanded. 'How do you know what I want to be? You obviously don't know me at all.'

She fumbled the catch of the Zinnia and allowed the pendant to drop onto the floor.

'I'm sorry,' she said again.

Then she ran out of the shop.

The journey back to her flat was a blur. She couldn't remember walking to the bus stop, or getting on the bus, or the drive home. It seemed to her that one minute she was in Warren's and the next she was stumbling up the stairs and putting her key in the door. Shirley was already home and was preparing to put some bacon and sausages on the grill when she walked in.

'Jeez, Lola, you're as white as a sheet!' she exclaimed. 'What's wrong?'

'Philip asked me to marry him,' she said.

'Oh my God! How brilliant. Congratulations!' Shirley flung her arms around her. 'I always knew you two would do it some day no matter what you said.'

'I said no.'

'You what?' Shirley stared at her.

'I said no.'

'Oh, Lola,' Shirley groaned. 'What have you done?'

'What d'you mean, what have I done?' cried Lola. 'I've said no to getting married to a man I don't love.'

'But you *do* love him,' said Shirley. 'You've said so.'

'Not enough,' said Lola.

'Flipping hell,' said Shirley.

'If you like him so much, why don't *you* marry him!' Lola's voice trembled.

'Ah, look, I'm sorry. I'm just shocked, that's all,' said Shirley. She turned the flame of the grill off. 'I know you've been in two minds about him. I just thought that when push came to shove, you'd realise what a good thing he was.'

'He is a good thing. I know that,' said Lola. 'I just . . .'

'Is it his mother?'

'He asked me that too.' Lola attempted a smile. 'It's not, though. It's me.'

'Oh well. Plenty more fish in the sea,' said Shirley.

'Yeah,' said Lola. 'Though maybe I've blown my only chance at catching one.'

'No point in catching it if you don't want it.' Shirley hugged her again. 'In those cases it's always better to throw it back.'

Shirley opened the bottle of wine that was in the kitchen cupboard. Who would have guessed that Chianti was a perfect accompaniment to sausages and rashers? mused Lola as she poured herself another glass. Why hadn't anyone told her that before?

'Are you drowning your sorrows or celebrating?' asked Fidelma when she got home and Shirley filled her in.

'I dunno,' said Lola. 'Maybe I'm drinking to forget that I'm a bad person who's let down a really good guy.'

'Rubbish,' said Crona, the fourth flatmate, when she arrived and was also brought up to speed. The bottle of wine was nearly finished, so she'd gone out again and returned with another. 'You were right to say you needed time to think. And if he didn't understand that, then you're well rid of him. Besides, you're too young to tie yourself down to one guy.'

'Ah well, we all know you're stringing along a dozen at the same time,' said Shirley.

'Excuse me!' Crona made a face. 'I have a number of friends who happen to be men. That doesn't make me some kind of siren, you know.'

Fidelma laughed. 'Siren. What a word.'

'He was really pissed off at me,' said Lola. 'I was a bit scared of him, to be honest.'

'You should've said yes,' Fidelma said. 'Then you could've broken it off later and maybe kept the ring.'

'I never thought of that,' said Shirley. 'You missed a trick there, Lo-Lo.'

'It was a gorgeous ring.' Lola held her hands out in front of her and looked at her naked fingers. 'I don't know if I'll ever own one as beautiful. Or as expensive.'

'Of course you will,' said Shirley. 'Don't you keep saying that you want to buy your own jewellery when you're successful?'

'I probably have as much chance of being successful as I have of getting engaged again.'

'You're not regretting saying no, are you?' asked Crona.

Lola shook her head as she pushed her glass at her and signalled her to refill it. 'It was the right thing. But . . .'

'You'll be grand,' said Fidelma. 'You'll find someone else when you're ready and you'll want to say yes.'

'All the same,' muttered Shirley later, when Lola had shuffled off to bed, 'she'll have her work cut out finding a better man than Philip Warren. If you ask me, she's going to regret this decision one day.'

Philip Warren had put the jewellery in the safe, hardly noticing what he was doing because he was shaking with anger and humiliation. He couldn't believe Lola Fitzpatrick had turned him down. Didn't she realise how lucky she was that he'd asked her to marry him in the first place? Didn't she understand what it meant? He was a Warren. She was nobody. He'd brought her into his world and she should have been grateful instead of bleating that she wasn't ready. His mother had been right about her after all, he muttered to himself as he set the alarm and then locked the door. She wasn't worthy of him. He'd misjudged her completely.

He went into the Duke pub and ordered himself a pint of lager. The jovial atmosphere soothed him a little. Then he remembered the dinner reservations he'd made at the upmarket Dobbins restaurant. He'd told them to have a bottle of champagne on ice. He'd bet any money she'd never had one bottle of champagne in her life before, let alone two. He ordered another pint, and when he'd finished it, he went outside and phoned the restaurant from the public phone box to cancel the reservation. Then he returned to the pub and had another drink. Three was enough, he decided as he downed it in a couple of long gulps. People were beginning to get edgy about driving after having alcohol. Which he agreed was understandable in some cases, but not his own, because he was a good driver and he was able to hold his drink too.

He retrieved his father's Volkswagen from the car park and headed back to Rathgar. He drove cautiously, both because of the beer and because his father treated his car the same way as he treated everything – with care and consideration – and expected his son to do the same. He put Lola and her treachery to the back of his mind, although it nagged at him constantly. As did the fact that he'd remembered he hadn't put the jewellery in the correct boxes before he'd placed them in the safe. He'd been so angry, he'd just shoved it all in together. He'd have to get in early in the morning and make sure he was the one to take them out and put them in the display cases. He couldn't leave it to Lorraine to sort out. It was fortunate that his father had stayed in Basle for an additional meeting with one of their suppliers. Richard wouldn't have accepted being upset as an excuse for not treating the jewellery properly.

Philip was mulling over his father's possible reaction to his actions when the woman stepped out in front of him. He felt a surge of adrenaline take over as he caught sight of her, and heard her startled cry. He stamped on the brakes and hauled at the steering wheel. He'd never had an accident in his life. But because of Lola Fitzpatrick, he was going to have one now.

Afterwards, he congratulated himself for missing both the woman who'd stepped onto the road in front of him and the nearby lamp post. What he didn't avoid was the low wall around the grass verge. The car went straight into it with surprising force. Philip, who'd never even scratched the car before, felt his rage with Lola intensify as the engine cut out. It took him a minute or two to regain his equilibrium, but when he eventually gathered his wits enough to open the door, he realised he couldn't put any weight on his right foot.

He stood on one leg, holding the door for support, as he surveyed the damage. The front of the car was now wedged over the wall and the front fender was crumpled. Meanwhile, the woman who'd caused it all was nowhere to be seen. Philip flexed his foot and a stab of pain juddered through him. Two small boys who'd been playing football on the street had come over to look.

'You've wrecked the wall, mister,' said one.

'And your car,' added the other.

'Thanks for that information, lads.' Philip scowled at them.

'My dad's a panel beater,' added the first helpfully. 'He could fix that for you.'

'If I need him, I'll ask,' said Philip.

He locked the car door and hobbled painfully to his parents' house, where Adele could see from his face that something had happened. When he told her, she immediately called Dick Roche, a nearby garage owner, who promised to tow the car away immediately.

'Nobody was hurt except you, of course, but the wall is damaged and someone might report it,' she told Philip, who was sitting at the kitchen table, his foot propped up on a chair and covered by a bag of Bird's Eye peas that Adele had taken from the freezer. 'We don't want questions asked. I can smell alcohol on your breath.'

'I was under the limit,' he said. 'If that old fruitcake hadn't tried to cross the road without looking, everything would've been fine. As it is, it's only because of my quick reactions that she wasn't flattened.'

'I appreciate that,' said Adele. 'Nevertheless, we don't want a brush with the law, regardless of the rights of the situation.' She looked at him quizzically. 'Why were you here anyway? I thought you were going out with Lola tonight.'

'Yeah, well, I didn't bother,' said Philip.

'Why not?'

'What d'you mean, why not? I didn't go out with her, that's all.'

'Has something happened?'

'You'd be delighted, wouldn't you?' asked Philip.

'Not for you, I wouldn't,' replied Adele.

'Well, delight away,' he said. 'Because we've split up.'

For a moment Adele's eyes gleamed, then she arranged her face into an expression of sympathy.

'I'm sorry,' she said. 'I know you liked her. What happened?'

'If you must know, I asked her to marry me,' said Philip. 'She said no.'

'What?' Adele was stunned. She hadn't known that Philip intended to propose to Lola. She'd have tried to talk him out of it if she had. On the other hand, the fact that the farmer's daughter had turned him down was cheering. Except that the ungrateful wretch had no right to reject him. She'd never get as good an offer again.

'She said she wasn't ready,' said Philip.

'The cheek of her. But you're young and she's immature.'

'Great. Thanks. The one time in your life you're on her side.'

'I'm not on anyone's side,' said Adele. 'I want you to be happy, that's all.'

'Marrying Lola would've made me happy,' said Philip.

'We'd better get that looked at.' Adele ignored his comment as she removed the frozen peas and looked critically at his foot, which was now swollen. 'You might have broken a bone.'

'It's ironic, isn't it,' said Philip. 'Most men get their hearts broken. I get a broken foot.'

'Let's go and get it checked out,' said Adele. 'It's probably just a sprain. So it's not that bad really.'

Nevertheless, thought Philip, as his mother went to the phone, he didn't know which part of him hurt most. His foot or his feelings.

Chapter 6

Kyanite: a blue or green layered crystal with a pearly sheen

Lola's hangover was the worst she'd ever had, and she spent the following morning alternating between throwing up and lying on her bed with a damp flannel across her forehead. Her flatmates went out – 'to let you suffer in peace', as Shirley put it – but when they returned that afternoon, she was still feeling wretched and confessed that she'd been sick on the hour every hour despite not having anything left to bring up.

Crona, a nurse, made her drink some flat 7 Up, which she said would help, but Lola barely allowed a sip to pass her lips before handing the glass back.

'Ah, don't worry, you'll be better before you're twice married,' Shirley told her later as she sat in the darkened bedroom.

'Though I've passed up the first opportunity I got.' Lola's voice was weak but held a hint of humour. 'So that might be a good deal further in the future than we think.'

Shirley was glad that her friend was able to make a joke, even if it was feeble. She was horrified at how pale and sick

Lola was looking, and would have suggested she had food poisoning except for the fact that they'd all eaten much the same thing the previous night. She was about to reply but she saw that Lola had closed her eyes again, and decided it would be better to let her sleep. After all, thought Shirley as she tiptoed out of the room, it wasn't every day you turned down the most eligible man in the country. It was hardly surprising she was feeling miserable. But hopefully she'd be right as rain tomorrow. Lola normally had the constitution of an ox. She hadn't been sick after eating a plateful of snails at the Warren home, something that Shirley was pretty certain would have made her puke on the spot. She decided that her flatmate's illness now was as much emotional as physical.

And after making that judgement, she told Crona and Fidelma that turning down marriage proposals was clearly a bad idea, and that if anyone ever asked her, she'd say yes straight away in order to avoid ending up in the same state as their friend.

An X-ray at the nearest emergency clinic had shown that Philip had cracked a bone, and as a result he'd been given a surgical boot to wear. That meant he hadn't been able to go into the shop to sort out the jewellery he'd shoved higgledy-piggledy into the safe the previous evening.

It was Lorraine who opened up, and it was Lorraine who called the house in some concern when she saw the state of the safe.

'It's my fault,' Philip told her. 'I left in a hurry last night. I'm very sorry.'

'I was worried there'd been some kind of botched burglary

attempt,' confessed Lorraine. 'Though I couldn't understand why the thieves would leave things jumbled up in the safe.'

'I'm sorry,' repeated Philip. 'And I'm also sorry you'll be short handed today. Hopefully I'll be in on Monday. And my father will be back then too.'

'Oh, it's OK,' said Lorraine. 'I'll manage.'

'Thank you,' said Philip. 'Call if you've any problems.'

He replaced the receiver and returned to the conservatory, where he'd been reading the *Irish Times*, his leg propped on a footstool.

Adele had fussed over him since the night before in a way that reminded him of when he was a small boy. Philip wasn't sure if her sudden rush of affection was due to her happiness at Lola's refusal to marry him, or her sympathy over his injured foot. But there was no doubt that she was in a better mood than he'd seen her in for quite a long time. From his vantage point in the sun he could hear her humming under her breath as she made him another cup of tea.

'You shouldn't be walking around,' she told him when she brought it in to him. 'I'll answer the phone if it rings.' She sat down opposite him. 'How are you feeling now?'

'I've taken the painkillers,' he said. 'But it still throbs.'

'I meant after the . . . situation with Lola.'

'There wasn't a situation,' said Philip. 'It's over. End of story.'

'Good.' Adele smiled. 'It's bad to mope.'

'I never mope,' said Philip.

'Because we can find you a much more suitable girl.'

'For heaven's sake, Mum. I don't need you to find me anyone.'

'A farmer's daughter was never going to work out,' said Adele.

'Can we stop talking about her?' asked Philip. 'You never wanted to when I was going out with her, so you don't need to now.'

'Of course.' Adele stood up again. 'I just want to be sure you're OK.'

'I'm fine,' said Philip. 'Absolutely fine.'

He closed his eyes and felt himself drifting off to sleep. He was back in the shop again, asking Lola to marry him, seeing the look of consternation on her face, hearing her say no. And then the phone rang again.

Lola eventually got out of bed and padded into the kitchen, where Shirley and Fidelma were having tea and toast. Crona had gone out with her boyfriend.

'Feeling better?' asked Shirley as Lola pulled out a wooden chair and sat down. 'There's tea in the pot and I can shove another slice in the toaster if you're hungry.'

Lola shuddered. 'I couldn't eat a thing,' she said.

'A drop of tea will do you the world of good,' said Shirley. 'There's nothing it won't cure.'

'I shouldn't have drunk all that wine,' said Lola. 'If I go out for a night on the lash, I usually have beer. It fills me up before I have time to get completely hammered.'

'Is your head at you? D'you want some Panadol?' asked Shirley.

'I don't actually have a headache.' Lola was surprised as she realised the fact. 'I just feel awful.'

'Stress,' said Fidelma. 'I'd feel awful too if I'd turned down a proposal from the handsomest man in Ireland.'

'It's probably a load of things.' Lola pushed the mug away without tasting the tea. 'Him, not getting promoted at work, getting pissed on Chianti . . .'

'Exactly,' said Fidelma. 'Don't worry, Lo-Lo, you'll be grand tomorrow.'

'I hope so,' said Lola, and rested her head on the table.

Shirley and Fidelma exchanged glances. They weren't sure if they should help her back to her room or leave her where she was. In the end, they left her. Sleep, said Fidelma, was probably the best thing for her, even if she ended up with a crick in her neck.

Philip's day of rest and recuperation had been ruined, although he hadn't yet said anything about it to his mother. It had been the second phone call from Lorraine that had shocked him.

'We've put everything out on display,' she said. 'One of the Troika engagement rings had fallen onto the safe floor and we missed it at first so we panicked a little bit about that.'

'There's no need to panic,' Philip told her. 'Everything's there. I'm certain of it.'

'Yes, well . . .' Lorraine hesitated.

'What?' he demanded.

'I wondered if you'd taken a pair of the Bluebell earrings with you,' she said. 'We're missing them.'

'You can't be,' said Philip. 'I put the earrings in the small box at the back . . . Oh!'

He'd just had a memory of putting his arms around Lola, trying to kiss her while she pushed him away. And he could see, as clearly as if he were there, the two small but perfect sapphires of the Bluebells shining in her ears.

72

'Philip?' Lorraine spoke enquiringly.

'You're absolutely right,' he said. 'I have them. I'd totally forgotten. Don't worry about it.'

'Are you sure?'

'Certain,' he said.

'That's a relief. There was a pair of cheap studs on the floor and I was afraid . . . well, I'm not sure what I was thinking.'

'I really do apologise.' He kept his tone relaxed and easy. 'Between leaving things in a mess last night and what happened afterwards, my head is all over the place.'

'I understand. No problem,' said Lorraine. 'I hope you feel better soon.'

'I'm sure I shall.'

Philip replaced the receiver slowly as Adele walked into the room.

'I told you I'd answer the phone,' she said. 'Was that Lorraine again?'

'Yes,' he said, and then added quickly, 'everything's fine, don't worry.'

'I wasn't worried,' said Adele. 'But our senior sales adviser should be able to look after things without having to resort to ringing you every ten minutes.'

'You're exaggerating,' said Philip. 'She had some legitimate queries, that's all.'

'Hmm.'

'Mum, I'm the store manager. I know my staff. Lorraine is very competent.'

'If you say so.' Adele shrugged and walked out again.

Philip hobbled back to his chair and ran his hands through his hair as he always did when he was worried. Had Lola deliberately taken those earrings? Had she intended to steal them from him? She'd practically thrown the other jewellery at him but had stormed off with the Bluebells in her ears. She must know by now she still had them. But she hadn't yet contacted him about returning them. It was possible that she didn't want to call. Maybe she was too embarrassed to talk to him. Perhaps she planned to bring them directly to the shop – although bringing them to the shop would mean having to see him face to face. She could hardly walk in and drop them on the counter.

One way or another he'd have to get them back from her as soon as possible. Even if Lorraine didn't say anything, his father would notice they were missing. He was razor sharp about the stock they held.

Philip stared ahead of him, wondering what the best thing to do was. Then he got up from the chair again and went to the phone. He dialled the number of Lola's flat. But nobody answered, and eventually he hung up.

When Crona got home in the early evening, Shirley told her that she was worried about Lola.

'I've never seen her so bad with a hangover before,' she said. 'I know she's upset too, but she hasn't kept a thing down all day.'

'She couldn't be pregnant, could she?' asked Crona.

Shirley looked horrified. 'She's on the pill. You were the one who told her condoms weren't reliable enough and made her go to the family planning clinic, remember?'

Crona nodded and went into the bedroom, where Lola was lying with her face buried in the pillow. She sat on the edge of the bed and took her friend's pulse.

'You should see a doctor,' she told her.

'No.' Lola shook her head.

'You really should,' said Crona. 'I'll bring you.'

'Oh, all right.' Lola didn't have the strength to protest any more. She didn't really have the strength for the ten-minute walk to the late-night surgery either, but supported by Crona on one side and Shirley on the other, she eventually made it. There were three people ahead of them. She closed her eyes and made a resolution never to drink red wine with sausages and rashers again.

Philip had phoned the flat twice more without success. He didn't know whether to be worried or not. But he assured himself that it was highly unlikely Lola Fitzpatrick had done a runner with the Bluebell earrings. She lived and worked in Dublin, for heaven's sake. She'd hardly be able to escape detection. If, indeed, she needed to be tracked down. He decided to give her until Monday to return them. He wouldn't ring the flat again because his mother would want to know who he was calling. Adele was looking after him brilliantly, but she wasn't giving him much time to himself. He certainly didn't want to accuse Lola of having the earrings with his mother beside him.

She'd return them, he said to himself as Adele put a tray with his evening meal on his lap. She *had* to return them. After all, she could have had an engagement ring worth more than the Bluebells if jewellery was what she wanted. But, he realised as he poked at the mashed potato in front of him, he'd never really known what Lola Fitzpatrick had wanted, had he?

He'd been played for a fool whichever way he looked at it.

Chapter 7

Sapphire: a transparent gemstone, usually blue, second only to diamond for hardness

When Lola left the doctor's consulting room, she was so white that her friends immediately thought she'd been given very bad news.

'I'm pregnant,' she told them and burst into tears.

Shirley and Crona exchanged glances.

'But . . . but . . . isn't the pill supposed to have a ninety-nine per cent success rate?' There was a sudden note of panic in Fidelma's voice.

'When taken properly,' said Crona. 'Did you miss taking it at all, Lola?' She put her arm around her friend's shoulder.

Lola nodded weakly. 'I don't like bringing it with me when I go back to Cloghdrom. It's not that my mother snoops, but . . .'

'Oh, Lola.' Shirley was close to tears too. 'What are you going to do?'

'I don't know.'

'Let's get you home first,' said Crona. 'Then we can talk about your options.'

They hurried out of the surgery and back to the flat, where Lola raced to the bathroom again.

'I can't believe being pregnant has made you so sick so suddenly,' Fidelma said. 'My mother had eight of us and was never once anything like you are now. And it's not just morning sickness, for heaven's sake. You were throwing up all day!'

'The doctor says I have hyper . . . hyper . . .'

'Hyperemesis gravidarum?' finished Crona.

Lola nodded.

'What the hell is that?' demanded Shirley. 'Is something wrong with the baby? Is that it?'

Crona shook her head and explained that it was a very severe form of morning sickness; although, she added, looking at Fidelma, sufferers could feel sick any time in the day. It could last until the end of the third month of pregnancy – sometimes even longer.

'Hard to keep it a secret so,' said Shirley.

The friends looked at each other in consternation. Although attitudes towards unmarried mothers were slowly changing in Ireland, many people, particularly in rural communities, still thought that a girl getting pregnant outside of marriage had brought shame on herself and her family. As a result, some chose to keep their pregnancies hidden. Occasionally a new arrival was said to be a baby of a relative who couldn't look after it; in some cases the girl's mother herself claimed to have had a late baby. Most people knew the truth. But appearances were everything.

'The doctor doesn't think I'm very far gone,' Lola said. 'It's like my body has just realised there's something else in there and is throwing a hissy fit. I've felt fine till now – well, once or twice a bit queasy, but everyone is a bit queasy from time to time for no apparent reason.' Suddenly overcome with the reality of her situation, she leaned her head on the table. 'I'm so fucked,' she whispered. 'I've made a mess of everything.'

'You have to phone Philip straight away,' said Shirley. 'Tell him that you were shocked by his proposal last night and that you didn't mean to say no. Tell him that you can't wait to marry him. And the sooner the better.'

Lola raised her head slowly and looked at Shirley from eyes that had darkened in her chalk-white face.

'Are you telling me to get married because of the baby?' she asked.

'What other option do you have?' demanded Shirley.

Lola said nothing.

'It's the right thing to do,' said Shirley. 'For everyone.'

'The doctor gave me information about places that can help,' Lola told her.

'Abortion clinics?' Fidelma couldn't keep the shock from her voice. Abortion was illegal, and a woman who wanted to terminate a pregnancy had to go to the UK. Nobody ever admitted to having had one. It was one of the great taboos.

'No. Just, you know, agencies who help with your pregnancy, and afterwards . . . well, they find a home for the baby.'

'D'you want to try to keep it a secret, Lo-Lo?' asked Crona.

'I might have,' said Lola. 'But with this hyperemesis thing . . . Shirley's right, it's not going to be easy.'

'For God's sake, Lola!' Shirley exclaimed. 'Why are you even thinking about anything other than Philip Warren? He's a man who wants to marry you! That solves all your problems.'

'I didn't want to marry him yesterday. Why should I want to marry him today?'

'Because everything has bloody well changed,' said Shirley. 'You're fecking pregnant. Pregnant! You need to get yourself married pronto.'

'I don't want to marry Philip Warren just because of a baby,' said Lola.

'It's not only about you any more,' said Fidelma. 'Think of what they'll all say if you rock up to Cloghdrom with a bump and no ring.'

'I'm not marrying somebody just because he's the father of my child.' Lola was adamant.

'Plenty of people do,' said Crona. 'And plenty of people make it work. You'd be one of them, and in a way better position because he's rich.'

'No!' Lola pushed the chair back and made another dash to the bathroom. 'I wouldn't.'

'She's out of her mind,' said Fidelma. 'Absolutely out of her mind.'

'And she won't listen to us,' Shirley said. 'She won't listen to anybody. She never does.'

The doctor had given her a sick cert for a month. Lola had never been off work for so long before. Although she didn't want to say it to her friends, she was frightened at how ill she was. And they were right about the enormity of her situation. There were no unmarried mothers in Cloghdrom, although she knew at least two girls who'd had babies an unfeasibly short time after they'd walked down the aisle. But nobody batted an eyelid at that. It was as though a ring on your finger made everything all right.

Would Philip accept her back if she phoned him and tried to persuade him that her refusal had simply been because she'd been overwhelmed? Or would he tell her that she'd had her chance and she'd blown it? Would he even believe that the baby was his?

'It's very early days,' she told Shirley the following morning. 'If I go to him and tell him about it and we get married just to make everything seem all right, and then I lose it anyway, I'll be trapped.'

'You can't make decisions on maybes,' said Shirley. 'You've got to see sense, Lola.'

'I thought I was doing the right thing yesterday.' Lola swallowed the antacid Crona had given her and made a face. 'In fact I was sort of proud of myself. I wasn't going to marry someone rich and handsome for the wrong reasons. I was being true to myself. And now . . .'

'You can still be true to yourself,' said Shirley. 'And, well, he has a right to know. It's his baby too.'

Lola gave her friend a scornful look. 'Like any of them care when you're pregnant,' she said. 'Like any of them want anything to do with you.'

'He wanted to marry you.'

'That was when I was a desirable single woman. Now I'm just someone who got herself knocked up.'

'You're not to think like that,' said Shirley.

'It's the truth. I wanted more from life than getting married and having kids. And now . . .'

'There's nothing wrong with being married and having kids,' said Shirley. 'And for the sake of your baby, you have to do it.'

Lola said nothing. But when she came back from the

bathroom, her face whiter than ever, she told Shirley that she wasn't going to say anything to anybody. At least for a few more weeks. Until she knew there was no other choice.

Telling her again what a massive mistake she was making would only make her more pig headed, thought Shirley. Instead she suggested Lola stay with her own older sister, Nuala, while she was on sick leave. Nuala lived in the pretty town of Virginia, about half an hour's drive from Cloghdrom. Her husband was in the Defence Forces and stationed with a peacekeeping mission in the Lebanon. Meantime Nuala, who worked at the local hospital, was alone in the house.

'She's the ideal person,' said Shirley. 'She doesn't really like being on her own, and even though she'll be working, she'll also be able to keep an eye on you.'

'It would be great to stay with her,' said Lola. 'But are you sure she'll want me?'

'I'll call her now.'

When Shirley returned after making the phone call, she said that Nuala would be delighted to take care of Lola for a while, and that she was going to drive to Dublin right now to bring her home with her. The good thing, Shirley added, was that Lola had been to Cloghdrom fairly recently, so she didn't need to go home again for a few weeks. As her mother never rang the office, Lola could call her from Nuala's and Eilis wouldn't know any different.

'Maybe that aul' hyper-whatsit will ease off while you're there too,' said Shirley. 'I know it's what the doc diagnosed, but he didn't take into account the fact that you were also absolutely wasted.'

Lola smiled faintly. Given that the antacids hadn't made much difference, she doubted it. The doctor had also given her some rehydration sachets, but Lola hadn't kept the liquid down for more than a few minutes.

'Nuala will look after you,' said Crona as Lola packed a small case. 'She'll make sure you're OK.'

'The thing is . . .' Lola looked at her friends, shamefaced. 'I'm honestly hoping I'm sick enough that I *will* lose the baby.'

'Don't talk like that!' Fidelma exclaimed. 'That's a terrible thought to have.'

'But it would definitely be better all round,' said Lola and rushed to the bathroom again.

Richard Warren was, like the vast majority of Irish people at the time, a Roman Catholic. Adele had been brought up as Church of England. They alternated their attendance at church between the two faiths, going to the local Church of Ireland one Sunday and the Catholic Church of the Three Patrons the other. Sometimes Philip attended with them, but this Sunday, given his crocked foot, he stayed at home. As soon as they'd left, he rang Lola's flat.

Lola was almost ready to leave when she heard the phone ringing in the hallway. Sarah, from one of the downstairs flats, yelled that it was her boyfriend.

'I can't talk to him.' Lola turned to Shirley. 'Will you? Tell him I've gone home for the weekend or something.'

'If I say that, he might try to call you at home,' she said.

'Oh crap, you're right. Tell him I'm staying with a friend. Tell him I'm upset. No,' she added, 'don't say that! He might think I'm going to change my mind. Just . . .'

'All right, all right,' said Shirley. 'Don't panic.'

Philip was getting impatient as he waited for Lola to come

to the phone. When he heard Shirley's voice, his hand tightened around the receiver.

'She's gone to see an old friend of ours in Cavan,' said Shirley. 'It was a kind of family emergency. I'm sorry, I don't have the number.'

'I need to talk to her urgently,' said Philip.

'If she rings, I'll give her the message.'

'Really urgently,' he said. 'It's important.'

'I'll tell her.'

'Is she back tomorrow?' he asked.

'I . . . I don't know.'

Philip didn't say anything else. He replaced the receiver with a bang. It didn't necessarily have to be suspicious that Lola had headed off. But he'd never known her to go and stay with a friend before. And he couldn't imagine what kind of family emergency would drag her back to Cavan. All the same . . . he told himself to breathe deeply . . . she still had to return to Dublin to work. The Bluebell earrings were worth a lot of money. But not enough for someone who'd stolen them to give up their job and disappear. He was making a mountain out of a molehill. Although he still had to get them back before his father realised they were gone.

The fact that he was unable to walk without crutches saved him on Monday. Lorraine didn't say anything to his father about the earrings as she assumed Philip would bring them with him when he next came into the shop. She'd replaced the Bluebell display with the Adele Rose collection, a perennial favourite with the customers of Warren's, so Richard didn't notice their absence.

When Adele went to her Ladies' Club meeting that

morning, Philip rang the Passport Office and discovered that Lola was on sick leave, a fact that left him feeling rather ill himself. He thought long and hard for a few minutes, then picked up the receiver again. He'd never phoned the farmhouse before, and he tapped his fingers impatiently as he waited for his call to be answered.

'Philip? Philip Warren? Lola's boyfriend? Is everything all right?' Eilis couldn't keep the anxiety out of her voice.

'I wanted to talk to Lola,' he said.

'Lola?' Eilis was astonished. 'She's not here.'

'I know she was going to stay with a friend, but now that she's off work sick, I thought she might have gone to you instead,' said Philip.

'Off work sick?' Eilis was even more worried. 'With what?'

'I don't know,' said Philip. 'She hasn't been in touch with me.'

'She hasn't been in touch with me either.'

'Well, look, if she does, will you tell her I'm looking for her? And if she calls me, I'll let you know.'

He hung up.

He was getting a really bad feeling about this.

Lola was feeling awful. She'd just been sick in Nuala's bath and she was now rinsing her mouth at the sink. Her normally glossy curls were falling in lank spirals around a face that was still deathly pale, and her eyes were dull and listless. She pushed her damp hair out of her eyes and tucked it behind her ears.

Which was when she saw the Bluebell earrings for the first time since she'd put them on in Warren's a couple of days earlier. She gasped in horror. She remembered pulling off all

84

the other jewellery and throwing it on the display counter, but she'd totally forgotten about the earrings, hidden as they were by her mass of hair, and very light despite the beauty of the stones.

She removed them with trembling fingers and, returning to the spare bedroom, put them into the pink plastic soap box in her sponge bag. The soap box was, she thought, an entirely inappropriate place for a pair of Adele Bluebells, but there was nowhere else to keep them. Not that she was keeping them, of course. She'd have to tell Philip. But how could she tell him about the earrings without telling him about the baby? She took a deep breath and gulped. And then sprinted for the bathroom again.

Eilis was far better at tracking down her daughter than Philip Warren had been. She phoned Shirley's library and told them that it was a matter of life and death and that she had to speak to her at once. Shirley, thinking that perhaps it was Lola herself, took the call and almost immediately confessed that Lola was with Nuala.

'But why?' asked Eilis.

'She needed a bit of time to herself.' Shirley wasn't going to break Lola's confidences, but she was uncomfortable at not telling Eilis the whole truth.

'Philip is going distracted,' said Eilis. 'Did they have a row?'

'Sort of.'

'Did he do something to upset her?' Eilis's voice hardened. 'Is she hiding from him?'

'Nothing like that,' Shirley assured her.

'Give me Nuala's number. I'll call her myself.'

'How about I ring Lola and get her to call you?' suggested Shirley.

'You will not. I'm her mother and I'll talk to her.'

'But Mrs Fitzpatrick—'

'Don't you Mrs Fitzpatrick me, Shirley Clooney,' said Eilis. 'Give me the number. Better still, give me the address.'

Which was how Eilis, driven by Milo, turned up at Nuala's doorstep later that afternoon and pressed the bell with such ferocity that Lola had no choice but to open it.

'Well, missy,' said Eilis as she walked into the hallway. 'Are you going to explain yourself?'

But Lola didn't need to. With just one look at her daughter, Eilis had guessed already.

She brought her to the farm and made her drink a cup of home-made broth, which Lola managed to keep down for fifteen minutes. After she came back from the bathroom, her eyes almost black in her paper-white face, Eilis insisted on full disclosure. She pursed her lips when Lola told her about the hyperemesis gravidarum.

'Your Aunt Madge suffered from it,' she said. 'That's why she only had one child. She said she couldn't go through it again.'

'I know how she feels,' muttered Lola.

'So what are your plans?' demanded Eilis. 'You know that boyfriend of yours is going frantic looking for you?'

'He is?' Lola was surprised. She'd thought that Philip would be too angry with her to ever want to talk to her again. And then it struck her. He knew about the earrings. He thought she'd taken them. That she was a thief. Her stomach lurched.

'He phoned here earlier. That's how I found out you were at Nuala's.'

'I didn't think he'd call,' said Lola.

'Why don't you want to talk to him? Have you had a row about this unplanned pregnancy? Is he trying to say it's nothing to do with him?' Eilis looked grimmer than ever.

'He doesn't know about it,' said Lola. She didn't say anything about the earrings. She didn't want to complicate matters with her mother.

'You'd better tell him right away, so that he can take care of his responsibilities.'

The baby wasn't Philip's responsibility, thought Lola. It was hers. She was the one who'd skipped the pill.

'I don't want him to know.'

Eilis stared at her.

Lola explained about Philip's proposal and how she'd turned him down. Eilis said the same to her as the girls had done – that things had changed and she had to think about the baby. But Lola was insistent that it would be more of a mistake to marry someone when she had doubts.

'It's a bit late to talk about mistakes!' cried Eilis. 'I'd say getting pregnant is a far bigger one.'

'No point in making two,' said Lola.

'So you're happy to bring disgrace on this family?'

'Oh, come on, Mam. It's not a disgrace.'

'Maybe not in Dublin. But in Cloghdrom . . .'

'You'd be happy for me to be married to someone I don't love?'

'You shouldn't have slept with him.'

'Girls do.' Lola kept her voice steady with difficulty. 'Girls sleep with boys and get blamed for falling pregnant. We're the ones who are looked down on and called sluts, while they get on with their lives, and it's bloody well not fair!'

'Life isn't fair! You know that.'

'I do know that, yes. But I'm not making a bad situation worse by marrying him. Besides, he probably wouldn't want me now.'

'The Warrens won't allow him to walk away from you. This baby is their grandchild too, you know.'

'Look, right now I'm only barely pregnant,' said Lola. 'You know yourself that nobody ever talks about it until they're around three months gone. I'm so sick, every time I throw up I think the baby will come with it! I'll tell him when I need to.'

'And when will that be?'

But Lola didn't answer.

And she didn't know which would be harder to confess to him. Being pregnant with his child or having a pair of Warren's earrings hidden in her soap box.

Chapter 8

Briolette: a faceted tear-drop-shaped stone

After she'd recovered from another bout of severe sickness the following morning, Lola rang the Warren's shop in Duke Lane. Lorraine told her that Philip wasn't there.

'Was he expecting to come in today?' she continued. 'I thought he was going to be at least a week on crutches.'

Lola was gobsmacked at the woman's words and immediately asked what on earth had happened.

'Don't you know?' said Lorraine. 'Haven't you seen him or phoned him?'

'Not since Friday,' she said. 'I've been sick.'

'Oh,' said Lorraine. 'Well . . . he crashed his car.'

'Oh my God! Is he OK?'

'He's broken a bone in his foot and he's in a surgical boot,' said Lorraine. 'So naturally he hasn't come into the shop. Look, I've got to go, there's a customer waiting.'

'Of course. Thanks, Lorraine.'

Lola replaced the receiver slowly. Then she picked it up again, took a deep breath and dialled the Warren house in Rathgar.

Philip, who'd been dozing in the conservatory, wasn't quick enough to pick it up before Adele answered. She came into the room and told him that Lola wanted to talk to him.

'She's probably changed her mind about splitting up with you,' she said. 'Realises which side her bread is buttered. I hope you hold firm.'

'Give it a rest, Mum.' Philip hauled himself out of the chair and went to the phone.

'Hello,' he said. 'I wondered if I'd ever hear from you again. I thought you were too much of a career girl to throw a sickie, but obviously work only matters when you're choosing it over me.'

'I *am* sick,' said Lola. 'I've come to the farm to recuperate.'

'Your mother said you weren't there.'

'I wasn't when you rang.'

'Where were you?'

'That doesn't matter. Look, I'm phoning you because I have those earrings.'

'Your conscience finally woke up, then?'

'I didn't realise I was still wearing them. I forgot to take them off in the shop, and—'

'And you were too sick to bother getting in touch straight away.'

'I told you, I didn't know I had them.'

'Yeah, right. You've probably spent the weekend out and about in them, throwing yourself at other men. Well listen to me, Lola Fitzpatrick, you'd better get them back to me right now.'

'I . . . I'm not sure how to do that,' said Lola. 'I'll be in Cloghdrom for a few weeks. Can you come and get them?'

'Haven't you heard about my accident?' he asked. 'Caused by how upset I was about you, by the way.'

'Lorraine told me. I rang the shop, you see, and—'

'I'm lucky I wasn't killed,' said Philip. 'Not that you'd care. In fact you'd probably have been delighted. That way you could have kept the Bluebells.'

'Don't be stupid,' she snapped, and then swallowed a couple of times as a wave of nausea hit her. 'I'm sorry you had an accident, but it wasn't my fault, and being sick . . .' She'd been about to say that wasn't her fault either, but of course it was. 'I can send them registered post,' she said. 'It will take a few days, though.'

'Are you out of your mind?' demanded Philip. 'They're worth thousands. Even with registered post I wouldn't risk them. You'll have to come back to Dublin with them.'

'I can't,' said Lola.

'Yes you bloody well can. Get the bus.'

'Please, Philip. It's not possible.'

'Listen to me. I want those earrings and I want them before Friday. Otherwise I'm going to the police.'

'Philip!'

'Just think,' he said. 'If you'd said yes, you'd be the owner of a diamond ring and maybe those earrings too. As it is, you don't own them; you've taken them without permission, which in anyone's book is stealing. You're lucky I haven't reported you already. I don't care how you get them to me, but you'd better do it, unless you want to end up on *Garda Patrol*.' He slammed the phone down.

Lola stared at the receiver.

Then she raced to the bathroom again.

* * *

Philip felt as though he'd dodged a bullet. The longer he'd gone without being able to contact Lola, the more he'd worried about having to confess to his father that she had the Bluebell earrings. Having made it clear to her that she'd have to get them back to him, he was feeling relieved. But his relief was short lived, because that evening Richard asked him about them himself.

'I was doing a stock check,' he said. 'They're missing, but Lorraine says you know all about it.'

'Well, yes,' said Philip. 'It's just that Lola has them, and—'

'Lola!' Adele, who was sitting in the armchair near the window, looked up sharply. 'But you've broken up with her. Did she buy them?'

'Of course not. She couldn't possibly afford them. She didn't realise she had them,' said Philip.

His parents stared at him.

'She was wearing them in the shop and she left still wearing them, and—'

'Was this before or after you asked her to marry you?' demanded Adele.

'After, but that—'

'She deliberately walked out of the shop with a pair of Bluebell earrings?'

'Yes, but—'

'I knew it,' said Adele. 'That girl had her eye on the jewellery from the start. She always intended to have something. She's nothing more than a common thief.'

'She could've had an engagement ring if she'd said yes,' Philip pointed out.

'But she would have had to marry you for that,' said Adele. 'Why hasn't she returned them?'

'Because she went home to the farm.'

'Why?'

'I don't know!' cried Philip. 'I suppose she was upset at not saying yes to me.'

Adele snorted. 'She probably went home for some country hoedown and decided she'd wear those beautiful earrings to impress people.'

'Maybe.' Philip sighed.

'She should have brought them back immediately,' said Richard. 'You should have made sure that she did.'

'In case it escaped your notice, I've been a bit incapacitated,' said Philip.

'It's almost as though she planned it.' Adele tapped her foot angrily.

'In fairness, she could hardly have planned Philip's car accident,' Richard pointed out.

'I'll get them back from her,' said Philip.

'You'd better,' Adele said. 'Otherwise we're calling the police.'

'I told her that already,' said Philip.

'So you think she's stolen them too?' asked Richard.

'I don't know what to think. Except that I thought I loved her, and I was a total idiot. And I guess you're both happy about that.'

Neither of his parents replied.

Philip was fuming. Lola Fitzpatrick had made an utter fool of him, and he'd never forgive her for that.

Ever.

The Agreement
Four years later

Chapter 9

Peridot: a green semi-precious gemstone

Your life could change in an instant, thought Lola as she looked out of the window to where her daughter was chasing the farm kittens, falling over as she rushed after them but getting up straight away and starting the chase again. In all her plans, she'd never considered being the unmarried mother of a three year old. She'd thought that crisis pregnancies happened to other people, dismissing unmarried mothers as stupid fools. Yet she'd been the foolish one. She'd been the one who'd had to go rushing back to her own mother when everything had gone so spectacularly pear shaped.

Even if she'd had the faintest thought of telling Philip Warren about her pregnancy, it had disappeared when Shirley had called her a few days after a visit to the farmhouse. Lola had given her the Bluebell earrings to return to him – wrapped in cotton wool and sealed in an envelope – and when Shirley phoned to tell her the deed was done, she also told her how angry Philip had been.

'He said you could rot in hell for all he cared.' She repeated his words exactly. 'He said you were lucky they didn't call the police.'

'I suppose I was,' said Lola. 'Adele never liked me; she'd probably have been delighted to see me arrested!'

'Ah, Lola . . .'

'I made such a mistake with all of them,' said Lola. 'But it's a whole new ball game for me now. I'm going to have my baby and I never need to talk to them again.'

'But you'll have to tell Philip when it's born,' said Shirley. 'You can't keep quiet.'

'Of course I can,' said Lola.

And she had. For three years. But now . . . she continued to watch the little girl through the kitchen window . . . now things were changing. And she wasn't as sure of everything as she'd been before.

It had been a simple moment that had caused her to think differently, the day Danny Coghlan, one of the farmhands, had come into the kitchen looking for her father.

'Dad's not here,' Lola told him. 'I'm not sure where he's gone.'

'Daddy!' Bey beamed at Danny. 'Daddy!'

Danny blushed deep scarlet as Lola burst out laughing.

'She calls every man who comes into the kitchen Daddy,' she reassured him. 'It's not just you.'

But when she was relating the story to the rest of the family over dinner, she suddenly realised it wasn't really a laughing matter. Right now, Bey didn't care who her father was. But one day she would. One day, just as everyone had said to Lola, she'd have a right to know.

'I've been selfish,' Lola told Eilis that night. 'I came here and took advantage of you and I didn't take proper responsibility for what I'd done.'

'Nonsense,' said Eilis. 'Sure where else would you go, pet? We're your family and we love you.'

'You've been brilliant,' said Lola. 'You haven't judged me, you've supported me and Bey, you've done everything a mother could do. But I have to stand on my own two feet again, Mam. And I have to think about what's right for Bey. She deserves to know that every man in wellington boots isn't her father. And Philip should know he has a daughter. Whatever his feelings are about it.'

'I'm glad you've finally recognised it,' Eilis said. 'You know your dad and I will always be happy to have you here. And we both love Bey to bits. But there's unfinished business between you and Philip Warren and you need to deal with it.'

'You're right,' said Lola and smiled at her. 'But then you're my mammy. You're always right.'

'Get away with you!' Eilis laughed. 'So what are your plans?'

'I called Shirley,' said Lola. 'I'm going to Dublin. I'll stay with her for a while and then I'll get in touch with Philip and tell him. I know he'll be furious with me, but I'll get over it. I've got over everything else, after all.'

'You won't regret it,' said Eilis.

'I hope not,' Lola said. 'I really do.'

Shirley was renting a small terraced cottage in North Strand, close to the city centre. Her former flatmates, Crona and Fidelma, had moved on. Crona was nursing in Oman, while

Fidelma was engaged and living with her fiancé. Shirley had split from her most recent boyfriend. 'I'm clearly congenitally incapable of having a relationship that lasts for more than three months,' she told Lola when she arrived a couple of weeks later. 'So I've decided to be a single lady around town and settle down in a place of my own instead of a scummy flatshare. It's not much, but it's home. I can't believe whole families used to live here in the past – there's hardly even room for me and a cat – but I suppose people's aspirations have changed.'

'It's fabulous,' said Lola as she settled Bey, who'd fallen asleep seconds before the taxi from the bus station had pulled up outside the door. 'I really have to start thinking about moving out of the farmhouse.'

'I thought you liked being at home. After all, you resigned from the Civil Service to stay there.'

'I had to resign. I would've been out sick for ages and I couldn't have stayed working there after Bey was born.' Lola took the big pink mug of tea that Shirley had made for her. 'Mam has been great over the last few years, but I can't rely on her forever. Besides, living at the farm makes me feel like a kid myself sometimes.'

'Would you marry Philip now?' asked Shirley. 'If he asked you?'

Lola laughed. 'I think Mam secretly hopes we'll get married and live happily ever after,' she said. 'But that's not going to happen.'

'Even if he asked you? Because of Bey?'

'That's highly unlikely,' said Lola. 'Especially after everything he said to you about me. No, I'm going to tell him he has a daughter, and assure him I'm not looking for anything from him. I'll say I'm looking for work in town so that he can see her if he wants. After that, it's up to him.'

'You're doing the right thing,' Shirley told her.

'I know,' said Lola. 'I should have told him at the start. You were all right about that. I was too stubborn to see it.'

'Ah, listen, you were sick as anything and in no fit state to make decent decisions,' said Shirley. 'The main thing is you're going to put things right now.'

'I hope Philip sees it that way,' said Lola.

She was allowing herself two days in Dublin before contacting him. Two days to remember the person she'd been before everything had changed so abruptly.

Even with Bey in tow, she was able to connect with the girl she'd been a few years earlier. She revelled in the anonymity of city life, of walking out of the house and not seeing anyone she knew, not being asked how she was and how Bey was getting along. She enjoyed the freedom of coming and going as she pleased without having to tell her mother her plans – or knowing that someone else would tell her anyway because nothing stayed secret in Cloghdrom for very long.

'I'm a city girl at heart,' she told Shirley as they drank iced smoothies in St Stephen's Green and luxuriated in an unexpected spell of fine weather. 'I know Cloghdrom is heavenly at this time of the year, but it's so damn quiet. Whereas here we're in a lovely park in the centre of the city and I can combine greenery and flowers with the sound of cars and planes.'

Shirley laughed. 'It's not Manhattan,' she said. 'It's just Dublin.'

'All the same' said Lola, 'it's great to be back.'

'And you being here makes it easier for Philip to see Bey,' said Shirley.

'I'm sort of hoping he won't want much access,' Lola admitted. 'I know loads of girls in my position would want the father to be involved, but . . .'

'He was pretty horrible about you when I brought back the earrings, but he's probably over that by now,' said Shirley. 'To tell you the truth, Lo-Lo, I never understood why you were so doubtful about him.'

'I think . . .' Lola took a deep breath as she considered what she was going to say. 'I think it was because he was so damn entitled. He thought he was doing me a favour by going out with me. He thought I wanted everything he had. He thought he was better than me and that I was lucky he'd chosen me.'

'I can understand that,' said Shirley. 'He does come from a different background, after all.'

'Yes, but . . . oh, I can't explain properly. He was almost . . . almost feudal about it. I don't remember if I told you this or not, but I wasn't just wearing the Bluebells. He made me put on loads of jewellery; it was hanging off me. And I suddenly realised that he wanted to own me. When I said I didn't want to marry him, he was so angry. He tried to kiss me even though I didn't want him to, and—'

'Lola! He didn't try to rape you, did he?'

'No!' cried Lola. 'I think he thought that if he kissed me . . . People don't say no to the Warrens. He didn't say no to his mother when she insisted I come for dinner that time. He didn't say no when she served me those bloody snails. He was on her side all the time even though she was being horrible to me because I wasn't good enough. I just feel . . . they'll never think I'm good enough. And me turning him down will only have made them worse, you know?'

'I think so,' said Shirley.

'Anyhow, this isn't about me or him or even Adele; it's about Bey. She deserves to know her father and I'm going to call him tomorrow to set it all up. He can lose the rag as much as he likes, but at least it will be out in the open.'

'You won't regret it.' Shirley got up from the grass where they'd been sitting and brushed stray blades from her skirt. 'I'd better get back to work. I'll see you later this evening.'

'OK,' said Lola. 'Have a nice day.'

Left alone with her daughter, Lola brought her to feed the ducks, something everyone with children did when they were in the city's favourite park. She thought about what she'd say to Philip, and how she should react to however he himself reacted. She would be calm, she promised herself. She was a more mature woman than the girl who'd fled Dublin four years earlier. She was a mother, and her responsibility was to her daughter before anything else.

She smiled as Bey shrieked with excitement when she threw scraps of the bread roll she'd bought for that purpose and the ducks paddled over to the side of the pond and fought over them. She was doing a good job raising her. But Bey had a right to a father too. Lola would do what was necessary even though she didn't want to.

'Ducks!' Bey cried. 'Ducks, ducks, ducks.'

Lola took her camera from her bag and took a photograph of Bey throwing bread to the ducks. It was as she was putting it back that she became aware of the man watching them from the path.

Her first thought was that Richard Warren looked more patriarchal than ever.

'Lola.' He spoke when he realised that she'd seen him.

'Mr Warren.'

'I wasn't sure it was you. We did only meet the one time. But you're a very striking young lady.'

'Am I?'

'Sparky, too, I remember thinking. Knew your own mind.'

Lola shrugged and steered Bey away from the water's edge.

'A pretty child,' said Richard. 'Yours?'

Lola wanted to say no, but that would have been a betrayal of her daughter, so she nodded.

'Ducks!' cried Bey again as they clustered around looking for more bread.

'Tomorrow,' promised Lola. 'We'll feed the ducks again tomorrow.'

'How old is she?' asked Richard.

'Just gone three.'

'You turned my son down because you weren't ready for marriage, but now you're a mother of a three year old?' He raised an eyebrow.

'I wasn't ready to marry *him*,' said Lola.

'Why?'

'I really don't think that's any business of yours, Mr Warren,' she said as she lifted Bey into her arms. 'It was . . . nice to see you again. But I've got to go.'

Her heart was hammering in her chest. This was her opportunity, but it was the wrong opportunity. She'd rehearsed what she'd say to Philip, not to his father. And she wasn't ready. Not here. Not now.

'I didn't recognise you at first.' Richard detained her. 'Like

I said, we only met the one time. I was staring because of the little girl.'

'Excuse me?'

'I recognised her.'

'I'm sorry, but I doubt you've seen her before.'

'Not her,' agreed Richard. 'But I've seen someone the image of her at that age. Philip.'

Lola stared at him.

'Oh for heaven's sake,' said Richard impatiently. 'Do you really think I can't spot a resemblance? I have a photograph of him in this park feeding the ducks too. And you'd be hard pressed to tell the difference between the two of them.'

'I know. I know. I was going to . . .'

'To what?'

'To tell him,' said Lola. 'Tomorrow. I was going to call to the shop and—'

'You'll do no such thing,' said Richard. 'I absolutely forbid it.'

She stared at him. 'I have to have a conversation with him,' she said. 'I realise that I should have done it before.'

'You're definitely going to have a conversation,' Richard told her. 'But it's going to be with me, not Philip. And you're most certainly not coming to the shop to create a scene. Are you crazy?'

'But . . .'

'This evening,' said Richard. 'We'll talk. Where do you live?'

'I'm staying with a friend.'

'I'm coming to see you,' he said. 'Whether you like it or not.'

She thought about it for a moment. Then she gave him Shirley's address.

After he left, she was shaking so much she had to sit back down on the grass.

Chapter 10

Bloodstone: a green gemstone spotted or streaked with red

As soon as she felt she could stand up again, Lola left St Stephen's Green and took a taxi she couldn't really afford back to Shirley's house in North Strand. When her friend arrived home at 5.30, she had to repeat the story of her encounter with Richard more than once because she was so overwrought that nothing she said made sense.

'He's coming here?' Shirley squeaked when she eventually realised what Lola was saying. 'Richard Warren? Will Philip be with him?'

'I don't know.' Lola's expression was stricken.

'We'd better be prepared.'

'For what?'

'For why you didn't say anything. For why you were only going to tell him tomorrow. For why I didn't say anything either when I brought Philip the earrings.'

'You were a messenger, that's all,' Lola said. 'None of it is your fault.'

'Ducks.' Bey, who'd been sitting on the kitchen floor with a sheet of paper and a set of crayons, held her picture up to

107

show her mother. Lola praised the coloured blobs and told her that she was very, very clever. Bey smiled and returned to her drawing, her tongue sticking out of the side of her mouth while she concentrated on what she was doing.

'What time will he be here?' asked Shirley later in the evening, after Lola had put her daughter to bed.

'I don't know. He didn't say.'

And at that moment a knock came to the door, causing both their hearts to start racing.

'Mr Warren,' said Lola when she opened it. 'Come in.'

He followed her into the tiny living room, where she introduced Shirley.

'You're the one who returned the Bluebells Lola took, aren't you?' asked Richard. 'Are you part of this conspiracy?'

'There's no conspiracy,' retorted Shirley.

'Not telling my son he's a father is most certainly a conspiracy,' said Richard.

'Philip didn't want to be a father,' said Lola. 'He had ambitions of his own.'

'That's what you think?'

'Yes,' said Lola.

'He asked you to marry him.' Richard's voice was cool. 'You rejected him. You ran away to your family's farm, taking some valuable jewellery of ours with you. You behaved disgracefully.'

'Lola had hyperemesis gravidarum when she was pregnant,' said Shirley. 'She was very sick. That was why she had to rush home. She wasn't trying to rob your silly earrings.'

'I thought I was going to lose the baby,' Lola explained when Richard looked confused. 'I didn't want to say anything to Philip, especially after turning him down. I didn't want him to think that I'd marry him just because I was pregnant.'

'And afterwards?' asked Richard.

'Afterwards there didn't seem to be any point,' said Lola. 'My reasons for not marrying him hadn't changed. Plus, I was in Cloghdrom and he was in Dublin.'

'You didn't think he had a right to know about his daughter?'

At Richard's words, the same ones she had used herself, Shirley shot a glance at Lola, who shook her head.

'Bey was my responsibility,' she said. 'I made the decisions. And I didn't see the point in involving Philip.'

'You didn't give him a chance,' said Richard.

'Oh for crying out loud!' exclaimed Lola. 'Even if I'd been head over heels in love with him, you and your wife made it perfectly clear I wasn't a suitable girlfriend, let alone wife. But I didn't love him and I didn't want to marry him and I didn't want to spend my life feeling inadequate. I wanted to be independent.'

'And now?' asked Richard. 'You said you wanted to tell him now. Why?'

'I made my decision for what I thought were the right reasons, but Bey needs to know her father,' said Lola. 'And he has a right to know her too.'

'Are you married?' asked Richard.

Lola shook her head.

'So you're looking after the child yourself.'

'I'm looking after Bey, yes,' she said.

'And it's difficult, I suppose.'

'No,' said Lola. 'She's a pet, she really is. I love her and I wouldn't be without her.'

'Are you working?'

Lola explained about staying on the farm, but added that her ambition was to return to Dublin and find a job.

'You talked about ambition before,' said Richard. 'When you came to dinner in our house. You wanted to be something ridiculous in the Civil Service.'

'A principal officer,' said Lola. 'Obviously that didn't work out.'

'So you're looking for a job. Do you live here?' He looked around the small house with a critical gaze.

'No,' said Lola. 'Shirley has let us stay for a while, but I'm going to find somewhere for Bey and me to live.'

'Ah,' said Richard. 'I understand now.'

'What?'

'You want to tell him for the money.'

'Money?'

'Oh, don't go all doe eyed on me!' Richard looked at her with disdain. 'I know your type. You get yourself in trouble and then you come looking for money. Maintenance, you'll call it, but you'll use it for living your life the way you want to at his expense.'

'That's totally unfair,' said Lola. 'If I'd wanted money from Philip, I would've told him about Bey a long time ago. And yes, I got pregnant, but there were two of us involved in that. So don't try to make it all about me.'

'But it *is* all about you, isn't it?' said Richard. 'You're the one who made the choices for everyone. And now you're regretting them. Because you realise that you can't stay with your mother and father forever and you need to find a way to live by yourself. So you're coming after my son to help you.'

'You're so wrong!'

'You want to ruin his life to enhance yours.'

'Lola is only here to tell Philip about his daughter,' said Shirley. 'He's entitled to know.'

'Actually he's entitled to live his life without someone else's mistake catching up with him,' said Richard.

'Hello!' cried Shirley. 'It takes two to tango, like Lola said.'

'I'm going to see him tomorrow,' said Lola. 'I don't care what sort of character assassination you want to do first.'

'You're not going to see him at all,' said Richard.

'Why not?' she asked.

'Because you're not going to destroy his life on a damn whim.'

'Bey won't destroy his life,' Lola said. 'She's the loveliest, happiest little girl in the world. He'll be proud to have her as his daughter.'

'Philip already has a family of his own to be proud of,' said Richard. 'He's married. His wife is pregnant. Surely you must know that already.'

Lola stared at him in shock.

'How the hell would I know?' she asked eventually.

'There was a notice in the paper,' said Richard. 'He married the year after you broke up with him. Her name is Donna. She's a lovely girl, from a good background, and she's very suitable for him.'

'So that's what you're worried about.' Lola spoke slowly. 'That knowing about Bey will mess things up for him and his new wife and family.'

'This is not a good time for him to hear about another child,' said Richard. 'And although I'd love to say that the child isn't his, it was clear to me at once that she is.'

111

'Why are you here?' Shirley felt she had to say something. 'What do you want?'

'What I *don't* want are loose ends,' he said.

'I'm not a loose end,' said Lola.

'I rather think your daughter is,' said Richard. 'And you thinking that she should know her father and he should know her – that's something I don't want to happen.'

'She'll find out one day,' said Shirley. 'Better now than later.'

'I'll be the judge of that,' said Richard. 'And I have a lot more experience at making judgements than two silly young girls.'

'You can't lie to Philip,' said Lola.

'I'm not proposing to lie to anyone. I'm proposing that you keep doing what you've done so successfully for the last four years. Which is to say nothing. Not now or in the future.' Richard took a folded sheet of paper out of his pocket. 'You said you needed to find work and a place to live. But you'll also have expenses for your daughter. For as long as you stay away from Philip and ensure she knows nothing about him, I'm prepared to pay those expenses by way of a monthly sum.'

'You're joking!' Lola stared at him.

'I most certainly am not.'

He handed her the paper and she read through it. The amount he was offering was close to what she'd been earning in the Civil Service. It would make all the difference to her plans to move back to Dublin.

'For all your fine words, the main reason you want to talk to Philip is money,' said Richard. 'So you can have it if you sign this.'

'I . . .' She stared at the agreement. 'It's not about the money. It really isn't.'

'Don't sign it,' said Shirley. 'However much it is, it's not worth it. Do the right thing. Tell Philip.'

'And wreck his marriage?' Lola's voice was full of concern.

'You don't know that it would be wrecked,' said Shirley. 'You don't know anything other than what this old fart is telling you.'

'I've made enough mistakes already,' said Lola. 'I want to be sure . . .'

'Sign it,' said Richard. 'It's the best offer you're ever going to get in your life.'

'If you don't tell Philip now, Bey might resent you in the future,' Shirley warned. 'He's a grown-up. He can look after himself.'

'But his wife doesn't deserve this stress, not now,' said Richard. 'She's been very ill with her pregnancy too. She's expecting twins, by the way.'

Lola looked at him, then looked at Shirley. She got up from the sofa and went into the bedroom. Bey was asleep, her red curls vibrant against the white pillow. She leaned against the door frame, uncertain of what to do. It seemed to her that every time she had to make an important decision, she made the wrong one. And this decision wasn't just about her. It was also about Bey. And Donna, who she didn't even know. And Donna's babies. And Philip. It was about everyone.

She turned back into the room and sat down again. She read through the agreement. She looked at the amount of money. She wondered if Judas had felt this way when he'd been offered the thirty pieces of silver. But that was money for himself. This was for Bey. This was to make sure everything would be all right. It would give her daughter a better life than Lola could provide on her own.

She rubbed the back of her neck as she thought about all the options. This would be the most important decision she ever made in her life. And she was making it for Bey, not for herself. For once, she had to get it right.

'Philip might offer you something better,' said Shirley.

Richard snorted. 'And you both wanted to convince me it wasn't about the money.'

'That's not what I meant,' said Shirley.

'Sign it and there'll be an additional sweetener for you and you alone,' Richard told Lola. 'This is a one-time offer.'

Philip had said the same thing to her when he'd asked her to marry him. She'd turned him down for all the right reasons, and yet perhaps it had been the biggest mistake of her life. Would not signing this piece of paper be an even bigger one?

She took the pen that Richard Warren was offering her, hesitated for a moment and then with a quick stroke signed her name.

'You've done the right thing,' said Richard. 'Fill in your bank details and the first payment will arrive next week.'

Lola exhaled slowly and looked at Shirley. Her friend shrugged, then gave her a sympathetic smile.

'I promised you a sweetener,' said Richard. 'For yourself.'

He handed her a sealed padded envelope. Lola put it on the table. She didn't want to look at a wad of cash right now. She'd feel like a total traitor if she did.

'Does the Ice Dragon know about this?' she asked.

'Ice Dragon?'

'Adele,' said Lola.

The faintest flicker of a smile crossed Richard's lips.

'This isn't something she needs to worry about,' he said.

'So you've basically brushed me out of your family's life,' said Lola.

'You were never a part of it,' Richard said. 'You're a silly, headstrong girl, but at least for the first time in your life you've made a sensible decision.'

But later that night, after she'd put the unopened envelope away, unable to face looking at her money, Lola still didn't know if it had been sensible or the most stupid thing she'd ever done.

The Theft
Nine years later

Chapter 11

Chalcedony: a semi-transparent or translucent type of quartz

Adele Warren sat in front of the desktop computer that Richard had installed in the room he used as a home office. She switched it on and waited as it whirred into life, excited by the new technology. It was far removed from her early years as an accounts clerk, when she'd carefully written income and expenditure into huge ledgers every day. Now she used the computer to keep track of the household expenses. She'd always been in charge of the finances at home, Richard being quite happy to leave that to her while he concentrated on the business. Her younger son, Peter, had set up a simple program for her to use, and she enjoyed tapping at the keyboard once a week as she inputted the various bills that had been paid and made projections for future payments too.

She was engrossed in her work when the doorbell rang. Irritated, she went to the door, only to find it was someone trying to sell her a new phone package. That was the down-side of the surge in technology-related things, she thought. New companies were springing up all over the place, claiming to offer better services than the older, trusted ones. It was happening in the retail sector too, with more glamorous jewellery shops opening in the city, trying to lure customers away. But none of them had the cachet of Warren's, Adele thought. And so far their customers had remained loyal.

On her return to the home office, she glanced out of the window at the young door-to-door salesman she'd sent off with a curt 'no thank you'. He might be working for a start-up company with an impressive-sounding name, she thought, but he was still drumming up business in an old-fashioned way. She smiled to herself as she turned back to the desk, and then cried out in annoyance as she knocked against the pile of folders on the desk, spilling their contents out onto the floor.

Her annoyance was as much with her husband as with herself. She'd been the one to knock them over, but it drove her crazy that he never put anything away properly, even though he had a perfectly good filing cabinet in the corner of the room.

Well, she thought, as she kneeled down and started to pick up Richard's papers, she'd tidy this lot up once and for all, and then she'd tell him that if they were sharing the beautiful mahogany desk he'd bought when they first moved into the house, the least he could do was to keep it clear of mess.

Most of the papers were fact sheets on the stones he was interested in for the Adele collections. She paused at a grading report for a diamond described as 'Fancy Intense Green'. She wondered if Richard was thinking of green diamonds for the next Adele range. She hoped not. Green stones should always be emeralds, and she preferred the purity of white diamonds.

'Get on with it, woman,' she murmured to herself as she

glanced through a memo he'd sent Peter about payment schedules. 'This isn't your business.'

Ever since Peter had taken over as the accountant at Warren's, Adele had tried to keep her nose out of the company finances, although she found it difficult. She'd enjoyed her limited involvement in the business when she was younger, but Richard had warned her that the boys needed to take more control of Warren's now, and that they couldn't interfere too much.

Which was easy for him to say, she thought as she smoothed out the bank statement in front of her. After all, he still went into the shop every day. And she was quite sure that he interfered as much as ever, no matter what he said to her.

She found her place in the accounting program again and then frowned as she looked at the statement. Nothing matched what she'd already inputted. She scrolled up and down the screen, then studied the statement more carefully. It was a few seconds before she realised that the reason nothing matched was because she was looking at Richard's personal bank statement, and not the household expense account.

Adele had never looked at her husband's bank statement before. She'd never felt the need to. He had always paid a substantial monthly sum into the household account and he never asked her how she spent it. He'd told her that she could take as much out of it as she liked for her personal use and to run the house with the rest. Which was what she'd done for their entire married life. She didn't mind what he did with his own money because he had always looked after her and the children extremely well.

Nevertheless, with the statement in front of her, she couldn't help looking at the numbers. She immediately identified the monthly payment to the household account, and the regular deduction for his car loan. But what she couldn't figure out was the other, quite substantial direct debit that came out of the account at the end of every month. It was too high to be an insurance premium, or a subscription. It wasn't a loan because the code was wrong for that. So what was it?

Adele told herself that it didn't matter.

But somehow, deep inside, she knew that it did.

She said nothing to Richard when he came home from the shop that evening. And she said nothing the next day either, because they'd been invited to Philip and Donna's for dinner and she didn't want to sour the mood. Adele enjoyed visiting her son and daughter-in-law. Donna was the perfect wife for Philip, quiet and self-effacing and always putting his needs first. Their two children, Anthony and Astrid, were both well behaved if a little overindulged from Adele's point of view. She was happy that Philip had settled down after his disastrous relationship with the farmer's daughter. She had to admit that Lola Fitzpatrick had had the kind of looks that would turn any man's head, but she was wild and unpredictable and would never have made a good wife for Philip. The whole business with the earrings had been unsettling too. Adele was sure there was something more to it than a simple mistake. She couldn't see how anyone could waltz off with earrings worth thousands in their ears and not know it. No, she thought, he'd had a lucky escape from Lola Fitzpatrick and it was a good thing that she was completely out of his life.

It would be nice to have her other son settled too, she mused as she got ready for bed that night. With both her boys married, she'd feel her work as a mother was done.

Although maybe not. A mother always worried about her children, no matter how grown up they were. And a wife worried about her husband too, even if he'd never given reason to worry before.

Lola Fitzpatrick hardly ever worried about Bey. A statement she made when she met Shirley for coffee one afternoon and which caused her friend to chuckle.

'What about the time she climbed that tree at Powerscourt and wouldn't come down?' Shirley reminded her. 'And when she and Áine decided to get the Dart to Howth on their own and none of us knew where they were?'

Lola grinned. 'Normal moments of anxiety,' she clarified. 'But generally, for a twelve year old, she's great.'

'I suppose it's because she's been around adults so much,' observed Shirley. 'She can be disconcertingly mature about things sometimes.'

'Far more mature than me, to be honest,' Lola said. 'Sometimes I feel she's the adult in our relationship.'

'She's a great kid and a total credit to you.' Shirley smiled. 'And even though I had my doubts about . . . well, you know . . . I think you did the right thing.'

'Hmm.' Lola spooned some of the froth from her cappuccino. 'She *has* asked about her dad from time to time, you know. A little more in the last year or so.'

'And what have you told her?'

'I've fudged things,' replied Lola. 'But it's getting harder and harder.'

'Richard's still paying for her, isn't he?'

Lola nodded. 'I have to admit, the money was very important when I moved back to Dublin and was looking for a place to live. It helped me find somewhere suitable. And since then, I've been able to put it into a college fund for Bey. So I have to be grateful.'

'Grateful?' Shirley snorted. 'For him stepping in and taking over his son's responsibilities?'

'He did what he thought was right. So did I.'

Shirley's expression softened. 'I know you did.'

'Besides,' said Lola, 'it's worked out all right. I'm happy in the house in Ringsend, I love my job at the property management company, and Bey's a great kid. But . . .' She hesitated. 'But not telling Philip about her right at the start simply stored things up for the future. The problem is, I think that future is now. I said as much to Richard the last time I saw him.'

'Meeting him every year wasn't part of the original deal,' said Shirley.

'No,' agreed Lola. 'But when he contacted me and said he wanted to be updated on how his money was being spent, I couldn't really say no.' She pushed her coffee cup away. 'He's an interesting man, Shirley. Very driven. Very clever.'

'Very bloody controlling, if you ask me,' said Shirley.

'That too,' Lola agreed. 'Still, he's been good to me.'

'You sound as though you like him. More than Philip.'

'He has more depth than Philip,' Lola said. 'Philip could be an arrogant shit from time to time. He loved to lecture me. Richard listens.'

'You sound smitten with him,' said Shirley. 'Like you might have got it on with him if the opportunity had presented itself.'

'Don't be daft!' Lola shook her head. 'At least . . .'

'Lola!'

'Oh, I don't fancy him like that. Not at all,' Lola assured her. 'But he's not as bad as I first thought. And he really does seem to care about Bey, which I didn't expect.'

'I wonder did he ever tell his wife?'

'I never asked him,' said Lola as she took out her purse to pay the bill. 'But if he did, Adele has shown no interest in wanting to know about us. And to be perfectly honest, I think I prefer it that way.'

She collected Bey on her way home. Her daughter, now a tall and leggy redhead with sea-blue eyes and a creamy complexion with a dusting of freckles across her nose, had spent the afternoon with her best friend Áine. The two girls were working on costumes for the end-of-term school concert.

'I'm not really into fairies and stuff,' said Bey as she showed her mother the gossamer wings she'd fashioned to go with the leotards and tutus that the girls would be wearing. 'But they look pretty, don't they?'

'They're lovely,' agreed Lola, who was truly impressed by her daughter's ability to make pretty things. 'Mrs Shaw will be delighted. Well done, both of you.'

'Oh, Bey did most of it.' Áine shrugged. 'I just cut out the material and helped stick on the sequins.'

'It's excellent work,' Lola assured her.

'And they've tidied up.' Beth Bellamy, Áine's mother, walked into the room. 'Which is the most excellent thing of all. Here you are, Bey, some of the cookies I made earlier.'

'Thank you, Mrs Bellamy,' said Bey.

'Next time, you can come to our house, Áine,' said Lola. 'Meantime, we'd better scoot. See you soon, Beth.'

She hustled her daughter out of the house and into the car.

'Áine's mum and dad have split up,' said Bey as Lola pulled away from the pavement.

'I'm sorry to hear that,' said Lola.

'Áine says it's better that way. They fought all the time. She says it's easier now he's moved out.'

'I'm sure it's not nice, all the same.'

'Her dad has custody rights,' said Bey. 'Áine and her brother will spend every second weekend with him. Although not at the same time, because he only has a one-bedroom flat and a sofa bed.'

'Has Áine stayed there already?' asked Lola.

'Yes,' replied Bey. 'But she's not sure she likes it very much.'

'She'll get used to it,' Lola told her. 'It's sad when adults mess up, but it happens.'

'Did my dad ever want custody rights?' asked Bey as they arrived outside their house, a two-up, two-down redbrick.

'That wasn't an option at the time,' Lola told her.

'Why?'

It was strange, Lola thought, how sometimes things seemed destined to happen. Today was the first time in months she'd spoken to Shirley about Richard and Philip. And today was the first time in a while that Bey had also decided to talk about her father.

She didn't reply until they were inside the house and were both sitting at the scrubbed-pine kitchen table, which had been a moving-in gift from her mum and dad.

'There were lots of reasons why your dad wasn't involved

with you when you were born,' she said. 'Maybe some of those reasons have changed and maybe they haven't.'

'Was it that he was too immature?' asked Bey.

Lola couldn't help smiling. Her daughter was so serious, so earnest. And so deserved to know about her dad.

'We were both immature,' she said. 'But of course we're older and more sensible now. So if you want me to contact him, I'll do my best.'

'Can you do that?' Bey looked at her in surprise. 'I thought he was sort of off the radar.'

Lola had never said that to her. But she knew that her own behaviour over the years might have given Bey that idea.

'If that's what you want, I'll try,' she said.

She'd expected Bey to say yes straight away and was surprised when her daughter frowned.

'I need to think about it,' Bey said eventually. 'I'll let you know.'

'Whenever you're ready, just say,' Lola said.

'I will,' said Bey, and went to her room.

Adele realised that she was becoming obsessed about the payments out of Richard's bank account. She kept coming up with reasons why he might need to spend that money on a monthly basis, and none of them were good. But to ask him about them would mean she'd have to admit to having looked at his statement, and that was something she was ashamed of doing, even if it had been accidental. Their relationship had always been built on trust. If she told him what she'd done, he might never trust her again. But right now, she didn't know if she could trust him either.

It was a week after she'd first seen it that she raised the

subject with him. And when she saw the expression in his eyes, she wished she'd never asked.

'Have you a mistress?' she demanded when he didn't speak. 'A child?'

'Of course not.' Being able to say no to her question made it easier for him. 'I would never cheat on you, Adele. You know that.'

'I don't know that at all,' she said. 'I want to believe it. I want to think you're not like my father. But I don't *know* it, Richard, do I?'

'You've always believed in me,' he said. 'Believed that I'll do the right thing for both of us. For our boys. For the business.'

'The business!' she exclaimed. 'Is it . . . are you paying hush money to someone?'

'Hush money?' He looked at her in astonishment. 'For what? No. Adele, sweetheart, it's nothing like that. Nothing at all. I've simply tried to . . .'

'What?' she asked.

Richard let out a slow breath. And then he told her about meeting Lola in St Stephen's Green, and of the existence of Bey.

'You're saying she's Philip's child?' asked Adele when he'd finished. 'And you expect me to believe that?'

'Because it's the truth.'

'Yet you've kept it from me.'

'I thought it was for the best.'

'And he doesn't know either?'

'No.'

'Have you seen her?'

'Who? Bey? Not since that first time.'

'Lola,' said Adele. 'You've been paying her money for nine years, Richard. Nine years! Have you asked her for anything in return during that time? Has she given you anything?'

'I . . . She . . .' Richard wanted to give her the answer she needed to hear. But he wasn't sure what that might be. 'I do a bit of an audit with her every year,' he said eventually. 'She tells me about the child and I reassure myself that she's looking after her properly.'

'I'm not convinced you need to do that.' Adele's voice was as hard as her eyes. 'I can't understand why you're involved at all.'

'She wanted to go to Philip when Donna was expecting the twins,' Richard reminded her. 'I couldn't let that happen, Adele. I couldn't. I had to step in and stop it.'

'I suppose you did,' Adele conceded. 'That damned girl! I knew she was trouble from the moment I saw her. All that fuss she kicked up about those snails.'

'To be fair, darling, it was a bit of a challenge.'

'I liked to challenge his girlfriends,' Adele said. 'Particularly the ones who needed challenging.'

'You didn't give Donna snails.'

'My challenge to Donna was quite different,' said Adele in a tone that told him not to ask.

'Maybe it was the snails that made Lola turn down his proposal,' he suggested.

'I'm glad if they did.' Adele snorted. 'Though she had a damn nerve saying no. So she was going to tell him about this child until you intervened, was she?'

'Yes.'

'Maybe it's money well spent,' said Adele. 'Although it's certainly far more than she deserves.'

129

'But it's kept her quiet for nine years,' said Richard.

'And you kept quiet about it for nine years too.'

'I should have told you,' Richard said. 'But I didn't want to stress you.'

Which was all very well, thought Adele that night as she lay in bed beside him. But they'd always shared everything in their lives, good and bad, stressful or not. He should have consulted her about paying off the gold-digging farmer's daughter. He'd been far more generous to the young woman than he'd needed to be. Adele wanted to trust him, but she found it difficult to believe everything he'd said. It was plausible, of course, but men could always come up with plausible excuses when they needed to. Richard had liked Lola Fitzpatrick even though he'd agreed with her that she might not be a suitable wife for their son. But had her husband considered her suitable for an affair of his own? Was he convering up his own infidelity and not the unwanted outcome of Philip's relationship with her? It wasn't entirely an impossible scenario. And she hated Lola Fitzpatrick and her inconvenient child for making her think about it at all.

Chapter 12

*Tiger's Eye: a semi-precious quartz with a silky lustre
and characteristic stripes*

Bey spent the summer at the farm in Cloghdrom, happy to be running around the fields with her cousins, helping to bring the cows in for milking and hosing down the shed, as well as collecting eggs from the hens and learning the art of baking soda bread from her grandmother.

'I don't think I'll ever be much of a cook,' she told Eilis one evening. 'And I'm not really cut out for farming either.'

Eilis grinned at her. Bey had promised to be up for the milking that morning but had slept through the alarm.

'But . . .' Bey held up an eggshell triumphantly. 'If anyone needs decorated eggshells, I'm your girl!'

'It's very clever.'

Bey had copied the design from a picture of a Fabergé egg, and had painted it a delicate pink before using narrow gold braid and small coloured beads to decorate it.

'It's for you,' she said. 'To say thank you for having me.'

'You know you're always welcome here.' Eilis hugged her.

'Sometimes I wish me and Mum still lived here with you,'

said Bey. 'It would be nice to see Uncle Milo and Auntie Claire and the boys every day. Auntie Gretta and Uncle Tony too. It's a pity we're so far away.'

'Lola was always a city girl at heart,' said Eilis. 'I bet you are too really.'

'I guess.' Bey smiled at her. 'I don't really mind where I live, as long as I can do my stuff.'

Eilis looked at the egg again. It really was exquisite. If she hadn't seen Bey working on it herself, she'd have thought it had been done by a professional.

'I'm going to make a necklace next,' Bey said. 'I saw a lovely picture in Auntie Gretta's magazine. It was a proper necklace with real gems in it, but I reckon I could do a nice one with coloured stones. I'll show you.'

She got up from the table and returned with the magazine, which she opened at the advertisement. *For the Tiger in your Life*, it said. *The Adele Tiger Lily. Only from Warren's the Jewellers.* Eilis stared at it.

'What d'you think, Gran? Isn't it pretty?' asked Bey.

'Lovely,' said Eilis faintly.

'I like the way they've set the stones,' Bey said. 'I don't know if I could do it exactly the same myself, but I bet I could give it a try.'

'I couldn't believe it,' Eilis said to Lola, who'd come up for the weekend as she always did during the summer. 'There she was cooing over a piece of Adele jewellery, thinking she could do it too.'

'Genes will out.' Lola's voice was as faint as Eilis's had been earlier. 'My God, Mum, it's like . . . it's like they have control over her even though they don't know it.'

'Ah, well, not quite.' Eilis patted Lola on the arm. 'I didn't mean to make you think . . . It was just the matter-of-fact way she said it. And the egg she did for me – well, it's just amazing.'

'I suppose it would be surprising if she hadn't inherited something from that side of the family,' said Lola.

'Disconcerting, though,' said Eilis.

Lola didn't say anything to Bey about jewellery or decorated eggs on the way back to Dublin. In fact they didn't talk much at all, but listened to Bey's LeAnn Rimes CD for most of the drive. It wasn't until they were nearly home that Bey asked her mother whether she thought her interest in jewellery and decorating came from her father's side of the family.

'Perhaps,' said Lola.

'I think I need to meet him,' said Bey. 'Can I?'

'Leave it with me,' Lola told her. 'I'll do what I can.'

What she did was to ring Richard on his direct line at the shop.

'We'll talk,' he said. 'Clarke's at twelve thirty.'

Clarke's was a small coffee shop off Baggot Street, a fifteen-minute walk from both Warren's and the property management office where Lola worked. It was out of the way enough for them not to have to worry about bumping into Philip or Peter. Richard was already sitting at one of the wooden tables when Lola arrived, a chicken sandwich and a black coffee in front of him. She ordered coffee and a doughnut.

'You need to eat more than that,' said Richard.

'Not hungry.' Lola shrugged.

'Or watching the pennies,' said Richard. 'After all, if you go ahead with this insane plan, you know what will happen. Your golden goose will stop laying eggs.'

'Richard, I really appreciate the support you've given Bey over the last nine years,' said Lola. 'It's made a hell of a difference to our lives and I'd hate to lose it. But the truth is that I don't consider you to be a golden goose and I can manage without your money. I've been doing well at work. I've been promoted a couple of times. I can support myself and my daughter.'

'Not with the same sense of ease as before,' said Richard.

'I would always have managed without you,' Lola told him. 'I'd planned to.'

'Then I dangled the money in front of you and you did a quick one-eighty-degree turn.'

'I did what I thought was best. It wasn't only about support for Bey. It was also about Philip's life. His marriage, his family – just like you said. But everyone's older and wiser now. And it's time.'

'Interesting timing,' said Richard. 'Because Adele recently found out about our little arrangement.'

'Oh.' Lola looked at him from her dark blue eyes. 'What did she say?'

'She thought I was having an affair with you.'

'What!' Lola was shocked, and then she laughed. 'That would have been the biggest betrayal of all for her. She hates my guts.'

'Not really,' said Richard.

'Oh come on.' Lola shook her head. 'You know she does.'

'She didn't trust you,' he said. 'And now . . . if you go through with this, she'll know she was right.'

'Richard, I made a decision based on what I thought was right back then. The decision I'm making now is based on what I think is right at this time. Who knows how it will work out? But it's what Bey wants.'

'And what she wants trumps everything else?'

'She has a right to know,' said Lola.

'I wish I believed that,' said Richard. 'But I'd urge you to think about everyone – not just one little girl – before you put the cat among the pigeons.'

'I will,' said Lola.

But she already knew what she was going to do.

Philip was shocked to hear from her, but when she said she needed to see him, he told her that there wasn't a snowball's chance in hell, that she was a long-forgotten part of his past and that it wasn't something he needed to revisit. He told her he was a happily married family man and that she'd done him a favour by turning down his proposal. She said he was right about that, but that she had something really important to discuss with him. When he eventually gave in and met her at the Shelbourne Hotel on St Stephen's Green, he was totally unprepared for what she had to say.

'I have a daughter!' He stared at her. 'A twelve-year-old daughter. And you never told me about her. How could you, Lola? How the hell could you?'

'You were married with a family of your own,' she said. 'I couldn't get in the way of that.'

'But you kept secrets from me! You had no right to do that.'

'I thought it was best.'

'I never understood you,' said Philip. 'I never will.'

135

'That's why I knew we shouldn't get married,' said Lola.
Philip said nothing.

'She wants to meet you,' Lola said.

'I don't think that's a good idea.'

'Please.'

He looked at her. She was still beautiful, he thought, but in
a different way to before. The carefree look had gone from her
face, replaced by a quiet determination. Nevertheless, her eyes
were still that amazing blue and her hair was as dark and luxuriant as ever. She was one of the most beautiful women he'd
ever met, but he'd never forgive her for humiliating him over
the proposal. Nor would he forgive her for not telling him about
her pregnancy. He didn't want to give in to her demand about
his daughter. But he knew he was going to. Because there was
something about Lola Fitzpatrick that made you want to make
her happy whether it was the right thing for you or not.

Although Bey wasn't a girl who cared very much about her
appearance, she wore her best jeans and jumper to meet her
father for the first time. She'd already used an enormous
quantity of Lola's hair mousse to tame her wild red curls,
and spent at least ten minutes appraising herself from every
angle before coming downstairs to wait for him.

'You look lovely,' Lola reassured her as Bey examined her
face in the hall mirror.

'I wish I looked like you,' Bey said.

'The Warrens are a good-looking family and you take after
them,' Lola told her.

'Do I? Really?'

Lola nodded. And then Philip pulled up in his BMW and
she went to open the door.

He was complaining about the traffic when he walked into the living room, but stopped talking the moment he saw Bey. He turned to Lola.

'This is my daughter?' There was surprise in his voice.

'Yes,' she said. 'Bey. Short for Beibhinn. It was my grandmother's name. It means "fair lady".'

'Hardly fair, with that ginger mop.'

Philip had spoken in a cheery tone, but Bey bristled. Although Lola insisted they were pure Titian, she put up with a lot of teasing in school about her flame-coloured locks. She hated being called ginger, even though she secretly admitted that it was probably justified.

'You're blond and I'm dark, so I suppose it was always a possibility,' said Lola. She turned to Bey. 'Say hello to your dad.'

'Hello,' said Bey.

'It's good to finally meet you,' said Philip when she didn't say anything else.

'You too.'

Bey didn't understand why she couldn't find anything to say to him. Everyone knew that she was chatty; Lola often had to tell her to shut up and let someone else get a word in. But meeting Philip Warren had silenced her. She looked at his handsome face and saw traces of her own, just as Lola had said. It was more disconcerting than she'd expected.

'I guess we'd better go,' said Philip.

'Where?' Bey asked.

'I haven't decided yet.'

Bey was silent again. The scene was very different to the one she'd played out in her mind. The one in which her father rushed into the house and said that he'd always wanted

137

to meet her. The one in which he put his arms around Lola and said that they should be together. She'd thought they'd suddenly turn into a family. She couldn't believe how silly she'd been.

His choice was eventually the zoo, which, as Bey said to her mother afterwards, was the lamest thing ever. Áine's father had taken her to the zoo twice since he'd left her mother. Was it the only place that dads could think of? she demanded.

'Men can sometimes lack imagination when it comes to children's outings,' said Lola. 'But aside from that, did you have a good day?'

Bey considered the question carefully. None of it, from Philip's arrival at the house to him dropping her off outside, had been the way she'd wanted it to be. She hadn't felt connected to him. She didn't think he'd felt connected either.

'It takes time,' Lola told her. 'I'm sure after a few visits you'll get on like a house on fire.'

But Bey wasn't as certain. And as she curled up in bed that night, she couldn't help wondering if Philip really was her father after all. Because he hadn't treated her like a daughter. If she had to put a word to it, she would've said 'nuisance'.

Nobody had ever treated her like a nuisance before. It was a very unsettling feeling.

When Lola didn't hear anything from Philip about meeting Bey again, she called him at the shop. It was Richard who answered.

'You do know that I've stopped the payment, don't you?' he said. 'You broke your word.'

'I did what Bey wanted.'

'I hope you think it was worth it,' he said. 'You could always try to get maintenance from Philip. But it would be a tad cheeky under the circumstances.'

'You're far more obsessed about the money than I am,' said Lola.

Richard snorted.

'And you of all people should know that it was never about money,' Lola told him. 'We've met. We've talked. You know me.'

'True,' said Richard. 'By the way, although I told you that Adele now knows about our little arrangement, Philip doesn't. I'd rather keep it that way. And neither of them knows about the sweetener.'

'Fine by me,' said Lola.

'Did you tell Bey?' asked Richard.

'About your support up till now? No.'

'I'd rather keep that quiet too. I don't want her knowing that I was a soft-hearted old fool.'

'Soft hearted!' Lola sounded amused. 'As if. Now can I speak to Philip?'

Richard put the call through and Philip told Lola that he'd been too busy to think about Bey, but that if she liked, he'd take her out the following week.

'Not the zoo,' said Lola. 'She's outgrown the zoo.'

'I'll pick somewhere appropriately glamorous.' His tone was laced with sarcasm. 'I've done what you wanted. I've met her. But I don't want it to be a regular thing. I'm living a different life, Lola. I don't need complications.'

'That's fine.' Lola kept her voice steady. 'I'm sure she'll be delighted to see you again. Especially as you're going to so much trouble.'

Bey wasn't delighted. In fact she was distinctly lukewarm when Lola told her when her father would be picking her up.

'I was planning to go to Áine's,' she said. 'We were going to put sparkles on our trainers.'

'You can do that another time,' Lola said. 'And your dad said he was taking you somewhere nice.'

Bey made a face. She wore her older, less fashionable jeans for the outing and didn't bother with the hair mousse. But when Philip brought her to an upmarket burger restaurant, she wished she had made an effort, because waiting for them at the table were Donna, Anthony and Astrid. And they were looking at her with undisguised interest.

Although Donna wasn't a beauty like Lola, she was an attractive woman with pale blond hair and wide grey-blue eyes. Anthony and Astrid, the twins, were fair haired too. Astrid was a mini-Donna, and had clearly dressed in her best for the day. Bey couldn't help thinking that although she was almost four years older than Astrid, the younger girl was far more sophisticated than she was. Both of the twins were. They ordered their meals with a confidence and authority that Bey herself lacked, and instead of being simply grateful for being out to dinner, they criticised the chips (not crispy enough) and the salad (too boring) and were only happy when the desserts were brought out.

Bey didn't have a sweet tooth and opted out of dessert, causing Astrid to ask her if she was on a diet. Before she had the chance to reply, the younger girl murmured that it probably wasn't a bad idea, as Bey seemed rather big for her age.

When the meal was finally over and they were saying goodbye – the twins and Donna were going home while Philip dropped Bey back to Ringsend – Astrid leaned towards her and whispered that their dad loved them more than her and she shouldn't ever forget that. Bey was too shocked to reply.

That night, she told Lola that it might be a good idea to leave meeting with Philip for a while. After all, she said, she was very busy with school and her art project, so she didn't really have time for socialising.

'Hardly socialising,' Lola said.

But Bey was adamant. She'd had enough of the Warrens for a while. And so there were no more visits.

Until the Christmas invitation arrived.

Chapter 13

Ruby: a rich, red, extremely hard gemstone

Philip had phoned Lola with the suggestion that Bey come to his home, Cleevaun House, for a Warren family Christmas. It had been his father's idea, he admitted. Richard had felt that it was important to welcome Bey into the fold.

'Really?' Lola was surprised. She'd thought that Richard would still be too angry at her failure to keep her word to want to have Bey anywhere around. Maybe, she thought, with a pang of contrition, he was soft hearted after all.

'I have to be honest, I'm not convinced about it,' said Philip. 'She's hardly what you'd call an easy child to get on with – though that's not entirely surprising given that she's lived with you all her life – but I'm prepared to give it a shot.'

'That's very good of you,' said Lola.

'I'm a good person,' said Philip. 'You never gave me a chance.'

'I'm sorry.' Lola wondered if she'd have to spend the rest of her life apologising to Philip Warren.

'Drop her to us in the early afternoon,' said Philip. 'She can stay overnight.'

'OK,' said Lola.

When she told Bey about the plan, her daughter looked at her dubiously.

'Are you sure that's what he said?' she asked. 'A whole day?'

'A whole day and a sleepover,' Lola confirmed. 'It'll be fun.'

Bey looked even more dubious.

'Don't you want to go?' asked Lola.

'Not really,' Bey said. 'I thought we were going to Cloghdrom, like always.'

'I realise it's not what we normally do,' said Lola. 'But your dad is making a huge effort and you should be glad he wants you there.'

'What about you?' asked Bey. 'Are you going to Cloghdrom without me?'

'Of course not,' replied Lola. 'We'll go the next day. I'll help out at the Golden Apples senior centre with Shirley.'

Bey looked at her uncertainly. This wasn't what she'd expected when she'd asked to meet her dad. And it wasn't what she wanted. But it looked like it was what she was going to get.

At first, on Christmas morning, she thought she wouldn't be going to Cleevaun House after all. Snow was coming down in frenzied flurries from dark grey clouds, spinning dizzily outside the window and covering the ground with a thin sheet of white. But by midday it had stopped, and although the sky was still grey and heavy, the forecast was for no more snow that day.

I should've kept my mouth shut, Bey thought as she packed

her overnight bag. I should never have asked about my dad. Mum and I were fine on our own. I've messed thing up for no reason at all.

And yet she knew that she'd had to find out. Lola had always been so reserved and cautious when she'd asked her about him in the past that Bey had been quite sure there was some glorious mystery about her father. She'd imagined him as a fairy-tale prince who'd been in love with her mother but had had to go back to his country to marry a woman he hated. She'd thought that perhaps her parents had been torn apart for some other tragic or romantic reason that Lola hadn't been able to tell her. Or that for some reason she hadn't yet decided on he was living alone and miserable in a dreary house, wishing he had a family who loved him.

She'd invested a lot of emotional time and energy in building up a picture of a father who wanted to be with her. Yet she couldn't help feeling that Philip was irritated by her more than anything else. And it was perfectly clear that he resented her mother. Which was sort of unbelievable, Bey thought, because Lola was one of the nicest, kindest people you could ever meet.

'Parents are weird,' Áine had commented after the Bellamys' separation. 'They tell you to be nice and polite and respectful and to love each other and then they don't do any of it themselves!'

Bey was very conscious that Lola, who was one of the most capable and serene people in the whole word, was stressed about her relationship with Philip Warren. She was bemused by it. Áine's mother wasn't flustered about Johnny Bellamy, although as Áine said, they were like complete

144

strangers when they talked to each other now. Far too polite, she'd said; it freaked her out.

Bey had desperately wanted to love her father and for him to love her too. But on that first outing together she'd found herself looking at the Swatch on her wrist more often than she'd expected, willing the time to pass as they walked around the zoo. She'd been taken aback at how much he'd talked about Donna and their twins. He hadn't asked her much about herself at all.

She realised her dreams of them all being a family together had evaporated the moment he'd walked through the front door. And she felt guilty about having thought that way in the first place because she and Lola – as well as everyone in Cloghdrom – were a family already.

She'd heard her mother and Shirley talking about it over coffee one Saturday, although they'd clammed up when she'd walked into the kitchen. Lola had been saying that it had all been very unnerving and perhaps she shouldn't have been persuaded by Richard after all, to which Shirley had remarked that Lola could only do what she thought was right at the time and that it had been a good deal. Then Shirley had asked if she'd ever got any use out of the sweetener and Lola had laughed and said no, and that was when Bey had joined them and they'd changed the subject to other things.

'Stop fidgeting,' Lola ordered now as she turned carefully onto the narrow road, still lightly dusted with snow, that led to her father's home. Bey already knew that this area near Killiney Hill was popular with rock stars and other celebrities, along with anyone else well heeled enough to afford the expensive houses with views over the sea. The reason Philip and his family could afford to live here was down to the ever-increasing success of the family business. Bey hadn't been to the flagship store in Duke Lane; she hadn't even realised at first that the Warrens were Warren's the Jewellers. Nor had it occurred to her that the necklace design she'd copied that summer had been from one of the famous Adele collections. But when her father had started talking about the shop, she'd been entranced. It had been the only time in their outings together that she'd listened to him properly.

Cleevaun House was set behind a high wall and wooden gates that effectively hid it from view. Lola eased the car to a gentle stop beside a steel post into which a grey intercom was set.

'Do I *have* to stay tonight?' asked Bey while they waited for someone to answer Lola's buzz. 'Couldn't you just come and get me later?'

'You're going to have a great time and you won't want me turning up,' Lola assured her. 'Besides, as soon as I get back from the Golden Apples dinner, I'm going to put my feet up in front of the fire. You wouldn't be so heartless as to ask me to come out in the snow again, would you?'

'I suppose not,' conceded Bey.

'Honestly, sweetheart, you'll be fine,' said Lola. 'I bet your dad and Donna have a wonderful day planned. I'm sure you'll have great fun with the twins.'

Bey stared ahead of her and said nothing.

'It's Christmas,' Lola reminded her. 'Everything's fun at Christmas.'

It was Astrid who was the problem, Bey realised. She was afraid of what other barbs the younger girl might throw at her. Because it was perfectly clear that her half-sister didn't like her one little bit. And Bey didn't like Astrid either.

But she didn't say this to Lola, who was looking at her anxiously. Instead she smiled and said that she was sorry she was being a bit of a pain about everything but it was just that this would be the first Christmas they hadn't spent together and it felt strange. And then Lola hugged her and told her that there'd be lots more Christmases in the future and that she was to enjoy herself as much as she possibly could.

Bey took a deep breath and nodded. She'd make an effort, she decided. After all, it was only one day.

The gates glided open to reveal a house and garden that looked exactly like a scene from a traditional Christmas card. The wide lawn was still and serene beneath its sugary dusting of snow. Snow also covered the branches of the trees that lined the driveway, while white lights had been arranged around the eaves of the house to look like falling icicles. The enormous wreath of holly on the red-painted front door added the finishing seasonal touch.

Lola stopped the car outside the front door, which opened as she switched off the engine.

'Hello, Bey,' said Philip as his daughter stepped out onto the snow-covered gravel. 'Happy Christmas. Welcome to Cleevaun House.'

'Thank you,' she said. 'It's lovely to be here.'

'Happy Christmas, Philip,' said Lola.

'Same to you,' he said, although, to Bey's ears at least, it didn't sound like he meant it.

They stood in an awkward circle for a moment, then Lola told them that she had to get back to town. 'I'm helping Shirley with the senior citizens' Christmas Day lunch,' she explained to Philip. 'I said I'd be there about an hour from now.'

'I'm sure you'll get your reward one day.' The edge to Philip's voice was unmistakable.

'I'll get it sooner than that,' Lola told him. 'The seniors are a great laugh.'

'Yes, well . . .' Philip shrugged. 'I'd better get Bey inside before all the heat goes out the door.'

'I'll be back for you in the morning.' Lola bent towards Bey and whispered, 'Have a good time. Behave yourself,' before kissing her and getting back into the car. Bey stayed at the door clutching her overnight bag until Lola had driven through the gates and they'd closed behind her again.

'Right,' said her father. 'That's that. Come on.'

Bey followed him across the wide hallway with its polished parquet floor and deep-pile rug and into a spacious living room. She was already intimidated by the sheer size of her father's house. She reckoned that the entire downstairs of their own home would fit into Cleevaun's living room alone. It was very impressive, with pale carpets, high ceilings, and patio doors right across the back looking over more snow-dusted garden.

She took a deep breath. She wanted to turn around and run after her mum, but it was too late. Besides, Philip had his hand at the small of her back, ushering her forward. And she could hardly run away when the room seemed full of people.

All of whom were looking at her with undisguised interest.

It was Donna, slender and pretty, her silky fair hair held back by a red velvet band, who spoke first.

'Hello, Bey,' she said. 'I'm so pleased you could come. Happy Christmas.' She walked over to her and gave her an awkward hug. 'I'll take your bag and put it upstairs. You can go to your room later. Sit down and make yourself comfortable.'

148

'You're in the dormer guest room,' said Astrid. 'It's a very nice room. You're extremely lucky.'

Bey stared at her. She was convinced her half-sister was wearing make-up. There was a light silvery shimmer on her eyelids that could only have come from a palette, while her lips were suspiciously glossy. Her hair fell in a sheer curtain of pale blond just past her shoulders. She was wearing a pastel-pink dress and matching ballerina pumps and looked like the fairy on top of the Christmas tree.

Bey smoothed her own hair with her palms even though she was wasting her time; despite her robbing Lola's mousse again that morning, it had reverted to its usual wild tangle.

As on the previous occasion she'd met him, Anthony ignored her completely. Which was actually more comfortable from Bey's point of view than the scrutiny of the other people in the room.

'Say hello to your grandmother and grandfather,' said Philip, introducing them first.

Bey looked at them uncertainly. Adele Warren was a truly beautiful woman, as different from Granny Fitzpatrick as it was possible to be. Not, of course, Bey said to herself, that Granny Fitzpatrick wasn't beautiful in her own way. Her mum's mother was rounder and softer, and her steel-grey hair was permed into tight curls around her dimpled face. She was, Bey decided, a comfortable person. A proper grand-mother. Adele Warren could never have been described as comfortable. She was slim and angular, and her shoulder-length hair was a fine ash blond. She was wearing a berry-red satin dress with matching red shoes, and her expensive Warren jewellery – a stunning ruby necklace with matching earrings, bracelet and ring – glittered in the light of the lamp on the

149

wall behind her. Richard was handsome and, although in his sixties, still had an almost full head of silver hair. He was dressed in a smart suit with a tie that matched Adele's dress. His piercing blue eyes regarded Bey speculatively.

'Don't you speak?' asked Adele. 'Your father asked you to say hello.'

'Hello, Granny,' said Bey.

'Nobody calls me Granny,' Adele told her. 'It's ageing. You may call me Adele.'

Bey blinked a couple of times. She'd never be able to call this absolute dragon of a woman by her first name. It would be utterly impossible.

'It's nice to meet you, Bey,' said Richard. 'I hope you have a good day today.'

'I didn't think there'd be other people here.' Bey turned to her father. 'You didn't say anything about meeting anyone else.'

'Of course we're here,' said Adele. 'We always get together at Christmas. And you're lucky to be joining us.'

Bey didn't think she was lucky at all. Her feelings about the day were getting more and more unsettled by the second.

'I'm delighted to meet you,' said a man around the same age as her father. 'I'm your uncle Peter, your dad's younger brother, and I've heard a lot about you.'

'You have?'

'All good,' Peter assured her.

He was lying, thought Bey. He hadn't heard much about her at all. But it was nice of him to say so. She smiled tentatively.

'And this is Cushla,' he added. 'My girlfriend.'

Cushla gave her a beaming smile. Unlike the Warrens, she wasn't startlingly attractive; her dark hair was almost as unruly as Bey's own and she lacked the sense of style that was evident in Adele, Donna and even Astrid. Bey warmed to her immediately.

'Well,' said Donna. 'This is nice.'

'It's something we should have done sooner,' Richard said.

But not something they wanted to, thought Bey. The invitation had been extended out of some misplaced sense of duty. Not because they cared. Just because they felt they should. She thought longingly of the farmhouse at Cloghdrom, of the roaring fire in the hearth and the smell of the turkey roasting in the Aga, and wished that she was there, being teased by her cousins and teasing them in return, safe in the comfort that everybody in the room loved her and she loved them too and there was nothing going on that she didn't understand.

'Now that we're all finally here, we can open the presents,' said Philip when Donna came downstairs again.

'I hope you weren't waiting for me before you did that!' Bey looked at him in horror. It was nearly two o'clock. She and Lola had exchanged gifts at seven that morning. She couldn't imagine hanging around for hours to unwrap Christmas presents.

'We thought it would be polite to wait for you,' said Adele.

'Though it's been an awfully long time,' complained Anthony.

'I'm sorry,' said Bey. 'We came as quickly as we could. Mum couldn't drive fast because of the snow.'

'Your pile is over there.' Donna indicated some beautifully gift-wrapped packages beneath the tree.

'They're all for me? Thank you,' said Bey. 'I have presents for you too, but they're in my bag upstairs. I'll go and get them.'

'There's no rush; you can wait until these are opened,' said Donna.

'I'm afraid there's nothing from Cushla and me,' Peter told her apologetically. 'Your dad didn't tell us you'd be here until it was too late to do anything about it. But . . .' he reached into his pocket and took some notes out of his wallet, 'here you are. Buy yourself something nice with that.'

'Oh, Uncle Peter, that's very good of you, but I couldn't possibly take money.' Bey looked longingly at the two twenty-pound notes in his outstretched hand. 'Besides, it's far too much.'

'Not at all,' said Peter. 'I hardly ever see you. Look at it as a cumulative present stretching over a few years.'

'Are you sure?'

'Oh, go on and take it,' said Peter. 'It'll probably be ages before I see you again anyway.'

Bey glanced at her father, who shrugged. She took the notes and put them carefully into her denim purse.

'You always were one for the extravagant gesture, Peter,' murmured Adele. 'I do hope you're more careful with the Warren finances. It wouldn't do for our accountant to be so blasé with company funds.'

'A hundred quid would have been extravagant, Mum,' said Peter. 'Forty is just nice. And given that I've only just met my eldest niece, a bit of largesse is long overdue.'

'Very generous, Pete,' said Bey's grandfather.

Bey was conscious of a slight edge between the adults. She wasn't used to it. The Fitzpatricks never spoke to each other like that. Perhaps it's my fault, she thought. I'm messing the whole day up for them. She stayed silent, not wanting to say the wrong thing.

'Open your presents now,' said Donna. 'All of you.'

Although they hadn't opened the family gifts, Anthony and Astrid had already unwrapped the ones from Santa, which were a bike each and a Nintendo console with a Super Mario game between them. Bey couldn't remember when she'd stopped believing in Santa herself, but she had a feeling it was younger than eight. She hadn't wanted to stop, though. She would have liked to believe, or at least pretend to believe, a little bit longer. But she knew there was no point in kidding herself. It was Lola who bought the presents and Lola who deserved to be thanked, not some unknown man in a fur-trimmed suit.

The remainder of the gifts, all in individual piles, had each person's name written on a card sitting on top of their pile. Bey carefully removed the red and green paper from the first of hers, which was from her grandparents. It contained six scented soaps.

'Thank you.' She didn't say that she and Lola agreed that soap was the most horrible gift you could give anybody. Lola's view was that unless you lived on your own, it was always going to be shared with the rest of the household. And Bey reckoned that a present that dissolved into a slimy mess the more you used it was pretty gross even if it did smell, as these did, of freesias and lilies.

However, her next gift, from her father and Donna, was a pretty silver locket that could be opened to put a photo inside. It came in the distinctive Warren's plum-coloured box, embossed with the Warren name in gold and tied with a purple satin ribbon. Bey took it out and carefully fastened it around her neck. It was a lovely present and she said so.

'I'm glad you like it,' said her grandfather. 'It's part of a new range we're doing.'

'The girl doesn't need to know about our business, Dad.' There was a touch of impatience in Philip's voice. 'It's just a present, for heaven's sake.'

'It's the nicest present I've ever been given,' said Bey, although she crossed her fingers behind her back as she spoke. It was certainly the most expensive present she'd ever received, but the nicest was always whatever Lola had chosen, because it was handed over with love and joy. Perhaps there was love behind the locket too, she reminded herself. Lola insisted that it wasn't her father's fault he hadn't had the chance to love her the way she did. But that he did love her in his own way. Bey wished that adults didn't always make things so complicated.

Her final gift was from Astrid and Anthony and was a Cadbury's selection box.

'Excellent,' she said, and meant it. 'I'll go and get your stuff now.' She scrambled to her feet, then looked at Donna enquiringly.

'Up two flights of stairs and it's the third bedroom on the right,' she told her.

Bey scampered out of the room and hurried up the stairs. It was a relief to be on her own again, even if it was only for a few minutes. Being with her father's family was hard work, and she wondered fleetingly if she could pretend to be ill so that Lola would have to come back and get her. But that would be letting her mother down, and she didn't want to do that. Besides, after she'd handed out her presents, things might get easier. She certainly hoped so. Otherwise it was going to be a terribly long day.

The guest room was about twice the size of her bedroom at home. It was decorated in shades of pink that were pretty in what Bey thought was a rather girlie sort of way. Her bag had been placed on a low chest at the end of the bed. She opened it and took out the presents she'd wrapped carefully in silver paper the previous night.

When she returned to the living room, everyone stopped talking. She smiled apprehensively as she began to hand over her gifts: an expensive cigar for her father, an annual for Anthony and glass bead bracelets for Donna and Astrid that she'd made herself the previous week.

'I'm sorry.' She looked at her grandparents, her uncle and Cushla. 'I didn't know you'd be here so I didn't bring anything.'

'That's quite all right,' said Adele, who was looking at the beaded bracelet in Donna's hand. 'I only wear Warren's jewellery, so anything else would have been wasted on me.'

'It's very pretty,' said Donna as she fixed it around her wrist. 'Perhaps you've inherited the family talent.'

'Actually, it's like the Adele Tiger Lily,' remarked Richard. 'The ambers and greens are very similar.'

'I'm glad you think so!' Bey beamed at him. 'I copied it.'

'What!' Adele stared at her granddaughter.

'I like making stuff,' Bey explained. 'And I saw a picture for this in *Woman's Way*. So I thought it would be nice to copy it. I didn't know at the time that Dad was a Warren. It's sort of a coincidence, isn't it?'

'It's really quite clever,' said Peter as he looked more closely at the bracelet. 'See, Mum, she's got it exactly right.'

'I suppose anyone can do anything with a kit,' remarked Adele. 'But I don't really see the point in copying our beautiful classic jewellery in glass beads!'

Bey looked at her doubtfully. 'I thought it would be nice,' she said.

'It's still only beads,' said Astrid.

'They're very well made,' said Philip into the silence following his daughter's words.

'Thank you,' said Bey.

'I think they're lovely,' said Cushla. 'I'm hopeless at anything like that.'

'I'd have made one for you too if I'd known you'd be here,' Bey said.

'You can have mine.' Astrid handed her bracelet to Cushla. 'I have other bracelets.'

'Oh, I couldn't possibly take your lovely Christmas present,' protested Cushla. 'Perhaps Bey will make me a bracelet of my own another time.'

'Sure.' Bey didn't allow herself to feel hurt at Astrid's rejection of her gift. She'd already decided that her half-sister – and it pained her to even think the word – was a grade A wagon and that they'd never like each other.

'I'll just wear my locket.' Astrid had received a similar one to Bey's from her parents and she adjusted it around her neck. 'It's the prettiest thing ever.'

'I'm glad you like it, sweetheart,' said Adele. She turned to Philip. 'Of course, if I had my way, we wouldn't be doing them at all. Warren's is about precious gemstones, not silver lockets.'

'I know, I know,' said Philip. 'But we've decided to run this range and we'll stick with it for a while.'

156

'Nothing can compare to a real gemstone,' said Adele.

'Luckily for us,' Richard said. 'Because they're what draw the customers in. Colour and sparkle.'

'I like colour and sparkle,' Bey said. 'It makes you want to pick something up the minute you see it.'

Richard looked at her appraisingly. 'Why do you think that is?' he asked.

'Because . . . because it makes it alive,' she said.

'Perhaps you can get a Saturday job in the shop when you're a little older.' Peter smiled. 'Warren's could do with someone like you.'

'I hardly think that's appropriate,' said Adele.

Bey couldn't imagine working in the Warren's shop either. Although it would be nice to be able to look at beautiful jewellery every day.

'Did you sell a lot for Christmas?' asked Cushla into the silence that had suddenly fallen.

'We certainly did. It's shaping up to be an excellent year.' Richard looked pleased. 'The Adele Dahlia was very popular.'

'It's stunning.' Cushla looked at Adele's magnificent dark ruby ring, which Bey had noticed earlier.

'The Adele rings were what took Warren's from a high-street jeweller to an iconic brand,' said Richard. 'But of course my beautiful wife was their inspiration. And turning the range into complete sets has made them inspirational for our customers too.'

Adele looked complacent.

'I was thinking of buying one for Cushla,' Peter said, and then cleared his throat. 'Though not the Dahlia. The Snowdrop. That's the one people choose as an engagement ring, isn't it?'

'Peter!' They all exclaimed at once, while Cushla stared at him.

'Well,' he said. 'It's as good a time to ask as any. Cushla Morrissey, will you marry me?'

Behind her enormous glasses, Cushla's expression was astonished.

'Well?' He looked anxiously at her.

'This is . . . unexpected,' she said.

'Unexpected but not unwelcome, I hope,' said Peter.

'Of course not unwelcome.' She smiled at him. 'And of course I'll marry you.'

Peter's proposal changed the atmosphere completely. Everyone clustered around them, congratulating them and asking them questions about when they planned to get married and where they were going to live – questions that Peter batted away with 'We've only just got engaged' while Cushla said that she hadn't been thinking about anything like that but hoped it would be soon.

Bey had never seen anyone propose or been accepted before, and she was totally caught up in the emotion of it. She wondered if anyone would ask her to marry them one day. There were girls in her year in school who already had boyfriends, but she wasn't one of them. Her experience of boys was limited to her cousins in Cloghdrom, and those experiences had all been about climbing trees and getting into mischief. She hadn't yet met a boy who'd made her think differently.

'When I get engaged, I'll have an Adele ring too,' said Astrid.

'Of course you will.' Donna hugged her. 'Just like me.'

Donna's engagement ring was the Adele Rose, a stunning

pink diamond that had been the first in the Adele range. Even to Bey's inexperienced eye the quality and workmanship was evident. She wondered what it would be like to own one. She didn't expect she'd ever know. Her grandfather might make them, but he certainly wouldn't ever give her anything so beautiful. And she'd never, ever be able to afford one for herself, even if they gave her a discount for being the outsider in the family dynasty.

Chapter 14

Tanzanite: a popular blue gemstone

Bey knew that Warren's was a dynasty, because when Lola had told her about her father, she'd told her all about his family too. She'd explained how the shop that had been founded by Bey's grandfather had grown from small beginnings, and how the Adele collections had become classics over the years. The most famous were the Rose, which featured pink diamonds, the Snowdrop, where the diamonds were white, and the Bouquet, which contained pink tourmaline, tanzanite, emeralds and, of course, diamonds too.

Bey had wondered if Lola would like to own the sort of jewellery that the Warrens sold, but Lola shook her head and said no, that Bey was the jewel in her life, which always made Bey smile.

'Dinner is ready,' announced Donna, who'd been flitting in and out of the kitchen while the rest of them were talking in the living room. 'Would you like to take yourselves off to the dining room and sit down.'

The dining room was another spacious room. It had a

long oval table covered by a crisp white linen tablecloth and laid with silver cutlery. A red and purple floral decoration was placed in the exact centre, and foil crackers inscribed with each person's name were set at their place. Bey couldn't help comparing it to Granny Fitzpatrick's scrubbed-pine table and the blue Willow Pattern china, which was kept for 'good'. There was always a free-for-all when it came to the seating arrangements, and as soon as Granny put the food on the table everyone helped themselves from the big tureens filled with home-grown vegetables and potatoes. The ham was farm reared too, although the turkey came from Bohane's on the other side of Cloghdrom. She felt a pang for the easiness of it all, for the banter and the teasing of anyone who took more than their fair share of carrots or cauliflower or broccoli or sprouts. (Not that there was much demand for the sprouts. Their only fan was her mother's older brother, her uncle Milo.)

But then Philip switched on the hi-fi in the corner, and the familiar sound of Christmas carols filled the room. It didn't matter that Christmas was different at the Warrens', thought Bey. Not everyone's had to be like Granny Fitzpatrick's. Or even the Christmas dinner at the Golden Apples centre, which was filled with laughter at the feeble jokes from the crackers they pulled as soon as they sat down. Christmas was Christmas wherever you were.

Reading the names on the crackers at each place setting, Bey saw that Donna and her father were at either end of the table, while she was on one side, between him and Cushla. Astrid was at the far end, between Donna and Uncle Peter. Anthony was in the middle, beside their grandfather. Richard Warren said grace, just as they did in Cloghdrom, though

161

the words were slightly different, and then Donna served a salmon mousse that everyone agreed was melt-in-the-mouth. Bey knew that the food at Granny Fitzpatrick's was good and nourishing and bursting with flavour. But she'd never tasted anything like Donna's salmon mousse before.

When the starters were cleared away, Philip made a big fuss of sharpening the carving knife while Donna brought out the turkey and ham. Bey stopped comparing things to Cloghdrom and just tucked in to what was a well-cooked meal while listening to Richard and Cushla talking about Warren's. Her grandfather was explaining more about the shop's history, telling her about the Adele rings and how they were designed.

'Norman and David, our designer and consultant, brainstorm ideas,' he said. 'Because the collections are named after flowers there's a theme there already. So then Norman sketches them up and shows them to me. Well, to both of us now.' He nodded at Philip. 'We have a think about it and maybe ask some questions and then we give the go-ahead.'

'Where do the jewels come from?' Bey was fascinated and couldn't help butting into the conversation.

'For the Adele ranges I go and meet people who buy and sell gemstones,' explained Richard. 'Your dad sometimes comes with me. We travel to places like South Africa and Amsterdam and New York. Then our designers work on the pieces.'

'It sounds very exciting.'

'It is,' said Richard. 'And then when you get the right stone the designer has to do his very best with it to turn it into something really beautiful.'

Bey wanted to ask more questions but she didn't think

Richard would appreciate her peppering him with them, especially as his conversation was really with Cushla, so she allowed her mind to drift instead to the bead bracelets she'd made for Donna and Astrid. She supposed her grandmother was right and it had been impertinent to copy the beautiful Warren designs, which had been intended for precious stones and not coloured glass. She wondered how much the Adele Tiger Lilies actually cost – in the magazine ads she'd seen there had been no mention of prices. Granny Fitzpatrick always said that if you had to ask, you couldn't afford it, so it was clear that Warren's jewellery was aimed at really rich people, not just someone looking for a pretty bracelet or ring.

But the jewellery her grandfather was now talking about was out of the reach of even averagely rich people. These were pieces that were made to be seen only on the very wealthy and famous as they got out of a car at the Cannes film festival, or appeared on stage at the Oscars. Warren's didn't make that sort of jewellery. 'True haute joaillerie – high-class hand-made jewellery – is out of our reach,' Richard told Cushla. 'But we do a great job with what we have.'

'I'm going to buy all the jewellery for Warren's when I grow up,' said Anthony. 'And then I'm going to own the business.'

'Are you really?' It was Cushla who asked the question.

'Dad says so,' replied Anthony. 'It's my inheritance.'

There was a burst of laughter from the adults at the table, then Philip nodded at Anthony and told him that he was indeed the heir to the Warren's throne. But Bey wondered why it had to be Anthony's inheritance and not Astrid's. And what if Peter and Cushla had a baby? Why wouldn't it be his or her inheritance? Why Anthony's?

'Because I'm the eldest, of course,' he said when she asked. 'You're a twin,' she objected. 'Astrid's the same age.' 'But she's a girl.' His voice was scornful.

'Astrid will wear the Warren jewellery and people will admire her style and elegance,' said Adele. 'Anthony will make it and sell it. Just like with Richard and me.'

Bey glanced at Astrid, wondering if she was happy at being relegated to the status of someone who simply wore the family's products rather than being involved in their manufacture in any way. But her half-sister was fiddling with the locket around her neck and wasn't listening.

And then the thought struck her. *She* was the eldest. Not Anthony or Astrid. So if that was how they measured it, the inheritance should be hers. But then she remembered that her name was Fitzpatrick and not Warren. And that was why it wasn't.

Dessert was Christmas pudding, which Donna placed on the table before pouring warmed whiskey over it and setting it alight. The effect, along with the fairy lights twinkling in the early-evening gloom, was totally magical.

'Having fun?' Philip asked Bey as she tasted it.

It wasn't the same sort of fun she'd have had in Cloghdrom, but she'd relaxed a little and the food was truly amazing. Cooking was never a high priority for Lola, but it was obvious that Donna, who was so quiet when she was among the rest of the family, was properly talented in the kitchen. Bey nodded because her mouth was full, and he smiled and patted her on the back. At that moment she felt part of it all. Part of the glamour and the elegance and the wonder of being a Warren. Then she thought of her mother home from the

Golden Apples dinner without her, and felt alone and guilty at the same time.

The crackers were pulled over tea and coffee. Whether you won or lost at the pulling, you still received the token inside the cracker with your name on it. Bey's gift was a small key ring with a leather fob, the letter B tooled into it.

'That's a coincidence,' she said in surprise.

'Isn't it?' Richard chuckled, and she smiled back at him, feeling part of it again. Of all the Warrens, she liked her grandfather the best. He was the only one who seemed perfectly at ease with her being there, and when he talked to her, he treated her like the young adult she wanted to believe she was.

'Help your mother,' Adele said to Astrid when Donna began to clear the table. 'You too.' She nodded at Bey. 'You've had a good day. Show your appreciation.'

'Of course,' she agreed. 'Thank you very much, Donna. Come on, Anthony.' She glanced at her half-brother, who was fiddling with his watch, a present from his grandparents.

'I don't do washing-up,' said Anthony. 'That's girls' work.'

'Rubbish,' said Bey. 'We should all help with the dishes.'

'Anthony will be pouring the drinks in the living room,' said Philip. 'That's his job.'

Bey opened her mouth to say that it was an easy job in comparison with washing and drying up after an entire Christmas dinner, but she saw the steel in her grandmother's eyes and stayed silent. She carried crockery into the kitchen, followed by Astrid, who brought the used linen napkins.

If Bey thought the living and dining rooms of Cleevaun House were big, she was blown away by the enormity of the kitchen. There was an island counter in the centre that she reckoned was the absolute height of modernity, a state-of-the-art cooker, a huge American-style fridge and – best of all – a dishwasher, which Donna was busy stacking. They didn't have one in Ringsend because her mother didn't see the point when there were only two of them, but Bey had always longed for one. She felt bad that she'd thought Anthony had an easy job, because stacking the dishwasher was actually fun.

'We have to wash the glasses and the cutlery by hand,' Donna told her. 'I'll do the glasses and you girls can do the cutlery.'

'I'll wash,' said Astrid. 'You can dry.'

That surprised Bey. She'd always thought most people preferred drying, as she did. However, when all the glasses were done, Astrid added more water to the sink and dumped the knives and forks into it, then swirled them around and simply began lifting them out in bundles.

'Hey!' cried Bey. 'There's still potato stuck to the forks. Wash them properly.'

'They're fine,' Astrid said.

'They're not.' Bey threw the offending forks back into the sink.

'I'm not doing them again!'

'You have to.'

'No. Stop it! I've done those already.'

They were glaring at each other as Donna walked back into the kitchen. When she asked what the matter was, Astrid told her that Bey was making her wash the cutlery a second time, and Bey jumped in to explain why. Donna told Astrid to wash them properly and then left them alone again. Bey smiled with satisfaction at her victory and Astrid shot her a daggered look.

'I can't do them because I don't want to get my ring wet,' she said.

'Take it off, then.'

The ring had been Astrid's Christmas cracker gift. It was a small blue stone on a narrow hoop, and although Astrid had put it on, she'd complained that it was too big for her. Richard had looked surprised, but Donna had told her it would probably fit her in a few weeks because she was growing so quickly.

Astrid heaved an exaggerated sigh and put the ring on the windowsill above the sink. 'I don't really like it anyhow,' she said as she swirled the cutlery around again. 'Blue isn't my favourite colour.'

'I guess it's pot luck with Christmas crackers,' said Bey. 'Last year I got a miniature spanner in mine.'

Astrid said nothing, but rattled some more knives and forks onto the draining board. Then she removed the apron Donna had made her wear before starting and said she was finished.

'You have to wait until I've dried them,' Bey protested. 'The washer-up puts them away. That's how we always do it at home.'

'Well you're not at home now, are you? You're in our house being made a fuss of even if you don't deserve it.'

Bey gasped at Astrid's words. She'd already decided her half-sister was bitchy. But she was taken aback by her blatant rudeness.

'Wait,' she said as Astrid walked toward the door. 'I don't know where to put stuff.'

'Are you thick? The box on the table, of course.' Astrid didn't turn around.

Bey hadn't noticed the red box with its velvet lining, which was obviously where the best cutlery was kept.

'Your ring!' Bey called towards her retreating back.

'Don't want it!' Astrid replied.

Bey sighed and returned to the drying-up. When she'd finished, she slotted the cutlery into the spaces in the box. Then she wiped down the draining board. Nobody had come into the kitchen to see how she was getting on, and she was feeling a little bit like Cinderella, cast out from the fun. When she'd seen the movie, years after her mother had read her the fairy tale, she'd thought Cinderella was a bit of a wimp in not standing up for herself more. But right now she understood her, even if the circumstances were entirely different.

Astrid's Christmas cracker ring was still on the windowsill. Bey couldn't see why she didn't like it. Even though it was plastic, the blue stone sparkled under the bright kitchen light. Unlike most rings from Christmas crackers, there wasn't a break in the hoop so you couldn't change the size, which was why it was too big for Astrid. Bey supposed it would be too small for her, but when she slipped it on, it fitted perfectly.

She wriggled her fingers in front of her. There was a vitality about it that enchanted her. She wondered if Astrid would swap it for the key ring. Though from what she was beginning to know of her half-sister, she doubted she would, especially as it had the wrong initial on the fob. But she'd said she didn't want this ring. She was clearly one of those people who only liked expensive things. She'd been happy to give away her cheap bracelet, even though it was a gift. She'd probably be equally happy to give away her Christmas cracker ring too. Although maybe not to Bey. In fact, definitely not to Bey. But what she didn't know wouldn't hurt her, would it?

Bey left the kitchen and went upstairs to her room. She took the ring off and left it on the dressing table. It was OK to keep it, she rationalised. There were other Christmas crackers still unpulled. Astrid would probably get something she liked much better the next time.

Chapter 15

Inclusion: a particle of foreign matter within a gemstone

When she arrived downstairs again, everyone was gathered in front of the TV.

'What on earth have you been doing?' demanded her father. 'We've been waiting for you.'

'Is everything OK?' asked Donna. 'I looked for you in the kitchen but you weren't there.'

'I went up to my room for a few minutes,' said Bey.

'Right,' said Peter. 'Fire her up, Phil!' He grinned at Philip, who pressed a button on the remote he was holding and the opening credits to *Mary Poppins* came up.

'Haven't we seen this before?' asked Adele.

'It's a limited-edition re-release,' said Philip. 'I picked it up in the States.'

'You were in America?' asked Bey. 'When?'

'Dad's always going to America,' said Astrid. 'We went too last year. To Disneyland. It was great.'

'I thought US cassettes didn't work in Europe,' said Cushla.

'This one does,' said Philip.

'I love *Mary Poppins*,' said Astrid.

'It's lame.' Anthony made a face.

Philip took another cassette from a box and handed it to him.

'If you'd rather watch this, you can go into the den,' he said.

'Oh, wow!' Anthony grinned as he saw the copy of *Star Trek: Insurrection*. 'That's more like it.'

Philip laughed as Anthony disappeared, followed by Peter, who said he'd keep him company.

'I'll join you both shortly,' he said. 'I want to see it too.'

Bey decided to stick with *Mary Poppins*, even though she would have preferred *Star Trek*. But nobody else was leaving the living room and she felt awkward about saying she'd prefer to be with the others in the den.

'Mary Poppins was a better au pair than Sabine,' said Astrid at the end of the film.

'She was a nanny,' Bey pointed out. 'Do you have a nanny?'

'We're not *babies*!' Astrid was outraged. 'Sabine was with us last summer. To help Mum and do stuff with us. She was great with hair,' she added. 'She used to do mine in plaits around my head. They wear their hair like that in Germany, you know.'

'Yes,' said Bey. 'I did know.'

'You couldn't do it with yours,' said Astrid. 'It would look stupid.'

'Why?'

'Because you're a ginger nut, of course.'

'It's Titian.' Bey had learned not to rise to the bait when people called her ginger, but Astrid had a definite ability to rub her up the wrong way.

171

'Ha ha. You wish. Carrot top!'

Bey made a face at her and Astrid made one back. She took the cassette out of the player and replaced it in its case.

'Where's your ring?' Donna asked her.

Astrid glanced at her hand. 'I left it in the kitchen.'

'You shouldn't leave things lying around,' said Donna. 'Go and get it.'

She added a quick 'now', which stifled the objection that Astrid seemed about to raise.

Bey knew she should say something but she wasn't sure what it should be. It would sound crazy to say that she'd taken the ring and put it in her bedroom, as though she was so overcome by everything the Warrens had that she wanted to keep an extra trinket from the Christmas crackers. She didn't want to seem that pathetic.

Astrid came back into the room and told her mum that the ring wasn't there.

'It must be,' said Philip, who'd returned from the den with Anthony and Peter. 'Look again, properly this time.'

'I looked all over,' said Astrid.

'When did you have it last?' asked Donna.

'I told you. In the kitchen. I took it off when we were washing up.'

'Where did you put it?'

'On the windowsill. I looked there. And on the floor.'

'Oh for heaven's sake.' There was a note of exasperation in Donna's voice. 'It can't have disappeared.'

Bey couldn't understand the fuss over a silly token from a cracker, but she was scrambling to her feet to say that she'd help look (her plan was to rush upstairs and get the ring, then drop it on the kitchen floor and 'find' it herself) when Astrid turned and pointed at her.

'She was alone in there,' cried the younger girl melodramatically. 'She could have robbed it when nobody was looking!'

'I . . . Of course I didn't rob it.' Bey knew that her next remark should be that she'd tried it on and accidentally left it upstairs. But facing their accusatory looks, the words that came out of her mouth instead were: 'Why would I take her stupid ring?'

'Because it's from Warren's,' said Astrid.

'It came out of a cracker!' Bey retorted. 'Not everything in the world belongs to the Warrens, you know!'

'Did you take it, Bey?' Cushla's voice was gentle. 'It doesn't matter if you did. It really doesn't.'

'Of course it matters!' cried Astrid. 'It's mine and she stole it! She's a thief, that's what she is.'

'I didn't steal it!' Bey shouted. 'I don't want your crappy stuff.'

'Bey!' Philip grabbed her by the hand. 'Let's check if you do have it, shall we?'

Bey felt dizzy. She wished she'd hidden the ring in her bag. But she'd left it in plain sight on the dressing table, and now her father was going to think she was both a thief and a liar. He'd think she'd taken it deliberately, which of course she had, but she hadn't intended to . . . Well, she didn't quite know what she had or hadn't intended when it had come to the ring. All she'd known was that Astrid didn't like it and she did. She told herself that it was only a plastic ring from a Christmas cracker. It wasn't as though she'd actually robbed something out of a Warren's shop! But she felt as though she had.

When her father opened the door to her room, Bey thought she was going to faint.

He stepped inside and immediately saw the ring. He turned to her, an unfathomable expression on his face.

'You lied to me,' he said. 'This is how you repay me after everything we did for you today. I'm very disappointed in you, Bey.'

'It was a mistake,' she said.

'What was?' asked Philip. 'Stealing it or lying about stealing it?'

'I didn't steal it. Not . . . not really. I just tried it on and . . .'

'And?'

'And came up here.'

'And left it in your room.'

'I was going to ask her to swap it,' she said.

'Why?'

'Astrid didn't want it. But I thought she mightn't do the swap, so when she left it there I . . . I took it.'

'That ring came out of a Warren's cracker,' said Philip. 'She wouldn't dream of swapping it.'

'Why not?' Bey asked. 'We swap things all the time in Cloghdrom.'

'That's completely different,' Philip told her. 'You're going to come downstairs with me now and apologise to Astrid, and give her her ring back.'

'I didn't mean to take it without saying anything. But she was being mean to me and—'

'Stop making excuses,' said her father. 'You took something that wasn't yours. That's a very serious issue, Bey. You must know that.'

'You don't have to make it such a big deal!' cried Bey.

'A Warren's ring from a Warren's Christmas cracker is a big deal,' said Philip. 'You should know that already.'

'What d'you mean, a Warren's ring?' Bey suddenly felt a hollow in the pit of her stomach.

'Every Warren's cracker contains a piece of jewellery,' said her father. 'Even if your mother didn't tell you, you can't have missed our ads on TV.'

Bey swallowed hard. Lola always switched channels when the Warren's ads came on.

'Some more expensive than others, of course,' he added. 'The ones I bring home aren't the most expensive. But they're nice.'

'You mean it's not plastic?' Bey gasped.

'Of course it's not plastic,' said Philip. 'Don't be ridiculous.'

'I'm not being ridiculous!' exclaimed Bey. 'How was I supposed to . . . I wouldn't have . . . It's actually a real jewel? A sapphire?'

'A small one,' said her father. 'But yes.'

'You put jewellery in Christmas crackers?!' Bey thought of the miniature yo-yos, the tiny spinning tops and the fortune-telling fish that were the usual fare at Granny Fitzpatrick's. 'Actual jewellery?'

'It's a signature thing for Warren's,' said her father. 'They're made to order.'

'But . . .' Bey thought about it for a moment and then looked at her father in confusion. 'I only got a key ring.'

'A very good key ring,' he reminded her. 'Stainless steel and leather.'

'That's why you didn't want me to swap. Astrid's ring is

a lot better than the key ring. It's probably more expensive.'

'The value has nothing to do with it,' said Philip. 'Look, I'm prepared to accept that you didn't realise the worth of the ring when you took it, but the principle is the same. You did take it and you lied about it too. So you need to apologise to Astrid right now.'

Bey felt as though she'd been punched in the stomach. She'd actually taken a real, proper piece of jewellery. Her father was right: the fact that she hadn't known it was valuable was irrelevant. It hadn't been hers to take. And taking it from Astrid somehow made things worse. The younger girl would never let her forget it.

'I'm not going down,' she said. 'You can give her the ring. And I don't think it's fair to make such a big deal about it. Everyone swaps things from crackers. It wasn't my fault that I didn't know it was real.'

'You knew enough to call it a sapphire.'

'It's a blue stone. Some of my blue beads are called sapphire. It doesn't make them real.'

She was trying hard not to cry. He was making her feel like some kind of master criminal specialising in sapphire thefts. She'd never seen a real sapphire in her life. And yet from the moment she'd seen the ring, she'd known it was special, and hadn't understood why Astrid didn't like it. So perhaps deep down she'd guessed it was valuable. Perhaps she was a proper thief after all. She blinked the tears from her eyes while her father stood looking at her.

'All right,' he said eventually, putting the ring in his pocket. 'You can stay here. I'll tell the others that your punishment for stealing and lying is being sent to your room.'

He walked out and closed the door firmly behind him.

Bey threw herself on the bed and buried her face in the covers. All day, even in the moments when she'd been enjoying herself the most, a part of her had been thinking that Christmas at Cleevaun House might be stylish, but it still couldn't compare with Christmas at Cloghdrom. She'd allowed herself a slight feeling of superiority, thinking that flashier didn't necessarily mean better. But she wasn't superior to them at all. She'd taken something that didn't belong to her.

She was a jewel thief.

And that was how they'd think of her forever.

She lay on the bed, the top cover wrapped around her. She wished she could phone her mother and ask her to come and get her, but despite her nagging at Lola to buy her a mobile phone for Christmas, Lola dismissed them as nothing more than expensive toys. There was no way of communicating with her from the sanctuary of her bedroom. And even if she could, what was she going to say? That she'd let herself and Lola down by stealing Astrid's sapphire ring? Her mother would freak out. She'd tell Bey that she thought she'd brought her up better than that. Before they'd set out that day, she'd begged her to be on her best behaviour and Bey had promised her she would be, because she wanted to prove to her father that they'd done OK without him. She wanted him to know that they hadn't needed the Warrens behind them to be happy. Which was true. But now his family were probably all thinking that, faced with a bit of Warren glamour, she'd completely lost the plot. They'd think she envied them. That she wanted to be like them. She should have spoken up sooner. She was an idiot.

She sniffed a few times and wiped away her tears. She'd been right not to want to come here today but she wasn't going to cry like a stupid kid. She'd wait in her bedroom until the morning, when her mother would come and get her, and then she'd drive away with her and never have to see her dad or any of the Warrens again. And that, as far as she was concerned, would be a good thing.

She sat up and took her book from her bag. She was reading the Chalet School stories in paperback editions that had belonged to her mum and her aunt Gretta, and even though they were practically historical, she longed to be at a lovely school in the Alps where the kind-hearted mistresses cared deeply about all the pupils under their care, and where stupid misunderstandings like accidentally robbed jewels were always ironed out. Even the current book, where the girls had to flee Austria before war broke out, seemed a better proposition to Bey than her own circumstances. At least they were all with people who cared about them and were looking after them. She was stuck in a house with people who hated her.

There was a tap at the door and Adele walked in. She looked at the book Bey had put on the bed and raised an eyebrow.

'A little childish for you, surely,' she said. 'I'd have thought you'd have progressed more by now.'

'To what? A manual for cat burglars?' Bey didn't know why she was cheeking her grandmother, but she couldn't help herself.

'Your father said you were contrite. I see you were merely fooling him,' she said.

'I *am* sorry,' said Bey. 'I didn't mean to take it.'

'Why did you?' asked Adele.

'Because Astrid left it there.'

'That was your only reason?'

'Yes.'

'Surely you knew it was wrong.'

'I didn't think it mattered because it came out of a cracker,' said Bey. 'I've never heard of expensive stuff in crackers before. Besides, she said she didn't even like it and that it was too big for her.'

'It shouldn't have been too big,' said Adele. 'Your father knows her size.'

'He got it wrong all the same.'

'What were you going to do with it?'

'Wear it, I suppose.' Bey shrugged.

'You don't want to be here, do you?' asked her grandmother.

Bey shrugged again.

'I knew it was a mistake,' said Adele. 'You mother chose a different life for you and that was her decision. It's important to stick to your decisions, to live with the consequences of your actions.'

'I wanted to know about him,' said Bey.

'And you get everything you want, do you?'

'Not like Anthony and Astrid,' muttered Bey.

'Excuse me?'

'They got expensive stuff. I got a key ring.'

'And you're making a fuss over that?'

'It's sort of putting me in my place, isn't it?'

'You're very rude for a twelve year old,' said Adele.

'They're rude too.'

'Let's accept that nobody has been on their best behaviour,'

179

said Adele. 'But it's Christmas and you've been punished enough. So come downstairs and apologise to Astrid and that can be the end of it.'

'Why should I be the one to apologise if nobody has been on their best behaviour?' asked Bey.

'Because nobody else stole something that didn't belong to them.'

'I didn't steal it!' cried Bey.

'You took it and it didn't belong to you,' Adele reminded her. 'That's stealing, young lady. So you have to come down and apologise.'

'Only if she says sorry too.'

'For heaven's sake!' Adele was exasperated. 'She's a little girl. You're practically grown up. You're the one who should do the right thing.'

Bey knew she ought to do as her grandmother asked, but her temper was as fiery as her hair, and she simply couldn't back down.

'Are you coming downstairs or not?' demanded Adele.

Bey was afraid she'd cry if she said anything else. And she didn't want to cry in front of Adele Warren. So she picked up her book and stared unseeingly at the jumble of words on the page in front of her.

She only looked up when she heard the bedroom door close and she was alone again.

Bey wondered if Astrid would come and apologise to her, but she didn't, and the bedroom door remained resolutely shut. She knew she should go downstairs, but she simply couldn't face them all. After a while, she lay down again and closed her eyes, the book upturned beside her.

180

She had no idea what time it was when she woke up, but the snow was falling more heavily and beginning to stick to the dormer window. She wondered if anyone else had come up to see her; if they had, they'd decided not to disturb her. She didn't know if that had been out of kindness to her or to themselves.

She turned on the bedside light and looked at her watch. It was after eleven and she was thirsty. There was no water in the room and she thought about sneaking down to the kitchen to get some. Not that she particularly wanted to return to the scene of her crime, especially as if they caught her wandering around the house in the middle of the night they'd probably assume she was looking for more Warren loot to take. But her throat was as dry as a desert now and she desperately wanted something to drink.

She stood hesitantly beside the door, then opened it cautiously. The lights were still on on the landing and in the hallway. She tiptoed along the landing and down the first few stairs. She could hear the faint hum of conversation but she couldn't tell who was speaking or what they were saying. Then the living-room door opened and she scurried to the top of the staircase again. She heard footsteps in the hallway, and then the same footsteps heading back to the living room.

'Leave the door open for a few minutes, Peter.' It was Adele's voice. 'It's quite stuffy in here now.'

'That's because of the cigar,' said Peter. 'Really and truly, I can't believe you'd even dream of smoking one indoors, Phil. They stink.'

'I like the smell of cigar smoke,' said Donna.

'I'm allowed one vice,' said Philip. 'And whatever I think

about Lola's choices in some things, at least she made sure the child brought me a decent cigar.'

'I can't believe she didn't come downstairs again,' said Donna. 'Astrid always caves in after five minutes alone in her room.'

'I'm afraid Bey is a lost cause,' said Adele. 'Her manners are appalling and she's nothing more than a thief.'

Huddled on the stairs, Bey stiffened at her grandmother's words.

'She didn't know the ring was real,' said Cushla. 'I mean, who'd ever imagine it was, Mrs Warren? Not a child, surely.'

'She certainly couldn't have thought it was a cheap bit of coloured glass. In those magnificent crackers!'

'Perhaps we were thoughtless in not explaining it to her,' said Donna. 'Still, regardless of what she did or didn't know, taking Astrid's ring was wrong and her behaviour afterwards was unforgivable.'

'Theft.' Adele's voice was clear. 'No point in sugar-coating it. But there you go, like mother, like daughter. They're both the same.'

Bey felt her body go rigid with shock. What on earth did her grandmother mean? Lola wouldn't steal anything. She was the most honest person in the world.

'Mum!' This time it was Philip's voice.

'Make all the excuses you like,' said Adele. 'But I remember how it was back then. How she treated you and how she treated us. And quite frankly, even if the circumstances are different, Bey's behaviour is exactly the same!'

Bey wrapped her arms around her legs as she strained to hear what else was being said.

'Did her mother steal from you?' asked Cushla. 'Really?'

'It's complicated,' said Philip.

'Even if she did, you can't take it out on Bey,' said Cushla.

'We're not taking it out on anyone,' said Adele. 'You don't know anything about it. You don't know anything about Lola. She behaved absolutely disgracefully towards Philip on more than one occasion. Let's just say that neither Bey nor Lola are really our sort of people.'

Bey felt rage surge through her and she clenched her fists. They were talking about her as if she were some kind of object, not a real, living person. And they had no right to say the kind of things they were saying. Fine, she was a thief. But she hadn't meant . . . she hadn't . . . and here she ran out of excuses, because she *had* meant to keep the ring, and the Warrens were right: she was practically a hardened criminal.

'What time is Lola coming to pick her up tomorrow?' Donna's voice was soft.

'I said I'd phone after breakfast,' said Philip. 'Although if it keeps snowing like this . . .'

'Oh my God, don't say she'll be stuck here!' cried Adele. 'Bad enough to have Christmas Day ruined by her, but tomorrow too!'

Bey clenched her fists even tighter. She was seething now, her contrition forgotten. She hated all of them as much as they hated her.

She got up and tiptoed back to her room, her dry throat forgotten, her eyes stinging with tears of rage. The flurries of snow danced in front of the window and she peered out anxiously. What if it became heavier overnight? What if her mother couldn't get here to pick her up? What if she was stuck for another day among people who thought she was a thief? And who seemed to think Lola was one too? It was hard to tell who'd be most upset, her or the Warrens.

Well, she thought furiously, as she opened the wardrobe and took out her white quilted jacket, they needn't worry about her outstaying her already outstayed welcome. She was going to leave right now. Or at least as soon as she could get out of the house without them noticing her. She was going to find a phone and call Lola and go home. And she was never going to set foot inside Cleevaun House again.

Chapter 16

Tourmaline: a versatile gemstone found in every colour

Bey sat in her room and waited for the sounds of people going to bed. When she eventually heard doors opening and closing, she jumped under the duvet and pulled it up under her chin in case anyone looked in on her. But nobody did and eventually the house settled into silence.

When she was certain there was no one about, she put on her jacket and picked up her bag. She left the Warren key ring and the locket in the centre of the dressing table. She didn't want either of them. They could return them both to the shop and sell them to someone else for all she cared.

She opened the bedroom door and this time there were no lights on. She waited for her eyes to adjust to the darkness and then slowly made her way downstairs. She tiptoed into the kitchen and poured herself a glass of water before walking stealthily along the hallway. It suddenly occurred to her that there might be a burglar alarm, but she hadn't heard the telltale beeping of one being set. Nevertheless she checked in the little cubby space under the stairs in case there was a control panel there. That was where the panel for the alarm in her own house was. She exhaled slowly. There was an alarm, but the light was green, indicating it hadn't been set. It would serve them right, she thought, if a real burglar broke in and took every bit of their damn jewellery!

She was still worried about all hell breaking loose when she opened the front door, but although it creaked slightly on its hinges as it swung inwards, there were no other sounds.

She caught her breath as she stepped into the cold night air. The snow had stopped falling and the sky was clear, but the temperature had definitely fallen. The steps to the house sparkled beneath the light of the moon, and were slippy underfoot. It was easier to walk across the lawn than on the driveway. She reached the gates and pressed the button marked 'Exit'. They slid open and she stepped outside. A few moments later, they'd closed automatically behind her.

The breath she'd been holding formed a misty cloud in front of her face as she slowly exhaled. She rubbed her hands together and set off along the road. She remembered passing a phone box on the way here. It had been beside a small row of shops, close to a housing estate. She couldn't recall exactly where she'd seen it, but she reckoned it was no more than five or ten minutes away.

The narrow pavement was as slippy as the steps to the house had been, and it was an effort to keep her balance as she walked. On the other hand, having to concentrate on staying upright meant that she wasn't thinking about the cold.

There was a spooky quality about the deserted road that unnerved her. Everything looked different in the moonlight. It was eerily quiet, too, the only sound the faint thud of the sea as the waves hit the shore.

After what seemed like an age, there was still no sign of the shops she'd remembered. She hadn't exactly been paying attention to the route, but she was certain the housing estate must be nearby. She knew that if she kept walking – or, more accurately, sliding – with the sea to her right, she'd eventually arrive somewhere close to home, because Ringsend was near the mouth of the River Liffey as it entered Dublin Bay. But that would take all night. Plus, she wasn't wearing walking shoes, and her feet were already freezing. She was beginning to wish she'd stuck it out in the warmth of Cleevaun House after all.

When she finally saw the cluster of yellow street lights in the distance, she felt a surge of energy. Five minutes later, she allowed herself a whoop of satisfaction as she arrived at her destination, which had been a lot further from the house than she'd expected.

But there wasn't a phone box. She looked around helplessly. She was positive she'd seen one earlier. She wondered if she'd imagined it simply because there were nearly always phone boxes near shops. Maybe everyone in this posh part of town had mobile phones already and didn't need public phone boxes any more. Bey wished she'd snooped around Cleevaun House before she'd left to see if her father had a mobile himself. She could have borrowed it to phone her mum and given it back to him afterwards. Although, she thought bitterly, it'd probably be another thing he'd accuse her of stealing.

She felt hot tears prick the back of her eyelids even as she shivered in the raw night air. She knew that stalking out of Cleevaun House in a temper had been stupid. As always, she'd acted first and thought later. What she should have done when she heard her father and the rest of the family being horrible about her and Lola was to march into the living room and demand to go home. But instead she'd been her usual irrational and impulsive self, and the result was that she was shivering in front of a row of deserted shops on Christmas night when everyone else was at home.

'Are you all right?'

The sound of the approaching car had been muffled by the snow. But it had pulled up beside her and the driver had lowered the window.

'Are you all right?' he repeated. He was a middle-aged man, wearing a traditional Irish tweed cap and a pair of black-rimmed glasses. 'Can I give you a lift somewhere?' he added.

From the moment Bey was first allowed outside on her own, her mother had warned her of the dangers of accepting lifts from strangers. 'Never get into a car,' she'd said. 'Even if the person says I've sent them. Don't believe them. Don't trust them. There are some bad people out there, Bey, and you don't want to meet one of them.'

She kept her mother's words in mind as she told the driver she was fine.

'What are you doing out on your own tonight?' he asked. 'It's Christmas.'

She didn't answer.

'Are you waiting for someone? Did they stand you up? Would you like to phone them?'

Bey looked at him hopefully. 'You have a phone?'

'Of course,' he said. 'Hop in and you can use it.'

Getting into a car and being driven off was one thing, but getting into a car to use a phone was something else entirely, she thought. She walked around to the passenger side, opened the door and slid inside. A blast of warm air from the front heaters hit her in the face. She sighed with pleasure and held her hands over the vents.

'Where's the phone?' she asked.

'Just down the road,' he told her as he put the car into gear.

'But you said . . .'

He ignored her, and the car started to pick up speed.

'I thought you meant you had a mobile phone in the car!' cried Bey. 'I wouldn't have got in otherwise.'

'We'll only be a minute.' He didn't look at her.

'I don't care.' She tried not to sound anxious. 'Stop here. I want to get out.'

'Don't be silly,' he told her. 'We'll be at the house in a second and you can phone from there.'

Bey knew with a horrible certainty that she'd made her second terrible mistake of the day. And this one was even more serious. She was in the car of a complete stranger, with no idea where he was taking her and nobody knowing where she was. The warnings that were supposed to have stopped her getting into it in the first place were now terrifying her as she hunched over in the front seat. Lola had never actually been graphic about the things that could happen, but Bey had seen news reports about missing girls in the past and she couldn't recall a single one that had worked out well.

She knew the man was going to do horrible things to her and then kill her. She would be forever remembered for being the girl who was murdered on Christmas Day.

'Oh God, oh God, oh God.' Her words were a whimper.

'Be quiet.' He reached out without looking at her and

patted her knee. 'There's no need for that. You'll be fine.'

The touch of his hand as he moved it along her leg made her want to be sick. Then the car lost some traction on the road and he took it away to hold the steering wheel again.

'Let me out.'

'When we get to the house.'

'I want to get out now.'

They were on the coast road, and driving towards Cleevaun, because the sea was on their left. Bey could make out the railway lines of the Dart suburban train, which hugged the coastline. She wasn't interested in the train, though. It didn't run in the middle of the night. All she cared about was finding a way out of the situation she'd allowed herself to get into.

Maybe it'll be OK, she comforted herself. Maybe I'm getting into a state over nothing. Maybe he's just a weirdo. After all, who'd be bothered prowling for young girls on Christmas night, when most people are at home? Maybe he'll bring me to his house and let me use the phone just as he'd said. It'll probably be a dump of a place, with crappy furniture and dirty surfaces, because he's a sad old man with nobody to look after him. Everything will be fine. There's no need to panic.

She wanted to believe her own words. But she didn't.

He turned onto another road that ran alongside the railway tracks, then turned again, too quickly, into a narrow country lane, where the car skidded slightly on the icy surface. As he tried to correct it, Bey, acting without thinking, grabbed the steering wheel and pushed it towards the driver's side. The man lashed out at her, losing what little control he had. The car slid to the right and then, in what Bey afterwards thought was the single luckiest moment of her life, did a complete turn-around and ended up on the verge.

As she realised what was happening, Bey undid the seat belt she'd automatically fastened earlier.

'Hey!' cried the man as she pushed at the passenger door. 'No you don't.'

But he was still secured by his own belt, and although he grabbed her by the wrist, Bey managed to pull free and jump out before he could stop her. She raced along the snowy verge until she reached the turn to the road beside the railway tracks. The railway line itself was protected by a mesh wire fence and she knew she'd never be able to climb over it. But on the other side of the road, through the brambles and bushes, were some small cottages with long gardens. The problem as far as Bey was concerned was that one of those cottages might be his.

She could hear him running unsteadily down the lane himself now, cursing as he slipped on an icy patch. She pushed herself deep into the centre of the bushes. Some were bare and stark, but others were evergreen – holly, she thought, as she felt the leaves scratch her face and hands. What were the chances of being saved by a holly bush on Christmas Day? The metallic taste of fear in her mouth told her that she didn't rate them very highly. She was grateful for her creamy-white jacket, which both protected her and helped to camouflage her as she burrowed down, keeping her face hidden from the light of the moon and hoping that her flame-coloured hair might blend in with the colours of the bare branches.

She remembered the games of hide-and-seek she'd played with her mother, crouching behind a sofa or curtains, thinking that because she couldn't see her mum, her mum couldn't see her. She couldn't see the man and she'd no idea if he could see her or not, but she could hear him breathing heavily and she knew he wasn't far away. Snow and frost crunched beneath his feet as he walked slowly past the bushes. She burrowed down even further.

'Dammit,' she heard him say.

She held her breath even as the snow on the collar of her jacket started to melt and drip onto her neck. Her cheeks were wet too. She didn't know if it was her own tears or more melting snow.

'Little bitch.'

His footsteps were loud on the frozen surface. Bey was sure her heartbeat was equally loud. She was terrified he could hear it. She couldn't believe this was actually happening to her. She stifled a sob. Finding her frozen body in a hedgerow would certainly mess up everyone's Christmas, she thought, as a tear rolled down her cheek and plopped onto the frosted leaf beside her. She wondered if the Warrens would feel bad that she'd been murdered.

She knew it was only a matter of time before he saw her among the bushes and hauled her out. She was breathing so fast that her head was spinning, just like when she'd broken her mother's favourite vase. She'd been terrified of Lola's reaction, but after her initial annoyance, Lola had simply glued it back together. She'd told Bey that nothing was so terrible it couldn't be fixed.

Only perhaps this was.

He was taking a long time to find her. Bey clamped down on her chattering teeth as she wondered what he was doing now. She couldn't hear his footsteps any more. She thought perhaps he was just standing there, waiting. Knowing she'd have to leave the sanctuary of the holly bush sometime. Knowing there was no rush. He was right. There wasn't.

She tried not to shiver as she focused on the holly in front of her. The snow sat on the leaves and sparkled in the shaft of moonlight. She kept her eyes fixed on them, staring so intently that she felt she could see each individual snowflake. She'd heard that no two were exactly alike. She could see one now, a six-sided figure of spikes and triangles, delicate and intricate. And another, a star shape with circles on the edge of every point. She suddenly realised that she was looking at a cobweb, dusted with snow and ice. She saw it tremble slightly beneath the weight of snow and held her breath again. It was a barrier, she thought. He couldn't pass it. Wouldn't pass it. It was protecting her. Like magic. She kept telling herself this as though by repeating it over and over it might be true.

And then she heard the car. The engine turning over, whirring, spluttering. Turning over again. And coughing into life. Revving loudly. Then the sound of tyres across the ground. Was it him? His car? It had to be. But was he leaving or had he another plan? Ram it into the bushes, perhaps? In which case he'd either kill her outright or frighten her into running again. Her already racing heart was now pumping so hard she was afraid it would burst. Her entire body was shaking with a mixture of cold and terror. She didn't know what to do. She couldn't think. Her brain was as frozen as the rest of her.

The cobweb fluttered as she exhaled sharply. But it didn't break.

She heard the distinctive whine of a car reversing down

the laneway. And then turning. And driving along the road again. At speed. Driving away from her. It could be a trick, she thought. He might be trying to flush her out. She stayed where she was, immobile except for her shivering.

An age after the sound of the car had disappeared, she risked looking up. Through the leaves and branches she could make out the moon and stars. She couldn't see the car. She couldn't see anyone standing waiting for her. The night was utterly silent. No sound. No animals. No trains. No cars. Nothing. But she didn't move. She couldn't.

She kept her eyes fixed on the cobweb. She could see thousands of individual flakes adhering to it. Miniature works of art. Intricate and perfect. Beautiful to look at.

She started to count them, but her brain wasn't working properly and she stopped at a hundred.

She waited a little longer.

He didn't return.

She moved slightly.

The cobweb broke and the snowflakes fluttered to the ground.

But he wasn't there.

She crawled out of the hedge.

She was on her own.

Chapter 17

Quartz: an abundant crystal mineral

She couldn't stay there. He might come back, or she might freeze to death. She hauled herself to her feet and began to walk cautiously towards the main road, listening out for the sound of the car or of footsteps, thinking that he could have parked around the corner and be waiting for her to appear. As she reached the turn, she dropped to her hands and knees and crawled close to the verge. She peered around the corner. There was no car, but she could hear the sound of an engine approaching so she hid in the icy ditch. But this car went past without slowing down and Bey knew that it hadn't been him. Nevertheless, she waited until everything was quiet before beginning to walk again.

Eventually she came to a proper pavement. A hundred metres or so in the distance was a big white house. Christmas lights twinkled around the windows although the house itself was in darkness. Like her father's home, it was walled and gated, with an intercom set into the pillar. She looked at the intercom and then the wall. She didn't want to stand outside while she waited to see if someone would answer, in case the man drove past. She thought it was unlikely now, but she couldn't be certain. Even though the wall was high, it would be easy to climb because there was a tree nearby with branches that hung over it. Which meant it wasn't very secure really. Any thief worth his salt could get over. And she was a thief, wasn't she? Her father had said so. So had her grandmother.

She used her icy hands to haul herself up the tree, then dropped over the other side and ran unsteadily across the frosty lawn to the front door. There was a bell on the porch pillar too, which she rang frantically before starting to bang loudly on the door itself. Tears had started to stream down her face but she didn't bother to wipe them away.

What if this is his house? she thought suddenly. What if I've made another mistake? She stopped banging and stood on the doorstep, unsure of what to do next. And then an internal light came on and she heard footsteps in the hallway. She thought about running, but she couldn't move. The door opened. She was looking at another middle-aged man. Only this one was wearing bright yellow pyjamas and was staring at her in absolute astonishment.

'It's a girl!' he called up the stairs. 'A young girl.'

'What!' A woman hurried down, tying the belt of a dressing gown as she descended. 'Oh my God,' she said as she saw Bey, dishevelled and sobbing, on the step. 'What on earth . . . Come in, come in . . .'

And then she was in the warmth of a strange house and two people she'd never set eyes on before were ushering her into their kitchen, where the woman began heating up milk in the microwave.

'Don't talk,' she said as she stirred hot chocolate into the mug. 'Drink this and then you can tell me what happened. My name is Sandra and this is my husband Nick.'

Even if Bey had wanted to talk, she couldn't. Her voice seemed to have frozen along with the rest of her. She shivered and trembled and her teeth chattered on the rim of the mug. As soon as she'd taken a couple of mouthfuls of the hot chocolate, Sandra told her to come upstairs with her and take off her wet things.

'We need to get you into something warmer,' she said as she handed her a T-shirt and a tracksuit that were way too big for her but were fleecy and comforting. 'We don't want you dying of hypothermia.'

Bey put them on wordlessly.

'Who do we phone?' asked Sandra.

Bey still couldn't speak. She wanted to but she simply couldn't form the words.

'Your mum? Your dad? Anyone?'

She nodded.

'Why don't you write down the number?' suggested Sandra. 'Oh, and write down your name too. Can you do that for me?'

Bey nodded again and Sandra gave her a piece of paper and a pen. Her hands were still shaking, but not from the cold. Sandra and Nick had obviously left the heating on, and the house was comfortably warm. But Bey still couldn't stop trembling and she was finding it hard to hold the pen. Eventually, though, she managed to print her name and her mother's phone number.

'I guess your mum will be worried about you, Bey,' said Sandra as she read it. 'Is it OK to phone her now? Or would you rather I called the gardai?'

Bey's eyes widened in horror. The police were the last people she wanted to see. They would find out about the ring. They might arrest her. And maybe the Warrens would make the accusations about her mum again too. She wasn't dragging Lola into something that involved the police. She shook her head and pushed the number towards Sandra. The older woman asked if she was sure; then, when Bey nodded vigorously, she picked up the phone and began to dial.

When Lola answered, Sandra spoke calmly and clearly, explaining who she was (a receptionist at a local doctor's surgery and the wife of a professor at University College; a statement clearly made with the intention of putting Lola's mind at ease) and telling her that Bey was at her house in Killiney. She gave Lola the address.

'But . . . but . . . what on earth is she doing there?' asked Lola. 'She's meant to be with her father. What's happened? What has she done? Is she all right? Can I talk to her?'

'She's fine, Mrs Fitzpatrick. She's just cold and a bit scared and she's not really able to talk right now.'

'Oh my God! I'll be right there. Give me ten minutes.'

'Take your time,' said Sandra. 'The roads are dangerous and Bey's perfectly safe with us. We're taking good care of her. Please don't worry.'

But Bey knew her mother *would* be worrying. Lola was usually a calm sort of person, but it would take someone without any emotions at all not to be panicked by getting a phone call in the middle of the night from a perfect stranger to say that their daughter had taken refuge in their house.

Lola would never stop worrying about her now.

And that made Bey feel even worse.

*　　*　　*

198

She was sitting in a big armchair, arms wrapped around her body, when the doorbell rang a mere twenty minutes later. Sandra answered it immediately and Lola pushed past her into the living room. She was wearing jeans and a jumper and a mismatched pair of boots. She'd bought both a black and a brown pair in Marks & Spencer earlier in the winter because they were so comfortable. She clearly hadn't bothered to check before she'd rushed out of the house.

'What in God's name are you doing here?' she demanded after she'd hugged her daughter close to her. 'I phoned your father at eleven. He said you were in bed asleep.'

Bey still couldn't speak. She gave her mother an anguished look.

'Bey doesn't feel able to talk about it just yet,' said Sandra. 'I know I'm only the receptionist at the surgery, but I've done a number of first-aid courses and I'm quite experienced. I've checked her over and as far as I can tell, apart from those scrapes and a couple of bruises, she's physically fine.'

'How did you get them?' Lola kept her arms around Bey as she spoke. 'Did someone . . . hurt you?'

Bey shook her head.

'You'd tell me?' Lola's voice was urgent. 'Bey, if something happened, anything at all, it's OK to tell me.'

Bey shook her head again.

'We can go to the police right now,' said Lola. 'If there's anything they should know, we'd be better off not losing time.'

This time Bey struggled from her arms and shook her head vigorously.

'Perhaps when you get home and she's had a night's sleep she'll be able to talk to you a little more about it,' Sandra said. 'Dr Carroll's surgery reopens the day after tomorrow – well, given the time, I guess it actually opens tomorrow – and if you think she needs to see him, just ring me and I'll schedule her in.'

'You've been more than kind,' said Lola. 'I really don't know . . .'

'It's not a problem,' said Sandra. 'Honestly.'

'Come on then.' Lola put her arm around Bey again. 'Let's get you home.'

'Here are her clothes.' Sandra picked up the plastic bag she'd put them in earlier.

'Thank you,' said Lola. 'I'll get your things washed and returned to you as soon as possible. And I'll be in touch again when I know . . . when Bey . . .'

'It's not a problem,' said Sandra. 'Safe home, Mrs Fitzpatrick. Happy Christmas.'

Neither of them spoke on the drive home, but Bey sighed in relief when her mother parked outside their house. As soon as they were inside, Lola called Philip. She had to wait a long time for the phone to be picked up, and when it was, it was Donna who answered. When Lola told her that Bey was with her, Bey herself could hear Donna's cry of surprise. She listened as her mother gave Donna the sketchiest outline of what had happened, saying that she really didn't know yet how Bey had managed to leave Cleevaun House and end up on a complete stranger's doorstep.

Philip took over the call, peppering Lola with questions, which she answered with a terse 'I don't know yet' or 'She hasn't said', finishing up with an angry 'You were supposed to be in charge of her, for God's sake. I'm picking up the pieces. As soon as I know, I'll call you.' After which she put the phone down and stared at her daughter.

'That saint of a woman Sandra is right; you need to get to bed,' she said. 'We'll talk in the morning, OK?'

Bey nodded. The two of them looked at each other in silence for a moment and then Lola put her arms around her again and held her more tightly than she ever had before. Over the last few months Bey had struggled free from Lola's hugs, thinking she was too old for that sort of thing, but right now she felt safe and comforted and didn't want her mother to let go.

Lola brought Bey upstairs to bed and stayed holding her hand until her daughter finally fell asleep. When her breathing was slow and even, Lola tucked her old teddy bear in beside her and went downstairs to make herself a coffee. It was still dark outside, but she knew she wasn't going to be able to sleep. She kept asking herself why Bey had slipped out of Cleevaun House. And she was terrified of what might have happened to her to make her end up asking a complete stranger for help. Lola understood why Sandra hadn't called the police, but if her daughter had been assaulted, despite her denials that anyone had hurt her, potential evidence would have been lost given that Sandra had undressed her. Lola rubbed her forehead. She was consumed with guilt. Bey hadn't wanted to spend Christmas with the Warrens but she'd insisted. If she'd listened to her daughter, this would never have happened.

Whatever had driven Bey to leave the warmth of Cleevaun House in the middle of the night must have been pretty awful. Lola sighed and rested her head on the table. For all her superiority, for all that she liked to think she knew best, she'd failed as a mother. But that shouldn't have surprised her, she thought. The more she tried to do what was right, the more dreadful her mistakes seemed to be.

It was nine o'clock the following morning when she heard the car pull up outside the door. She was on her third cup of coffee, and was back in Bey's room, watching over her. Her daughter was still sleeping, her face slightly flushed, her hair fanned out across the pillow. Lola looked out of the window and saw Philip getting out of his BMW. She hurried downstairs before he could ring the bell.

'Hello,' she said shakily as she opened the door.

'What the hell is all this about?' He walked past her into the kitchen.

'I should ask you that,' said Lola. 'You were the one she was supposed to be with.'

'I might have guessed you'd start the blame game straight away,' said Philip.

'Oh for heaven's sake!' Lola cried. 'We're not here to talk about us. We're here because of Bey. Because of what might have happened to her.'

'What might have . . . What exactly did happen to her?' asked Philip.

As Lola told him what little she knew, he looked at her in complete bewilderment.

'Normally we set the alarm at night, but because Mum and Dad and Peter and Cushla were staying over, we didn't,' he said.

'You didn't tell me your parents would be there.' Lola was

taken aback. 'Your brother, too? I'm guessing Cushla is his . . . wife, girlfriend?'

'Fiancée,' said Philip. 'Since yesterday. At least Pete didn't suffer the ignominy of being turned down.'

'Actually, Peter's marital state is irrelevant,' said Lola. 'More pressing is the fact that Bey did get out of the house and ended up with complete strangers. Did something happen to upset her? To make her want to come home?'

Philip said nothing.

'What?' demanded Lola. 'What did you say? What did you do?'

'I did nothing!' Philip was angry. 'Stop looking at me as though I'm some kind of monster.'

'I'm sorry,' she said. 'I'm not trying to . . . It's just . . . she ran away, Philip. In the middle of the night. In the snow. And she's only twelve years old.'

'Nothing happened that should've made her do that,' said Philip. 'Yes, there was a slight contretemps. But honestly, Lola, it was . . . in the grand scheme of things, it was just a bit of a dust-up.'

'What sort of dust-up?'

'I stole Astrid's ring.'

They both turned around at the sound of Bey's voice. She was standing in the doorway, hugging her red dressing gown around her and looking at them from anxious eyes.

'You what?' Lola stared at her.

'I saw the ring and I took it,' said Bey. 'It was real sapphire, not a glass stone. They said I was a thief and a liar and they were right. But I'm not going to the police. I'm not talking to them about anything. I'm not.'

And then she burst into tears.

Chapter 18

*Opal: a delicate, semi-transparent gem with points
of shifting colour*

Even though Lola's arms were around her in an instant, Bey
knew that her mother would be as disgusted with her as she
was with herself when she heard the full story. But as Philip
began to explain what had happened, she realised that her
mother's anger was directed at him rather than her.

'Oh my God!' Lola's voice was shaking with anger. 'What
sort of . . . of . . . emotional fuckwit are you to talk like this?
Your daughter – who's still only a child, for God's sake – ran
away in the middle of the night because your entire lunatic
family made her feel so bad that she didn't think she could
stay in the house. Anything could have happened to her.'

'She behaved like a drama queen, just like you.' Philip's
face was red. 'Running away instead of facing up to things.
Making everything into a bigger deal than it needed to be.
Staying silent when she should have spoken up. Making
everyone dance to her tune. All I asked for was an apology
for stealing Astrid's ring, and she wasn't prepared to give it.
She deserved to be punished.'

'I'm sure she would have said sorry eventually,' said Lola. 'You didn't have to make her feel so horrible about it.'

'You mean I shouldn't have pointed out the difference between right and wrong,' said Philip. 'Some father I would have been then.'

'I know the difference,' Bey whispered. 'I really do. I'm sorry.'

'It's a bit late now,' said Philip. 'But I hope you've learned your lesson, young lady, and you'll never take anything that doesn't belong to you again.' He sent an angry glance in Lola's direction before turning back to Bey. 'Now, tell me truthfully, how on earth did you arrive at that house in Killiney? Why didn't you simply phone your mother and ask her to bring you home?'

She swallowed a couple of times and then told them about getting into the car. Her explanation faltered when she saw both her parents looking at her with horror in their eyes.

'Did you mother teach you nothing?' demanded Philip before Lola could speak. 'You were lucky that he left you at that house. He could have . . .'

Lola's hand on his arm stopped him from completing the sentence. Bey stayed silent. She wasn't going to elaborate on exactly what had happened, even though her heart was racing and she trembled at the memory of hiding among the snow-covered bushes. She was afraid he'd be even angrier with her than before.

'I want you to promise me you'll never do anything like that again,' said her father. 'It's the only promise I've ever asked of you and the only way I'll ever forgive you for what you've done.'

205

She nodded, and he continued with the words that would remain etched on her mind for ever afterwards.

'You clearly don't know how to judge men. Even if it's someone you know, don't get into their car unless they've been specifically sent by your mother or by me. And when you're older and going out with boys, be careful where you go with them and always tell someone where you are. Don't let anyone you don't know near enough to touch you. Girls disappear, you know. You could have been one of them. You could have totally ruined Christmas for everyone in the family forever by going missing and never being found. If the worst had happened, we'd be reminded every single year. You should have been more thoughtful.'

Bey nodded again. Lola didn't trust herself to speak.

'Anyway,' he finished, 'I'm glad you're all right. Everyone is glad you're all right. In fact Astrid was so pleased, she asked me to give you this.'

He put his hand in his pocket and withdrew a purple Warren box. He handed it to Bey, who took it uncertainly.

'Open it,' said Philip.

Bey didn't need to open it to know what was inside. But she did anyway.

The sapphire ring twinkled at her.

She closed the box again.

'Well,' said Philip. 'Can I tell her thank you?'

'I don't—'

'You'd better not say you don't want it,' said Philip. 'Not after all the trouble you've caused and not after she's been so generous in giving it to you. Just say thank you. Properly.'

'Thank you,' said Bey.

'You also left this behind.' He took another box from his pocket. 'It's your locket.'

Bey took that too.

'All's well that ends well,' said Philip. 'I'll let myself out.'

But Bey knew that wasn't the end of it. She'd seen the expression on her mother's face. She knew that Lola would have more questions. She went into the kitchen and sat at the table with her sketchbook while her mother saw her father to the door. She'd nearly finished her detailed drawing of a snowflake when Lola came and sat down opposite her.

'Tell me about this man in the car,' she said. 'Where did you meet him and why did he bring you to Killiney?'

'It doesn't matter now.' Bey concentrated on her drawing. 'Can we forget about it? We're supposed to be going to Cloghdrom today. Gran and Grandad will be expecting us.'

'We're not going anywhere until you tell me everything,' said Lola. 'Look at me. Now.'

Bey knew from the tone of Lola's voice that she was deadly serious. So she looked up. And then she told her. And they didn't go to Cloghdrom because Lola insisted on bringing Bey to the police station, where they asked her lots of questions about the man and what he'd looked like and where he'd taken her and how she'd escaped. Yet somehow, the frightening journey with her abductor, her frenzied escape from his car and the time she'd spent hiding in the snowy hedgerow at the side of the road seemed less real and less vivid than the moment when she'd had to admit to stealing Astrid's ring. Her abduction and escape had taken on a surreal quality, as though it had happened to someone else entirely, but the shame and humiliation she felt about Astrid's ring was deeper and personal.

The policewoman who was taking her statement praised her quick thinking and resourcefulness, although later Bey heard her murmur to Lola how lucky they were that things had turned out as they had. When they'd finally finished questioning her, the policewoman told Lola that they'd keep them informed if they heard of any other incidents that might be relevant. Bey didn't want to know. All she wanted to do was forget about how stupid she'd been in the first place. Being abducted was, she thought, an entirely appropriate punishment for a jewel thief.

But at least the garda hadn't asked her why exactly she'd left Cleevaun House.

Which meant that Lola's criminal past – if it existed – remained a secret.

And she was very relieved about that.

The Raid
Ten years later

Chapter 19

Sunstone: a spangled red-orange gemstone

The workshop was at the top of a three-storey whitewashed building near Córdoba cathedral. A row of wooden benches lined the wall and a selection of jeweller's tools hung from a dried tree stump in the centre of the room. All the benches were empty except one. And the young woman sitting at it was far too engrossed in the silver ring she was working on to hear the laugher and excited chatter of the tourists in the narrow street below through the open window.

She was about to solder the two ends together. She used pliers to hold the ring, and was just focusing the flame from her torch on the area she wanted the solder to go when her mobile phone, which was in the bag at her feet, began to vibrate, followed by her 'Single Ladies' ringtone at full volume. She jumped in surprise and singed her finger with the flame.

'Oh bloody, bloody hell!' Bey Fitzpatrick exclaimed, switching off the torch before pushing her safety goggles onto her head. 'Ow, ow, ow!'

'Everything OK?'

She whirled around, nearly as startled by the voice as she'd been by the phone, which had now stopped ringing.

Martín Jurado, son of the owner of the jewellery design studio where Bey had been working as an apprentice for the past few months, was already reaching for the first-aid box.

'I got distracted by my phone,' she said, waving her hand around.

'Here you are.' Martín took a tube of cream from the box and handed it to her.

'Thanks,' she said as she dabbed it on her finger. 'I'm an idiot.'

'Accidents happen,' said Martín. 'That's why we have the box.'

Bey's phone began to ring again, and she frowned.

'It's Mum's ringtone,' she said as she reached into her bag with her uninjured hand and retrieved the phone. 'She's not normally so insistent. I hope everything's OK.'

Even though her finger was still throbbing, she kept her voice light and carefree as she answered.

'I have some bad news,' said Lola after they'd exchanged greetings.

'What's wrong?' Despite the warmth of the workshop, Bey felt a chill run through her. 'Is it Gran?'

Eilis had had a hip replacement the previous month. Bey had thought about going back to Ireland to see her, but her grandmother had insisted that she was fine and that she'd see her later in the year. Now Bey was feeling guilty that she hadn't gone home after all.

'No, no, your gran is OK,' Lola assured her. 'It's Richard Warren. There was a raid on the shop today by masked men with a gun. Your grandfather and the store manager were on the shop floor, your dad was upstairs in the office. They weren't injured, but your grandfather has had a heart attack.'

'Oh my God!' exclaimed Bey. 'That's . . . that's dreadful. Is he OK? Have they caught the raiders?'

'Not yet,' said Lola. 'Although according to the news they're following a definite line of enquiry.'

'That's good.'

'But the news about your grandfather isn't. He's very poorly and . . . well, they're not sure he'll make it through the night.'

'Oh.' Bey didn't know what to say.

'So I need you to come home.'

'But . . . but why? I haven't seen him in years! I haven't seen any of the Warrens in years. There's no need for me to be there.'

'He's your grandfather.'

'So what?'

'Bey. Please. This is serious. You have to come back.'

Bey hadn't thought of the Warrens in a long time. They were part of a past she'd long since put behind her. A past that had changed her. And she had no desire to revisit it. But she recognised the tone of her mother's voice. She knew there was no point in arguing.

She took off her green work apron and dropped it on her bench.

She was leaving Córdoba.

She was going home.

And she was going to see them all again.

Martín drove her to the train station the next morning to catch the first train to Madrid. At such short notice, the only available flight was via London. Which wasn't ideal, said Bey as she said goodbye to him, but at least it got her home.

'I'm so sorry this has happened,' he said. 'Take care of yourself, Bey. Let us know how things are. Come back soon.'

'I left the ring on the workbench,' she told him. 'Hopefully I'll be back in a couple of days to work on it again. Hopefully . . .' Her voice petered out.

'Don't worry,' he said. 'Don't worry about anything but your family.'

He didn't know about the fractured nature of her relationship with them. The Jurados were a warm, big-hearted clan, more like the Fitzpatricks than the Warrens. There were no hidden depths to their relationships and no hidden meanings in the words they spoke to each other.

'Safe travels,' he added when she reached the barrier. 'Come back soon.'

He hugged her and then kissed her gently on the lips. She put her arms around him, holding him tightly as the desire to stay with him, safe and secure, threatened to overwhelm her. He continued to hold her too, and in the end she was the one to disentangle herself.

'I'll be in touch,' she said.

'*Hasta pronto.*'

She boarded the train and checked her phone to see if there were any messages from Lola. But the only one was her mother's acknowledgement of her travel plans and her confirmation that she'd pick her up at Dublin airport later that evening.

Such a nuisance you have to come through London, Lola had texted. *And horrible circumstances for your journey. But I'm looking forward to seeing you.*

214

Despite herself, Bey couldn't help a brief smile. Lola never used text speak or abbreviations and insisted on using perfect capitalisation and punctuation too, which always made her messages longer than they needed to be.

The timing between her arrival at the train station in Madrid and the departure of her flight from the airport was tight, and Bey arrived at the gate just as it started to board. She sat back in her seat and closed her eyes. She hadn't slept much the previous night and tiredness was catching up with her. Even though she hadn't wanted to think about the Warrens, she couldn't help picturing what it must have been like in the shop when the raiders had burst in, her imagination drawing on crime movies she'd seen on TV. Had they worn masks? Fired their guns? Destroyed the displays as they grabbed the diamonds and rubies and sapphires? It was hard to reconcile her Hollywood interpretation of a heist with something that had happened in Dublin. She simply couldn't get her head around it.

When she transferred at Heathrow, she bought an Irish newspaper and saw the story on the second page. *Masked Raiders Swoop On Iconic City Store*, she read. *Unknown quantity of precious jewellery taken. Founder critically ill in hospital.* The report didn't tell her anything new. It talked about Warren's and its history and included photos of Adele and Richard, as well as a close-up of the Nightshade collection and thumbnails of the Rose and Snowdrop rings. Bey wondered which jewels the raiders had got away with. It was horrible to think about the gems in the hands of people who didn't appreciate them for their beauty, only for their monetary value. But of course it was even more horrible to think that Richard might die because of them being stolen.

215

Of all the Warrens – her father included – Richard was the only one with whom she felt the slightest empathy, although she'd only met him once following that horrible Christmas. He'd called to the house about a week later to speak to Lola. Her grandfather and her mother had sat together in the kitchen while Bey watched a movie on TV. After they'd finished their conversation, he'd walked into the living room. He hadn't said anything, but he had sat beside her until the movie had ended. Then he'd asked how she was feeling.

'Fine,' she'd replied, though the truth was she still had nightmares in which she was burrowed into the holly bush waiting for the cobweb to break.

'It was a silly thing you did,' he told her.

'I know. Mum said so. Dad said so. You don't have to tell me too.'

'I suppose not. I'm glad you're OK, Bey. I think you were really brave.'

'I thought you said I was silly.'

'Silly to get into the situation. Brave to deal with it. But what would've been braver still would've been to come downstairs and talk to us all instead of running away in the middle of the night.'

'I didn't need to be called a thief again,' she said. 'And Adele . . .' she stumbled over saying her grandmother's name, 'well, she definitely thinks I'm a kind of Pink Panther.'

Richard smiled. 'Not really.'

'She doesn't like me,' said Bey. 'She's happy to think the worst of me.'

'What makes you say that?'

'The way she looks at me,' said Bey.

216

Richard nodded slowly. 'That's probably my fault. Mine and your mum's. Sometimes adults can be really silly too.'

Bey smiled faintly at him.

He stood up. 'I'm glad you're OK,' he repeated. 'I hope I'll see you again.'

But she hadn't seen him. She hadn't seen any of them. It had been her choice and it seemed the Warrens were happy enough to embrace it. When she'd told Lola that she didn't want to see her father for a while, Lola had acquiesced. Neither of them had expected that 'a while' would drift into an almost permanent state of affairs. But Lola was worried more about Bey herself than the relationship she'd hoped she'd have with Philip. She was particularly concerned that Bey was spending more and more time alone in her room with her sketchpad, drawing leaves, snowflakes and spider's webs.

Bey herself still believed that being abducted was a perfectly reasonable punishment for being a jewel thief. She knew she'd done the wrong thing. And she knew, because of the sleep-walking, that her mistake had become part of her.

Her nocturnal adventures had started a few days after they'd visited the police station. Lola had gone to investigate sounds coming from the kitchen in the middle of the night. She'd found Bey sitting at the table polishing knives and forks. Bey hadn't acknowledged her or woken up, even when she'd touched her on the shoulder to lead her back to bed. She hadn't entirely believed Lola's account of what had occurred, but it happened again when she went to Cloghdrom for a few days, a trip that Lola had thought would be good for her. Until then, Lola's main concern had been that Bey hadn't been eating, and she'd hoped that farmhouse cooking would restore her appetite, although even her grandmother's best efforts hadn't tempted her. The sleepwalking had been the final straw.

She'd brought her daughter to see a counsellor. The sessions with Paige Pentony were still clear in Bey's mind.

'What worries *you*?' Paige asked one day when Bey had told her that she knew getting into the car with a stranger had been a crazy thing to do and that nobody had to worry, she wasn't likely to repeat it.

'Wanting beautiful things,' she replied immediately. 'Even when they're not mine.'

'Everybody wants things they don't have,' Paige said. 'That's normal.'

'Not everybody takes them,' said Bey. 'Not everyone's a thief.'

'You're not a thief,' said Paige. 'You made a mistake, that's all.'

But it was a mistake Bey could never forgive herself for making. And although Paige had insisted it wouldn't define her forever, Bey knew that she'd become two people. The girl she'd been before meeting her father and before her abduction – cheerful, open and trusting. And the one from afterwards – quieter, more introverted and significantly less trusting than before.

Leaving Dublin had helped her come closer to rediscovering the version of herself that she wanted to be. It had put a distance between her and the incident that still defined her. Each time she'd returned, it had been on her own terms. This was something different. And thinking about the people she would have to see brought anxieties she wanted to put behind her to the surface all over again.

218

Chapter 20

Amethyst: the most precious quartz gemstone

The London-to-Dublin flight was full and she was seated in the centre of a row. She closed the paper and folded it when a tall man arrived to claim the vacant aisle seat. He couldn't find space in the overhead bin for his cabin bag, which he had to squash under the seat in front of him. This left him struggling to find a comfortable place to put his feet, which he eventually placed on either side of the protruding bag. Bey, sympathetic to his predicament but slightly irked by the fact that he was encroaching on her space, suggested he might like to put the bag under the seat in front of her, as her legs were shorter and it was less of a deal for her. He looked at her in surprise, thanked her and then said that as it was such a short flight and the bag was now firmly wedged in place, it would be easier to leave things as they were.

Bey sat at an angle to avoid his foot and closed her eyes. But despite her exhaustion, she was unable to sleep. She knew it wasn't surprising that she kept thinking about the Warrens, but she wished she could keep them in the locked room in her head that she used to shut away things she didn't want to deal with.

After her abduction ordeal, Lola had accepted that she didn't want to see her father again. In fact his name hadn't been mentioned between them until Bey began to look at her college options, and only then because, after much soul searching, she'd decided to study jewellery design.

She'd stopped making bead necklaces and bracelets after that disastrous Christmas, but in her school transition year, when pupils focused on activities outside the academic curriculum, she started again. Each student had to come up with a business project as part of their programme, and Bey chose to make jewellery. Her pretty snowflake pendants and matching bracelets sold out almost at once, and she was awarded a prize for the most profitable small business at the end of the year.

'I think it's what I want to do,' she'd told Lola. 'But . . .'

'But what?'

'Isn't it copying the Warrens?' Her voice was agonised. 'I mean, that's them, not me really.'

'Nobody has a monopoly on making bracelets,' Lola said. 'If it's what you want to do, sweetheart, you have to be true to yourself.'

It was very much what she wanted to do, she realised, as she researched courses. The truth was, she couldn't imagine doing anything else.

What she hadn't expected was to go away to study. She'd downloaded the prospectus from Birmingham University more for comparison purposes than anything else, but when she'd read it, she'd been enthusiastic. Lola, seeing her engrossed in the pages, had asked about it, and when Bey had explained that she'd go like a shot if only she could afford the fees, Lola had asked why.

'The course is brilliant,' Bey said. 'And it would be fantastic to get away. Not from you,' she'd added hastily, seeing Lola's eyes cloud over. 'Just, you know, out of Dublin. Somewhere else. Somewhere I didn't have to . . . where I didn't feel . . . well, somewhere different.'

Lola didn't want to let her go. Lola wanted to protect her precious child forever. But Bey wasn't a child any more. She was almost an adult. She had a right to do what made her happy. And more than anything else, Lola wanted her to be happy. She wanted to believe that Bey could live a life without always having a slightly anxious air about her. Without always seeming to be careful about whom she met and whom she allowed to get close to her. Without looking over her shoulder and blaming herself for everything that went wrong. Lola wanted her to feel safe. And to feel free.

'If this is what you want, then we can afford the fees,' said Lola. 'I have money saved for your education.'

Bey looked at her in astonishment. She'd never got the impression that they'd been well off enough to save money for anything. But her mother was nothing if not amazing. She flung her arms around Lola's neck and told her that she was the luckiest daughter in the world. And that one day she'd repay her.

She hadn't got around to that, she thought, as she wriggled in her seat once again. But hopefully after she'd finished her apprenticeship with the Jurados, she'd get a decent job and start contributing properly at home. More than anything, she wanted to make Lola proud. Her mother had been there for her when she needed her most. Which was the only reason, she told herself, that she was coming back to Dublin now.

Lola switched off the TV. The lead news had been about the raid on the Warren's store, but there were no hard facts about the incident and the report was padded out with shots of well-known Irish celebrities wearing pieces from the Adele collections. Richard would hate the personal publicity, she thought, but he'd be delighted to think that the shop was in the news, even for such a horrible reason.

Despite the prognosis of the doctors, Lola couldn't help hoping that he'd pull through. Richard was a good deal tougher than he seemed and she was well aware of his fighting qualities. Although she didn't talk to Bey about the Warrens any more, she'd kept in touch with him even after Bey's Christmas escapade.

'Maybe I'm just used to our annual meeting,' he'd said to her the first time they'd met after it. 'Or maybe it's that I'm concerned about my granddaughter.'

Lola didn't tell Bey about these meetings. There was no reason to.

The last time they'd met had been after he'd been hospitalised for bypass surgery a couple of years earlier. Lola had gone to visit him and seen him looking greyer and older, but with his blue eyes still as determined as ever.

'Why are you here?' he'd asked her.

'I was worried about you,' she replied. 'I've no ulterior motive,' she added. 'Just in case you thought I had.'

'Oh, I never truly knew your motives, Lola Fitzpatrick.' Richard had laughed then, a slightly pained laugh. 'I never will.'

She'd been laughing too when Adele Warren walked into the room. Despite the fact that it was over twenty years since Lola had seen her, Adele hardly seemed to have aged at all. She was as slim and elegant as ever in a fashionable three-quarter-length grey coat over a red wool dress. The Snowdrop necklace glittered around her throat. But when she saw Lola, and recognised her immediately, her eyes had flashed in anger.

'You have no right to be here,' she'd hissed. 'Get out at once.'

'I came to see how Richard was,' Lola told her. 'I'm sorry. I didn't realise you'd be here at this hour.'

'Why do you need to know how he is? Were you hoping he was at death's door? Were you thinking you could force him into supporting you and your dreadful daughter all over again?'

'Don't you dare talk about Bey like that,' said Lola. 'And the only reason I came was because . . . because I care.'

Adele had stared at her wordlessly. Richard had looked between the two of them, his expression wary.

'You have no right to care.' Adele's voice was icy. 'You have no right to be here. You have no rights at all.'

'It's not about rights,' Lola had said. 'It's about . . .' But she didn't know what to say to Adele. Philip's mother had been one of the deciding factors in Lola's decision not to marry him. Of course it hadn't all been down to her, but Lola realised that when she'd told everyone she didn't love Philip enough, that included that she didn't love him enough to put up with his mother. If Adele had been softer, kinder and more welcoming, Lola had sometimes thought, then perhaps she might have thought about things differently.

'I asked you to leave,' said Adele. 'I don't know why they even let you in.'

Lola picked up her bag from the windowsill and slung it over her shoulder.

'I'm glad you're recovering, Richard,' she said. 'I hope you're home soon.'

But Richard Warren had said nothing in reply. And Lola wondered if she'd ever hear from him again.

Despite the turmoil that was going on in her mind, Bey eventually drifted into a state of semi-consciousness. So when the plane hit a sudden patch of turbulence, she wasn't quick enough to catch the almost-empty coffee cup on the tray top in front of her. It slid sideways and landed upside down on the keyboard of the notebook computer that the passenger beside her was working on.

'Oh crap!' she gasped as he swore loudly. 'I'm so sorry.'

The coffee was rolling off the keyboard and onto his trousers as she offered him her crumpled napkin, continuing to apologise.

'It wasn't your fault.' His accent was more Celtic than English, and the softer cadences almost hid the irritation in his voice.

'You should turn off the computer,' she told him. 'Ideally you need to open the case as well and let the liquid drain out, but there wasn't that much in it . . . I hope.'

He hesitated for a moment, then powered down the notebook. 'Are you a tech person?' he asked, fixing her with a look from eyes that immediately made her think of violet amethysts.

'No,' she said. 'But my best friend's brother is pretty good

224

with technology. His other bit of advice is to let it dry out thoroughly before you try switching it on again. Three days is his recommendation.'

'Three days!' The man looked horrified. 'I need to use it in three hours.'

'I really am sorry. It just . . . it was so sudden, I didn't have time . . . I . . .' She shrugged helplessly.

'Don't worry about it,' he said, although this time he couldn't hide his exasperation. 'Really and truly, air travel is shit. Nobody would dream of breaking out a trolley full of drinks on a bus journey that lasted an hour. This desire to pour stuff down you on planes is beyond me.'

He was being grumpy beyond his years, thought Bey, as he shoved the computer back into its bag. He didn't appear to be much older than her, after all.

'I appreciate you didn't do it deliberately.' His tone had softened a little.

'Thanks.'

'And I apologise if I was a little abrupt.'

'That's OK,' she said.

'But I'm right about air travel,' he said. 'It really is shit.'

She felt as though she should say something else, but she was hopeless at small talk, especially with men she didn't know, and couldn't think of anything. So she simply gave him a slight smile and then busied herself with the newspaper again.

A few minutes later, the cabin crew announced their descent into Dublin airport. They rushed through the aircraft clearing up the rubbish while the passengers began to organise themselves for landing. As the plane bumped its way through the grey clouds, Bey craned her head to see past the passenger at the window and spotted Howth harbour, with the green fields of north Dublin beyond.

As soon as the aircraft had come to a stop, the man next to her pulled his leather cabin bag from beneath the seat in front and then asked Bey if she had any luggage in the overhead bin.

'A green case,' she said.

He took it down for her, and she thanked him. Then he took his mobile from his pocket and switched it on. It immediately beeped with a message. He looked at it and dialled a number.

'I have a problem with my computer,' he said to the person on the other end. 'I'll have to work my way through it.'

Bey gave him another apologetic smile, but he was intent on his conversation and didn't notice.

He was still talking as they began to disembark and was soon caught up in the flow of people streaming through the terminal. Bey walked more slowly. She was looking forward to seeing her mother again. But everything else was sure to be a nightmare.

She saw Lola at once, standing beside one of the pillars in the arrivals hall, and hurried over to her.

Lola's first words were that Bey had lost weight.

'Mum. For heaven's sake.' Bey gave her an exasperated look. 'You say that every time you see me, and every time I tell you that I haven't lost a pound. Not only that, but I've actually put on a few over the last couple of months.'

'Hmm.' Lola held her daughter by her shoulders and looked at her. 'Are you sure about that?'

'I'm certain,' said Bey. 'How could I not? I've been eating all sorts of great food in Córdoba.'

'Oh, all right.' Lola kissed her. 'It's just that you always look thin.'

'I'm long and leggy,' Bey said. 'I seem thinner than I am, that's all.'

Bey knew that her mother had never quite got over a fear that she'd decided to stop eating in order to make herself unattractive to men. After Lola had admitted as much to her, Bey had done her best to reassure her that this wasn't the case; that she'd simply lost her appetite for a while. But she wasn't sure Lola truly believed her, and whenever they were together, she was conscious that her mother monitored her eating habits like a hawk.

'Anyway,' said Bey as they began to walk to the car park. 'What's the news on Richard?'

'None yet,' replied Lola. 'I haven't heard anything more from Philip, but he said he'd let me know if there was any change.'

'I'm astonished that he called you at all,' said Bey.

'When I heard the news, I sent him a message,' said Lola. 'He phoned me back.'

Bey nodded silently. It always surprised her that despite the fact that her parents were virtual strangers to each other these days, they'd never entirely broken off the tenuous connection that sharing a daughter gave them.

'How's Dad?' asked Bey. 'You said he was in the office when it happened. Did he walk in on them, or did they storm the office too? And what about the store manager? Is it still . . . um . . . Lorraine?'

'Lorraine retired a while ago,' said Lola. 'I don't know who the store manager is, but I didn't hear of any injuries. I only spoke briefly to your father when I heard the news.'

Bey shot a sideways look at her. The connection might be tenuous, but Lola still stressed out on the rare occasions she talked to Philip. And she knew that Philip always spoke to her mother as though he were superior to her in every way. It surprised her that Lola, who normally stood up for herself very well, never quite seemed to manage to keep her composure when talking to him.

They reached the car park and Bey put her green bag in the boot before sitting in the passenger seat and heaving a sigh.

'Are you all right?' asked Lola.

'A bit tired, that's all,' replied Bey. 'A couple of hours in a train followed by two flights takes it out of a girl.'

'You've probably been burning the candle at both ends while you were away. Maybe a spell in Dublin will be good for you. Get you eating and sleeping properly again. How has your sleeping been, by the way? Nothing you need to tell me about?'

'Please get off my case,' said Bey. 'My weight, my sleeping – what's next? My love life?'

'Sorry.' That had, in fact, been the next question Lola was about to ask. 'I kind of forget you're not my baby any more.'

'I'm twenty-two.' Bey sat upright again. 'I've graduated from college. I've sold my own jewellery for actual money. I'm training in another country – where, by the way, I'm not burning the candle at both ends because I'm too busy learning stuff to ever have time for mad socialising. There's no reason to think of me as a baby.'

'I know I shouldn't,' said Lola. 'I just can't help it sometimes.'

Bey settled back into her seat, pleased that Lola had accepted the point.

'So how are things going in Córdoba?' asked Lola as they exited the car park. 'Everyone says it's a lovely city. Are you having fun?'

'It's beautiful,' agreed Bey. 'There's history oozing out of every building. And of course the jewellery quarter is fabulous. I was so lucky to meet the Jurados at the fair and get the opportunity to intern with them.'

It had been during her last year at college. She and her friend Vika had taken a stand to exhibit their designs. Martín and his father, Manolo, had been attracted to her silver snowflake pendants and bracelets, and after talking to her for a while, Manolo had offered her the apprenticeship.

'Are you learning much?'

'Loads,' Bey replied. 'The Jurados take such care about their work. Their cutting is exquisite and they polish and polish until the silver is like a glass lake.'

'What about your own designs?'

Bey told her about the ring she was working on, and said that the Jurados wanted an entire collection of her designs for their shop.

'Would you like to stay there with them?'

Bey shook her head. 'They couldn't afford to take on an extra person full time. Besides, I really want to work with precious gems. The Jurados use crystals and glass stones. They're lovely, but they're not diamonds.'

'You're such a snob!' Lola laughed. 'I like Swarovski myself. And it's a lot less scary to lose a crystal necklace than a diamond one.'

'I'm working on the kind of clasp that will mean you'll

never lose your jewellery at all,' said Bey. 'And don't tell me you prefer crystals over diamonds. You're not fooling me for an instant.'

'I don't suppose I ever could,' said Lola.

'You've had it painted!' Bey put her case on the floor and looked around the small house. 'It's lovely, Mum, really lovely.'

'It is, isn't it?' Lola smiled in satisfaction.

'Totally. And you've had the floors redone too. It's totally a single-lady pad now.'

'Never think that.' Lola was aghast. 'It will always be your home, Bey. No matter what. You know that.'

'Of course I do,' said Bey. She gave her mother a hug. 'All I meant was that you can see your personality shining through. I love the artwork.'

Lola grinned. The canvas had been done by her fourteen-year-old nephew, Sean, her sister Gretta's oldest child. He'd won a prize in the Texaco Children's Art competition with it. It was called *Moo Cow*, and was an almost comic-strip rendition of a black and white cow on a yellow background. It brightened the living room considerably.

'I'm waiting for him to become famous,' she said. 'Then I'm going to sell it for a fortune.'

'He's really good, isn't he?' Bey looked at it critically. 'It's very clever.'

'We're an arty family,' said Lola.

'You think?'

'Of course. You. Sean. And Gretta does all the promotional stuff for the co-op, you know – the brochure design and everything. It's really good. If she wasn't such a hot-shot executive, she'd be an artist too.'

'I'm not an artist,' said Bey.

'What would you call yourself then?' demanded Lola.

'I guess I consider my design work to be art,' admitted Bey. 'But not everyone would. And of course the jewellery gene is from Dad's side, so it doesn't count on the art front.'

'Maybe your love of jewellery is from Philip's side,' said Lola. 'But the Warrens don't do the design themselves, you know that. So your arty side is entirely Fitzpatrick. Don't forget your gran and her egg cosies!'

Bey laughed. Eilis had taken up crocheting a couple of years earlier and had surprised them all by concentrating on quirky little egg cosies, which she'd started to sell along with some of the farm produce at farmers' markets around the country. They'd proved to be an astonishing hit with the buyers, and Eilis could hardly keep up with demand.

'What's she going to do about them while she's laid up?' asked Bey.

'Aodhan is going to go round the markets with them for her,' said Lola. 'It's good experience for him.'

Aodhan, three years younger than Bey, was studying agriculture. His father Milo, Lola's older brother, had taken over the farm on their father's sixtieth birthday. Billy Fitzpatrick had said he didn't want Milo hanging around forever waiting for him to die before getting his hands on the farm. So he'd sold a small field with road frontage to a local developer and used the money to build a pretty cottage near High Pasture for himself and Eilis. Everyone was happy with the arrangement. Neither Gretta nor Lola was interested in the farm. Lola had made her life in Dublin with Bey, and Gretta was a senior executive at the co-op.

Lola found it ironic that her sister, who'd planned to be

married and have a family by the time she was twenty-one, had turned into the kind of career woman she'd longed to be herself. Gretta had broken off her engagement to Mossy McCloskey shortly after Bey was born, saying that she wasn't ready to be a wife and mother, and had applied for a job at the creamery, where she rose rapidly through the ranks, becoming the first female director. Much to everyone's surprise, because she'd embraced the role of career woman so thoroughly, she then married Tony O'Mahony, who came from a nearby town. When they started a family, it was Tony who stayed at home with the children while Gretta continued to work. This had caused quite a bit of comment in Cloghdrom – they were the first family in the town where the term 'house husband' was used, but as Tony was also a carpenter and made bespoke furniture to order from a workshop in the garden, it was felt by the more traditional inhabitants that he hadn't been totally emasculated by the decision, and the arrangement worked well for everyone.

Although Lola didn't want to blame herself for Gretta's broken engagement, she knew her pregnancy had been a catalyst. Seeing her sister so ill had completely changed Gretta's view about marriage and babies and the direction of her life. Lola sometimes found it hard not to envy Gretta, who often stayed with her when she came to Dublin for meetings with agricultural organizations, and who always seemed so calm and self-assured.

'D'you think I'd have time to visit Cloghdrom?' Bey asked as she slipped off her jacket and draped it over a chair.

'I don't see why not,' said Lola. 'I'm sure your gran would love to see you.'

'I can't imagine being in Ireland without going to visit her,' said Bey.

'Well, let's wait for news from your dad and we'll make our plans. In the meantime, how about a cup of tea?' Lola headed for the kitchen.

'I'm dying for a decent cuppa.' Bey flopped onto the sofa and kicked off her shoes. 'And I'd forgotten how good it is to have someone who looks after my every need.'

'You lazy wretch!' But Lola was laughing as she switched on the kettle.

Chapter 21

*Clarity: one of the major factors in grading
and valuing gemstones*

They were drinking the tea and eating chocolate Kimberley biscuits when Lola's mobile rang.

'Oh, Philip. I'm so sorry,' she said after she'd listened for a few moments. 'Have you got any details yet? . . . I understand. OK.'

She hung up and looked at Bey.

'Your grandfather passed away a few hours ago,' she said.

Bey replaced the chocolate Kimberly on her plate. She hadn't honestly believed that Richard would die. And it had happened while she'd been upending coffee over a fellow passenger on the aeroplane, or coming in to land, or hurrying through security. While he'd been slipping out of the world, she'd been occupied with something mundane. She found herself suddenly choked up.

'Are you OK?' asked Lola.

'I'm fine,' said Bey as she pushed away the plate. 'It's just – well, we didn't know each other very well, but anyone dying is . . . it makes you think.'

'Life is short,' said Lola. 'Too short for squabbles and feuds and things that don't really matter in the end. Too short for manipulating people's lives for your own ends.'

'Huh.' Bey made a face. 'I don't think the Warrens could live without squabbling. As for manipulation – Grandfather was head of the business and probably had to make some big decisions, but I bet Adele was behind most of them.'

'Your grandmother might have ruled the roost,' agreed Lola. 'But Richard was his own man. Like all of us, though, he made some bad choices.'

'What were they?' asked Bey.

'None that matter now.' Lola had kept her promise to Richard and never said anything about the money he'd given her to keep Bey a secret from her father. Now that he was dead, she wondered whether she should tell her. But she hadn't thought it through enough yet.

Hearing the slight edge to Lola's voice, Bey decided to avoid the topic of her grandfather's bad choices for the time being.

'Was there any news on the raiders?' she asked. 'And does Grandfather dying turn it into a murder enquiry?'

'Nothing from your dad, at least,' replied Lola. 'As far as your grandfather's death is concerned, I don't think they can call it murder because they didn't actually shoot him or assault him physically. At least I don't think they did. Maybe it could be manslaughter. I've no idea.'

'It's horrible.' Bey shuddered. 'Really horrible.'

The doorbell buzzed and Lola got up to answer it. Bey heard a low murmur of voices and then her mother walked into the room followed by a stocky man with greying hair, wearing casual trousers, a T-shirt and a jumper.

'This is Des,' said Lola, a touch of apprehension in her voice. 'Des, this is my daughter, Bey.'

Bey knew all about Des. He was a client of the property management company Lola had been working for over the past few years. Her mother had mentioned him a number of times since Bey had gone to Córdoba, and then, when she'd asked her in exasperation if Des Halligan was the only client she had, Lola had admitted that she was seeing him outside of work.

'Dating him?' Bey had asked in surprise.

'Does it bother you? If it does . . .'

'Hey, I've no right to tell you how to live your life,' Bey replied. 'I'm delighted you're seeing someone. You've always been the one caring for people. It's nice to think there's someone caring about you for a change.'

She'd meant it at the time. But now, face to face with her mother's boyfriend – companion? Lover? She wasn't really sure what the appropriate word should be – she felt suddenly uncertain.

'Hello,' she said as she took his outstretched hand. 'It's nice to meet you.'

'It's nice to finally meet you too.' His handshake was firm and decisive. 'Your mum has told me a lot about you.'

'She has?'

'Not that much,' said Lola. 'Don't flatter yourself.' But she smiled.

'I stopped by to see how Lola was,' he explained as she boiled the kettle again. 'A terrible thing, that shooting. You never think something like that will happen to someone you know.'

'No, you don't,' agreed Bey.

'I was thinking it would be a good plan to go out for something to eat,' said Des. 'Unless there's something you need to do, Lola?'

'They haven't made any arrangements yet,' she told him.

'Go ahead and get yourselves some food,' said Bey. 'I'm not very hungry. I'll stay here in case . . . well . . .'

'Your father will call my mobile, not the house,' said Lola. 'You should come with us.'

Bey suddenly realised that Des's invitation to eat had been decided in advance.

'It would be good to get to know you,' he said.

She'd been telling the truth when she said she wasn't hungry, but she took her jacket from the back of the chair and slipped it on.

When they reached the pub, Des held the door open and Bey followed her mother inside. She remembered the place as dark and traditional, but like so much of the area it had been given a makeover, and now the interior wood was blond rather than mahogany and the ancient carpet had been replaced by high-gloss tiles. It also served a gastropub menu that included mushroom arancini balls and gambas in aioli, which was a far cry from the cheese and onion crisps and salted peanuts that had been on offer before.

'I can't believe how much Dublin has changed,' she remarked as she opted for a Caesar salad. 'It's like someone has airbrushed it into gorgeousness.'

'Let's hope it stays that way,' said Lola. 'The economy isn't doing as well as it was. Especially for property owners.'

'Like you?' Bey turned towards Des.

'Ah, I'm grand,' he said easily. 'My properties are all in

good locations, and a lot of them are in the UK or Florida. I'm diversified.'

'Do you live in them or rent them all out?' asked Bey.

'Rent them, of course,' he said. 'It's a business, and managing them all needs professionals. That's why I've got your mother's agency on board. Well, for the Irish and UK properties anyhow. I have different companies for the States and Eastern Europe.'

'It sounds like an empire,' said Bey.

'Just a business.' Des grinned.

'I've never known anyone who owned more than one house before,' she told him.

'Your dad has three,' remarked Lola. 'Cleevaun House, a villa in Marbella and a studio in New York.'

'Really?' Bey was surprised. 'The jewellery business must be doing well.'

'If he didn't rake it in over the last five years he's an eejit,' said Des. 'And even in a downturn the cream will always rise to the top. I keep telling your mum she should leave the agency and work for me full time. She'd certainly make a lot more money that way.'

'Are you thinking about it?' Bey glanced at her mother.

'Perhaps in the future,' replied Lola.

Bey guessed that this was a conversation she and Des had had before.

'Are you two . . . serious?' She tried to keep a straight face, but then began to laugh. 'I'm sorry,' she said. 'I'm sitting here between my mum and her boyfriend, about to quiz them about their relationship. It seems a bit arse-over-tit to me.'

Des laughed too and Lola grinned at her daughter.

'I suppose you have to make sure it's not some irresponsible fling,' she said.

'You can have as many flings as you like. It's not up to me,' Bey told her.

'I care about your mum a lot,' said Des. 'We're making decisions about the next level.'

Bey smothered a giggle and Lola shot her an amused look.

'You're enjoying this, aren't you?'

'I'm remembering all the times you asked me about my boyfriends at college,' she said. 'And how you lectured me on responsible sex and stuff.'

'Oh God.' Des hid his face in his hands.

'We're very responsible,' Lola said. 'And as for the next level – I'll keep you informed.'

'As long as Des can keep you in the style to which you should be accustomed, I guess I'm fine with it,' said Bey.

'I'm not sure I can keep up with the Warrens,' said Des. 'But I'll do all right.'

'The Warrens.' Bey returned to the real reason she was in Dublin. 'This must all be so dreadful for them.'

'And they have to think about the business even while they're grieving,' said Lola.

'What d'you think will happen?' asked Bey. 'Who's in charge?'

'You dad has been the managing director for a few years already,' said Lola. 'So nothing fundamental will change. I guess Richard's role has been more honorary recently.'

'And there's always Anthony,' Bey commented.

'Anthony?' Des looked at Lola.

'Philip's son,' she said. 'Bey's half-brother. But it'll be

quite a while before he has anything to do with it. He's still only a teenager.'

'They talked about it the year I went to them for Christmas,' Bey told them. 'They said that Anthony was the heir.'

'That's a cheering kind of conversation to have over the turkey,' said Des.

'I asked why it wasn't Astrid, and they said because Anthony was older.'

'The eldest usually gets the top job,' agreed Des.

'But Anthony isn't the eldest.' Bey looked at her mother, an amused gleam in her eyes. 'I remember thinking it at the time. Strictly speaking, I am.'

Lola looked startled, but it was Des who asked if she thought she should or would have a stake in the firm in the future.

'Mum clearly hasn't told you much about them.' Bey shook her head. 'I wouldn't want to work with them and they certainly wouldn't want to work with me. All I'm saying is that Anthony isn't the eldest of Dad's children.'

Lola said nothing. But she couldn't help mulling over Bey's words.

It had never occurred to her before, but her daughter had a point.

It was after nine by the time they left the pub. Lola invited Des back to the house, but he said he needed to get home as he had some more work to do. Even as he spoke, he raised his arm and hailed a passing cab, giving Lola a quick peck on the cheek before getting inside.

'He's nice,' said Bey as the cab pulled away and they began to walk down the road.

'I was hoping you'd think more than just nice,' said Lola.

'I think he cares about you a lot,' Bey said. 'And I think you totally deserve that. Has he been married before?'

'He got divorced a couple of years ago,' said Lola. 'He has a son and a daughter, aged twenty and seventeen. I've met Rory, who's in college. Ciara, his daughter, is at school in Cork. She lives with her mum, who moved back there after the divorce.'

'So if you marry him, I'll have a stepbrother and stepsister to add to Anthony and Astrid,' said Bey. 'Families can become very complicated, can't they?'

'I'm not planning on marrying him yet,' said Lola. 'If at all.'

'Why not?'

'I've lasted this long without getting married,' she said. 'I'm not sure I need to.'

Bey looked at her thoughtfully.

'Does Des want to marry you?'

'He's asked,' said Lola. 'I told him I needed time to think. And that you'd have to meet him first, of course.'

'It's not up to me,' said Bey.

'It is.'

'No.' Bey shook her head so vigorously that her tumble of red curls fell over her face and she had to push them back again. 'In the same way it's not up to you to tell me who to marry either.'

'Is there someone?' Lola sounded excited. 'Have you and the sultry Spaniard got it together at last?'

'Mum!' cried Bey. 'That's totally not a question to ask me.'

241

'Why not?' demanded Lola. 'I've laid my love life out for you. You should do the same for me.'

'I should *not*,' said Bey firmly. 'Martín and I are . . . are . . .'

'Don't say friends with benefits,' begged Lola. 'Please don't.'

Bey grinned. 'We're close,' she admitted. 'But he's not the One.'

'You never give any man the chance to be the One,' protested Lola. 'At college you kept telling me about this guy and that guy, and none of them lasted longer than a jar of coffee.'

This time Bey laughed. 'I'm far too young for long-lasting relationships,' she said. 'Coffee-jar men work just fine for me.'

Lola frowned. She knew mothers worried about everything to do with their children, and she knew Bey had to live her own life, but she couldn't help feeling that her daughter's attitude towards relationships was too dismissive. That she would never see a man as forever.

'Anyway, you're one to talk,' Bey added. 'You turn down all your marriage proposals.'

'There were only two,' said Lola. 'And I haven't completely written Des off yet.'

'But you did write Dad off,' Bey remarked. 'You said you didn't love him enough. I certainly haven't met anyone I love enough yet either . . . Oh!'

Her exclamation came as she saw a group of people standing outside another gastropub on the opposite side of the road.

'What?' asked Lola.

'That man,' she said. 'The one on the end, not smoking. He was on the flight from London.'

242

'And?'

'I dumped a cup of coffee over him.'

'Bey Fitzpatrick! You didn't.' Lola smothered a horrified laugh when Bey explained what had happened. 'Although,' she added appraisingly, 'if I was going to drench someone in coffee, he wouldn't be a bad choice. He's got quite a sexy vibe going on there, and he's about the right age for you.'

'Would you stop it!' demanded Bey. 'Honestly, if this is what being in love – even with someone you might not want to marry – has done to you, I'm glad I'm going to die alone and single in an attic, mourned only by my cat.'

Lola made a face at her. Bey made a face in return. And neither of them noticed that the man across the road, who'd heard their guffaws, was watching them as they turned the corner arm in arm.

They turned on the late news out of what Lola called a morbid curiosity to see how the story of the raid on Warren's was being treated by the media. Bey looked at footage of the gardai outside the Duke Lane shop, which then cut to Philip on the steps of his parents' house thanking people for their support and saying that there was no further information. Despite the tragedy, she thought he looked well in his tailored suit and dark tie, and he spoke courteously to the reporters standing on the pavement.

'He's classy,' she said. 'Very confident.'

'He'll need to be now he's in charge of everything,' said Lola. 'I used to think he wouldn't be any good at it, but I was wrong. I suppose with a family firm you grow into it.'

'Maybe.' Bey picked idly at the cuticle of her thumb.

'Leave your nails alone,' said Lola.

Bey sighed but stopped. It had been a long-running battle when she was younger. She used to pick and pick until she tore the skin, which drove Lola mad.

'I'm not—' She broke off and stared at the TV screen, her face frozen in shock.

'What's the matter?' asked Lola.

Bey didn't answer. She was transfixed by the story that had come on after the report on Warren's.

'. . . Mr Fenton's body was identified by dental records,' the reporter was saying. 'It's believed that it had lain undisturbed for at least ten years before its discovery two months ago.'

'Bey?' Lola looked at her daughter and then at the screen, where they'd moved back to the studio.

'It's him,' said Bey, her voice barely above a whisper.

'Who?' asked Lola.

'Him.' Bey swallowed. 'The man whose car I got into.'

'What!' Lola stared at the screen and then cried out in frustration as the news moved on to something else. 'Are you sure?'

Bey nodded. 'Absolutely.'

'You said you couldn't remember what he looked like,' said Lola.

'I couldn't,' said Bey. 'I didn't want to. I completely blocked him out of my head. But that picture – with the flat cap and the glasses – it's him, Mum, I'm certain.'

'Oh my God.' Lola wasn't sure what to say or do.

'Do you know anything about it?' asked Bey. 'They said his body was discovered two months ago.'

'I remember the initial report,' said Lola. 'A man walking his dog in the Dublin mountains found him. I don't recall exactly where. In a wood, I think. There was an appeal for anyone who knew him to come forward.'

'I didn't hear anything,' said Bey.

'It was a local story, so why would you?' Lola took her by the hand. 'Are you all right?'

'I . . . think so.' Bey's heart was racing. She didn't know how she felt. Except that, even as she was sitting there, she could feel a burden she hadn't known she was carrying slide from her in a way she'd never expected. Seeing the news story had been a shock, but the greater shock was the realisation that she didn't have to be afraid of seeing her abductor again. Or that one day she'd feel a hand on her shoulder and it would be his. She'd always told her mother that she wasn't scared of him, but deep down a nugget of fear had remained. Nor did she have to be afraid that he might succeed in doing to some other girl what he'd nearly done to her, which had also preyed on her mind. She took a deep breath and then exhaled slowly.

'You're really sure it's him?' asked Lola.

'I couldn't possibly mistake him for anyone else,' said Bey. 'Oh, Mum . . .'

And then she burst into tears.

Chapter 22

Amber: the fossilised hardened resin of the pine tree

Lola went out early to get the paper the following morning. The story about Raymond Fenton, aged sixty-four, was on the inside page. He'd been reported missing by his son a month after Bey had got into the car with him.

'Hopefully that means he didn't get the chance to take anyone else.' Bey released her breath slowly. 'Every time I heard anything about someone going missing, I was afraid it was him. I blamed myself for not remembering what he looked like. For not being able to help the police. For being afraid they'd . . .' She stopped. Her fear had been that the police would ask about Lola rather than her abductor. That they'd find out she really had stolen something from the Warrens in the past. That Adele's words would turn out to be true no matter how much Bey believed they couldn't possibly be. It may have been a childish fear. But it had been real nonetheless.

Lola wrapped her arms around her and held her close.

'If it hadn't been for Grandad dying, I never would have known,' Bey said suddenly. 'It's like . . . it's fate, Mum. I feel I should thank Grandad for . . .well, not for dying, that's ridiculous, but . . .'

'Plenty of strange things happen in life – and in death,' said Lola. 'You know I'm not religious, or even very spiritual. But perhaps somehow your grandfather's spirit influenced the identification of that man.'

'I like to think so,' said Bey. 'He was the kindest of the Warrens.'

'Why do you think that?' Lola's voice was suddenly tight, but Bey, still overcome by the discovery of Raymond Fenton's body, didn't notice.

'He talked to me like I mattered,' she replied. 'Like I was a real person.'

'We should go to the police,' said Lola after a moment. 'I don't know if they still have a file open on your case, but it would be the right thing to do.'

Bey swallowed hard a few times, then nodded. She still couldn't quite believe that the man who'd been in her head for so many years was finally gone. She was astonished at how strong that suddenly made her feel.

Philip rang shortly afterwards to give Lola information about the funeral arrangements. Richard's body would be brought to the house in Rathgar, where he would remain overnight ahead of the funeral service that would take place the following day.

'The house is private,' Philip said. 'Immediate family only.'

'OK,' said Lola, who'd decided not to say anything to him about Raymond Fenton until a more appropriate time. 'We'll see you at the funeral. I really am sorry, Philip.'

'He was in his seventies,' said Philip. 'He'd had double

heart bypass surgery. Two thugs came at him with sawn-off shotguns. It would have been a miracle if he hadn't had a heart attack.'

'No news on the raiders yet?'

'They're not saying much, but I think they know who did it.'

'It must have been horrifying for you.'

'Yes. Well, I'm in charge of things now and I have to get over the horror and step up to the plate,' said Philip. 'The shops will be closed as a mark of respect but I'll talk to all the managers after the funeral and set out a strategy for them. I need to work on that. I have to talk to Peter, too.'

Lola knew that Philip was still in shock about the raid, but he was certainly revelling in his elevation to head of the family. There was an authority in his voice that she'd never heard before. Despite Philip's designation as managing director for a number of years, Lola knew that Richard hadn't handed over the reins to his elder son quite as completely as her own father had handed over the farm to Milo. Richard had always been the one who made the final decisions on the things that mattered, which she was sure would have irritated Philip, especially since she was aware that his father didn't interfere quite so much with the financial side of the business, happily leaving that to Peter. Even when she'd first known him, Lola had been aware of a certain friction between the brothers caused by the fact that while Richard had absolute faith in his younger son's ability with numbers, he didn't seem able to accept that Philip would be equally good at running the stores. She wondered if the tension was still there, and if it was, whether Richard's death would change anything.

something about those Warrens that invites trouble. Some people are like that and they mess up everyone close to them.'

'Richard had . . . good intentions,' said Lola. 'He always put his family first. He always wanted to do what was best.'

'That doesn't always mean doing the right thing,' Eilis said.

'We've given the Warrens enough time today.' Lola's voice was firm in her determination to change the subject. 'How's Gretta?'

'Ah, now, she's doing great,' began Eilis.

Bey smiled as she listened to her mother and grandmother chat. There was a comfort factor in being at Cloghdrom that didn't exist anywhere else. Something about the farm seemed to reach out and envelop her in warmth and love. In Cloghdrom she was always the Bey she wanted to be. She wondered if she'd ever find a place of her own to make her feel that way. But Cloghdrom was more than a place, she reminded herself. It was people. And Bey knew she wasn't good with people. She didn't like getting close to them. That was why her men never lasted longer than a jar of coffee.

And that was the legacy Christmas Day with the Warrens had left her.

Chapter 23

Onyx: a banded or layered chalcedony, usually black

There were television cameras outside the inter-faith chapel at the crematorium, and a reporter was speaking into a mic as he described the scene for that evening's news. Because Richard had been such a well-known business figure in the city, the mourners included local politicians, gardai and members of the jewellery trade.

Lola and Bey stood among them and waited for the cortège to arrive. Since the only person they recognised was one of the politicians, who also happened to be a cabinet minister, they kept to themselves and didn't speak to anybody else. Lola had never met any of Richard's own family. She knew he was the third of four siblings – he had two older sisters, one of whom was married and lived abroad and the other who'd died in her early twenties from tuberculosis. His younger sister was also married and had a family, but that was as much as Lola knew. As for Adele's relatives, the Pendletons, she was completely in the dark there.

There was a low murmur from the assembled crowd as the hearse, followed by two large Daimlers, turned into the

gravel driveway leading to the chapel. It stopped outside the door and the undertakers slid the coffin out. Then Philip and Peter along with two men Lola didn't recognise heaved it onto their shoulders and carried it into the chapel.

They were followed by Adele, looking strong and elegant in a black linen dress and a short black jacket. Her patent-leather shoes had a higher heel than either Lola or Bey felt comfortable wearing. Her silver hair was styled into her trademark chignon and held in place by an ebony comb. She was also wearing the Adele Nightshade collection, the onyx and garnets dark and sombre against her black dress. She kept her eyes fixed straight ahead of her as she walked into the chapel, flanked by Donna and a much older woman who Lola guessed was Richard's sister.

Behind them were Anthony and Astrid. Now eighteen, they looked more alike than they had done when they were younger. Both were tall and fair, with Adele's fine features, and both wore their expensive clothes well. They were the new generation of Warrens, confident in themselves and their surroundings despite the sombre occasion.

There was total silence among the mourners. Bey slid her hand into her mother's, who squeezed it gently while the minister gave a eulogy, listing Richard's business achievements and calling him a pillar of the community. But, he said, more important were his qualities as a father and a husband. He had been a loving man, said the minister, whose main priority had always been his family.

And that might be true, thought Lola as she glanced around the church, but not necessarily in the way that the minister meant.

* * *

At the end of the service, Philip stepped up to the lectern and invited everyone present to the house at Rathgar for a brief celebration of his father's life.

'Not us, though,' said Bey as they filed out of the chapel. 'We don't know anyone and we're not part of anything.'

'This is different,' said Lola. 'Funerals . . . well, there are expectations around them. As for being part of it, I made a huge mistake about that when you were small, and—'

'And you've been trying to fix it ever since,' Bey interrupted her. 'But it never worked and you don't have to try any more. Let's go home. There's no place for us here.'

As Lola hesitated, Peter Warren walked over to them, a quizzical expression on his face.

'Lola?' he said. 'Bey?'

'Uncle Peter.' Bey had recognised him straight away.

He smiled at her. 'You've grown considerably since the last time we met.'

'I hope so. And you haven't changed at all,' she said.

'I'm sorry for your loss, Peter,' said Lola. 'And for what happened at the store. It must have been awful.'

'It was pretty dreadful all right.' Peter heaved a sigh. 'Thank you both for coming. I know we haven't been close over the years, but it's nice to know that you cared enough to be here.'

Bey, knowing that she hadn't really wanted be there at all, felt guilty and then grateful that Lola had made her do the right thing.

'You're coming back to the house?' said Peter.

'We were just deciding what to do about that,' said Lola.

'Please come,' he said. 'Phil has organised a retrospective about Dad. Some photos of his life, that sort of thing. I

know Mum would like to have as many people as possible there.'

'Even us?' asked Bey.

Peter smiled. 'Everyone who knew Dad is welcome. And he liked you, Bey.'

'He did?'

'Oh yes,' said Peter. 'He was very taken with those bracelets you made. Do you still do stuff like that?'

'Bey is working for a jewellery company in Córdoba,' Lola told him, and Peter's eyes widened in surprise.

'Really?'

'It's a small silversmith's,' Bey said. 'I'm just learning.'

'Nature over nurture,' said Peter. 'I shouldn't be surprised. Dad was right about your bracelets. They were very pretty.'

'Adele didn't think much of them,' said Bey. 'She thought I'd made them from a kit.'

'Oh well, unless they're diamonds or rubies, Mum wouldn't give them the time of day.' Peter grinned.

'I haven't quite got to diamonds or rubies yet,' said Bey. 'I kind of feel I'm better off away from them.'

'Don't be silly,' said Peter. 'I'm sure you'd do wonderful work with them. Cushla loved your bracelets too, you know.'

'Mum told me you didn't get married in the end. Can I ask why?'

'We didn't cover ourselves in glory that Christmas,' Peter replied. 'Cushla realised she'd be making a mistake.'

'What d'you mean?'

'Oh, Bey,' he said. 'It was a difficult day . . . and night.'

'Was it because I ran away?' Bey was aghast. 'How could that have affected you and Cushla?'

'It brought out our worst sides,' Peter said. 'Things were

257

said that shouldn't have been. And Cushla decided she didn't much care for it. Or us.'

'I'm so sorry if I had something to do with it,' said Bey in distress.

'It wasn't your fault,' said Lola. 'You were the child. They were the adults.'

'Mum, please.' Bey put her hand on Lola's arm and turned to Peter. 'Did you ever marry anyone else?'

'No,' said Peter. 'I never quite found anyone I wanted to spend the rest of my life with. Or maybe it was that nobody I met wanted to spend the rest of her life with me.'

Bey was struggling with the feelings of guilt that were washing over her. It was hard to accept that the consequences of her actions had affected lives apart from her own. She was spared having to say anything else, however, because at that point a man neither she nor Lola recognised came over to express his condolences and Peter moved to talk to him.

'Let's go get a coffee,' suggested Lola. 'Afterwards we'll head on to the house. But we'll just stay long enough to pay our respects.'

Bey nodded. The Warrens were an insignificant part of her life and yet they were taking up a substantial part of her emotional memory right now. And she wasn't at all sure she was equipped to deal with it.

The small café close to the crematorium was nearly full, but they didn't know if any of the occupants had also been at Richard's funeral. They sat at a table near the back while they drank their coffee in silence. Bey was thinking about precious gemstones and the unpolished ring on her work-bench when Lola nudged her.

'Time to go,' she said. 'Time to face the Ice Dragon in her lair.'

'Ice Dragon? Mum!'

Lola grinned. 'It suits her, don't you think?'

'Did you have one for Grandfather too?' asked Bey.

'Mack,' admitted Lola.

'Mack?' Bey looked confused. 'After who?'

'Machiavelli,' replied Lola. 'Not that your grandfather was as devious as him, but he had his moments.'

'I thought we agreed he was the nicest of the lot,' said Bey in surprise. 'When was he devious?'

'Oh, I'm just being silly,' said Lola as she stood up. 'Come on. Let's go.'

And she swept out of the café, leaving Bey to rush after her.

Lola could hardly believe that so much time had passed since she'd first walked up the steps to the Warrens' house, wearing her navy dress with the white collar, for dinner with Richard, Adele and Philip. For a fleeting moment she wondered what her life would have been like if she'd said yes to his proposal. She wondered most of all if things would have been better for Bey. If she could have been sure they would have been, she wouldn't have hesitated. She'd have married Philip Warren without question. But she couldn't change the past. What was done was done. She took a deep breath and walked through the open door.

It was no surprise that the house had changed. The fussy decor that she remembered from her solitary visit had been replaced with light creams, pale greens and muted taupes. The walls in the hallway were covered with stylised photos

of the Adele collections, while a large portrait of Richard and Adele hung on the main living-room wall. The marble fireplace had been removed and replaced with an old-fashioned cast-iron one, which Lola supposed had been the original style for the room. The furniture was quietly elegant. The entire house gave off an air of understated wealth.

Three large albums containing photos of Richard from boy to man, at home and at the Warren shops, with his family and with members of the trade, had been left on a table in the window alcove, and earlier arrivals were already looking through them. Meanwhile, other people gravitated towards the dining room, which was linked to the living room by double doors. From there, French doors leading to the well-kept garden were also open. Another table had been set up where two waiters were serving drinks, while three more offered canapés and neatly cut sandwiches to the mourners.

'Crikey,' said Bey as she took an egg and watercress. 'This is more like a cocktail party than a funeral.'

She'd only been to one funeral before, that of Hetty Banks, the grandmother of one of her school friends, from the adjoining farm in Cloghdrom. It had been an altogether more traditional event, with soup and sandwiches at the local pub after the burial. Nobody in Cloghdrom got cremated. They were all laid to rest in one of the town's two churchyards.

'Adele clearly likes to keep up standards,' murmured Lola. 'No matter what the circumstances.'

'She looks amazing, doesn't she?' said Bey. 'All sort of regal and superior. That dress and those shoes are fabulous, and although I'm not crazy about the Nightshade collection,

she wears it well. Oh look. Here's Donna, come to give us the once-over.'

Donna, wearing a black dress and jacket, and the Bouquet collection, was making her way towards them.

'Lola,' she said, extending a perfectly manicured hand. 'It was kind of you to come.'

'Of course we came,' said Lola. 'We were both stunned when we heard the news.'

'It's awful.' Donna's voice lost some of its polished politeness. 'The boys are devastated and Adele is still in shock herself.'

'I hope they find who did it,' said Lola.

'The Garda have a good idea who they were,' said Donna. 'Known criminals apparently. I don't know what we're paying our taxes for when these thugs can roam the streets with impunity. And even if they're caught, a decent solicitor will probably get them off. Maybe not for robbing the shop, but they'll say Richard had a heart condition and could have dropped dead any time.'

'I'm sorry,' said Lola.

Bey, feeling uncomfortable standing beside them with no idea what to say, sidled away and got a drink of water. While she was sipping it, Astrid came up to her.

'I hardly recognised you,' said the younger girl. 'You look completely different.'

'And you look great,' said Bey.

Astrid was as groomed as a fashion model, with her perfectly made-up face and artfully styled hair.

'Thank you,' she said.

'I'm sorry about what happened.'

Astrid's lip quivered.

'Poor Grandfather,' she said. 'Those awful people. They could have killed anyone. Me even, if I'd been there.'

Bey gave her a sympathetic smile.

'Dad says we have to review security,' Astrid continued. 'Not that we don't have a lot at the house and shops anyway, but we have to be more careful. I asked him if I needed a bodyguard, but he said that was probably going a bit far.'

'Probably,' agreed Bey. 'After all, they were only after the stuff in the shop, not you personally.'

'All the same,' said Astrid, 'it'd be terrible to be snatched and ransomed.'

Bey nodded.

'Of course, you know all about that,' Astrid said. 'After all, you were kidnapped yourself, weren't you?'

Her words were spoken in such a matter-of-fact way that they took Bey totally by surprise.

'I wasn't kidnapped,' she said when she'd recovered. 'I was just . . . abducted.' Her voice faltered.

'You never know,' Astrid said. 'If he'd seen you leave Cleevaun House, he could've thought you were from a rich family and we'd have to pay a ransom for your safe return.'

'I doubt he was hanging around Cleevaun House at that hour of the night waiting for me to come out,' said Bey. 'Besides, I was miles away when it happened.'

'He could have been casing the joint for a robbery,' said Astrid. 'And then taken a different opportunity when you appeared. I heard them talking about it,' she added. 'Dad thought it was a possibility.'

'He was wrong.' Bey frowned. Despite the counselling sessions where Paige Pentony had tried to make her remember events so that she could deal with them, Bey had worked

262

very hard to lock them away as much she could. She didn't want to recall the moment when she'd realised she'd made the biggest mistake of her life. And she definitely didn't want to relive the sheer terror of crouching in the snow, trying not to breathe, waiting to be found by her captor. All she wanted was to forget. And the knowledge that Raymond Fenton was dead was making that easier by the second.

'Were you scared?' Astrid's voice was eager and interested.

'Yes,' Bey said. 'I was scared.'

'But you escaped.'

'I was lucky.'

'That's what Adele says.' Astrid smiled slightly. 'She says you live a charmed life.'

'I don't think so,' said Bey.

'You're wearing the same earrings as me.' Astrid brushed a strand of her golden locks from her eyes as she changed the subject. 'The Bluebells. Where did you get them?'

'Mum gave them to me before I went to college,' said Bey.

'That was an extravagant gift, don't you think?'

Bey bit back the retort she'd been about to make, although she agreed with Astrid that it had been very extravagant indeed. She'd been shocked when her mother had produced the earrings, and asked if she'd actually gone to Duke Lane to buy them for her. But Lola had said they'd been a gift to her when she was younger, and now she wanted Bey to have them. Bey had asked if the gift had been from her father, but Lola had shaken her head and said that there had been more men in her life than Philip. Bey had wondered why she'd never worn them herself, and her mother had said that she'd wanted to keep them as an heirloom for Bey. But even

as Bey had hugged her and told her they were the nicest present anyone had ever given her, she couldn't help thinking that Lola was keeping something from her and that the earrings meant more than she'd ever know.

'They suit you,' said Astrid when she realised that Bey was remaining silent. 'But then, you like Warren jewellery, don't you?'

'These are all I have,' Bey told her.

'And the ring.' Astrid's smile didn't reach her eyes. 'My ring. From the Christmas cracker.'

After all this time, she hasn't forgiven me for taking it, Bey realised. She still thinks of me as a thief. She felt her face flush.

'Dad made me give it to you,' Astrid continued. 'He said it was the least I could do after your ordeal.'

'I didn't want it,' said Bey.

'But you took it all the same.'

Bey had no answer. The silence between them was growing increasingly uncomfortable, and she was relieved when a young man she didn't know came over to them and asked Astrid how she was feeling.

'Tired,' Astrid replied. 'It's been a difficult day.'

'Of course it has.' The man put his arm around her shoulders. 'Come on, sweetheart. Let's sit in the garden for a while.'

Astrid allowed herself to be led away without saying another word. Bey hadn't realised she'd been holding her breath until she exhaled in relief. Then she opened her small leather handbag and looked inside.

She'd begun to walk towards the kitchen, but stopped in complete astonishment when she saw the tall, dark-haired

man standing close to the door. It took a moment for her to be sure it was the same man who'd sat beside her on the flight from London, and who she'd seen standing outside the pub that same evening. Bey didn't believe in coincidences or karma or things that were meant to be, but it was startling to see him here and now in a completely different context. He turned suddenly and a flash of recognition passed over his face.

'Hello again,' he said. 'I didn't expect to see you again so soon. And here of all places.'

'I was thinking the same. And I saw you before.' She blurted out the words. 'The other night. Outside a pub.'

'You say that with a slightly accusing tone.' He grinned. 'As though I shouldn't have been. And this might freak you out, but I saw you too.'

'Really?'

'But I stayed well away in case you wanted to dump my drink all over me.'

'Do I need to apologise for that again? Is your notebook OK?'

'Surprisingly, yes. I was going to yell across the road to you and tell you, but you were engrossed in conversation.'

'I was out with my mum,' she said. 'I'm glad to hear the notebook wasn't ruined. I was feeling pretty bad about it.'

'No need to feel bad any more,' he said.

'So as you're here, you must have known Richard?' said Bey.

He nodded. 'I did business with him a few times. When I heard the news, I stayed on in Dublin to pay my respects. He was a good man to work with. And you?'

'Oh, he's . . . he was a distant relative.' Bey felt that was the best approach to take regarding her relationship to her late grandfather.

'In that case, I'm sorry,' said the man. He held out his hand. 'Will Murdoch.'

'Bey Fitzpatrick.'

His grip was confident and businesslike.

'I was in a shop that was raided myself once,' he said. 'Horrible thing.'

'Really?' Bey's eyes widened. 'What happened?'

'Masked men burst in, told us all to get down and stay down, fired a shot into the ceiling and then made off with as much as they could,' said Will. 'It seemed to last forever, but apparently it took less than a minute.'

'Scary.'

'At least none of us was killed,' he said. 'We were gutted about the jewellery, of course, but in the end, no matter how beautiful it was, people's lives were more important.'

'So you're in the trade?' she said.

'A wholesaler,' he told her. 'We supply diamonds and other gemstones.'

She nodded.

'I like your Adele Bluebells,' he added. 'Sapphires are my favourite stones.'

This time she smiled. 'Mine too. There's something about the deep blue of a sapphire that tugs at me,' she confessed.

'It's an emotional thing, isn't it?' he said. 'You see a stone and it seems to speak to you and . . .' He gave a slightly embarrassed laugh. 'Sorry, I get a bit carried away sometimes.'

'But I think the same thing,' she said. 'They're not just pieces of rock.'

266

'Of course some people only like them for what they're worth,' Will said. 'But I see them as living history. Here before us, here after we go.'

'Exactly.' And as their eyes met, she was struck once again by the dark amethyst of his. Whereas mine, she thought, are more like aquamarines.

'If you're ever thinking of having a piece made, you should contact me.' He broke their gaze and took a business card from his inside pocket. 'I love matching stones to people and I know I could get a really good one for you. Though what am I saying?' he added. 'You probably get a family discount at Warren's. You don't need anything from me.'

'No,' she said. 'I don't get a discount. And I'll keep you in mind if I ever need precious gems. It's unlikely,' she added. 'I might be as much of a sucker as the next girl for a flawless diamond, but right now I'd be pushing it to afford a decent cubic zirconia.'

He laughed. 'Are you involved in the jewellery trade yourself?'

'Sort of,' she admitted, and told him about her apprenticeship with the Jurados.

'I don't know them,' he said. 'What sort of stuff do you design?'

Bey pulled at the silver chain around her neck. It was one of the earliest pieces she'd done in Córdoba, a crescent moon with a small black stone at the very tip. She'd made it so that Manolo could assess her skills. Even though there was nothing difficult in it, he'd made comments to her at every stage of the process, and as a result she thought it was one of her best pieces of work.

'Striking,' said Will as he turned it over between his fingers.

'I realise it's not much.' Bey was feeling embarrassed now. After all, if Will dealt with Warren's, he was probably used to far more intricate work that this. And of course nothing in the Warren's line contained glass stones.

'I like the style,' he said. 'There's something eye catching about its simplicity. Do you have others?'

'I'm working on them at the moment,' she said.

'I'd love to see them.'

'I can email you photos if you like.' Bey knew that he was probably being polite and that a gemstone wholesaler wouldn't have a lot of use for her designs, but it was nice of him to ask.

'My details are on the card I gave you,' he said. 'Give me a call any time.'

'You're based in London,' she said as she looked at it.

He nodded. 'But we also have offices in New York.'

'Do you travel a lot?'

'Yes, and usually long haul. Which is why I'm so crap with luggage on short-hop flights.' He gave her an apologetic look. 'I was a bit of an arse the other day. I'm sorry.'

'I retaliated by dumping my coffee all over you, so we're quits.' She smiled. Perhaps it was because of their shared views on precious gems, but the walls and barriers she normally put up around men she didn't know seemed unnecessary with Will Murdoch.

She would have enjoyed talking a little more, but at that moment she saw Adele making her way across the room. As her grandmother said hello, she effectively excluded Will, who murmured a quick goodbye and left them alone.

'You're looking surprisingly elegant today,' Adele said when Bey remained silent. 'You've improved with age.'

'Thank you.' Bey was getting a little tired of people commenting on her appearance. The last time she'd seen any of them, she'd been a child. Now she was a grown-up.

'I appreciate that you and your mother came to the service. It wasn't necessary for you to come to the house, but I believe Peter insisted.' Adele's words were jerky and her voice was uneven.

'We only dropped by for a few minutes,' said Bey. 'I'm sure Mum will want to leave soon.'

'Richard had a softer spot than was necessary as far as you were concerned,' said Adele, her long, slender fingers playing unconsciously with her Nightshade necklace. 'Regardless of my personal feelings, he'd be glad to know you were here.'

'Oh.' Bey didn't know what else to say.

'How are you getting on with your life?' her grandmother finally asked.

'Pretty well,' said Bey. 'I graduated last year.'

'Have you got a job?'

'Unpaid except for a very small living allowance, but I'm learning a lot,' she said.

'And what are you learning?' asked Adele.

'Design.'

'Designing what?'

Bey didn't think her grandmother would appreciate hearing that she was following in her grandfather's footsteps and studying jewellery. She was pretty sure Adele would consider it an affront. So she simply shrugged and said, 'This and that.'

'And are you planning to get a proper job?' asked Adele.

'I hope so,' said Bey. 'I have to pay the rent somehow.'

'Don't you live with your mother any more?'

Bey explained about studying in Birmingham and now being in Córdoba.

'Isn't it expensive to study outside Ireland?' asked Adele.

'Mum saved up for me,' said Bey. 'She always made sure that I was looked after. She's amazing like that.'

Adele said nothing, but her expression hardened and the silence between them grew. Bey looked around to see if she could catch Lola's eye, but her mother was in deep conversation with a woman Bey didn't know.

'Did you ever meet Richard again?'

Adele's question was so unexpected that Bey looked at her in astonishment.

'Grandfather? Why on earth would I?' she responded.

'When he was ill, some time ago,' said Adele. 'When he had his bypass. You didn't come to see him?'

'No,' said Bey. 'How would I? I was at college.'

Adele's shoulders relaxed a little. 'Well, I don't suppose we'll see each other after today,' she said. 'Thank you for coming.'

She turned and walked away.

Bey stared after her, completely bewildered by Adele's remarks. It was as though her grandmother was trying to elicit some kind of secret from her, she thought. But the one sure thing in Bey's life was that she didn't have any secrets.

She glanced at her watch. They'd been here for almost an hour and she really wanted to leave. But she had something she needed to do first. She walked out of the room and crossed the hallway, moving away from the noise of the two reception rooms. She opened one of the closed doors and looked inside.

A big mahogany desk with a closed laptop in the centre

270

of it dominated the room. Bookshelves lined the walls and there were two wooden filing cabinets in one of the corners.

This will do perfectly, thought Bey, as she rooted in her handbag. Nestled at the bottom were two small boxes. She took them out and opened them. One contained a small sapphire ring. The other a silver locket.

She'd almost given the ring to Astrid when she'd started talking about it, but she'd been afraid of making a scene. Anyway, a scene hadn't been part of her plan. But from the moment her father had given her Astrid's ring, she'd wanted to give it back. She simply hadn't known the best way to go about it. As for the locket, she'd never worn it.

Adele would be happy to have them, she thought. And she herself was happy not to.

She placed the boxes side by side on the desk and closed them again. Then she walked out of Richard's study and went to find her mother.

Lola was talking to Philip while Donna stood awkwardly to one side when Bey came up to her.

'We should probably go, Mum,' she said.

'I haven't had time to talk to you,' said Philip. 'I know these aren't ideal circumstances, but it's the first time I've seen you for ages and we should at least have a moment's conversation.'

'We've managed fine without it till now, don't you think?' said Bey.

Her father looked at her thoughtfully. 'I would've—'

'Please don't,' said Bey. 'Don't say you would've got in touch or we should've got in touch. We didn't and that's all that counts.'

'Your mother—'

'And please don't blame my mother for anything.' Bey's voice was firm. 'She's been brilliant. She always is.'

'I wasn't going to blame her,' said Philip. 'Although—'

'We really need to go.' Bey interrupted him for the third time. 'I have a flight to catch tomorrow.'

'Fine,' said Philip. 'Just don't say I didn't try.'

'I won't.'

'You were a bit rude to your dad,' Lola told her as they walked out of the front door. 'He was making an effort.'

'He doesn't like me,' Bey said. 'Same as Adele.'

'They don't know you,' Lola reminded her. 'And like I've said a million times before, that's my fault as much as theirs. I didn't think your dad and I would be good together and I . . . I made the decision that it was better for both of us to go it alone.'

'It was the right decision.' Bey linked her arm with Lola's. 'You always make the right decisions, Mum.'

'Oh Bey—'

But Lola was interrupted by the sound of Bey's name being called. They turned around. Will Murdoch was standing on the steps.

'I just wanted to catch you before you leave,' he said. 'I meant what I said about your designs. I'd really love to see them, so don't forget to send them.'

'Thank you.' Bey smiled at him. 'And if you hear of anyone hiring promising young designers, please let me know.'

'Of course I will,' he said.

'It was good to meet you.'

'You too.'

272

She waved and then caught up with her mother, who was waiting for her at the gate.

'Who was he?' asked Lola. 'He looked vaguely familiar.'

'The man I spilled the coffee over.'

'You're not serious! What on earth was he doing here?'

Bey explained Will's connection to the Warrens.

'And he wants you to send him designs?'

Bey nodded.

'So drowning him in coffee might have been a good career move,' said Lola.

'You never know.'

But that night, as she looked at his business card, Bey realised with a jolt that it wasn't her career she was thinking of.

It was just him.

Which was a complete surprise.

Chapter 24

Lapis lazuli: a unique deep blue gemstone

It was silly to think that Will Murdoch had meant what he said, Bey thought a few months later as she sat at the big dining table with the Jurados, who'd organised a farewell dinner for her the night before she left Córdoba. She'd sent him pictures of her designs as he'd asked, and had received an automatic response saying that he was away on business and would get back to her as soon as possible. But she hadn't heard anything from him since, and the excitement that she'd felt about someone being interested in her work had dissipated with each passing day. As had the unaccustomed feeling of having met someone who mattered to her in a way she couldn't quite explain even to herself. Even though she'd only exchanged a few words with him, she'd felt a connection with him that she'd never felt with a man before. But it had been fleeting, she told herself, and he clearly hadn't felt anything at all. His request to see her designs had simply been a kindness on his part. He worked with fine jewellery. He had no interest in silver trinkets. And no interest in her either. She'd foolishly hoped that he'd be so enchanted by

her designs he'd immediately recommend her to a famous jewellery house like Van Cleef or Tiffany's. But she had to accept that she was nobody as far as he was concerned. And that his promise of letting her know about new opportunities had been part of social conversation, nothing more. So, with no other options on the horizon, she was returning to Dublin.

'. . . but we hope you will come back to us someday.' Manolo's voice broke into her thoughts. He was standing at the head of the table and raising a wine glass to her. 'Because you have a good eye for beautiful design and you are a quick learner of our methods.'

'Thank you,' she said in response. 'It's been wonderful being here and . . . and I'm sorry to be leaving you.' Her voice broke at the end because she was speaking the truth. She was sad that her time with the Jurados, who'd treated her more and more as part of the family, had come to an end.

'I'll miss you most of all.' It was Martín who spoke next. 'Having you here has made me think differently about our own designs. And other things.'

She smiled at him. She hadn't said it to Lola, but Martín had been another coffee-jar man in her life. She'd felt the spark of attraction when they'd first met at Birmingham and then when he'd collected her from the train station at Córdoba. And she'd allowed herself to be drawn closer and closer to him as she honed her silversmithing skills, culminating in a night of frenzied passion in the studio apartment above the workshop where she was staying.

But, as with all the men she'd dated, she'd held a part of herself back. She didn't know why it was that she couldn't lose her heart to anyone. She told herself it was a good thing,

because the world probably had enough broken-hearted women in it already. She ignored the fact that, at the back of her mind, she could still hear her father's words, the day after she'd run away. *You clearly don't know how to judge men.* Because she didn't want to think that he could be right.

When she arrived back in Dublin, she got a taxi from the airport to the house in Ringsend. Lola was still at work – the agency was pitching to a new corporate client and she was leading the proposal.

'I've got to be there,' she'd told Bey. 'I'm the one who's been in touch with their directors and I'm the one who needs to close this deal.'

'Don't worry,' Bey had responded. 'I know how to make myself feel at home.'

Now, however, as she walked through the familiar rooms, she felt an unaccustomed sense of not belonging. More than her years in college, her months with the Jurados had made her feel independent. As though she was finally living a life that wasn't predictable. But now she was back. And instead of Bey Fitzpatrick, the talented Irish designer, she was just Lola's daughter. The daughter, she knew, that Lola continued to worry about despite all the progress she'd made in her life.

'Oh, mothers worry about their daughters forever,' Lola had said one evening when she'd phoned Bey, not having heard from her for over a week. 'Your gran still worries about me.'

'Nobody could possibly worry about you!' Bey had exclaimed. 'You're Superwoman.'

And they'd laughed. But it was true, Bey thought. Her

mother had an inner strength and an inner confidence that Bey knew she lacked herself. Lola always knew what to do. And despite the fact that they both agreed she'd made mistakes in the past, she could move on from them. Bey wished she could feel as free from the past. But even though the spectre of Raymond Fenton had finally disappeared, the knowledge that she herself had been to blame for what had happened never would.

Being back in Dublin was more problematic than she'd expected. The economic downturn, which Des had been so blasé about a few months earlier, seemed to have the country in a vice-like grip. Companies were shedding jobs, house prices were falling and everybody was stressed. Nobody wanted to take on a design graduate, and even temporary jobs like working in a pub or a coffee shop were hard to come by. Bey had originally assumed she'd be staying with Lola for a few weeks, but a couple of months after her return she was still there and still sending out her CV to prospective employers. So far her only success had been reprising her college job as a part-time barista in a coffee shop on the quays.

'I'm one of these boomerang kids,' she wailed as once again she checked her email fruitlessly in the hope that a job offer would have arrived. 'I'm back and I'm afraid I'll never be able to leave again.'

'Of course you will,' said Lola. 'But in the meantime, I love having you here.'

Des didn't, though. Bey knew that he was increasingly irritated by her presence in the house, and once or twice he had greeted her with a jokey 'Still here?' that was anything but funny. Lola spent occasional nights in his apartment, and

those were the nights in which Bey was at her most relaxed, as she didn't feel that she was casting a cloud over their relationship. One day she asked Des if he knew anyone who could give her a job, and he replied tersely that if she read the papers she'd know that the housing market was in free fall and that he had far more important things to worry about than a NEET.

'A what?' she asked.

'Not in education, employment or training,' he responded.

'I wish I *was* in any of those things,' she retorted. 'I'm doing my best.'

She didn't tell her mother that Des was needling her. He had a point. Though she wished he'd do it in front of Lola and not when she wasn't there.

Much to her relief and surprise, she was eventually offered a job at a jewellery design studio in Dun Laoghaire. She hoped she'd be adding to the experience she'd already gained with the Jurados, but she realised quickly that Tina Garavan simply wanted an assistant and not someone who was interested in doing her own thing. Bey felt as though her career had taken a backwards step as she spent her day cleaning moulds and tidying up the workshop, but it had the advantage of finally removing her from NEET status, a phrase she used when she took Lola out to dinner with her first pay cheque.

'A what?' asked Lola in exactly the same bewildered tone that Bey had used when she'd first heard the expression.

Bey explained it to her mother, who laughed.

'It's true, though,' Bey said. 'I was pretty much sponging off you for a while. And to be honest, I still will be. I'm not earning enough to move out yet. I feel so hopeless!'

'I'm happy to have you,' said Lola. 'And I'm sure you'll get what you want eventually.'

Bey wasn't as confident as her mother. To help supplement her income she set up a workbench in the shed at Ringsend, having bought it and a set of tools cheaply from Tina. She was going to work on her own designs, she told Lola, and try to sell them at various markets. Like Gran and her tea cosies, she added, which made Lola smile.

'You've come on a lot,' said her mother one night when she dropped by the shed to see how things were going. 'That really is beautiful.' The pendant, inlaid with glass stones, was one of Bey's spider's web designs.

'It's for you,' she said as she handed it to Lola. 'To say thanks.'

'You don't need to make me things to thank me,' said Lola. 'I've told you a million times I love having you here.'

'I'm in the way,' said Bey. 'I bet Des would normally drop by a lot more than he does.'

Lola shrugged. 'Possibly. But he's very busy at the moment. The downturn . . . well, it's becoming a crisis for him too at this stage.'

'I thought he said he was grand.'

'He has mortgages on all the properties. Some of the tenants have lost their jobs and have to move out. It's difficult. It's difficult for me too.'

'With him or at work?' asked Bey.

'Both,' replied Lola. 'We're losing clients too, which isn't altogether surprising. Things will be tricky for a while.'

'You won't lose your own job, will you?'

'I hope not,' said Lola. 'But nothing's certain in this world. Except,' she added with a smile, 'that the most important person in my life is you.'

'I shouldn't always be,' said Bey.

'You're my only daughter. My only child. You'll always be the most important person to me.'

'It's a lot of responsibility,' Bey said as she used a cloth to buff a pendant. 'Being the repository of all your hopes and dreams.'

Lola looked at her anxiously. 'Do you really feel that way?' she asked.

'All I meant was that your love should be shared,' Bey assured her. 'And I suppose . . .' She hesitated.

'What?'

'You want so much for me,' Bey told her. 'I didn't realise it before, but I see it now. You want me to have the best life and the best job.'

'Of course I do!' cried Lola. 'That's what all mothers want for their children.'

'But I get it wrong sometimes,' said Bey. 'And I'll undoubtedly get it wrong again. I don't like to think of you letting opportunities for your own happiness go begging while you're waiting to pick up the pieces for me.'

'I hope all your mistakes are minor ones,' Lola said. 'But I'll always be here to pick up the pieces.'

'Oh, Mum, you've been wonderful to me forever!' Bey hugged her. 'All I'm saying is lighten up a bit and enjoy your own life too. And don't . . . don't fall out with Des because of me.'

'I do enjoy my life,' protested Lola as they left the shed together. 'I know things get tricky from time to time, but I'm doing all right. And as for Des – he's a completely separate issue to you.'

'Can I ask you a question?' asked Bey when they were back in the house and sipping coffee at the kitchen table.

'Sure you can.' Lola smiled at her. It was a long time since she'd had a heart-to-heart with her daughter and she was enjoying it.

'Did you and Dad ever love each other?' asked Bey. 'You know, were you ever properly in love? Did he make your heart race and stuff like that?'

'Yes,' said Lola. 'Yes, he did. But there was always something missing and I never really knew what it was. Plus,' she added, 'he imagined me as the girl he dreamed of marrying, not the girl I actually was. Have you found someone who makes your heart race, Bey?' She looked at her daughter hopefully.

'Nothing makes my heart race like jewellery.' Bey grinned.

'Hopefully one day you'll think differently,' said Lola.

Bey thought for a few moments before asking her mother if she'd ever thought that marrying Philip would've been a good option. Or that the money might have been nice.

'The last reason for marrying anyone is money,' Lola said. 'But I'd be lying if I didn't wonder sometimes whether marrying your dad wouldn't have been an easier choice.'

Bey was surprised by the vehemence of her mother's words. She got up and hugged her.

'I do love you, you know, Mum. I probably don't say it enough.'

'You don't need to.' Lola hugged her back. 'I know it already.'

Because it was Saturday, both of them slept late. Over breakfast, Lola suggested it might be nice to have a girlie day in town together, so they walked to Grafton Street and spent a couple of happy hours wandering around the shops before grabbing lunch in one of Dawson Street's brasseries.

'D'you mind if we walk past Warren's?' asked Bey when they'd finished.

'Why?'

'I'd just like to see it,' she replied.

Lola shrugged and they turned towards Duke Lane. The shop had recently been renovated. Lola said there'd been a piece about it in the *Irish Times*, showcasing the brand-new interior and the most recent range – the Adele Hyacinth – which was designed with lapis lazuli stones.

'It's not my favourite,' she confessed as they stood outside and looked at the complex necklace and earrings on display. 'I suppose there'll be a new design this year in time for the Christmas market.'

'They always start with a ring, don't they?' remarked Bey.

'Then they add the rest over the course of a few years.' Lola nodded. 'Though I'm not sure that's a great way of doing it any more. I think they should try to launch it as a complete set every time. Not everyone would buy all of it, but it would give them a choice.'

'You're absolutely right,' said Bey.

'Still, your dad knows what he's doing. He's been running things on his own for a while now, and perhaps being cautious with the releases while the economy is flatlining is a good thing.'

'I wonder will they still do the range when Adele dies?' mused Bey. 'Or will they launch a new one? They could call it the Donna, although I can't really imagine her stepping into Adele's shoes, can you?'

'Donna is terribly unassuming,' agreed Lola. 'I can see why they loved her after me, but it's hard to see her as the face of Warren's. The Ice Dragon still casts her spell over them all.'

'You really shouldn't call her that,' said Bey. 'Though it's quite stunningly appropriate.'

The two of them walked away and their conversation turned to other things. But Bey couldn't help wondering what life would have been like as part of the Warren empire. And what difference it would have made to her own life if her mother had made different choices.

As she continued to work at the studio in Dun Laoghaire during the day and in the shed at night, Bey considered ways in which she might kick-start her career. Even if she hadn't learned much about design from Tina, she was picking up a lot of tips on how to run a small business. Tina was very focused on the practical side of things, which hadn't been a high priority for Bey, but she realised that dealing with suppliers and keeping up to date with the bank accounts and other administrative paperwork was just as important as turning out good design. Because, Tina had said one day, if the company went bust, they weren't much good to anyone.

And then the email from Will Murdoch arrived. It was brisk and businesslike but made her gasp with excitement.

He was suggesting that she apply for a job with Van Aelten and Schaap, a family firm based in London and Amsterdam who were looking for an assistant designer. Bey had heard of the two-hundred-year-old firm before. They specialised in haute joaillerie – high-class, luxury jewellery – and working for them would be an amazing opportunity.

I do a lot of work for them, he wrote. *They're a great company and don't hire that often. But I think you'd be well suited if you were interested.*

Bey couldn't wait until Lola got home that night to tell her.

'Of course I mightn't get the job,' she said in order to temper their excitement. 'In fact I probably won't. I'm sure there are plenty of other designers out there who'd be just as good.'

'Would you be based in Amsterdam or London?' Lola's only reservation about it was that Bey would be leaving Dublin again. She'd grown used to having her around and she loved the fact that her daughter was a more confident, outgoing person than she'd been before she left. Both Birmingham and Córdoba had been good for her, she thought, suddenly seeing Bey as a young woman and not simply her only child. And this job might be the making of her.

'Everyone is employed by the head office in Amsterdam but I'd be working in London,' said Bey as she skimmed through the printout she already knew by heart. 'Oh, Mum! I'd be working with proper gemstones! Can you imagine?'

Even as Lola smiled at her, she could see in Bey's eyes something of the enthusiasm she'd once seen in Philip when he'd talked about rubies and diamonds. It's in the genes, she thought. No matter how much I try not to think it, she's a Warren too.

Bey spent a few days crafting her CV before sending it off. An almost immediate reply asked her to come for interview, and two weeks later she was sitting in front of Clara Kotze, the company's head designer, at the Bond Street store and workshop.

'This was made for the Tsarina Alexandra,' Clara said as

she showed her a photo of a magnificent tiara from a bound book of Van Aelten and Schaap designs. 'Like with many of the imperial jewels, she sewed them into her corset when the family was taken prisoner by the Bolsheviks.'

It was the sort of thing Adele might do, thought Bey. Perhaps if the Tsarina had possessed as sharp a tongue as Adele Warren, the fate of the Russian royal family might have been different. She couldn't imagine anyone having the nerve to shoot her grandmother even if they were ordered to. Adele would fix them with her basilisk glare and they would wilt on the spot.

She continued to turn the pages of the book, exclaiming over the photographs of some of the more memorable pieces.

'Of course we take a more modern approach to our designs now,' said Clara. 'But we're a firm built on tradition and our customers know what they want from us. We like to think of ourselves as classic jewellery makers.'

'I can see that.' Bey nodded. 'I'd love the chance to work here. I really would.'

Her excitement knew no bounds when she was asked to a second interview in Amsterdam.

'They must really want you if they're flying you to London *and* Amsterdam,' said Lola.

'I hope so,' said Bey as she danced around the kitchen with delight.

She'd emailed Will after her first interview, thanking him profusely for telling her about the job. When they asked her for the second interview, she emailed him again.

I'm in Amsterdam myself right now, he replied. *Would you like to meet for coffee afterwards?*

*   *   *

She arrived close to the Van Aelten and Schaap Amsterdam headquarters on Grimburgwal with plenty of time to spare, so she took a little time to explore the warren of narrow streets, lined by traditional buildings with curved gable roofs and neatly painted doors and windows. There were quite a few jewellery shops, she realised, many of them new and funky but others specialising in more traditional work. But of them all, Van Aelten and Schaap's was the most impressive, having a wider street frontage and overlooking one of the city's many canals.

She was nervous as she pressed the old-fashioned bell, and when she was admitted to the reception area – which was decorated as though it were a turn-of-the-century salon – she realised her heart was racing.

But she relaxed once she was brought upstairs to the meeting room, where she was welcomed by Gerritt Van Aelten, who looked after the London business, and Rolf Schaap, who was based in Amsterdam.

'We're a traditional company,' Rolf told her when she remarked that the building was like a perfectly preserved piece of history. 'But we also know that we must move forward. That's why we're looking for a new designer for our team.'

Bey had already emailed them her portfolio of designs, but she'd brought samples with her that she laid on the walnut desk in front of her. Gerritt and Rolf looked at them critically, exchanging glances from time to time but not saying anything, which left her feeling very nervous. Finally Rolf said that the designs were beautiful and the work was pretty good too, which, he added, impressed him because he liked to know that his designers understood form and function and could make pieces themselves.

'Not that you'd be making anything.' Gerritt smiled at her. 'We have a great team to do that. All we want from you is innovative designs that fit in with our ethos.'

'I'm confident I can do that,' said Bey. Which was perfectly true. There were things in her life that she wasn't in the slightest bit confident about – her relationships with men, her looks, her fashion sense and her inability to drive a car being chief among them – but when it came to design she had a self-belief that had been enhanced by her months in Córdoba and the encouragement of the Jurados.

'It's tradition that keeps us in Amsterdam, but our main design centre is in London,' Gerritt said. 'You'd be reporting directly to Clara Kotze and to me.'

'It all sounds fabulous.' Bey's interview face finally slipped and she beamed at him. 'I'd love to work with you. Your jewellery is absolutely amazing and I'd give anything to be part of it.'

Gerritt smiled. So did Rolf.

And when they shook hands with her and told her they'd be in touch very soon, she knew that this was the only job in the world she wanted.

Will had suggested meeting in a coffee shop on Singel, a short walk away. She crossed the narrow bridge, enchanted by the sheer volume of bicycles chained to it, as well as by the sparkle of the sunlight on the grey-green water of the canal. Then she turned towards the café, which she'd marked on her local map. For a moment she didn't recognise Will, sitting at one of the pavement tables at the water's edge. In his faded jeans and cotton T-shirt he looked considerably younger and less intimidating than on the previous occasions

she'd met him, and she told him this even as he gave her a formal handshake and her heart did a backwards flip.

'I think that's a compliment,' he said. 'I'll take it as one anyhow.'

'Sorry, was I horribly rude?' she asked as she sat down. 'It was just that at the funeral you looked like a total businessman. Now you're like a real person.'

He laughed. 'Well the tables are turned, because you look very executive,' he said.

Bey was wearing a pair of navy trousers and a matching jacket she'd bought in Zara. The dangling earrings and matching pendant around her neck were ones she'd made herself. Rolf and Gerritt had commented on the clever way she'd set the glass stones so that they appeared to float in their settings.

'I wanted to make a good impression,' she said.

'I'm sure it was your talent and not your clothes that made the impression,' said Will.

'I hope so.' She smiled. 'Thanks so much again for telling me about this job. Even if I don't get it, the whole thing has been a great experience.'

'Fingers crossed you do,' said Will.

'You said in your email that you do quite a lot of work for Van Aelten's,' she said when the coffee had arrived and she'd tipped some sugar into the froth of her cappuccino.

'Actually, I'll be joining them full time at the end of the month,' he said. 'I used to work for myself but they made me an offer I couldn't refuse.'

'I hope they do the same for me,' she said. 'I like working for myself but working for Van Aelten and Schaap would be

a dream come true. My only worry is that my designs are more contemporary than theirs.'

'Obviously the whole vintage look is a big part of the company,' said Will. 'But they don't want to miss out on other markets too. I think you'd be a good fit.'

'I hope so.' Her words were fervent. 'And . . . and it would be great to work with you too.'

'I spend most of my time on the road looking for the perfect stone,' he said. 'You only see me when I turn up with something that needs lots of TLC to turn it into a thing of beauty.'

Bey smiled, but her heart sank a little. Being with Will Murdoch seemed to spark something inside her. A light she hadn't known she had. In him she could sense a kindred spirit. Someone who felt passionately about glamour and sparkle in the same way she did. Someone who made everything fall into place.

He was staying in Amsterdam that night but she was booked on a flight later in the afternoon, so when they finished their coffees he walked with her to the stop for the airport express.

'I'm really looking forward to working with you,' he said as she prepared to board the bus.

'I haven't got the job yet,' she reminded him.

'You will,' said Will. 'I know it.'

She hoped he was right.

The email offering her the job arrived the next morning. Bey and Lola did a little jig of happiness and then Bey hugged her mother and thanked her for everything.

'Especially for allowing me to put my workbench in the shed,' she said. 'In fact I've taken over the whole house these last few months and you've been great about it.'

'To be honest, I'm sorry you're leaving,' said Lola. 'I've enjoyed knowing you're here. But I'm pleased at the same time. I so want you to be happy. In life, in love, in everything.'

'Happy with work will be a good start.' Bey kissed her. 'As for the rest . . .' She thought about Will Murdoch again. 'Maybe it'll follow.'

Lola had asked her if she wanted her to come to London with her and help look for somewhere to live, but Bey had good news on that front too. She'd called her old college friend Vika, who was living in a house share with three other girls off the Uxbridge Road and who said that there'd be a spare room the following month. In the meantime, Van Aelten were putting her up in a London flat.

'That's very good of them.' Lola was astonished.

'The family lives in Hertfordshire but have some apartments in the city,' said Bey. 'One of them is empty and they said I can use it.'

'You're mixing in properly rich circles now, my girl,' said Lola. 'Country houses and flats in the city.'

'Though I'm not the one who's got the money.' Bey chuckled. 'Oh, Mum, it's great though. I felt comfortable the minute I walked in the door.'

'You must have made an impression on that guy Will, too,' said Lola. 'It was wonderful of him to remember you and tell you about the job.'

'If you recall, I tried to scald him with coffee,' Bey reminded her. 'That tends to mark you out.'

'All the same, he clearly thought a lot of your work to recommend you.'

'Which is great,' said Bey.

She was hoping that it wasn't just her work he thought a lot of.

Chapter 25

Emerald: a bright green precious stone

The next time Bey saw him was a month after she joined Van Aelten and Schaap. He walked into the office where she was studying a silver ring, sliding it on and off her finger as she assessed it for ease of wear. The design was far fussier than anything she would have come up with herself, but the ring was surprisingly comfortable. The final version would be in gold and set with two diamonds, but the silver one had been made so that she could test it for wearability.

'Having fun?' he asked when she didn't look up.

'Will!' She put the ring on the desk in front of her. 'It's great to see you. I'm loving the job.'

'I knew it would suit you.' He gave her a complacent smile. 'I knew you'd suit them too.'

'The vintage jewellery is great fun,' she said. 'I never thought I'd enjoy it as much as I do. At the moment I'm working on engagement rings for the Renaissance line.'

'This is one?' He picked it up. 'Nice.'

'It'll be very glamorous,' agreed Bey. 'I'd prefer some-

thing simpler myself, but this is great to wear. In any case, I wouldn't say no to anyone who proposed to me with the final version.'

He grinned at her. 'I didn't realise you were so easily persuaded.'

'Well, I guess it would depend on the man too,' she conceded.

Will laughed.

'But this way . . .' she continued, 'this way I get to play with the ring without having to make the commitment. Truthfully, working here is a dream come true for me.' She gave him a rueful look. 'Does that make me sound completely shallow? I know I'm not saving the world. I know there are plenty of people doing far more important jobs. But . . .'

'But you're making beautiful things,' said Will. 'And that's art, Bey. Just as much as a great painting or a piece of music.'

'Exactly.'

'If I didn't think so too, I'd feel pretty useless wandering around the globe looking at grubby pieces of stone.'

'The Stone Man.' She grinned. 'Did you know that's what they call you? It's because you always know the ones that'll look great after they're cut and polished.'

Her fingers went to the Adele Bluebells in her ears. Since she'd started working at Van Aelten, she'd taken to wearing them every day. She felt as though her job now merited wearing expensive pieces on a regular basis, although when she was meeting clients she always borrowed from the Van Aelten and Schaap stock.

'They suit you,' observed Will. 'I think Warren's sourced Ceylon sapphires for the Bluebell collection. Richard always went for the best he could get.'

'I've never thought about where the stones themselves came from,' said Bey. 'Mum gave me the earrings before I went to college.'

'Lovely present,' said Will. 'And of course you'd have to have at least one Warren design. I should have asked before, I guess, but how exactly are you related?'

At Richard's funeral she'd told him she was only a distant relation. But there was no reason not to tell him the truth now. He looked at her in total astonishment.

'So why on earth didn't you get a job with Warren's?' he asked.

'We're not close,' she explained. 'Mum and Dad didn't have a great relationship and I don't get on with the rest of them either.'

'That's a shame,' said Will. 'I'm sure you would've been a real asset to them.'

'Oh, they're happy enough the way things are,' said Bey. 'They already have someone for the Adele ranges, and everything else they buy in on exclusive terms. They don't need me.'

'They're making a mistake letting you work for someone else. If I'd realised you were actually a Warren . . .'

'I'm not. A Warren, I mean,' she added. 'I hardly know them, and they . . .' She shrugged. 'They're not part of my life. Besides, Warren's isn't like Cartier or Tiffany or Boodles. It's a small Irish outfit that punches above its weight. It doesn't have the history or the client list of the big companies.'

'I suppose not,' acknowledged Will. 'All the same . . .'

'Wouldn't you have suggested me for the job if you'd realised?' She tried to hide the concern in her voice.

294

'I might have thought differently about it,' he admitted. 'But it would've been a mistake. Everyone thinks you're great.'

She smiled with relief and then looked up as Clara and her assistant, Henry, walked into the office.

'Hi, Will,' said Clara. 'D'you want to see what I've done for the tennis trophy?'

Van Aelten and Schaap had been asked to design the trophy for a new tournament being held in the Middle East. Bey had seen Clara's initial design, which looked like a sail encrusted with precious stones. The trophy itself was a metre high, and the tournament winner would receive a replica. Bey hadn't thought about the other things that jewellers made, but she was enthusiastic about the idea of designing something like the trophy herself one day.

'Sure,' he said. 'We need to have a chat about that bracelet you were talking about too.'

Will and Clara disappeared into her office, while Henry went downstairs to the shop and Bey got back to the silver ring. She was beginning to put everything away for the evening when they came out again. Clara said she was going to see Gerritt for a few minutes and Will stayed in the outer office and waited for Bey to finish up.

'I wondered if you'd like to have a bite to eat with me,' he said. 'To celebrate your job here.'

'That would be lovely,' she said. 'But please don't feel you have to look after me because you got me the job.'

'You got yourself the job,' said Will. 'I was just the messenger. Anyhow, I wasn't thinking of something extravagant. How about a pizza? Or is that a little too downmarket for Van Aelten and Schaap's latest designer?'

She smiled. 'I'd love pizza. I skipped lunch today and I'm absolutely starving.'

'There's a good place down the road,' he said. 'Let's go.'

It was a warm evening and the streets were busy and bustling. Bey was enjoying the feeling of belonging in the city, of having a job she loved and walking alongside a man who made her feel alive inside. It was a long time since she'd walked alongside a man at all, she thought. Her brief romance with Martín Jurado had been tied up with being in a new and wonderful place, and feeling freer than she'd done in years. But she'd known that it hadn't meant anything deep to either of them. He was rebounding from a break-up and she didn't want to let anyone into her heart. She was afraid that, like with her parents, it would all go wrong. And she didn't want to make that kind of mistake.

Getting involved with Will Murdoch would be a truly terrible mistake, she told herself as they sat at a patio table outside the restaurant. Why she was even thinking of him like that was a mystery to her. Will had been friendly but professional when they'd met. That was all. Yet she felt a delight in being with him that had nothing to do with being professional. And everything to do with his easy charm and good looks.

'Prosecco?' he asked as the waiter came to take their order.

'Oh, I couldn't . . .'

'We're celebrating,' he reminded her.

'But . . .'

'If you don't drink alcohol, that's fine,' Will said. 'But you should mark the occasion.'

'You've twisted my arm,' she said, although she looked at

him in consternation when he only ordered one glass because, he told her, he had to drive home later.

'Enjoy it.' He shrugged dismissively. 'I'll toast you with sparkling water.'

She relaxed into relishing the cold, fizzy wine, which came with a strawberry on the rim.

'Five a day,' she said as she ate the strawberry and then tucked into the ham and pineapple pizza she'd ordered.

'I don't know how you do it,' said Will when she'd finished before him.

'Do what?'

'Pack away the pizza like that and still look as slender as a reed.'

'Metabolism,' she told him. 'And skipping lunch.'

Will said that skipping lunch was a very bad idea. She said it wouldn't become a habit, and he said it was as well to remember that. Then she made some other comment and suddenly they were talking and talking as though conversation had only just been invented.

She felt more alive sitting beside Will Murdoch than she had in years. Yet being with him was also comfortable and comforting. There was an unexpected calmness about him that allowed her to talk to him as though she'd known him all her life.

She learned that he'd been born and raised in Scotland. His father was an estate manager, his mother a teacher. His interest in gemstones had been forged by a fascination with geology and the landscape around him, but he'd been introduced to it as a career by a neighbouring landowner whose family had mined diamonds in Johannesburg. She loved hearing the cadences of his voice as he spoke, picturing a *Monarch of the Glen* existence within a strong, secure family.

Two sisters, both pharmacists. A younger brother who ran a local hotel. Close but not in each other's pockets. A little like the Fitzpatricks, she thought.

He asked her to tell him more about herself and the Warrens and she simply said that her visits to her father had never been successful and that her mother and her mother's parents were her proper family.

'It's a shame that things sometimes work out that way,' he said. 'But we're not defined by our families, you know.'

He might have a different opinion if he was related to the Warrens, she thought. She couldn't help defining herself based on their opinions of her, no matter how many times she told herself they weren't important.

'We're lucky to work in the jewellery trade,' remarked Will, realising that talking about the Warrens made her uncomfortable. 'No matter what goes on, it's a make-believe world. We only ever see people when they're rich and happy.'

She laughed at his words and told him that she wasn't rich. But, she realised, she had the Bluebells. And she had her dream job. So she was very definitely happy.

It was late by the time they got up to leave. He asked where she lived and she told him about the house share she'd moved into with Vika.

'I'll drop you off,' he said.

Even though it was Will and she felt as though she'd known him for ever, she hesitated for a moment. Her father's words of warning were still burned into her brain, influencing every move she made when it came to men. She'd never got into a car alone with any of her coffee-jar men. She'd always had an excuse thought up in advance. But now, even though Philip's voice was clear and insistent, she ignored it.

'I don't want to put you to any trouble,' she said.

'Even if I was heading back to Scotland, I'd drop you home first.' He grinned at her. 'You're an important member of the company now. It's no trouble.'

He paid the bill, waving aside her offer to split it, and then led her to Burlington Road, where he'd left his car.

'Nice,' she said as she got into the passenger seat of the white Audi Q7.

'To be honest, it's a bit of a pain in the city,' he said. 'But a dream for driving up to Scotland, and handy in the hills, of course.' His accent broadened as he spoke, and she laughed.

He continued to make her laugh as he regaled her with stories of his childhood on the journey back to the three-storey house she shared with Vika and the others.

'Would you like to come in for coffee?' she asked when he pulled up outside, a question that made her wince because it sounded so crass and obvious when all she really wanted was to keep talking to him for a little longer.

'Better not,' said Will. 'I've a few calls to make to the States this evening and I need to get home.'

'Don't let me keep you a minute longer,' she said. 'Thank you so much for driving me. I'm really sorry if it's messed up your evening.'

'I was the one who suggested dinner, remember?' He smiled at her as she opened the door. 'You didn't mess up a thing. And it was the nicest evening I've had in ages.'

She felt a warm glow envelop her. And as she watched him pull away, she wondered how much coffee was left in the jar on the cupboard shelf.

* * *

She climbed the creaking stairs to the office the following morning with a sense of anticipation, but although she was at her desk for the entire day and hoped that Will would drop by – to see either her or Clara – there was no sign of him. Later in the week, she heard Nico, the manager of the Bond Street store, saying that he'd gone to New York. She felt hollow inside, even though Clara asked her for ideas about additions to the Van Aelten and Schaap vintage range and gave time and attention to her suggestions. However, she cheered up immensely when the head designer asked her to work on a bracelet. Clara's faith in her and her ability was confidence-boosting. And yet, although she was engrossed in what she was doing, her head still jerked up every time the door to the office opened, hoping that Will had returned.

She didn't see him again until the staff monthly meeting, when Gerritt Van Aelten talked about their upcoming customer event at the Savoy. Will was already sitting at the round table in the small meeting room when she walked in, but was engrossed in conversation with Gerritt and simply acknowledged her presence with a brief nod.

'The economic climate is difficult,' said Gerritt once everyone had arrived and the meeting proper had begun. 'But we want to remind our clients that no matter what, haute joaillerie is a good investment and Van Aelten and Schaap can put on a great show.'

Henry Austen, Clara's assistant, had already told Bey about the events to which selected customers were invited and where Van Aelten and Schaap showed off their latest collections. The theme for this one was opera. The models for the night would be representing various operatic heroines; there would also be performances from rising stars of the Royal

Opera, and each of the tables was named for one of the great works. Display cases were to be arranged around the room so that clients could try on the jewellery in a relaxed atmosphere.

'Is it a good selling opportunity?' Bey asked Nico, who was sitting beside her.

'Naturally we want to sell as much as we can,' he told her. 'But it's also a way of thanking our customers for their business during the year. All the same . . .' he smiled, 'yes, it is a good selling opportunity. And of course you'll be wearing lots of Van Aelten and Schaap jewellery that night too.'

Which was something she was really looking forward to.

'Are you going to be there?' she asked Will when the meeting broke up.

'Oh yes,' he replied. 'Some of our biggest clients are coming along. They ask for specific stones and I have to source them. It can take months to get the right ones.'

She glanced at her watch and saw that it was nearly 12.30.

'Would you like to have a sandwich with me?' she asked.

'That's sweet of you,' he said. 'But I'm rushing off to the airport shortly.'

'You're going away *again*?' She kept the disappointment out of her voice. 'What a jet-set life you lead.'

'Not this time,' he said. 'I'm just picking someone up. See you soon.'

She stared after him. He was like a different person to the man she'd had the pizza with in the London sunshine, the man who'd made her drink Prosecco and laughed when she'd got tomato sauce on her chin. He was brisk and businesslike and totally focused on what he had to do.

But it didn't matter. She'd made her mind up about one thing.

She wasn't a girl who didn't know how to fall in love any more.

Because she just had.

Chapter 26

Citrine: a yellow-gold transparent quartz

Being in love – even if the object of her affection was totally unaware of it – was a bewildering yet exciting sensation. Every day, whether she saw him or not, Will Murdoch was always in her thoughts. Not necessarily at the front of them – after all, she was working hard on the projects Clara had given her and they needed her concentration – but she was conscious of his existence, of the fact that he was on the planet, that even when she couldn't see him, he was out there somewhere. She was always alert for the sound of his footsteps on the stairs, or the moment when he might push open the door and say hello. The fact that he was away more than he was in the office didn't matter. Her happiness was inextricably linked with his presence. Every day she didn't see him was a crushing blow, but every passing day brought her closer to one when she would.

It was the day of the opera event before she spoke to him again.

He walked into the function room while she was arranging a selection of earrings in a display case.

'Wow,' he said.

'They're lovely, aren't they?' She held up some rubies for his inspection.

'I wasn't talking about them. The wow was for you.'

Bey's heart flipped. She knew she looked good. Her dress was a vibrant green, which contrasted with her flaming hair, she was wearing Van Aelten and Schaap diamonds from one of their vintage lines, and now that Will was here, the excitement that had been building up within her about the event bubbled over.

'I feel amazing,' she confessed. 'No wonder truly rich people are always so confident. How can you not be when you're dripping with fabulous rocks? You look great yourself,' she added, with an approving look at his tux.

'I hate dressing up,' he said.

'It's good for you,' she told him. 'Men are usually so hopeless at it. On a night out women will pull out all the stops with dresses and high heels and make-up and hair, but the men think a brightly coloured polo shirt outside their jeans is enough.'

'Guilty as charged,' admitted Will.

Though he'd look good in anything, reflected Bey, aware that she was staring at him rather too intently and immediately turning her attention back to the display case.

'Who's at your table tonight?' he asked.

She rearranged the jewellery as she replied.

'A finance guru and his wife. A tech mogul and his girl-friend. Afton Hall, the actress, and her husband. And,' she lowered her voice, 'someone called the Contessa and her guest.'

'An interesting bunch,' said Will. 'You'll like the Contessa.

She's good fun as well as frighteningly clever. Scares the pants off me when she asks me questions.'

'Nothing would scare you.' She looked up at him again.

'You'd be surprised,' said Will. 'I've got to talk to Gerritt. See you later.'

She watched as he weaved his way around the displays.

She was still in love with him.

Which was crazy. But true.

The Contessa was just as much fun as Will had said. She was tall and striking, handsome rather than beautiful; once seen, never forgotten. She wasn't really a member of the aristocracy but was the only granddaughter of an ex-Mafia boss and had inherited the bulk of the family's wealth. She had homes in the US and the UK as well as a farmhouse in Tuscany from where she ran an exclusive Italian food company. She had never married, although whenever she was seen at social events she always had an attractive man by her side. Her companion for the evening, Tyson Jett, was her US attorney, and as taciturn as she was outgoing. He reminded Bey of Denzel Washington in *Crimson Tide*, which was one of her mother's favourite movies.

The conversation around their table was wide ranging, but because she was sitting beside them, Bey found herself talking to the Contessa and her attorney more than the other guests. The Contessa asked her about her design work and Bey told her that she while she adored Van Aelten's vintage lines, she hoped to work on more contemporary designs in the future. The Contessa regarded her thoughtfully from dark brown eyes and assured her that she was looking forward to seeing them.

Then the opera singers did their thing while the models strode down a catwalk between the tables, glittering in Van Aelten and Schaap's newest ranges, which left the guests cooing in delight. The Contessa was particularly taken by a necklace modelled on Queen Mary's diamond rivière, which she insisted on trying on. The original had consisted of thirty-four cut diamonds set in gold and diamond – valued, Clara had told Bey when she first saw the design, at around two million dollars. The Van Aelten version was a more modest piece, with fewer stones, but it was still utterly fabulous and, despite their obvious wealth, out of the reach of many people in the room. The Contessa was charmed by the necklace but eventually decided that a pair of pink topaz and diamond earrings called the Marie Antoinette were the pieces going home with her that night.

'I'll wear them now,' she said, removing her garnet studs and putting them into a box, much to the dismay of Tyson, who murmured that she should really wait until she had the new ones insured.

'Not a bit of it,' retorted the Contessa. 'They're perfect with this dress.'

Bey agreed. They were fabulous.

Afton Hall wanted to try on a bracelet she'd seen earlier, so Bey went off to find it for her. Despite wearing diamonds herself, she was feeling slightly overwhelmed by the glitz and glamour. She wondered if Warren's had ever held an event like this. She knew they invited guests to sporting events (she remembered Lola being particularly sniffy about them sponsoring races at Cheltenham), but she couldn't imagine her father and Donna in this sort of crowd. Although Adele was a different story. She wouldn't be fazed by any of them, not even the Contessa.

As more and more guests asked to try on jewellery, Bey found herself busily fetching and returning various pieces. Her feet were beginning to ache and she longed to be able to kick off her high heels and sit down in a corner. And it was probably because of her tired feet that she did eventually almost tumble from her spindly shoes and was saved from falling by a woman standing nearby who reached out a hand to steady her.

'Thank you,' gasped Bey. 'I would've made such an ass of myself if I'd landed on the floor.'

'That's OK.' The woman, who Bey realised was closer to her own age than she'd originally thought, smiled at her. She was very striking, with cropped blond hair, wide blue eyes and a rosebud mouth. 'Are you Bey?'

'Yes. I'm sorry, I don't know you. But you're obviously a good client.' She nodded at the woman's citrine necklace and matching bracelet, which were from a popular Van Aelten and Schaap collection, while at the same time noting that she wore an enormous diamond ring on her engagement finger.

'I'd love to own them all, but only the diamond is mine. I borrowed the rest for tonight. I'm Callista,' the woman added.

Bey racked her brains but couldn't remember a client named Callista.

'Callista Cox,' said the woman. 'Will Murdoch's fiancée.'

Bey suddenly knew what it meant when people said that the bottom had fallen out of their world. She could hear Callista talking and she knew that she was replying to her, but she couldn't think of anything other than that Will Murdoch was

engaged to the most beautiful woman in the room and she hadn't known about it. She felt herself grow hot and cold as she remembered falling for him over pizza and inviting him in for coffee. And then asking him if he'd like to join her for a sandwich. Both of which invitations he'd politely turned down. The truth was that while she'd been falling in love with him, he was simply being friendly towards the new girl, trying to make her feel part of the company team. The humiliation was almost on a par with the moment she'd had to admit to stealing Astrid's sapphire ring. Although thankfully, on this occasion, she could keep her embarrassment to herself.

Of course it hadn't been love. How could it have been? She'd been besotted, that was all. Because he'd been kind and generous and had found her her dream job. How could she ever have imagined that what she was feeling was love? But, of course, she wasn't good at love. Her father was absolutely right. She wasn't a good judge of men. Or herself.

Thank God she hadn't said anything remotely romantic to him.

Thank God she hadn't said anything to anyone else.

'Are you OK?' Callista paused in the middle of the story she was telling. It was something to do with a loose bull in a field. Bey had no idea how the conversation had turned to farmyard tales.

'I . . . oh, yes. I'm sorry. I thought I saw . . .'

But she didn't finish her sentence because just then Will came over to them.

'You've met,' he said. 'I was going to introduce you earlier, but Bey was totally caught up with the Contessa, weren't you?'

'Yes,' said Bey.

'She bought the pink topaz earrings.'

'Yes,' said Bey again.

'Good sale,' said Will.

'Oh look!' Callista cut in. 'There's Gerritt. I haven't spoken to him yet. Back in a sec.' She waved across the room and Bey saw her magnificent diamond engagement ring flash in the light.

'Sorry I didn't get to talk to you before now,' said Will. 'It's been manic, hasn't it?'

'Yes.' Bey was beginning to think her entire vocabulary had shrunk to just one word.

'I was actually hoping to introduce you to Cally before the guests arrived,' Will said. 'But she was delayed getting here. Mind you, she's never on time for anything, so I guess that's nothing new.'

'Yes,' said Bey.

'Bey?' He looked at her. 'Are you feeling all right?'

'Yes.' She cleared her throat. 'Yes, of course. A bit tired, and my feet are sore in these silly shoes. It's been a long day. And I'm sure you want to join Callista.'

'Oh, she's happy with Gerritt,' said Will. 'How are you?'

'Fine. Why wouldn't I be?'

'It's your first Van Aelten and Schaap event,' said Will. 'We like to think it's fun, but it can also be stressful.'

'It was very glamorous, but in the end it's just selling things.'

Will looked surprised. 'I've never heard you talk about jewellery like that before.'

'It's true though, isn't it?' She shrugged. 'Like you said, we see people when they're rich and happy. We made them

happy tonight. They were in the mood to buy stuff. And they did.'

'Are you sure you're OK?'

'Of course.'

'Would you like to nab a drink at the bar?' he asked. 'Most of the clients have gone home and the displays won't be disassembled till tomorrow. You deserve a little time to let your hair down. Though it's doing that by itself,' he added as he reached out and his fingers brushed a lock of her red curls that had come loose from its clip.

Bey froze. 'Don't touch me,' she said.

He jerked his hand back as though she'd slapped him.

'I'm sorry.' He looked shocked. 'I didn't mean to upset you.'

'No,' she said. 'It's me. Sometimes I . . . It doesn't matter. I have to tidy up. See you later.'

'Bey . . .'

She looked at him without speaking. Then she adjusted the strap of her high heels and walked out of the room.

Haute Joaillerie
Four years later

Chapter 27

*Fancy diamond: a coloured diamond. Pink is associated
with joy and happiness*

The sound of Iolanda groaning distracted Bey from the image
she'd been studying on the screen in front of her. She looked
up and saw her colleague make a face at her own computer
screen.

'What's the matter?' she asked.

'I can't seem to get this right,' complained Iolanda. 'It
looks like I'm just shoving the diamond in the middle of the
setting any old way.'

'Let me take a peek.' Bey got up from her desk near the
window and crossed the room while Iolanda stood up and
stretched her arms over her head.

'I've been at it all morning and I'm making things worse
not better,' she said as Bey slid into her seat and clicked the
mouse in front of her. 'I know it's a nice commission, but
Mrs Semenova loses it completely if she doesn't like the work,
and she's certainly not going to like this.'

Bey grinned at her. In the course of her four years as a
designer at Van Aelten and Schaap, she'd dealt with the Russian

oligarch's wife on a number of occasions. Raisa Semenova was demanding, changed her mind frequently and was apt to throw spectacular tantrums when the design of the jewellery she commissioned didn't live up to her expectations. So Bey understood why Iolanda was getting frazzled, even though Raisa would have looked fabulous wearing a glass stone from a market stall, let alone a bespoke piece from Van Aelten and Schaap. Until her marriage, she'd worked as a model and had appeared in campaigns for H&M and Zara, but now she owned a contemporary art gallery off the New King's Road. She regarded her own appearance as a work of art too, and her clothes, accessories and jewellery were an important part of her image.

Iolanda, the junior designer, had been asked to remodel a necklace using gems from a piece that Raisa didn't like. Her husband had given her the original necklace, rumoured to have been owned by a Russian princess, for their wedding anniversary, but although Raisa loved the stones – and who wouldn't, thought Bey as she examined them; they were stunning – she didn't think the fussy style of the necklace itself suited her, and had asked the team at Van Aelten and Schaap to come up with something different.

'I can't make a mess of it,' Iolanda said as Bey continued to manipulate the onscreen drawing. 'She's a great customer and Clara will go nuts if we don't get it right.'

'Let's not panic.' Bey's fingers slid over the trackpad. 'Look,' she said. 'If you lengthen this here . . . and then bring this out a little more . . .' The image changed and Iolanda clapped her hands.

'You've got it!' she exclaimed. 'How the hell do you do that?'

'Do what?'

'Look at something and just know what has to be done to fix it?'

'I don't always—'

'You do,' Iolanda interrupted. 'Every bloody time. You're a jewellery genius.'

'I'm not really.' Bey was uncomfortable with her colleague's effusive praise. 'Honestly, I'm not. I get things wrong as often as I get them right.'

'But you get them right more often than anyone,' proclaimed Iolanda as she saved the image in front of her. 'In a million years I'll never be as good as you.'

'Would you stop it?' demanded Bey. 'You've probably put a hex on me now and I'll never be able to do a decent drawing again.'

Iolanda laughed and Bey returned to her own computer. She opened a page of sketches that she'd previously saved and gazed at them. They were part of a new design she'd been thinking of for their next collection, but she knew she wasn't ready to show them to Clara yet. She glanced towards the head designer's office. The door, normally open, was shut; Clara had been in a meeting with Gerritt for the past half-hour. Bey wondered what they were talking about – the heavy doors and thick carpets effectively muffled any conversation.

Then the outer door to their own office opened and Will Murdoch walked in.

'Will!' Iolanda jumped up from her seat and flung her arms around him. 'Welcome back! How were your travels?'

'Not bad at all,' he said, kissing her on the cheek. 'And how have you all been keeping? Working on anything nice?'

'Do we ever work on anything that isn't?' asked Iolanda. 'A necklace for Raisa Semenova.'

'The demanding Raisa.' Will smiled. 'I'm sure it'll be gorgeous.'

'Of course it will,' said Iolanda. 'Bey has sprinkled some of her magic dust over it.'

'As always.' Will turned to Bey, who'd remained sitting at her desk. 'So what do you think of these?' He opened the leather briefcase he'd been carrying, took out a brifka and spilled its contents onto a sheet of paper on the desk in front of her.

'Oh. My. God,' breathed Bey.

The three cushion-cut diamonds in front of her were a light pink. They were almost identical in size and were dazzlingly beautiful.

'Two carats each,' said Will. 'They're amazing, aren't they?'

'And exactly what the Contessa asked for.'

'Almost exactly.' Will grinned.

Bey picked one up and held it between her fingers, moving it so that it caught the light.

'I'm speechless,' she said after a long time when she had, indeed, been unable to say anything. 'It's so perfect.'

'I'm glad you think so,' said Will. 'Hopefully Clara will too.'

'How can she not?' asked Bey. She glanced at the closed office door. 'She's in a meeting with Gerritt at the moment, but I'm sure both of them will want to see these.'

'I emailed them a photo last night,' said Will. 'I think she was pleased. So was he.'

'They should go down on their knees thanking God for the day you became their buyer,' said Bey. 'Honestly, Will, these are utterly divine.'

He laughed. 'You know how to pander to my ego,' he said.

'I know great stones when I see them.' Bey exhaled slowly. 'I wonder how she'll use them for the Contessa's piece?'

Everyone in Van Aelten and Schaap knew that the Italian businesswoman had expressed a desire to have a pink diamond set made for her fortieth birthday. It had been the talk of the company for weeks. Now that Will had sourced the diamonds, they would have to come up with a design that the Contessa would like and that did justice to the stones. Bey felt sure that Clara would succeed. She was instinctively brilliant, steeped in the tradition of the company and very in tune with the tastes of their individual clients.

'What would you do with them?' asked Will as she continued to examine the biggest of the diamonds.

'I'd like them in something summery and light. A gold setting. Some white diamonds too, of course.'

'Of course.' Will grinned.

'Candyfloss,' said Bey suddenly. 'That's what they make me think of. So something . . . well, candy-ish.'

'I don't think the Contessa is candyfloss,' remarked Iolanda.

'That's why it's better for Clara to do the piece.'

'What the hell are they talking about?' Will frowned. 'I want to barge in, but—'

'Don't!' Bey and Iolanda spoke at the same time.

'She gets very cranky if you interrupt her,' said Iolanda.

'I know.' Will sat on the deep window ledge. 'I suppose I'll just wait here.'

'Want some coffee?' Iolanda asked.

'Yes please.'

'For you too, Bey?'

Bey nodded, and Iolanda went out of the room to the small kitchen.

'Did you enjoy your treasure hunt?' asked Bey when they were alone together.

'Of course I did. I got what I wanted,' replied Will.

'You always get what you want,' said Bey. 'The Stone Man is unstoppable in pursuit of the perfect gem.'

'I don't *always* get what I want,' Will disagreed. 'But I do my best.'

'True. It was a long trip. Are you glad to be back?'

'Yes,' said Will. 'Cally suggested I meet her in Barbados, but I'm looking forward to sleeping in my own bed again.'

'What's she doing in Barbados?' Bey continued to look at the stones.

'Hen party.'

'You might have been a little out of place,' Bey remarked.

Will grinned. 'That's what I told her. She said she'd stay on a few days if I wanted.'

'Hen parties in Barbados.' Bey finally put the diamonds down and looked at Will. 'Whatever happened to putting on a trashy veil and an L plate and trotting off to the local pub?'

'I don't think any of Callista's friends have tried that,' said Will. 'They went to a Highland castle for hers. It was spa treatments and champagne all the way.'

There was a moment of silence during which Bey tried to think of something light hearted to say. Not coming up with anything, she pulled at her already perfectly neat fishtail plait, jabbing clips into it to keep it securely in place, her favourite way of regaining her equilibrium. Meanwhile Will replaced the pink diamonds in the brifka. When she looked at him again, her expression was neutral. She was good at neutral expressions as far as Will Murdoch was concerned. She'd certainly had plenty of practice over the last four years.

When she'd gone home after the opera event, she'd told herself, as sternly as she could, that her infatuation with Will had been based on his kindness towards her and – because there was no getting away from it – the fact that he was very, very attractive. Also, she'd repeated as she'd sat alone in her room that night, she was a bad judge of men. She'd misjudged Will Murdoch quite spectacularly. But no harm done, she thought, even though her heart still felt as though it would break. She hadn't given herself away. She hadn't let herself down. She hadn't tried to take something – or someone – that belonged to someone else. She'd got away unscathed.

The next day she'd arrived into the office and started work on a minor commission that Clara had assigned to her, her pencil flying over the paper as though by firmly closing the door on the idea that she could be in love with somebody – no matter how unsuitably – she'd opened a different one into her own creativity. When she'd shown her drawings to Clara, the chief designer had nodded approvingly. She hadn't made a single change to them, which, Bey learned later, was unheard of.

As she grew into her role with Van Aelten and Schaap, Bey lavished the same attention to detail on every design she worked on. She completed a necklace and earring set for Raisa Semenova, which the Russian woman said was one of her favourites ever; a pretty tiara for a young European princess who was featured wearing it in *Hello!* magazine, and an engagement ring for one of the singers who had appeared at the opera event and who was now making a name for herself around the world.

She allowed her heart to mend and didn't give herself time to think about crushes or infatuations or potential boyfriends

or husbands. She didn't swear off men entirely – it was impossible when she ended up going to a lot of social functions – but she was never in danger of having even the briefest of relationships, let alone falling for anyone. There was no chance of Bey Fitzpatrick needing a ring for her finger. No chance at all.

In this she was almost the polar opposite of practically all of her close friends, because since beginning to work at Van Aelten and Schaap, she'd gone to more engagement parties and weddings than ever before.

She'd visited Dublin for first the engagement party and then the wedding of her old schoolfriend Áine; and then Córdoba, where Martín Jurado had married his childhood sweetheart. Their wedding day had been beautiful, at a time when the patios of the city had been overflowing with the magnificent floral displays that the householders put on every year. The scent of jasmine and orange had filled the air, and Martín and Paloma had looked radiantly happy. Bey had been happy for them too.

Her next trip was back to Birmingham, because despite always insisting that she had no interest in marrying anyone, her college friend and flatmate Vika had also tied the knot, with a man she'd gone out with for less than six months. And the most unexpected of them all had been Clara, who never seemed to have much of a personal life but who'd issued invitations to the entire company when she'd married her boyfriend the previous year.

Bey had had no choice but to attend Will and Callista's wedding too, which had taken place shortly after the opera event. She hadn't gone to the ceremony itself, but had been invited to the party afterwards, another glittering evening of

jewellery and high fashion. It had been impossible to turn down the invitation as everyone in Van Aelten and Schaap had been asked and had accepted, and it would have looked odd for her to refuse. Callista's father worked in the City, and the wedding had taken place at their country house in Derbyshire, a Grade I listed property that had taken Bey's breath away. It was nothing like her grandparents' farm in Cloghdrom, nothing like anywhere else she'd ever been before. And nothing like anywhere she'd ever go in the future either. She'd realised that Will Murdoch wasn't the man she'd imagined the night he'd dropped her home. He wasn't a farmer's son from Scotland. He belonged here, with the rich and happy people. And she belonged somewhere else.

Anyhow, she'd told herself as she strolled through the gardens with a glass of Krug in her hand, jewellery and gemstones were her passion. They were far more reliable than men.

After Will's marriage, she'd focused on her work with an intensity that impressed everyone around her. When Henry Austen left Van Aelten and Schaap, she was immediately promoted to assistant designer. She began to work on some of the more exclusive collections and with some of the company's most prestigious clients. Now she was considered to be one of the best hires Van Aelten and Schaap had ever made.

She worked hardest of all to ensure that she had a great relationship with Will Murdoch and that he never, ever suspected that she'd once been in love with him. After all, he was the chief buyer for the company and it was important they understood each other. Leaving everything else out of it, they shared a deep understanding of precious stones. As soon as Will showed her his latest acquisitions, Bey could see

why he'd bought them. Whenever he looked at her designs he could see why they were faultless. Iolanda, brought in when Bey was promoted, often said that they were like two sides of the same coin and that was why they made a great team. Bey would reply that she could work with anyone who had an eye for fabulous stones. Iolanda would say that Will had a better eye than most. Bey would snort and say there were plenty of good people out there. But, she'd finally concede, Will was undoubtedly one of the best. And then, sometimes, Iolanda would sigh and say that it was a pity he was married, because he was the sort of man any girl would like to spend the rest of her life with. And Bey would shake her head and tell her not to be silly, that basically it was all about the precious gems.

At last the door opened and Clara looked out.

'Hey!' Will smiled at her. 'Here I am, bearing gifts.'

'Not just yet,' she said. 'Bey, could you come in for a moment.'

Bey got up from her desk. She knew there was no reason for her to be concerned, and yet there'd been something in Clara's voice that had unsettled her. She felt even more unsettled when she saw Gerritt's serious expression.

Clara closed the door behind them.

'Sit down,' she said.

Bey looked anxiously between her boss and the company owner.

'I have some news,' said Clara. 'I'm leaving Van Aelten and Schaap.'

'What!' Bey hadn't expected that. If she'd ever thought about it – and she hadn't – she'd have assumed that Clara

would be with the company until she retired. But the older girl was looking at her with an expression every bit as serious as Gerritt's.

'I'm moving to New Zealand,' she said. 'Malik has got a job there.'

Malik was Clara's husband. He was a doctor at Barts but had family in New Zealand. Now, said Clara, he'd been offered a great post there and he wanted to go.

'He's been supportive of me in the past,' she said. 'It's my turn to be supportive of him.'

He'd been supportive of her while they were living together, thought Bey. But now that they were husband and wife, things had clearly changed. That was something she'd noticed when her female friends married. They nearly always put their husbands first. Men – at least the ones she knew – put their careers ahead of everything. Now Clara, the most career-driven woman she'd ever met, was giving up her successful life to move to the other side of the world with her husband. Bey knew that it was what you did when you loved someone. But she wondered how hard a decision it would be.

'Couldn't you design from there?' she said. 'What with today's technology and everything, we could easily keep in touch.'

'That's always a possibility,' Clara acknowledged. 'But it's not the same as being here as part of the team. And there's the time difference to take into account. Besides, Malik and I may start a family, and I want to devote myself to that for a few years.'

'I see.' Bey was even more astonished. Clara had never spoken of children before. But then, she reminded herself,

nearly every conversation they'd had was about jewellery. They rarely discussed anything personal.

'That being the case,' said Gerritt. 'We need to replace Clara.'

'Of course,' said Bey. Her mind ranged over possible candidates. She wondered who the best fit for Van Aelten and Schaap might be. The company was a unique blend of tradition and innovation, and any new designer would need to understand that. After all, they had designed collections for royalty. They were part of history. Their heritage was important.

'We think you have everything the role needs,' said Gerritt.

'Me?' she squeaked. 'Me?'

'Why not you?' asked Clara.

'I . . . I . . .'

There was no reason why it couldn't be her, of course, and yet she simply couldn't believe that a mere four years after joining the company, she could be their chief designer. Although she'd wanted a great career with them, she hadn't expected a promotion like this just yet.

'You've worked well with us since the day you joined,' said Clara. 'You have a good relationship with the people in the workshop and with the retail staff too. You understand the difference between designing something you're going to make yourself and designing something someone else will make. You also have a grasp of the economics of it. You get on well with our clients. But most importantly, you design beautiful jewellery. Your Reed Flute Cave collection was quite brilliant.'

Bey blushed at the compliment. Her brief had been to design something contemporary and youthful. She'd based

her collection on the stalagmites and stalactites of the Reed Flute Cave in Guilin, China. During the Tang Dynasty, people who visited the cave wrote inscriptions on the stones, and each one of Bey's designs carried a small inscription too. They had proved to be immensely popular, especially among the younger customers.

'So we think you'll be well capable of succeeding Clara,' said Gerritt.

'I . . . I'd be honoured,' said Bey. 'But to be honest, I'm speechless.'

'Don't be speechless. Be proud.'

'I am.'

'And be as good a designer for us as we know you can be,' he added.

'I will,' she said.

'So let's go and tell the troops,' said Gerritt.

He opened the door, and they walked outside.

'Why are women always so . . . so lacking in confidence about their work?' demanded Will as he dumped a sachet of sugar into his coffee. He and Bey had gone to the nearby Starbucks after Clara's bombshell.

'We're not,' protested Bey.

'Of course you are,' he said impatiently. 'Since we sat down, you've done nothing except wonder if you're up to the job and if they wouldn't have been better getting in someone more senior than you – whatever the hell that means – when what you should be saying is that they're lucky that you're ready and able to step into Clara's shoes. If Henry had still been here, d'you think he would have hesitated for a nanosecond before trumpeting how great his new designs

were going to be and how he'd bring Van Aelten and Schaap to the next level?'

'Van Aelten doesn't need to be at another level,' said Bey.

'Every business needs to grow and change,' said Will. 'And if you don't see that, if you don't have ideas of your own, then perhaps I'm wrong and you're right and you're not ready.'

'Of course I'm ready.' Her voice was sharp. 'Of course I have ideas. Of course I'll move the company forward.'

Will laughed. 'You see?' he said. 'Passion and confidence. That's what you need, instead of saying things like "I think this is an excellent design, but if anyone has a better idea . . ."'

'I do say that sometimes, don't I?' Bey picked up a spoon and scooped some froth from the top of her cappuccino. 'You're right. Dammit.'

'Clara is a great designer, but the reason she's successful is that she always projects that belief,' he said. 'You're as good a designer, if not better, but you need to believe in yourself more.'

'I *do* believe in myself,' said Bey. 'And they clearly believe in me enough to promote me.'

'Yes. But you've got to take a grip on things. Don't defer to people like Iolanda – or me, for that matter. I know jack-all about design but I know a good stone when I see one, and I also know that it will make a good piece. But it's not until you show me something that I know that's what I was thinking of all the time.'

'I wish you didn't have to tell me this stuff.' Bey put the spoon back on her saucer. 'You're right, of course. I can be a bit . . .'

'. . . too modest,' he finished when she hesitated. 'But don't be. You're the best at what you do. Let everyone know it.'

'It's not really me,' said Bey. 'I don't like blowing my own trumpet.'

'You have to make it you,' Will told her. 'You have to be proud of what you've achieved.'

'It's all thanks to you.' Bey took a sip of her coffee. 'If you hadn't got me the job in the first place, I could have ended up flogging silver charms on eBay.'

'You would have ended up somewhere just as good as Van Aelten,' he told her. 'I was the catalyst for this one, but talent will out, Bey. Sometimes it needs a push, though.'

'I always feel totally motivated after talking to you.' She smiled at him. 'You're good for my ego.'

'I hope so,' said Will. 'We both want the same thing. To make our stones shine. To make Van Aelten and Schaap the best place to buy them. If you need a little encouragement from time to time, I'm the man to give it to you. And I'll tell you something else,' he added after he'd drained his cup. 'Your damn family should be rueing the day they didn't give you a job.'

'I told you before, they have their own people and their own way of doing things,' said Bey. 'Even if they'd wanted me, they certainly didn't need me.'

'It's bizarre all the same,' he said. 'If I were your father, I'd be moving heaven and earth to get you to design for me. And Warren's could do with someone new, you know.'

'They could?'

'Their last Adele collection didn't really take off,' Will said. 'They haven't been using the best gems. They won't pay the

price. Times have been tough, but their problems are more fundamental than the recession.'

'I didn't know that.'

'Because you don't listen to the gossip,' said Will. 'You're not out and about like I am.'

'Oh well, I suppose they can get through a few lean years,' said Bey. 'I know the recession was hard for everyone, but things are getting better now, and I'm sure it'll work out in the long run.'

'If they can wait for the long run,' said Will.

Bey frowned. 'They're not in real trouble, are they?'

'I hope not. Nobody in the industry wants a company to fail. But they've lost the cachet they had,' he replied. 'With lesser-quality stones and designs that are a little tired, it's easy to slip back.'

'I'm sure my father will pull things out of the fire,' Bey told him. 'According to my mum, he's single minded.'

'Like you?' Will grinned.

'I'm nothing like him,' she said quickly. 'Not at all.'

'But you *are* single minded,' he said. 'All work and no play, that's you.'

'Don't be silly.'

'People say that about you,' Will said. 'That gemstones are your life. That there's no room for anything else.'

'I would have said the same about Clara,' retorted Bey. 'But there she is, moving to the other side of the world to support her husband.'

'Would you do the same?' asked Will.

'It's not likely to be an option.'

'Why?' he asked.

'Because I love my job far too much to give it up for a man,' she said.

'Has there ever been anyone important to you?' he asked when she didn't answer. 'I know you've brought men to our events from time to time, but I've never seen you with the same one twice.'

Only you. She didn't say the words out loud, but she couldn't help thinking them.

Instead she smiled and said, 'Unlike men, the diamonds linger,' which was her favourite line ever. She hadn't thought much of the Bond movie the song had come from, but she had the track on one of her playlists.

'Oh, Bey!' Will couldn't help laughing. 'There are times when I really do love you.'

'And there are times when you drive me to distraction,' she said, and got up from the table, leaving him to pay the bill.

With Clara heading off to New Zealand, Bey took over the design of the pink diamond necklace for the Contessa. She put her original thoughts of candyfloss out of her mind and spent her days sitting at her desk filling her notebook with pencil drawings, and her nights in her room at the house she still shared studying them, refining them, then balling up the paper and throwing it across the room. None of her drawings captured the essence of the woman's dynamism, charm and heritage.

She spent a lot of time on Google before she came upon stills from a 1954 movie called *The Barefoot Contessa*, which starred Ava Gardner and Humphrey Bogart. The one that

caught her attention was Ava wearing a pink dress and a diamond necklace. Bey suddenly saw a way in which she could incorporate the pink diamonds Will had found into a modern lavaliere – a pendant suspended from a necklace – that would look wonderful on the Contessa. As the images came to her, her pencil flew over the pages and she sketched outlines and details without stopping, finally confident that she was on the right lines.

It was her phone ringing that finally pulled her away from her work. As it was Lola, she answered straight away.

'Two bits of news for you,' said her mother. 'Shirley's getting married and Astrid Warren has just got engaged.'

'Shirley's getting married!' exclaimed Bey, putting the phone on loudspeaker so she could continue to shade one of her drawings. 'I didn't even know she was seeing anyone.'

'She hasn't known Ian that long, but she's utterly besotted,' said Lola. 'And I'm delighted for her.'

'Me too,' said Bey. 'I hope she's ecstatically happy. As for Astrid – isn't she quite young to be getting engaged?'

'Yes,' agreed Lola. 'But she's been going out with Jordan Hunt for the last year. He's the son of Kelvin Hunt, your dad's horse trainer.'

'The only time I watch a horse race is the Grand National,' said Bey. 'And any time I've ever been in a sweep or backed a horse, it's usually fallen at the first fence.'

'You went to the polo last year, didn't you?'

It had been a day sponsored by Van Aelten and Schaap and Cox Financial, the company owned by Callista Murdoch's father. Callista had presented the prizes. She'd looked stunning in a floral Stella McCartney dress and wedge shoes, her only jewellery her wedding and engagement rings.

'That's totally different,' said Bey. 'Not that I had a clue what was going on anyhow. But the trophy looked great.' She'd worked on the design of it with Iolanda.

'I'm sure Astrid would love polo,' said Lola. 'All that glamour.'

'It's not always glamorous.' Bey remembered stepping into some horse dung and ruining her shoes. It had been her own fault; she'd been watching Will and Callista laughing and joking with Gerritt van Aelten and hadn't been paying attention to where she was going. 'However, I'm sure you're right. Astrid would love it. How did you hear about her engagement?'

'It was in the papers, of course,' said Lola. 'Her ring is an Adele.'

'The latest is the Pansy, isn't it?' recalled Bey.

'Yes, but Astrid is sporting a Snowdrop.'

'That was always your favourite.'

'I'd still like to own one,' admitted Lola. 'But I've better things to spend my money on.'

'I can get you a discount on a Van Aelten and Schaap ring,' Bey reminded her. 'Even with that, though, they're blindingly expensive and I know it's not the same as your very own Snowdrop. Anyhow, Shirley is more important. When did she get engaged? When is she getting married?'

'Oh, they didn't bother getting engaged,' said Lola. 'They're just going ahead and getting married as soon as possible. She'll be sending out the invites shortly and she wanted to know if there was a name to put on yours.'

'Has she lost her mind or something?' Bey was puzzled. 'My name is my name.'

'For your plus-one, you idiot,' said her mother. 'Who d'you want to bring with you?'

331

'Oh, just "plus one" will be fine,' said Bey. 'Not that there is a plus-one at the moment. So it might just be me.'

'Right,' said Lola.

'Will Terry be coming with you?' asked Bey.

Lola was no longer seeing Des, who hadn't been as protected as he thought from the financial crisis and whose properties had been repossessed and sold off. Des himself had moved to the UK for a year to take advantage of the more lenient bankruptcy laws there, before emigrating to South Africa. Lola hadn't heard from him since. Bey knew that her mother had been upset by the breakdown of the relationship, but more upset by the fact that Des hadn't told her of his plans until the day before he left.

'I'm clearly not a good judge of men,' she'd said over the phone, and the echo of her father's words had caused Bey to catch her breath.

'Of course you are,' she'd said. 'After all, you held out against marrying him.'

'I seem to be better at not being married,' agreed Lola. 'Oh well, back to the drawing board.'

Some time later she'd begun seeing Terry O'Gorman, an architect who'd worked on an office block her company managed. Bey had now met him a couple of times and had confessed to Lola that she much preferred him to Des. There was a quiet thoughtfulness in Terry that had been missing in Des and that Bey thought suited her mother much better.

'Of course he'll be coming,' said Lola.

'Not thinking about issuing invites yourself?' Bey teased.

'Terry is lovely, but I've lasted this long without getting married and I'm not going to change the habit of a lifetime.'

'Is it because of me?' asked Bey. 'Do you not want to hurt my feelings because I'm still stuck on the shelf?'

'Don't be daft,' retorted her mother. 'I care about your feelings, but not that much.'

Bey laughed.

'Honestly,' said Lola. 'If I wanted to marry someone, I would. But I don't. I'm happier doing my own thing, knowing I can close my door at night and the only person I have to think about is myself.'

'Me too,' said Bey.

'Just because I've turned out that way doesn't mean you have to,' said Lola.

'I shouldn't have said anything,' Bey groaned. 'I knew the moment the words were out of my mouth that I was opening a Pandora's box. All I meant was that I like closing my door at night and only thinking about myself too.'

'You're a lot younger than me,' said Lola. 'You deserve a chance.'

'So do you. So does Terry,' said Bey. 'If the right one for me comes along, I'll let you know. But you have to trust me when I say that I'm perfectly happy.'

'I'm glad to hear it.'

'On another subject . . .' Bey looked at her drawing and then erased a line and redrew it. 'Have you heard anything about Warren's being in financial trouble?'

'No!' Lola sounded shocked. 'Are they? Have you heard something?'

'Just a comment one of the people here made,' said Bey. 'That they've lost their cachet.'

'I know they struggled during the recession,' said Lola. 'But I'm sure your dad knows what he's doing. Adele

would go crackers if she thought there was a problem.'

'That's what I thought.' Bey put her completed drawing on her desk.

'If there really was a problem, Philip would have to give up his horses. I'm not sure how Astrid's prospective father-in-law would feel about that! Or her husband-to-be, either.'

'It wouldn't be much of a marriage if it couldn't withstand a bit of pressure,' said Bey.

'I very much doubt Astrid Warren has ever been under pressure in her life,' Lola said.

'How do we know?' said Bey. 'Maybe she lives a very pressurised existence. Although,' she added, 'I seriously doubt it. She thinks she's a cut above everyone.'

'Takes after Adele so,' said Lola.

'You don't like her one little bit, do you?'

'Ah, I'm being silly,' Lola said. 'I'm dredging up my past feelings, which is bloody ridiculous because I only met her once when I was going out with your dad. Though in fairness, once was enough to finish us off.'

Bey chuckled.

'Anyhow, the past is the past,' said Lola. 'I gave too much of my emotional energy to trying to do the right thing as far as the Warrens were concerned, and only succeeded in making life far more complicated than it needed to be.'

'Have you seen Dad at all over the past few years, even on the street?' asked Bey. 'You work quite close by after all.'

'Never,' said Lola. 'But then he probably goes to flash places for his lunch while I have a sandwich at my desk. Different worlds, Bey. Different worlds.'

And yet I'm in that world now, Bey thought, after she'd ended the call. The world of the rich and happy people.

Because most of them *were* happy, she decided. At least once they had a diamond around their neck. Or on their finger.

She looked at her own hand. She wore a ring on her engagement finger, a small Van Alten and Schaap garnet in a simple bezel setting. She'd bought it to celebrate her promotion. She reckoned it would be the only ring she'd ever wear on that finger.

She couldn't understand why her mother was so keen for her to find someone to share her life with. Lola's own career had been derailed by Bey's arrival. Yet she seemed to think that Bey herself should be looking for love rather than professional success. Which only goes to prove, Bey murmured to herself, that mothers are experts in the 'do as I say and not as I do' department. As far as Bey was concerned, Lola was going to be disappointed. She had the job she'd always wanted. And no man in the world could compete with a flawless gemstone.

Lola was thinking about Bey's work–life balance too. She could never quite get a handle on her daughter's attitude towards men. She herself had always seen them as a distraction from her ambition. Until Philip Warren, she'd never gone out with anyone who came close to making her think that marriage was a viable option. And even then she'd turned him down. So she couldn't blame Bey for apparently thinking the same way. And yet Bey kept a distance between her and her boyfriends that Lola had never done. She seemed to regard them as an inconvenience to be endured rather than an important part of her life.

Lola wanted desperately to believe that her daughter's attitude had nothing to do with the night of her abduction,

but she was terribly afraid it might. And that made her feel guiltier than ever. Because she'd made Bey go to Cleevaun House that Christmas, and she'd done it for all the wrong reasons. Which meant that the person she loved most in the world was still suffering because of her bad decisions, and that was something she found very hard to bear.

Chapter 28

Moonstone: a stone with a silver-white reflection

A few days after the Contessa had approved the design for her pink diamond lavaliere, Bey sat at her desk and studied the Adele collections on the Warren website. Her conversation with Will had ignited her interest in her father's company and she wanted to see their newest designs. The latest collection, the Pansy, so far consisted of an amethyst ring. It was pretty, thought Bey as she looked at it critically, but she couldn't help feeling that the setting was a little dated. And the previous collection, the lapis lazuli Hyacinth, though extravagant, wasn't very beautiful. The more recent designs lacked the elegance of the stunning Snowdrop, which was Bey's favourite just as it had been Lola's. It was hard to judge the stones from the website photographs, but perhaps Will was right about those too. Maybe Philip wasn't willing to buy the very best any more. She felt sure that the Warrens had changed their designer – both David Hayes and Norman Jacobs had created showy pieces, but there had been a cohesion about them that was certainly missing from the Hyacinth and Pansy ranges. It was boastful to think that the necklace

she'd designed for the Contessa would be more beautiful than a classic Adele one, but Bey couldn't help feeling that it was. And as she sat there staring at the screen, she felt a jolt of pride in her work, and satisfaction that it stood up against anything the Warrens had come up with.

There was a tap at her door and Will himself walked in. Bey quickly closed her browser and motioned him to a chair on the other side of the desk. As he sat down, he looked around the office, noticing that the pictures and drawings on Clara's large mood board had now been replaced by Bey's own.

'The Contessa was on the phone to me,' said Will. 'She thanked me again for finding the stones and said that she thought the necklace was going to be the most beautiful thing she's ever had made.'

'She hasn't seen the finished product yet,' said Bey.

'No false modesty,' lectured Will. 'Everyone here thinks it looks amazing. And it's not boasting to admit that it is.'

Sometimes, thought Bey, it was as though Will Murdoch could step into her mind. She clamped down on the sudden unwanted thought that it would be wonderful if he could step into her bed.

'It'll definitely be amazing,' she said, and he grinned.

'The Contessa is already murmuring about rings and brace-lets,' he said. 'Although it was tricky enough to get fancy diamonds of that quality to start with. But I'll keep an eye out for her and you keep the thought in the background that she might want complementary pieces.'

Bey nodded. She liked creating sets of jewellery, although whenever she went to Van Aelten and Schaap events now, she enjoyed mixing and matching her favourites, wearing vintage and contemporary at the same time.

'Anyhow, I'm here because thanks to the Contessa, we might have another private commission,' said Will.

'Oh?'

'The proper aristocracy this time.' Will paused. 'It's the Duquesa de Olvera y Montecalmón.'

'And who might she be when she's at home?' enquired Bey.

'She's a friend of the Contessa,' said Will. 'Her family is one of the oldest in Spain. There are a couple of brothers who run the estates in both Spain and Argentina, where they also have land, but she herself is involved in the media – she owns a TV production company. She doesn't generally use her title, so she's just known as Isabella Olvera to the likes of you and me.'

'And she's looking for what?' asked Bey.

'She's getting married next year,' Will explained. 'The family has a collection of jewellery, but some was lost during the civil war in the thirties, including a tiara that Isabella's great-grandmother wore for her own wedding. She'd like a replica made – or at least an interpretation of the original. She only has one photo where her great-grandmother is wearing it, but there are also some family portraits that include it. I thought you'd be particularly keen as it incorporates sapphires, and I know you're a sapphire fan.'

Bey's fingers went involuntarily to the Bluebells in her ears, which she still wore regularly.

'So is she going to send us copies of the photo and the portraits?' she asked.

'No,' said Will. 'She wants us to go there and see them for ourselves.'

'Where?' Bey called up her diary. 'Does she have an office in London?'

339

'No,' said Will. 'Her house in Cádiz.'

'What!'

'You're dealing with the big time now,' he said with a smile. 'She'll be spending a lot of money on the tiara, so if she wants us to go to her, we will.'

'Us?' Bey frowned. 'Who is us?'

'You and me, of course,' replied Will. 'I need to talk about the stones and you'll need to see the design.'

Bey had worked hard to cultivate a warm and friendly relationship with Will as a colleague by shutting her more personal feelings into the locked room in her head. She felt that she'd succeeded. But the idea of travelling to Spain alone with him was deeply unsettling.

'I talked about going to Cádiz when I worked with the Jurados in Córdoba,' she said as she opened a bottle of water on her desk and took a sip. 'But I never got around to it.'

'I haven't been either,' confessed Will. 'But it'll be fun, don't you think?'

'Perhaps Callista would like to come too?' She made the suggestion as blandly as she could.

'Huh?' Will looked at her in astonishment. 'This is a business trip, not a holiday.'

'I just thought you might like to stay an extra few days or something,' said Bey. 'Besides, it might be useful to have her there. She has a lot more in common with the Duquesa than I'd ever have.'

Will snorted with laughter. 'I don't think the fact that her dad made a fortune in the City would cut much ice with someone whose family dates back over six hundred years,' he said.

'All our families date back just as far,' retorted Bey. 'It's just that we haven't kept track of them.'

'Good point,' acknowledged Will.

'And the only reason these ancient families are so rich is that their ancestors were better at raping and pillaging than ours.'

'You'd better not say that in front of the Duquesa,' said Will.

Bey grinned. 'Don't worry. I'll be as humble as a servant,' she said.

'We don't want you humble,' Will told her. 'We want you confident and sassy. As befits the chief designer of Van Aelten and Schaap. The woman who can bring diamonds and sapphires to life.'

'Confident and sassy it is, in that case,' said Bey as she turned away from him and clicked on her computer to google Isabella de Olvera y Montecalmón.

They left the following week, flying to Madrid for an onward connection to Jerez de la Frontera. A car would be waiting for them, Will said, to bring them to the Duquesa's house in the Puerto de Santa María, a few kilometres from Cádiz itself. As she boarded the plane and pushed her overnight bag into the overhead locker, Bey thought of the last time she'd been on a flight with Will Murdoch, when she'd dumped a cup of coffee over him.

'It's OK,' he said in amusement later as he watched her hold on to the filtered one she'd brought on board. 'As a precaution, I've left my computer in my bag.'

'Very funny.' She made a face at him. 'But I'm not going to risk you turning up to see the Duquesa in coffee-stained trousers.'

'Don't worry, I've brought a change or two, just in case.'

'That's a relief.' She took a gulp from her coffee and sighed. 'I'm *so* not a morning person.'

'We could have overnighted in Madrid,' said Will, 'and connected tomorrow.'

'No point in wasting time and money,' said Bey.

'If we get this commission, I don't think an extra overnight stay will worry us in the grand scheme of things,' Will remarked. 'But I applaud your frugality.'

'We're not the clients,' Bey reminded him. 'We don't buy the finished product.'

'Have you had any ideas yet?' he asked.

'The whole purpose of coming here is to meet this woman and get a feel for what she does and doesn't like,' said Bey. 'And to see the photos and portraits. There's no point in me having ideas yet. Though the prospect of meeting someone called Isabella de Olvera y Montecalmón does spark quite a few thoughts in my head.'

Will grinned. 'Good ones, I hope.'

'Ones that will probably be discarded the moment I meet her.' Bey handed her empty cup to a passing cabin crew member. 'Now, since even the caffeine in that coffee isn't enough to keep my eyes open, I'm going to have a sleep. Give me a nudge when we're there.'

Both of them nodded off on the first flight but were more alert on the shorter one from Madrid to Jerez and wide awake for the thirty-minute drive to the Duquesa's house, which was set in a carefully tended garden filled with palm trees and multicoloured flowers.

'My secret hideaway,' she told them after she'd greeted them. 'Everybody should have one.'

It was certainly tranquil, thought Bey, although it wasn't as isolated or as ancestral as she'd imagined. She reckoned it had only been built about fifty years earlier. It was pretty, but not remarkable.

'The view is from the upstairs salon,' said the Duquesa as she led them up a spiral staircase to a room that opened onto a wide terrace with panoramic views over the sea.

'Wow,' said Bey, revising her opinion. 'It's fabulous.'

'I think so too,' said the Duquesa, a tall, slender woman with a mane of dark hair, which she wore tied back. 'Can I get you anything to drink? Something cool? Water? Or a glass of wine, perhaps? I've arranged for some cold tapas. You've been travelling all day and must be hungry.'

'Water would be lovely, Doña Isabella, thank you,' said Bey. She'd emailed Martín before they'd left, asking him the correct way to address a Spanish duchess, and he'd sent her back a reply pointing out that he'd never actually met any duchesses and that her career had clearly moved on in leaps and bounds if she was now hobnobbing with the aristocracy. But he'd given her the information she wanted, as well as attaching a photo of his newly born daughter Helena, who he said was his own personal duchess. Bey had smiled at his reply and responded saying how lovely Helena was and that titles meant nothing, she just wanted to be polite.

'Call me Izzy,' said the Duquesa. Her accent was mid-Atlantic and her English perfect and idiomatic. 'It's not that I'm unconscious of my heritage; after all, I've asked you here so that I can re-create part of it, but honestly it freaks me out when people are too polite. In everyday life I'm Izzy Olvera, so can we stick to that, please.'

'I didn't want to create a diplomatic incident,' said Bey.

Izzy chucked. 'I'm sure we would've overcome it. Sit on the terrace for a moment and I'll bring the water.'

'I thought she'd have had servants to do that,' murmured Bey as she and Will stepped outside to lean on the white balustrade and gaze over the ocean.

'I bet she does,' said Will. 'Maybe she's trying to put us at our ease.'

'You're used to this stuff,' Bey told him. 'You know a few royals yourself.'

'No I don't,' protested Will.

'Wasn't Callista's father knighted last year? Doesn't that make him Sir Marcus of somewhere or other?'

'I think you have to be a lord to be "of" somewhere,' said Will. 'I'm afraid Callista's dad is just Sir Marcus. He got his award for services to finance. Though I'm not sure that making pots of money is really that great a service.'

'Will!'

'If you ask me, it's doctors and nurses who should be honoured, not financiers and other moguls,' said Will. 'But hey, I'm Scottish, so maybe I'm a rebel at heart.'

'Or a socialist.' Bey chuckled. 'And you'd better not let the Duquesa hear you spouting your revolutionary ideas, even if they are good ones.'

'I think honours are a bit daft, that's all,' said Will. 'I don't mind people who make pots of cash if they do it legally and don't cheat anyone, but I'd have thought having the money itself was enough reward.'

'You know, when I was younger and thinking about how my life would turn out, standing on the terrace of a duquesa's house having a conversation about titles certainly wasn't part of it,' said Bey.

Will laughed. 'Me neither, truth be told. But let's face it, to do what we do, there need to be people out there who can afford the product.'

Bey nodded and recalled the conversation she'd had with her mother earlier in the week when she'd rung her to tell her about the trip.

'I was talking to your gran last night,' Lola had said. 'She's absolutely delighted for you. She wants to know everything about it. She also said you're not to be nervous just because you're mixing with rich people these days – all that means is they can afford the stuff you make. She says to remind you that you grew up on a farm and that should equip you for anything.'

Which had made Bey laugh but had comforted her too. Regardless of where she'd started out, she was currently in a good place in her life. She'd overcome the things that might have held her back and was focused on what she wanted to do. She'd worked hard, served her time, moved ahead. She wasn't entirely convinced that the version of herself that existed right now was the best it could be, but it was better than it had been four years earlier. She had solid achievements behind her, and she'd done it all on her own merit, without the help of the Warrens. She had a lot to be proud of. So she had no intention of being intimidated by the Duquesa, but she couldn't help being in awe of the other woman's business success. After all, she had to know a thing or two if she owned media companies around the world, and from what she could tell, Izzy Olvera wasn't much older than her.

The Duquesa walked out onto the terrace carrying a silver tray covered with a starched white napkin and bearing three Waterford glasses and a large jug of minted iced water. She

set the tray on a tiled table and motioned Will and Bey to sit on the cushioned chairs.

'The food will be along in a moment,' she said as she handed Bey a glass of water. 'Meanwhile I have to tell you that Julia raves about you. She says you make gems come alive. And you,' she added, turning to Will, 'she thinks you're like a pig sniffing out truffles when it comes to finding the right stones.'

It took Bey a moment to remember that the Contessa's name was Julia, but it was the image of Will sniffing out stones that made her splutter into her water.

'I'm wrong?' asked the other woman.

'I think she's laughing at the idea of me snorting my way around the globe,' said Will.

'Perhaps it's not such a good analogy,' acknowledged Izzy. 'Ah, here we are.' She nodded as an older man dressed in a white shirt and black trousers laid some dishes of olives, chorizo, cheese and ham in front of them. 'Please help your-selves,' she said, picking up one of the small silver forks that had accompanied the dishes and spearing a piece of cheese.

Once they had finished the food, she wiped her hands on a napkin and opened a walnut box that had been on the table. 'I have the photo of my great-grandmother in her tiara and some of our other jewels to show you,' she said. She took the photo out and put it in front of Bey. Then she removed a selection of velvet pouches and laid their contents – a collection of bracelets and rings – on the table.

'These are wonderful.' Will picked up a bracelet and studied it carefully. 'How old is it?'

'Two hundred years.'

Bey was startled at the casual way the other woman spoke

about the bracelet, which truly was exquisite. No matter how confident she told herself she was, she couldn't help wondering what on earth she was doing here, with this woman, with these jewels, with a man who was looking at them appraisingly but knowledgeably. She remembered running around High Pasture with her cousins, watching a calf being born with her grandfather, collecting eggs with her grandmother. She also remembered sitting at the kitchen table in Ringsend decorating terracotta pots for her mother, and snuggling up beneath a duvet on the sofa while they watched TV together. Then, with a sudden jolt, she recalled hiding in the snow from the man who had abducted her – not because she was rich and worth anything, but simply because she was there and available. So many versions of me, she thought. And which is the real one?

'Bey?' Will's voice brought her back to reality.

'Sorry,' she said as she picked up the photo and looked at it carefully. 'This is a remarkable piece of work. The jewels . . . the silver . . . It would have weighed quite a bit – and cost more than a lot.'

'Yes, I'm aware of that,' said Izzy calmly. 'It belonged to a Spanish infanta who was sent to a nunnery after her husband died. Its history is a bit complicated after that, but it ended up in my father's family and was handed down to a number of women for their wedding days. But like I said, it disappeared during the war and we've no idea what happened to it. I hate to think it might have been melted down and the stones used for other things, but I have to allow the possibility. Anyhow, I adored my *bisabuela* and I thought it would be nice to wear something similar myself as a tribute to her.'

Bey nodded.

'I realise that I can't have anything quite as extravagant as this,' Izzy added. 'Times have changed. So what I want is something in the same style without it being the same. Something I can wear without getting a headache for starters!'

'This has at least a dozen sapphires,' said Bey. 'Are you thinking of having that many?' A dozen sapphires as well as the diamonds would move it into the stratospherically expensive bracket.

'What I want and what I can have are two different things,' said Izzy. 'I want something that captures the spirit of the original. I'll speak to Will about the amount I can spend, and between you perhaps you can work out how many big gemstones you can fit into it.'

'OK,' said Bey. 'I have thoughts . . .'

'Already?'

'Bey's mind is like a magical garden,' said Will. 'She sees jewels, she has ideas, she's extraordinary.'

'Not really,' said Bey.

'Oh yes.' The Duquesa looked at her from wide brown eyes. 'Yes, Julia says the same about you. That the gemstones talk to you. If you're good at something, Bey, you must say so. You must embrace it. I say so to all the women who work for me. Don't hide yourself. Don't pretend you're not good enough. Stand up and shout it.'

Bey glanced at Will, and sighed inwardly. What was the point in her thinking she was in a good place in her life if everyone else thought she lacked confidence? She took a deep breath and promised the Duquesa that she would design her a beautiful wedding tiara that would be a homage to her great-grandmother and an heirloom for her family.

'Thank you.' Izzy smiled. 'After talking to Julia, I was

certain you could. I needed to meet you to be sure. And now I am.'

The Duquesa had arranged for Will and Bey to stay overnight at the Parador de Cádiz, and after they'd finished looking at the photographs and portraits of her great-grandmother wearing the original tiara, the driver who'd picked them up from the airport left them outside the sleek, contemporary building set beside the sea.

'It's such a contrast to the old city,' remarked Bey as they walked across the stylish reception area to check in. Will nodded in agreement and said that he hoped they'd find a little time to do some exploring. The city had been used as a substitute for Havana in the movie *Die Another Day*, he said, and he could see why.

'You've been to Cuba?' she asked.

'When I was young and more rebellious,' he replied, which made her laugh.

They arranged to meet in the outdoor bar an hour later, but Bey left her room after twenty minutes, wanting to walk along the beautiful promenade and soak up the atmosphere by herself. The blue of the sea was making her think of the sapphires she'd use in the Duquesa's tiara, but as she arrived at a small park with mosaic pathways and intricate fountains, her thoughts veered off in other directions. This was always the way when she was contemplating a new design. Her brain went into sensory overload but eventually she'd pick the best colours and shapes for the work she was going to do. She leaned over the weather-beaten balustrade and looked towards the collection of whitewashed buildings that made up the old town. A seagull whirled overhead while a fisherman cast

his line. Old and new, the past and the present collided in her mind. That was what the tiara needed to be too, she thought. A piece that would honour the great-grandmother the Duquesa had loved while being something that a modern woman could wear. As yet Bey had no clear idea of how it would look. But she knew what her starting point would be.

A cool breeze from the sea made her shiver suddenly, and she slipped the fine wool cardigan she'd been carrying over her light floral dress. It was later than she'd realised, and when she hurried back to the parador, Will was sitting at one of the outside tables.

'I thought you'd stood me up,' he said. 'Then I saw you further along the promenade. You seemed lost in thought.'

'I got carried away by the beauty of it all,' said Bey. 'I'm sorry.'

'Don't be.' He smiled at her. 'It's nice to think that the beauty of a place can make us forget everything. Even dinner,' he added with a glance at his watch. 'Although it's probably a bit early for that.'

She smiled at him. 'Perhaps an aperitif first?'

'I was going to suggest that very thing,' said Will. 'We have to toast our fabulous commission.' He waved his hand and ordered two glasses of wine, but Bey asked for water instead.

'I need to keep thinking,' she explained. 'If I have wine, I'll forget.'

'You could let it go for a night,' he said.

'Never.'

The waiter returned with their drinks.

'Do you really think—' Bey began as she poured water into her glass.

350

'Don't say you're not good enough,' Will interrupted her. 'I've told you a million times you are, and even the Duquesa herself called you out on false modesty!'

'I wasn't going to ask if I was good enough,' retorted Bey. 'I was wondering if she was really going to have a traditional wedding. After all, she's a hugely successful woman in her own right. Clearly her wealth isn't only because of her family. Does she need to do the whole white dress and long veil thing?'

'Women seem to like it,' Will said. 'Cally certainly did. Wouldn't you?'

'I don't know.' Bey took a sip of water. 'I suppose there might have been a time in my life when I would have wanted it, but it seems to have passed me by. I can't help feeling that white dresses and tiaras and stuff is all very well when you're a virginal-looking twenty, but it becomes a little daft when you're an adult.'

'Gosh,' said Will. 'I didn't realise you were such a feminist.'

'That's not being a feminist!' cried Bey. 'That's just making a point. Really and truly, men can be so irritating sometimes.'

'Sorry,' he said. 'I didn't mean to annoy you.'

'I'm quite happy for girls – women even – to look like Disney princesses if they want,' said Bey. 'They've a right to choose. And let's face it, I design jewellery so that they can look gorgeous. It's just the wedding palaver that does my head in. I've been to quite a few over the last year or so and they were all really over the top. Even Vika . . .' She shook her head as she thought about her college friend. 'Vika designs spiky, ultra-modern stuff that she normally wears all the time. But for her wedding day she went the whole traditional route and it was like she was someone else entirely.'

351

'I suppose you thought mine and Cally's was excessive?' Bey could detect the slightest edge to his voice.

'Why wouldn't it have been?' she said. 'Callista's an only daughter. She was entitled to make a big day of it.'

'So what sort of wedding are you planning to have?' he asked. 'Sackcloth and ashes?'

She made a face at him. 'I haven't planned it,' she said.

'I thought all girls started planning their wedding from the age of five.'

'Really? I don't know anyone who did.' She poured more water into her glass. 'Oh, don't mind me,' she added. 'I'm being a bit weird today. I love wedding stuff – at least for other people – and I want to design that tiara. I know it'll look lovely.'

'It'll be spectacular,' said Will.

'Spectacular is the brief,' she agreed.

They sat in silence as the sun began to sink lower in the sky and flooded the water with a golden glow.

'It's still the best job in the world,' he said eventually. 'Even if you think it's silly.'

'That's not what I said,' Bey told him. 'I don't think making jewellery is silly at all. You know I love gemstones. I just think that grown women obsessing about a single day is silly. You should be true to yourself.'

'You are,' said Will. 'Always. Everyone says that about you.'

'I'm being an idiot,' said Bey. 'We're in this gorgeous place and I'm nit-picking over the client. Who, Nico would remind us, is always right.'

Will smiled. 'Have a glass of wine,' he said. 'You'll remember everything you need to remember. Chill out for once, Bey.'

'Oh, OK.'

When the wine arrived, he raised his glass to her. 'Here's to us,' he said.

'To our success,' she amended as she raised hers in return.

Chapter 29

Jasper: a grainy chalcedony, usually yellow-brown

It was properly dark by the time they'd finished the wine, and Will asked Bey if she was hungry yet.

'Starving,' she said. 'Those olives were all very well, but they don't exactly fill you up, do they.'

'Would you like to go to dinner? In town or in the parador?'

Bey glanced over her shoulder. Elegantly set tables with white tablecloths and individual flower arrangements were visible through the hotel's long picture windows.

'I was thinking a burger downtown would be lovely,' she confessed. 'I've had enough of starched linen and cut glass for the day.'

Will grinned.

'Don't feel you have to come with me,' continued Bey. 'If you'd rather eat here, that's fine by me.'

'A burger sounds great,' he said.

'Give me a minute to drop my notebook and stuff upstairs,' Bey said. 'Then we'll go.'

She returned a few minutes later in a pair of light trousers

and a denim jacket, a small bag over her shoulder in place of the leather satchel she'd carried with her earlier. Together they walked past the Gran Teatro, with its Moorish design, and along the narrow cobbled Calle Sacramento to the heart of the old town.

'This is like another movie set,' said Will as he pulled her to one side to avoid a Vespa whizzing along the street. 'I kind of expect the cobbles to be slick with rain beneath these pools of lamplight.'

'Idiot.' Bey's heartbeat returned to normal after the suddenness of his touch.

'Who's the idiot? Me or him.' He made a face after the scooter rider.

'You,' she said. 'With your talk of arty movies and whatever. He's probably used to zipping along these roads. Look – there seems to be a little plaza ahead of us.'

'Oh good,' said Will. 'I was thinking that this was going to get even narrower. It's astonishing, isn't it, how tiny the streets are.'

'It is a bit,' agreed Bey. 'Is that a bar over there? D'you think they do food?'

'Let's see.'

The place she'd pointed out did indeed serve food, although Will looked a bit doubtfully at the printed menu in its shabby plastic folder.

'It's fine,' said Bey.

'If you're sure.'

He ordered burgers, chips and two glasses of wine. Bey took a sip of hers and gasped.

'What's it like?' he asked.

'A sturdy little number.' She grimaced. 'But it's wine.'

'That's what you get for choosing a local bar over a flash dining room.'

'Don't the tourist guides always tell you local is better?' she demanded.

'Hmm. I'm not entirely convinced about getting down with the locals all the time,' he said.

'Too much high living is turning you into a proper snob, Will Murdoch,' she said. 'I bet the chipper in Auchtermuchty is quite good enough for you.'

He roared with laughter. 'I've never been to Auchtermuchty,' he said. 'But I'm sure you're right. And I only eat chips from the chippie if they're smothered in salt and vinegar.'

'Oooh.' She sighed. 'Total bliss. There was a wonderful chipper around the corner from us at home. Mum used to get fish and chips there as a treat. They were gorgeous.'

The bar owner arrived at their table with their food. The burgers looked big and juicy and the chips were home cooked.

'Y'see,' said Bey when Will had tasted one and given it the thumbs-up. 'The wine might be a little on the rough-and-ready side but the food is great.'

'You're a girl who's never lost touch with her roots,' he said.

'Oh, please.' She shook her head as she squeezed tomato sauce onto the side of her plate. 'I am who I am. I meet rich people. I'm not one of them. Much as I'd like to wear the jewels, I'm happier making them.'

As she said the words, she realised they were true, at least as far as some of the more extravagant pieces were concerned. Her fingers went to her ears. She didn't have the Adele Bluebells on today; for the meeting with the Duquesa she'd

worn a pair of Van Aelten and Schaap chandelier diamonds, which cost £25,000. She'd put them in the room safe before coming out and substituted them with a pair of silver studs from Jurado's.

'You're a good person, Bey Fitzpatrick,' said Will. 'I wish I'd known you sooner.'

'Sooner than when?' She dipped one of her chips into the tomato sauce.

'Sooner than . . . well . . .' He shook his head. 'Before now. Thing is, I feel like I've known you forever.'

'How odd. I feel the same about you.' Bey's expression was startled. 'I mean,' she continued quickly, 'we see things the same way and that makes us a good team. Today was great. The Duquesa . . . Izzy . . . is lovely. I'm looking forward to working on the tiara. I hope she goes for loads of sapphires.'

'You do, do you?' Will smiled. 'You don't care that I'm the one who has to go looking for them?'

'Leave no stone unturned,' she joked. 'Isn't that your motto?'

'Because it's true.'

She was happy that their conversation had returned to jewellery, which kept them occupied for quite some time. After a couple of coffees, Will paid the bill and they began to walk back.

They heard the sound of another motorbike on the road behind them, and once again Will pulled Bey to one side. But this time the rider didn't go straight past them. Instead he slowed down and in a single motion cut the thin strap holding Bey's bag on her shoulder and pulled it towards him. Then, with the bag under his arm, he speeded up again and

had disappeared out of sight before either of them had properly registered what had happened.

'Are you all right?' Will's arm was around her shoulder and he was looking at her anxiously. 'Did he hurt you?'

'No,' she said. 'No, I'm fine. Just . . . shocked.' She rubbed her arm where the strap of the bag had been. 'I can't quite believe that happened.'

'Sure you're OK?' asked Will.

'Honestly,' she said.

'We'd better go to the police. I'm sure the concierge at the hotel can—'

'No,' she said. 'No police.'

'But you've been mugged!' cried Will. 'What did you have in your bag?'

'Only my purse,' said Bey. 'Luckily I'd left everything else in my satchel. I didn't think I was going to need my cards, so I didn't bother taking them.'

'How about your phone? Your passport? Keys? Stuff like that?'

'All in the satchel,' Bey said. 'Mind you, he did get the Dior lipstick I treated myself to in duty-free, as well as my gorgeous bottle of Jo Malone, but that's it.' She gave him a shaky smile.

'How much was in your purse?'

'A hundred euros,' she said. 'It's not the end of the world.'

'We should still report it.'

'I'd rather not. You know what the police are like, everything takes forever, and we're in another country, we don't speak the language . . . it's too much trouble, really it is.'

'I don't like to think that he'll get away with it,' said Will.

'He will anyway.' Bey heard the tremor in her own voice. 'I didn't see him properly. I wouldn't be able to identify him.'

She'd said exactly the same thing to the lovely, caring garda who'd talked to her that Christmas. The woman had led her through what she had and hadn't seen, trying to unearth any information Bey might have, but all her efforts had been in vain. Bey could remember nothing but a tweed cap and dark-rimmed glasses. Which the garda said was fantastic anyhow, because it gave them something to work with. But despite that, they hadn't found the man who'd abducted her until his body had been unearthed years later. And in the meantime, Bey had been consumed with guilt that she hadn't tried to imprint every detail of him on her mind.

'If you don't want to report it, you don't have to.' Will had heard her voice shake and realised that she was upset. 'Let's get back to the hotel and have a drink to steady our nerves.'

'No,' said Bey as she unconsciously tidied her hair. 'You're right. We'll go to the police.'

'Are you sure?'

'Certain,' she said.

He took her arm and they walked back up the street again. She was angry with herself for not taking more care with her bag, for not wearing it on her other shoulder, away from the street, to make it more difficult for someone to snatch. Given that there'd been nothing that couldn't be easily replaced in it, the theft was a minor irritation rather than a catastrophe, but it was the violation that was upsetting; the fact that someone had pushed against her, touched her, treated her as an obstacle rather than a person.

They talked about me as though I wasn't there. As though I was an object.

Another memory. This time of saying those words about the Warrens to Paige Pentony, her counsellor, even as she felt guilty that Lola was having to shell out for her sessions. And then more – that she was worrying her mother by not eating, even though every bite of food tasted like cardboard. That Lola was sleeping as badly as Bey herself because she was afraid that one day she'd let herself out of the house in her sleep. As well as the guilt that she was the cause of even more animosity between her parents. Paige had told her that she had to let it go, that she could only be responsible for her own feelings, but Bey found that difficult to do.

The police station was in an old building that had been modernised inside. When Bey began to explain what had happened in her rusty Spanish, the kindly officer called an English-speaking colleague to take their statement.

'I doubt we will recover your items,' he told Bey. 'But you must list them and the value for your insurance claim.'

'Oh, I probably won't bother with that,' she said.

He looked horrified. 'You must. That is why you have insurance, no?'

She smiled at his outrage and then gave an approximate value for the bag, the purse and the other items. The whole process took over an hour, and she was exhausted by the time they were finished.

'We definitely need a drink after that,' said Will as they walked back to the hotel.

There weren't many people around when they arrived at the parador, and the small bar beside the outdoor area was closed.

'I thought everything in Spain stayed open till the early hours,' he said in dismay.

'It's OK,' Bey said. 'I'll just go to bed.' She was suddenly feeling teary, which she told herself was delayed shock. But she wasn't going to cry in front of Will Murdoch. She was a professional person. He was her colleague. She needed to pull herself together.

But when they got upstairs, she remembered that her key card had been in her bag too.

'I'll go to reception and get you another,' said Will.

'I don't think they'll give you my room key,' she told him. 'I'll have to get it myself.'

As she turned and began to walk along the corridor, she stumbled and reached out to the wall for support. Will was beside her in an instant.

'I'm fine, I'm fine,' she said as he steadied her. 'Just a little wobbly for a moment.'

The receptionist made no comment when she asked for another key, and simply coded one for her.

'You should have a drink before you head off to bed,' Will said. 'You're very definitely in shock.'

'I'm over it now,' she assured him. But quite suddenly she didn't want to be alone, so she nodded and followed him to his room. It was identical to hers, with a huge picture window leading to a wide balcony overlooking the illuminated swimming pools below.

'Oh.' Bey forgot her shock as she stepped outside and stared out at them. 'They're like two rectangles of tanzanite on a black cloth. You could . . .' Her words petered out as she studied the pools.

'You're not thinking jewellery right now, are you?' Will

had opened the minibar and was extracting a couple of bottles.

'Well, yes.' She turned towards him with a weak smile. 'That look is so geometric but so bright. It'd work really well in a collar, or a bracelet.'

'You're unbelievable,' he said. He handed her a glass.

She looked at the amber liquid inside. 'What's this?'

'Whisky,' he said.

'I don't drink whisky,' she told him. 'Honestly, Will, you're making me out to be some kind of traumatised victim. I'm not. I've never been a victim. I'm in charge of my own life and I can handle everything it throws at me. And if I've made a mistake, I can accept it and move on.'

He was startled by her tone and her words. She looked at him ruefully.

'Sorry. It's a bit of a mantra. I learned it when I was younger.'

'There's more to you than meets the eye, Bey Fitzpatrick,' he said.

'Maybe.' She sniffed at the whisky. 'I'm sorry. I truly can't drink this.'

'Wine?'

She sat down on one of the outdoor chairs. Perhaps a glass of wine, looking out onto those pools, was a good idea after all.

A minute later, Will put a glass of wine in front of her and joined her.

'It's a spectacular view,' he acknowledged.

'Beautiful by night, stunning by day,' she said. 'Can't you see it, though – blue stones, and diamonds behind, like the pool lights, and . . .' she frowned, 'a yellow jasper – what

on earth is that in the pool?' She got up, glass in hand, and leaned over the balcony. The yellow object she'd seen moving through the blue water was an automated pool cleaner. She turned to smile at Will, who'd followed her.

'Clever,' he said. 'I've never actually seen one working before.'

'It's kind of cute. But it doesn't really fit in with my design vision.'

'I guess not.'

They watched as the robotic cleaner moved methodically up and down the pool. It was strangely calming, thought Bey as she sipped the wine, which was immeasurably more palatable than the stuff at the local bar. She felt the tension in her shoulders ease and her mind started to drift back to the Duquesa and her tiara. The lighted swimming pools had sparked a flood of new ideas in her head, but there was a tranquillity to standing in the moonlight, her head resting against Will's shoulder, that made her want to stay where she was for a few minutes longer.

Her head against Will's shoulder! The moment she realised it, she jerked upright and wine splashed out of her glass and onto his shirt.

'Oh crap!' she cried. 'I'm sorry.'

'It does seem to be a habit of yours to drench me in liquids,' he observed as he mopped at the shirt with one of the paper napkins from the table. 'What the hell happened there?'

'I . . . I was leaning against you,' she said.

'And that was enough to make you decide to drown me in Viña Esmeralda?' he asked.

'I shouldn't have been . . . I'm so, so sorry.'

'It's perfectly OK,' said Will.

'No. No, it's not. I shouldn't have . . .'

'It's fine,' he insisted. 'You'd had a shock. You needed a moment.'

'Yes, and I had it. I'll leave you alone now. I'm sure you've plenty to do.'

'Like what?' he asked.

'Like . . . like . . . contact wholesalers. Source stones. Your usual stuff.'

'It might surprise you to know that I don't spend my entire life looking at pieces of rock,' said Will. 'I'm perfectly capable of spending an evening without feeling the need to examine diamonds or sapphires.'

'I guess.'

'Relax,' he said. 'Sit and talk to me. And not about jewellery; about anything else you like. But wait until I change out of this. D'you want another glass, by the way?' he called from the room. 'Most of that seems to have ended up on me.'

'Oh, OK.' She'd stopped caring about the alcohol. Besides, they didn't have to be up early in the morning. Will was right. She recognised that she was still a bit shocked. She needed to relax. She just wasn't sure she could do it with him.

But it turned out she could.

It was like the day he'd taken her for pizza. It was cheerful and fun and very, very soothing. She reminded herself every so often that whatever else she'd messed up in her life, she'd got it right with Will Murdoch, because they were a great working partnership and she liked to think of him as a friend too. It was good to have a man who was a friend and nothing more, she thought. It brought a different perspective to life.

'Sorry?' she said as he looked at her enquiringly. 'What did you say?'

'I knew you weren't listening to me.' He topped up her glass. 'I was asking about the Warrens. I know you said you weren't close, but how did that happen?'

The wine had loosened her tongue. She explained that Lola hadn't wanted her father to know about her.

'You're joking.' His eyes widened. 'That was a pretty big decision to make.'

'She didn't love him enough.' Bey gave the explanation that Lola had always given her. 'She didn't want to be pressurised into marrying him because she was pregnant. So it was better not to tell him. And it makes sense,' she added. 'It's easy to fool yourself into thinking you're in love but you need to be sure to get married. She did the right thing.'

'She didn't think she should marry him for your sake?' asked Will.

'That's a rubbish reason for anyone to get married,' said Bey. 'It would have been a mistake.'

'But she told him eventually.'

'Partly my fault,' said Bey. 'I nagged at her. I shouldn't have. I'd've been better off not knowing them.'

'Why?'

She'd never told anyone before. And she didn't know if it was the wine again, or the shock, or simply the closeness of Will Murdoch that made her talk of the night of her abduction for the first time in years.

'Oh my God,' he said when she'd finished. 'I never thought . . . That must have been totally traumatising.'

'I got over it,' she said.

'But you must sometimes still think about it,' said Will. 'I

still think about the time when I was eleven and Jamie McMurdo beat the crap out of me in the playground at school. I remember how scared I was and how humiliated I felt that I was so useless at fighting back. I went to tae kwon do classes afterwards. I was always hoping he'd do me over again and I could tell him to stay away, that my hands were lethal weapons, but his family moved to Newcastle shortly afterwards so I never got the chance.'

Bey smiled at him. 'I went to counselling, I did all the stuff they make you do, and I've pretty much forgotten all about it,' she said.

'Is that why you don't see the Warrens?' he asked.

'Perhaps partly,' she admitted. 'But I'm fine, Will, honestly. It was years ago.'

'I can't believe you jumped out of a car and hid in a holly bush,' said Will. 'That's amazing. *You're* amazing!'

'Not so amazing,' she said. 'I nicked a ring and ran away. I deserved what I got.'

'You did not!' cried Will. 'What you deserved was for someone to ask why you were all alone in the middle of the night and bring you home. Or call home for you, like those people whose house you ended up in.'

'The Connors,' said Bey. 'They were lovely. We still exchange Christmas cards every year.'

'And you said this guy's body was found in the woods years later?'

She nodded.

'I don't know what to say.' Will poured more wine into their glasses. 'To have that in your life. You never told me. You don't tell anyone.'

'I didn't want it to become the most interesting thing

about me. To be introduced as the girl who was abducted and escaped.'

'I can see that,' he said. 'And I can totally see why you and the Warrens have a difficult relationship.'

'It was always going to be difficult,' said Bey. 'Finding out about me was a shock to them. Poor Mum tried to make things OK, but it backfired on her massively. They're quite horrible about her and I've never quite figured out if it was because she wouldn't marry Dad or because she ran home when she was expecting me and didn't say anything until years later.'

'It must have been hard for her on her own,' observed Will.

'You called me amazing, but Mum is the amazing one,' said Bey. 'She got a great job, worked really hard, put me through college, did everything for me . . . she's the one constant in my life. Always was, always will be.'

'It's important to have someone you can trust completely,' said Will. 'Someone you can turn to.'

'You have Callista.' The words were out of Bey's mouth before she could stop them.

'Yes,' he said.

She shouldn't have said Callista's name. She shouldn't have made the conversation even more personal than it was already becoming. She stood up abruptly.

'I'm tired,' she said, swaying slightly. 'I need to sleep.'

'Careful.' He got up too. 'Maybe I was a bit generous with the wine.'

'It was nice,' she said. 'Really. Thank you for asking me to your room. Although that sounds horribly compromising.'

'You're welcome.' He put a hand out to guide her as she stepped in from the balcony.

'Oh God, I'm probably drunk,' she said. 'I don't get drunk, Will Murdoch. It's not my thing.'

'I know. I'm sorry. I thought you needed it.'

'Nobody *needs* alcohol.' There was mock severity in her tone. 'Our teachers in school told us that. But most of the class had already quaffed a fair few ciders behind the bike sheds by then.'

He laughed. So did she.

'I'm glad you were with me on this trip,' he said.

'I'm glad I came.'

She looked up at him then, and realised he was looking at her too. His eyes were more like violet amethysts than ever in the muted light of the room. Only more beautiful. She exhaled sharply. She couldn't think of Will as having beautiful eyes. She definitely shouldn't be comparing them to gemstones. This was why she didn't drink. It made her think stupid thoughts.

'You have amazing hair, did anyone ever tell you that?' He tucked a strand behind her ear.

She remembered when he'd tried to do it before, just after she'd discovered he was engaged to Callista, when she'd been younger and less experienced at life. She'd done the right thing then, because she'd practically run away from him. She should run away now, she thought. That would be the sensible thing to do.

But she didn't do the sensible thing.

She put her hand on his chest and felt the steady drumming of his heart.

She tilted her head.

And then she kissed him.

*　　*　　*

She was reasonably experienced in the art of kissing, although she was a little out of practice. But none of her past kisses, not with people she liked, or people she thought she loved, or people she knew she didn't love but who she thought she should kiss anyhow, had been like this. Never before had she surrendered to the moment and allowed the physical pleasure to take over from what was going on in her head.

This kiss was different.

This kiss was with someone she cared about.

This kiss was with Will Murdoch, and she'd wanted to kiss him for a very long time.

She felt the heat of his hand on her back and the strength of his body next to hers. It felt right. It felt perfect.

Because she was in love with him. She would always be in love with him. She couldn't help it.

Even though he was in love with someone else.

Even though he was married to someone else.

And she shouldn't be kissing him at all.

She pulled away from him abruptly. 'People blame alcohol when they do crazy things.' Her voice was shaking. 'I never believe them. But the only way I'll ever believe I did that was owing to having too much to drink. I'm so, so sorry.'

'I should be sorry too.' Will's eyes were searching her face. 'And I am. I really am. But—'

'No buts!' she cried. 'This was . . . totally inappropriate. We're work colleagues. You could sue me for sexual harassment.'

'Don't be silly,' said Will.

'I'm horrified at what I've just done,' she said. 'You should be horrified too.'

369

'I am.' There was a tremor in Will's voice. 'I promise you I am.'

'You're married to Callista. You shouldn't be kissing me.'

'I know. But listen to me, Bey—'

'No. There's nothing to say. Nothing at all.'

She strode to the door, thankful that she was at least able to walk straight, and fumbled at the handle, crying out in frustration when the door remained obstinately closed.

She felt the heat of him again as he reached around her to unlock it.

'Does this happen on all your overseas trips?' Her voice was tight.

'How could it?' he said. 'This is the only one you've ever been on with me.'

'You know quite well what I mean.'

'Yes, I do. And of course it doesn't. I've never even—'

'This was a big mistake,' Bey interrupted him. 'Bigger than all the other millions of mistakes I've made as I've blundered my way through life. I'm thinking that the shock and the drink left me in a vulnerable state and I made a fool of myself. I never, ever want to talk about this again. It didn't happen. OK?'

'Bey—'

'Not another bloody word!'

Their eyes locked and Bey saw her own desire reflected in his. She caught her breath, then walked rapidly towards her own room. She stopped outside the door. A moment later Will came up behind her and handed her the key card that she'd left on the table on his balcony.

'I know it was a mistake,' he said. 'I'm really sorry. I can forget about it, I promise.'

'Good,' said Bey and unlocked her door.

The problem was, she thought as she leaned against the wall of her room, she wasn't sure if she could.

Chapter 30

Cabochon: a stone cut with a domed top and flat bottom

It wasn't until the car arrived to bring them to the train station the following day that she saw him again. He'd texted her when she hadn't turned up for breakfast and she'd replied that she was having it in her room as she was working on her notes for the design of the Duquesa's tiara. Then he asked if she'd like to go for a stroll around the old town before they left and she replied with a brief *No thanks.* He didn't send any more texts but was waiting in the foyer when she got there herself.

She was wearing her jeans and a white shirt, her hair once again in its neat plait. She knew that despite her inner turmoil, she was outwardly calm and relaxed.

'Are you OK?' he asked as they got into the car.

'Of course.' She began to talk about the tiara, even though she normally never discussed her designs until she was confident about what she wanted to do, asking him questions about the availability of sapphires and diamonds of particular cut and clarity that he answered in the same casual yet professional tone. The atmosphere, while friendly, lacked the

God preserve me from a family business, she muttered as she replaced the phone. Maybe it was just as well that Bey had no romantic interest in Martín Jurado. Although she wished her daughter had a romantic interest in somebody. It wasn't right that a girl of her age had never had a serious boyfriend.

She was brewing coffee when Bey walked into the kitchen, rubbing her eyes.

'Did I hear the phone ring?' she asked.

Lola told her about the arrangements.

'So we're not invited to Rathgar tonight. That's a relief.' She popped some bread in the toaster. 'I've never seen a dead body before and I would've freaked to see Grandfather lying in a box in the living room.'

'You'd have been fine,' said her mother.

'I really don't think so.' Bey shuddered. 'Well, as we're not doing anything today, can we go to Cloghdrom?'

'I assumed you'd want to do that after the funeral,' said Lola.

'I need to get back to Córdoba afterwards,' Bey said. 'I hate leaving work sitting on the bench, and I made a mess of soldering a ring when you called.' She showed her mother her injured finger as proof. 'So if you don't mind, it would be great to visit today.'

'We'll go to the Garda station first,' Lola said. 'And then my wish is your command. As always.'

A kind and sympathetic garda took down their statement and told them that Raymond Fenton hadn't been known to them prior to Bey's experience. It was likely that she'd been his first attempt at snatching someone, and thanks to her resourcefulness, the outcome had been a good one. As they left the police station, Bey felt more relaxed than she'd done in Dublin for years.

She phoned her grandmother when they were on the road. Eilis was delighted to hear from her and was standing at the door of the cottage waiting to greet them when they arrived.

'Granny! How are you? Are you feeling OK? Can you walk better? Are you pain free?' Bey threw her arms around the older woman, who laughed at the force of her granddaughter's hug.

'I'm grand, not a bother on me,' she said. 'A bit stiff, but that's to be expected. It'll take me a while to get up to speed on the new hip, but it's so much better to be able to move without agony.'

She led the way into the kitchen, where the aroma of freshly baked bread filled the air.

'Oh, Gran! Soda bread. My favourite.' Bey hugged her again.

'Mine too,' said Lola, sniffing appreciatively.

'Sit yourselves down and I'll put the kettle on. Then you can tell me all your news, Bey. And your mother can tell me about the Warrens.' She blessed herself. 'That poor man. What a dreadful thing to have happened.'

'It was terrible,' said Lola, 'but we have other news first.'

Eilis looked at them in surprise and Lola told her about Raymond Fenton.

'Thank God.' Eilis's words were heartfelt. 'I've always prayed that one day that man would be found. And I'm delighted that Bey won't have to make any more statements or give evidence or anything horrible like that.'

'It's definitely good news,' agreed Lola.

'Are you all right about it, pet?' Eilis asked Bey.

'Totally,' she replied. 'I suppose I shouldn't be glad that he's dead, but at least he hasn't been able to harm anyone else.'

'Well it's uplifting that something good has come out of something terrible,' said Eilis. 'Billy will be glad to hear about it too.'

'Where's Dad now?' asked Lola.

'Low Pasture with Milo,' replied Eilis. 'In fairness, he's hands-off now as far as running things are concerned, but you can't keep him away from his cows.'

Bey laughed. Her grandfather very definitely cared for his cows as much as he did for his family.

'D'you want tea?' Eilis paused with the kettle in her hand. 'Or would you prefer a fancy coffee?'

'What sort of fancy coffee?' asked Bey, a little surprised by the offer. Eilis had always been a traditionalist when it came to hot beverages. Tea, strong with plenty of milk and two spoons of sugar, was her usual brew.

'Gretta bought me a machine for my birthday,' her grandmother said. 'She has one herself and she loves it. It does those lattes and cappuccinos and stuff that people seem happy to spend a small fortune on these days. It's a long way from how I was reared, but I have to say that I've taken a bit of a shine to them now.'

'I'll have one,' said Bey. She grinned as she picked a capsule from the box that Eilis had taken from the cupboard. 'I'm very impressed with you these days, Gran. Fancy coffees and a very fancy kitchen!'

'Ah well, when we were having this place built, we decided to make it as high tech and low maintenance as possible,' said Eilis. 'I have to say I miss my Aga, but I've got used to the new oven and hob. And of course the lighting is great so I can see what I'm doing. Anyhow, pet, it's lovely to see you, even if the circumstances are not ideal. D'you have any more information about the raid?' she added, turning to Lola.

Lola told her mother what little she knew, and Eilis said it was shocking and that she'd seen the TV pictures and read the papers and she never would have believed such an awful thing would happen to someone she knew. Or, she corrected herself, to someone she knew about, and who was connected to her even if they'd never met.

'Poor Grandfather,' said Bey. 'I can't imagine how he must have felt with someone waving a shotgun in his face.'

'No indeed,' agreed Eilis. 'I don't think I'd have done well with it myself. Of course we have one ourselves for security.'

'Mum!' Lola was horrified.

'We're isolated up here,' said Eilis. 'And you know how it is, the criminals can terrorise you if you're on your own. So we have the shotgun. It's licensed, of course.'

'Can you use it, Gran?' asked Bey.

'I practised up at High Pasture when your grandad got it.' Eilis nodded. 'And if I say so myself, I do a pretty good Annie Oakley impression.'

Bey rocked with laughter but Lola looked at her mother in despair.

'I don't like to think of you with a gun,' she said.

'And I don't like to think of myself without one,' said Eilis. 'Of course it's a whole different scenario for us up here than having someone raid your shop like that. There's just

252

warmth that normally existed between them, but neither of them made any reference to the evening before until they were on the flight to London.

'Look,' said Will, after the seat-belt signs had been turned off, 'you're obviously still very upset with me.'

'I'm not,' she said. 'I'm upset with myself. I can't believe I was so bloody unprofessional. Like I said, it was shock and alcohol, and I apologise for behaving in such an inappropriate way.'

'That's fine,' he said. 'I just—'

'Will, the only way I am ever going to be able to look you in the eye again is if we never, ever talk about it.' She loosened her seat belt. 'So can we agree that it's a topic that's not going to be raised again?'

'All I wanted to say was—'

'I meant what I said,' she interrupted him. 'Let's move on. Now, I've had more thoughts about the tiara given what you've already told me. If we use half a dozen sapphires . . .'

They took the Gatwick Express to Victoria and then separate cabs home. It wasn't until she'd closed the door behind her that Bey finally started to cry. And then she cried as though she would never stop. Because what had happened with Will confirmed everything she hated most about herself. The fact that she always wanted the one thing she couldn't have. That she still didn't have the self-control not to take it anyway. And that she'd learned nothing over the last fourteen years.

She'd composed herself by the next day and was in the office early, sitting at her desk and making more sketches of her tiara ideas. As well as the Duquesa's commission, she was also working on the next Van Aelten and Schaap collection, so she had plenty to keep her occupied. The problem, she realised as she looked up from her desk later, was that every time anybody approached her office, her heart leaped in her chest, hoping it was Will and yet at the same time not wanting it to be. She told herself that the flare-up of her long-buried crush would recede. That it had only happened because she hadn't been in control of her actions or her emotions. But that she was totally in control of herself now. And then her heart leaped again as she heard footsteps outside the door, but it was only a courier with a 3-D model of a ring design.

'I'm going for a walk, Iolanda.' She signed for the model and then got up from her desk. 'I'll be back in a while.'

'Are you all right?' Iolanda looked at her in surprise.

'Headache,' said Bey. 'I need some fresh air.'

She hurried down the stairs and outside. She strode towards Oxford Street, not taking any notice of the people around her, not thinking of anything because her head was in a whirl again. She'd worked successfully with Will for four years. In that time she'd dated other men. She could still work with him. She could date other men again. All she needed was to pull herself together.

She went into Starbucks and ordered a coffee, which she drank while leafing through a copy of *Metro* that had been left on the table. But she didn't take in anything she was reading, her mind filled with the touch of Will's lips on hers and the intensity of her feelings as he'd held her close. Why was such an insignificant moment taking up so much of her mental time? she asked herself angrily. Why was she letting it matter? Why was she wondering what it would be like to kiss him again? She had no right even to think about it. Will was married. She shouldn't fantasise about him. She couldn't. Besides, there were more important things for her to worry about. The collection. The tiara. All far more meaningful than ten seconds of madness in Cádiz.

But then I always seem to mess up my life with a few moments of madness, she mused as she refolded the paper. Everything would be going fine, and then she would do something stupid, like steal a ring or get into a stranger's car or kiss a married man, and the consequences were overwhelming, not just for her but for everyone around her. She finished the coffee and threw the waxed cup into the trash. This moment, this thing with Will, who knows what it could have started and how it could have ended. It might have cost him everything. And it would have been all her fault, just like every other time.

'How's your head?' asked Iolanda when she walked back into the office.

'Improving,' replied Bey. 'Anything happening?'

'Gerritt wants to have a chat about the Duquesa,' said her assistant. 'And Will Murdoch dropped by but I told him you'd gone out.'

Bey's heart missed a beat.

'Is he coming back?'

'He hung around for a while but he had a meeting. He said he'd be back around six.'

Bey nodded. She went back to her desk and started sketching.

At 5.45, she left for the evening.

Her days now seemed to be entirely measured around Will's timetable. It was all about avoiding him whenever she could and yet feeling the bitter sting of disappointment when she didn't see him.

When he did have to call into her office, she was very careful never to be alone with him – which wasn't that difficult as she always left her door open. She found a way of talking to him that sounded strained to her but that everyone else seemed to accept as perfectly normal. She never instigated conversations and always kept the ones they did have as brief as possible. She did her best not to allow her feelings to become apparent to anybody else. But after a few weeks Iolanda asked if she'd had a row with Will, and when Bey asked why, Iolanda said that she'd been very offhand with him lately and he seemed unhappy.

'We're both very busy,' Bey said. 'He's trying to source the stones for the tiara and I still haven't come up with a design that I like. It's stressful.'

'I've never known you to be stressed before,' said Iolanda.

'There's a first time for everything,' said Bey.

And a first time for not feeling comfortable with the design she was working on. It was as though her own conflicted emotions were reflected in her designs for the tiara. Her original sketches from before the kiss were still there and still something to work from, but they weren't progressing the way she wanted. She felt as though she were in a maze, unable to find her way out, taking random turns and panicking when they didn't lead her where she expected.

In the end she decided to return to Ireland for a couple of days. She caught an early-evening flight on Thursday and was having a takeaway in front of the TV with Lola by nine o'clock.

'It's lovely to have you back,' said Lola as she decanted Thai red curry into a bowl.

'It's nice to be back,' said Bey. 'It's been a while, I'm sorry.'

'You've been busy,' said Lola. 'Jetting off to Cádiz, getting important commissions from duchesses . . .' She smiled. 'You're a superstar now.'

'I'm not.' Bey dug her fork into the steaming rice. 'And if I'm strictly honest with you, the tiara isn't working out quite the way I'd hoped. That's why I'm here. I thought . . .' She looked up. 'I thought maybe I could go to Cloghdrom for a day. Walk the fields. Clear my mind. Talk to Granny.'

'I'm sure your gran would love to see you.' Lola looked at her daughter thoughtfully. 'Is there anything wrong?'

'Not wrong exactly,' said Bey after she'd swallowed a mouthful of chicken. 'Just . . .'

'Want to talk about it?'

'Not yet.'

'OK.' Lola knew better than to press her. Years before, Paige Pentony had told her that it would be better for Bey to be more open and honest about her feelings, but despite the outgoing person Bey had once been, she never blurted out her innermost thoughts. She didn't have social media accounts and preferred to keep her personal life personal. Lola loved that about her, although she sometimes yearned to have the kind of conversations that some of her colleagues seemed to have with their daughters – where nothing was off limits and everything was out in the open. Nevertheless, she respected Bey's sense of privacy and wouldn't dream of violating it.

'How's Terry?' asked Bey when she'd finished her curry and settled back on the sofa.

'He's fine,' said Lola.

'You're getting along well?'

'That's the kind of question I should be asking you about your boyfriend,' remarked Lola.

'You could if I had one at the moment,' said Bey.

'I thought perhaps you'd come home because you wanted my motherly advice on boyfriends past or future.'

Bey winced. 'I don't need advice,' she said. 'I know what I have to do.'

'There's someone?'

'Not the way you think.'

'Tell me.'

'He's unsuitable,' said Bey. 'It can't work out. I just need to get my head around it.'

'Oh, Bey.' Lola leaned across the sofa and hugged her. 'I'm sorry.'

'I'll be fine, Mum,' she said. 'I always am, you know.'

'You always seem to be,' said Lola. 'But that's another thing entirely.'

The following morning, Bey got the bus to Cloghdrom. Her grandmother was waiting at the door of the cottage to meet her when she walked up the pathway from the main house.

'You look fantastic, Gran,' said Bey after she'd thrown her arms around her and hugged her. 'Country living sure as hell keeps you looking young. I should try it myself.'

'Really?' Eilis kept her arm linked in her granddaughter's.

'Maybe not,' admitted Bey. 'But I should certainly come here more often. Is Grandad around?'

'He's in the farmhouse with Milo,' said Eilis. 'He'll be back later this afternoon. So you and I have plenty of time for a natter.'

She led the way into the kitchen and nodded towards the coffee machine.

'Make your fancy coffee,' she said. 'Make one for me too.'

'What would you like?' asked Bey as she took some capsules from the brightly coloured container on the worktop.

'Just plain black. I'll put milk into it myself,' said Eilis.

Bey fiddled with the machine and brought the two coffees to the table.

'So.' Eilis looked at her. 'D'you want to tell me right away what has you back here, or do you want to faff around with the pleasantries first.'

'Gran!'

'Well it's clear as day that there's something wrong,' said Eilis. 'You look positively gaunt.'

'I don't.'

'Black shadows under your eyes and a hangdog look on your face.'

'Even Mum didn't say that,' said Bey.

'She wouldn't,' Eilis said. 'She's afraid of you getting annoyed with her. But I'm your granny and I can say what I like. Man trouble, I'm guessing.'

'Oh, Gran.' Bey sighed. 'I've been very stupid.'

'Well you certainly aren't the first and you definitely won't be the last, so I don't know what you're worried about,' said Eilis. 'Tell me.'

Bey told her about Will Murdoch and Cádiz while the coffee in the cup in front of her went cold.

'Let me get this straight,' said Eilis when she'd finished.

'You've had a shine for this man since before he was married?'

'I just fancied him a bit,' said Bey. 'I thought there was a connection. I don't know why because he certainly didn't think so or he wouldn't have got married to someone else in the first place.'

Eilis said nothing.

'I know it was wrong, Granny. I didn't mean to kiss him.'

'Well, we all do things we don't mean to. That's as far as it went?' Eilis asked. 'A kiss?'

'It sounds so pathetic to say yes,' Bey replied. 'I mean, a kiss. What's in a kiss, after all? But it was still a kiss with someone I shouldn't have kissed and . . . and somehow it seemed to be a whole lot more.' She swallowed hard. 'And I want to do it again.'

'That's not great,' said her grandmother.

'I know. I know. That's why I had to get away!' cried Bey. 'You'd think it'd be easy, wouldn't you? To just put someone out of your head? But it's hard, Gran. It really is.'

'It's certainly hard if you've been carrying a torch for him ever since you started working with him,' said Eilis.

'I haven't been thinking about him all that time,' Bey told her. 'I've gone out with other men, you know.'

'You say that as though they were a penance for you.'

'Not at all,' protested Bey. She sighed. 'I don't pick the right ones. I can't stick with any of them. I can't seem to adapt to what they want me to be.'

'No woman should let herself be anything other than who she wants to be,' said Eilis, which made Bey give her a watery smile. 'As for not sticking with one man, your mum blames herself for that.'

'She does?' Bey was astonished. 'Why on earth would she?'

'She thinks she set you a bad example,' said Eilis. 'With the relationship she has with your dad.'

'I'd hardly measure relationships by the one Mum and Dad have,' said Bey.

'Lola never properly got over her decision not to tell your father about you. She wanted to and she didn't and she regrets that very much.'

'I thought I was the one who wanted him to know about me,' said Bey in surprise.

'When you were much smaller, she was going to tell him. And then she changed her mind. And she thinks that was a mistake.'

'She never told me that,' said Bey. 'She must have had her reasons, though, and I'm OK with them, whatever they were. But I don't have some kind of father complex – whatever other problems I might lay at Dad's door, my problems with men aren't one of them. They're nothing to do with Mum either. They're all my own.'

'So you blame yourself for this kiss business?' asked Eilis.

'It was my own silly fault.'

'He doesn't share any of it?'

'I don't want him to.' Bey looked into her coffee cup and then up at her grandmother again. 'I want him to be happy with Callista and have a great marriage and not think about me at all.'

'Men can compartmentalise,' said Eilis. 'Women are terrible at that. We keep going on and on about things, letting them take over our heads until we're wrecked. Meanwhile the men aren't in the slightest bit bothered. Your Will Murdoch probably hasn't given that kiss another thought.'

'I know.' Bey groaned. 'And despite what I just said, that makes me feel even worse. One, because it meant so little to him. And two, because he could forget about Callista like that and I didn't think he was that sort of person. Of course my judgement of men is terrible. We all know that.'

'You don't have a monopoly on misjudging men,' said Eilis. 'I had a bit of a mishap with one myself when I was younger. I thought he loved me. I was going to spend the night with him in a fancy hotel in Dublin. And then, when I got there, I discovered that he was a married man himself.'

'Gran!' Bey was shocked.

'Oh, you young things don't have a monopoly on messy relationships,' said Eilis. 'Sex didn't start with your generation, you know.'

'So . . . so what happened with you and him?' asked Bey.

'I turned on my heel and went straight back home,' said Eilis. 'I married your grandfather, who I'd always thought was boring, and we've had the best marriage a couple could have. And that's what will happen to you one day. You just have to open up to the right person coming along.'

Bey was silent.

'Will Murdoch is not the right person,' said Eilis.

'I keep telling myself that over and over,' said Bey. 'I'm truly terrible, Gran. I'm so ashamed of myself. I wish it wasn't part of me. Wanting something that belongs to someone else and just taking it. I have form in that department, as you well know.'

'Is that what this is really about?' cried Eilis. 'Are you banging on about that stupid ring again? You were twelve years old when that happened!'

'Stealing a ring, stealing someone's husband – it amounts

to the same thing. It really bothers me that I can't stop myself doing things I shouldn't.'

'How old are you?' demanded her grandmother.

'Twenty-seven. I should have more sense.'

'And in all those years, how many things have you done that you shouldn't?' Eilis continued as though Bey hadn't spoken.

'Millions, I should think,' she said.

'And life's gone on all the same,' said her grandmother. 'Remember when you were small and you played skittles with the fresh eggs on my kitchen floor? Turned it into a sea of yolk?'

'Oh gosh, yes.' Bey covered her mouth with her hand as she recalled the incident. Her grandmother had been incandescent with rage.

'And the time you got into the sheep dip with all your dolls?'

'Um . . . yes.'

'And the time you came to stay and offered to do the ironing and you went to answer the phone and burned my best blouse?'

'I . . .'

'And the time you opened the oven door to check my soufflés and ruined them?'

'Yes, but—'

'Millions is right,' said Eilis. 'But guess what, Bey. The world is still spinning and you're still standing and we all still love you.'

'Because you're my family and you have to,' said Bey.

'We love you because we know you. And we know you want to do the right thing.'

'But I don't always succeed.'

'Life would be boring if we always got it right first time,' said Eilis. 'You should know that it's how you react to your mistakes that's the important thing. What you learn and how you get back up after being knocked down. And you always get up, Bey.'

'Mostly my mistakes have been mistakes for me,' said Bey. 'But kissing Will . . .'

'Forget about it!' Her grandmother reached out and squeezed her hands. 'Of course you shouldn't have done it. But you've punished yourself enough.'

'I can't help feeling like I should be punished more,' admitted Bey. 'My punishment after taking the ring was being abducted by Raymond Fenton. I don't know what punishment will come to me for kissing Will.'

'How many times have you been told that being abducted wasn't a punishment?' demanded Eilis. 'It was something that happened, that's all. If you're waiting for a bolt of lightning to hit you because of a moment of madness with a colleague – well, you're far, far sillier than I ever thought. What you have to do, missy, is what they all tell you to do these days. Build a bridge and get over it.'

Bey laughed shakily.

'He's not important,' said Eilis. 'Your life is what matters.'

'But his marriage . . .'

'Is his problem, not yours.'

'I know that really,' said Bey. 'I do. I keep thinking I've got over it. But then I see him and . . .'

'You have a great job that you're good at,' said Eilis. 'But no job is more important than your own happiness.'

'I wish I hadn't done it.'

'The milk is already spilt,' said Eilis. 'The eggs are already broken. The soufflés are already flat. No wishing can change that. But it's only milk and eggs, pet.'

'I suppose you're right,' said Bey.

'I know I am. Now come on, let's put it behind us and have a lovely day.'

That evening, Bey went to the farmhouse to have dinner with Milo and Claire and her cousins. It brought her back to her childhood, when they'd all sat around the same table together, bickering and squabbling but having fun and believing that nothing but good things were around the corner.

We make our own happiness, she thought as she went to bed later that night. And we make our own good things.

I think I'd forgotten that until now.

By the time she returned to London, she'd made up her mind. She couldn't stay at Van Aelten and Schaap any longer. Haute joaillerie was all very well, but she needed to go back to Ireland, to be with the people who loved her and understood her. And she needed to be away from Will.

Having made the decision, she found her thought process about the tiara much clearer, and she moved from pencil sketches to computer design, rendering the piece in three dimensions and seeing clearly where the sapphires would sit and how the tiara would look on the Duquesa's head. She had a silver model of it made and asked Iolanda to try it, testing it for comfort and wearability, though obviously when the stones were set it would be much heavier. She mailed photos of it to the Duquesa, who was enchanted and said that it channelled the one her great-grandmother had owned while having its own contemporary style. Gerritt Van Aelten was delighted. Everyone in the company loved it. She basked in their admiration for a few days before calling into Gerritt's office to tell him of her decision to resign.

He was shocked.

'Perhaps a leave of absence?' he suggested when she told him that her reasons for leaving were personal.

'I'm afraid not,' she said. 'I'm sorry. I'm telling you now so that you can organise a replacement. I'll stay until the work on the next collection is completed, which should give you plenty of time.'

The only people who knew about her imminent departure were Gerritt and the management team. He said he didn't want to disrupt the general staff by telling them, and she was perfectly happy with that. Six weeks later, he called her in to say that they'd found their new chief designer.

'Clara is coming back,' he said.

Bey looked at him in astonishment.

'It appears that New Zealand wasn't all she expected it to be,' said Gerritt. 'She wanted to come home.'

'And her husband?'

'They're divorcing. It's a pity for her personally, but obviously it's come at an opportune time for us.'

Bey was sorry that things hadn't worked out for Clara and sent her an email saying so.

Onwards and upwards, Clara replied. *And thankfully it turned out that we didn't have children after all, so there's no trauma there. I'm looking forward to getting back in the saddle at Van Aelten. I like what you've done in my absence but I've got lots of new ideas.*

So that's that, Bey said to herself. You come, your star burns brightly for a while and then you leave and you're forgotten. Only the gemstones remain, glittering on, ready for the moment when someone rich and happy owns them.

Will arrived in her office unexpectedly one evening after her departure had been announced. He closed the door behind him then asked if her decision had anything to do with him.

'Why on earth should it?' she asked.

'You know perfectly well why,' he said. 'Ever since Cádiz, you've avoided me like the plague. And I wanted to say that if you're leaving because of me – please don't. I'll go if my being around you makes you uncomfortable. I can find somewhere else to work. You're too good at this to walk away, Bey. Especially if it's because of me.'

'Your arrogance is breathtaking,' she said. And then she gave him the warmest smile she could. 'Of course it's nothing to do with you. I've been away from home for too long, that's all.'

'But what are you going to do back in Ireland? There aren't any jewellers of Van Aelten and Schaap's standard there.'

'I'm sure some of them would disagree,' she said.

'Are you going to work for your family?'

'Not at all,' she said. 'I'm going to work for myself.'

'Bey . . .'

'Honestly, Will, it's what I want to do.'

'If I believed you, I'd be happy for you. But how can you go back to making cheap trinkets when you've designed for Van Aelten?'

'Cheap trinkets!' She made a face. 'Less expensive than the baubles here, certainly. Fewer contessas and duquesas and wives of Russian oligarchs, that's true. But I won't be making disposable jewellery, Will. I'll be making quality pieces at affordable prices.'

'Have you got a plan?' he demanded.

It was only a vague one, more in her head than on paper. But she nodded.

'I'll miss you,' he said.

'No you won't,' she assured him, reaching out gratefully to answer her phone. 'Not in the slightest.'

Before moving back to Dublin, she contacted Martín Jurado and asked if there was any chance of interning with his family firm again for a few weeks so that she could renew her silver-smithing skills. He was shocked to hear that she was leaving Van Aelten and Schaap but delighted that she'd called. The studio flat above the workshop was free, he told her. If she wanted to spend a couple of months there, they'd be delighted to have her.

And so she went back to Córdoba and once again walked the narrow twisting streets, soaking up the atmosphere of the city. The colours and the scents fired a million ideas in her brain and she visualised a range in the shape of the pretty flowers with brightly coloured stones at their centre. She showed her sketches to Martín, who nodded and then sat with her as she went back to basics, annealing her silver, shaping it carefully, hammering it, soldering it, polishing it and finally placing the complete piece on display.

'You haven't forgotten everything you learned,' remarked Manolo, when he came in to see her. 'In fact you're doing surprisingly well for someone who's spent the last few years at a desk instead of a workbench.'

She smiled at him. 'You were so strict with me when I was here before that it was impossible to forget,' she said. 'Although I'll never be as good as you.'

'I wouldn't expect you to be.' Manolo smiled in return. 'But it is nice to have you here again and nice to have some of your designs to sell. We still sell the snowflake, you know. It's popular at Christmas.'

'I'm glad,' said Bey. 'It's good to know that wherever I am, the design lives on.'

'Not just our designs,' said Manolo. 'Those you did for Van Aelten too. I've watched your career, Bey. You were doing some lovely work for them. Are you sure this is really what you want?'

'Very sure,' she said, and he accepted it.

She was anxious about moving back in with Lola yet again when she finished in Córdoba, afraid her presence would cramp her mother's style and that the two of them would find it hard to live together after such a long time apart. But Lola was adamant that Bey should stay with her and Bey herself was more than aware that she couldn't really afford to set up a workshop and a flat at the same time. Accommodation costs in the city had been increasing relentlessly over the past few years, and even though the economy was growing steadily after the recession, getting a small business loan was difficult.

It was Terry, her mother's boyfriend, who arranged a meeting with his own bank manager that resulted in her getting the money she needed, and Terry who found a small premises close to St Patrick's Cathedral that he thought might be suitable for her.

It had originally been a car mechanic's lock-up and over the last decade had variously housed a furniture repair shop, an antiques store, a dog-grooming parlour and a Pilates studio, but following a refurbishment it now contained the offices of a security company, a small electrical suppliers, and the unit Terry thought Bey could use. As she stood in the middle of it, she visualised where she would put her workbench and her tools, her mood boards and her desk. And she smiled. Because even though it wasn't a beautiful office at Van Aelten and Schaap, she knew it was right for her.

Lola had long since made an uneasy peace with the choices she'd made and the outcome of them. She still had regrets, but she tried to live in the present, not the past. Nevertheless, she knew that if she could change only one thing, it would be that stupid decision to insist on Bey spending Christmas with the Warrens. She could have said no. She should have said no. But she'd been selfish and pig headed because she'd wanted them to see what a success she'd made of raising her daughter on her own. She'd piled the pressure on Bey and her little girl had cracked. She could never get over the guilt she felt about it. She knew her daughter had come back from London because of a failed relationship, and it broke her heart to think that it was all her fault.

'It's not all about you,' Eilis told her when she rang her one night. 'You and Bey are very different people.'

'I want to fix it,' said Lola. 'I *need* to fix it.'

'Don't you dare interfere.' Eilis's voice was stern. 'You never listened to me in your life before, Lola Fitzpatrick, but you can listen to me now. Leave Bey to sort out her own problems. She can do it. She's the only one who can.'

For once Lola followed her mother's advice. Even though she didn't want to. Even though she was afraid it was another mistake.

Bijou
Two years later

Chapter 31

Aquamarine: a precious light blue or green-blue gemstone

Bey shook the raindrops from her umbrella and unlocked the door to her workshop. She turned off the alarm (an advantage of sharing the building with the security company was feeling that it was well protected) and plugged in the kettle. Then she hung up her coat and put her bag away before sitting down with a strong coffee and looking around her with satisfaction. The walls of the room were covered in drawings, posters and photos. The drawings were her own; the posters and photos were of images that inspired her. She'd added Post-it notes to some of them in case she used them in the future, jotting down phrases or ideas as they came to her. Her tools were hung neatly on the preserved tree stump in the middle of the floor, just as they had been at Jurado's. It was, she thought with a sense of fulfilment, a proper workshop. And it was hers.

She opened her laptop and checked her orders while she sipped the coffee, giving thanks for people who liked to do their Christmas shopping in advance. Sales were running ahead of the previous year, which was positive – with a bit of luck, she thought, as she drained her cup then rinsed it in the small sink, Bijou by Bey would actually make a profit this year. The idea of finally making money filled her with immense satisfaction.

A different type of satisfaction than she'd got from designing truly beautiful pieces for Van Aelten and Schaap, she admitted to herself. But still satisfying. Her time at the high-end jeweller's had been purely creative and artistic, based around using only the best and most beautiful stones that money could buy. The past couple of years had been about tapping into her inner creativity and using it to make beautiful things that ordinary people could afford, using the skills she'd learned from Manolo and Martín Jurado, but also the business expertise she'd acquired from her months working with Tina Garavan.

She'd kept in touch with Vika, who was running a small business and who devoted her mornings to making jewellery and her afternoons to her children. A year after Bey's return to Dublin, they took a stand at the Birmingham Jewellery Fair together and immediately increased their orders. It was definitely a case of back to the future, Bey remarked when Martín and Manolo Jurado dropped by to say hello. Just that they were all a little older.

'And wiser,' Vika said.

Bey liked to think she was wiser. But she wasn't a hundred per cent sure about that.

She spent the morning listening to the gentle hiss of rain on the window as she worked. She was adding to her spring collection for the following year. She had moulds for her most popular pieces, which meant they were easy to replicate, and she knew that floral designs were always popular. Having previously collaborated with Martín on a small collection they'd christened Jasmine, she'd added Crocus and Daffodil. She would've liked to include a Snowdrop too, but she was pretty sure that the Warrens would sue her if she did. Her use of floral names had been entirely unconscious at the time, but she sometimes wondered if there had been a demon in the back of her mind pushing her towards them, even though her simple designs were a million miles away from the extravagant Adeles.

Liesel Mieders arrived at lunchtime. The younger woman was working with her as part of an intern placement scheme, and Bey was determined to help her new assistant gain as much experience as possible. She set her to polishing some of the small charms she'd made for a Christmas bracelet, and the two of them worked steadily until there was a tap at the door and the owner of the electrical repair shop came in to ask if they had any spare milk, as he'd run out. Jim, a kindly man in his early forties, had taken Bey under his wing when she'd started the business.

'I have two young daughters myself,' he'd said when they first met. 'I like to see women getting on. You're a role model for them.'

Anyone less like a role model than her would be hard to find, Bey thought, but Jim had become a good friend.

'On a day like today, I bet you miss the glamour,' he said as he looked out the window. 'Wouldn't it be lovely to have someone like your Duquesa phone up now and offer to fly you to the south of Spain to knock up a nice necklace for her?'

'Yes.' Bey grinned. 'But even if she did, I wouldn't be

able to help her. I designed that tiara but the real experts were the people who made it. Their craftsmanship was awesome.'

'But you make awesome things too,' said Liesel after Jim had gone. 'I'm learning so much by being here. This is really pretty.' She looked at the silver ring with a raspberry-pink cabochon at its centre that she'd finished polishing. 'It makes me feel joyous just to look at it.'

The same thing had been said to Bey at Van Aelten and Schaap by the wife of a Formula 1 driver when she came to collect a ring that her husband had commissioned specially for her. It had been a yellow diamond to match his team colours. Will had spent three months looking for the right one.

'I'm glad you like it,' she told Liesel. 'I'm hoping it'll be our big seller.'

'How can it not be?' said Liesel. 'And,' she added as Bey's mobile began to ring, 'maybe that's a customer to buy it.'

Bey grinned and picked up her mobile, already aware that the call was a personal one.

'Hi, Lorcan,' she said. 'How's it going?'

Lorcan Keneally was the first man she'd dated since she'd come home. They'd met at a young entrepreneurs' conference held by Dublin City Council about six months after she'd first set up her business, and when he'd asked if she'd like to meet for a drink, she'd agreed. She knew that her acceptance was based as much on the fact that her mother had complained that she was turning into a total recluse, only happy when she was working, as it was on her enjoyment of Lorcan's company. But it had been satisfying to return to the house in Ringsend and tell Lola that she had a date. And the date itself had been a lot more fun than she'd expected. She was halfway through the jar of coffee, and so far they were still together.

'I'm back in town for a couple of weeks,' he said. 'Want to meet tonight?'

Lorcan ran his own IT company. Bey had no idea what it actually did, but she did know that he spent a lot of his time FaceTiming people in California and going to meetings in various European capitals, which all seemed very buzzy and exciting to her. He had a duplex apartment in Dublin's Smithfield and was never short of money. She liked having him in her life because his need to be with her was as flexible as her need to be with him. As far as she knew, they were exclusive to each other, but they also tacitly accepted that they had other priorities in their lives.

He was five years younger than her and at least ten times more successful. But he was easy to be with and never made demands. So she said she'd be delighted to see him and ended the call with a smile.

Almost immediately the phone rang again, and when she heard the voice at the other end, she dropped it to the floor.

The screen was cracked but the call was still active when she picked it up again.

'Hello,' she said, and then, because it had been a long time and she couldn't be absolutely certain, 'who's calling?'

'It's me,' he said. 'Your father. Philip. What the hell happened there?'

'Oh, nothing. I was distracted for a moment. Um . . . why on earth are you calling me?'

'I want to meet you,' said Philip.

'What? After all this time? Why?'

'I'll explain when I see you. Is tonight OK for you?'

'I'm sorry, I can't make it tonight.' Bey had recovered her equilibrium a little. 'I'm busy.'

'If you're out with Lola, I'm sure she won't mind.'

'Actually, no,' Bey said. 'I have a date.'

'Oh. Right.' Philip sounded flustered. 'Tomorrow night, then?'

'Can't you just tell me whatever it is over the phone?'

'I'd really rather talk face to face,' said Philip. 'It would be better.'

'Where?' asked Bey.

'The Westbury?' The five-star hotel was off Grafton Street and a short distance from the Warren's store.

'OK.'

'Six o'clock,' said Philip.

'Six o'clock,' repeated Bey and ended the call.

She was too gobsmacked to do any more work that day.

Later that afternoon, Lorcan texted her to say that something had come up and could they take a rain check. This was a common feature of their relationship, and although his last-minute cancellations could be annoying, this time Bey was relieved. Her mind was in such a whirl that she wasn't sure she'd have been good company. She was also relieved when she arrived home to see a note from Lola saying that she'd gone out with Shirley and her husband Ian. Bey was happy to sit in front of the TV alone and think of all the reasons her father might have for wanting to see her for the first time since Richard Warren's funeral. But she couldn't come up with anything sensible.

She went to bed before Lola returned, although she was still awake when she heard her mother's key in the door. She was tempted to get up and tell her about Philip's call, but she knew they'd end up talking about it for half the night. But by two in the morning she still hadn't nodded off and her mind was in a whirl.

She didn't know what time it was when she opened her eyes, but when she did, she was sitting at the kitchen table, Lola opposite her, watching her anxiously.

'Oh crap,' she said as she realised she was holding a carving knife and a tea towel. 'I don't believe it.'

'Did something happen?' asked Lola. 'I heard noises, and when I got up, here you were, polishing like billy-o.'

Bey put the knife down. 'Everything's fine,' she said. 'It really is. I just had a bit of a surprise yesterday. But why it should have made me do this again . . .'

'What sort of a surprise?' Lola was still anxious.

Bey took a deep breath. 'Dad phoned me.'

'What!' Lola stared at her. 'Philip? Called you? Directly? Himself?'

'Yup.'

'How did he even know how to find you?' she asked.

'I suppose he googled me.' Bey was properly awake now. 'I know I hate it personally, but I've had to do a lot of social media stuff for Bijou by Bey. And my mobile number is on the site.'

'What did he want?' asked Lola.

'To meet me,' replied Bey.

'He should've spoken to me first.'

'I'm a grown-up, Mum,' said Bey. 'He's entitled to call me if he wants.'

401

'All the same . . .'

'I realise there's something a little disturbing about the fact that a phone call from my father seems to have triggered off a bout of midnight cutlery cleaning,' said Bey. 'But I'm sure it's nothing important.'

'I still can't believe he rang,' said Lola.

'Yes, well, neither can I. But I'll find out what it's all about later.' She glanced at the kitchen clock. It was four in the morning. 'I'm so sorry for waking you,' she said.

'That's OK,' said Lola. 'Do you . . . do you want me to come with you to see him?'

'Of course not,' said Bey. 'I've been around the block a few times. I'm not going to be fazed by my dad any more.'

Although, she thought as she replaced the cutlery in the drawer, he'd clearly fazed her already.

She couldn't concentrate on anything. She managed to make a mess of a simple bangle with pearls she was adding to her Christmas collection and was annoyed with herself for not focusing properly on the task in hand. Eventually she abandoned her attempts at making jewellery and instead looked through her online presence to see what her father might have found out about her.

There was more than she'd expected. As well as Bijou by Bey on Facebook, Twitter and Instagram, and a Pinterest page where she posted pictures of her pieces, there were links to magazine articles she'd completely forgotten about, including an interview she'd done for a luxury goods magazine when she'd been promoted to head designer at Van Aelten and Schaap. There were also feature pieces about the company itself, which included more photos. Her attention was caught by one in particular, of the management group at the Bond Street headquarters, where she was standing between Gerritt and Will. It had been taken shortly after the launch of Cascade, her first collection as head designer, which had been inspired by a small waterfall near her grandparents' farm at Cloghdrom. 'I tried to reflect the brilliance of drops of water caught in the sunlight,' she'd explained to the reporter. 'I hope I succeeded.'

She had. Demand for the pieces had been huge. She remembered talking to Will about the stones, his assurance that he'd source the perfect ones for her and that the cutters in Amsterdam would be able to get them exactly right. She'd gone to the workshop on the Grimburgwal and watched as they worked on the diamonds, marvelling at how the initial dull stone was turned into something of beauty. The newspaper article had been gushing about the collection, saying that in Bey Fitzpatrick, Van Aelten had sourced the best jewel of them all.

She closed the web page and opened Bijou for Bey. After the brilliance of the diamonds and other precious gems, her silver pieces looked very ordinary, and although her costume jewellery was more extravagant, it was still very affordable. Just like my life, she thought. For a few years I was immersed in the rich and happy. I basked in the success of what I was doing. I thought I had a real chance of being great at it forever. But it wasn't real. It was never real. This is who I am. Bijou Bey. The girl who makes nice things for everyone, not just people with a lot of money to spend.

Her phone pinged with a message from Lorcan to say that he was sorry about last night and that he was now up against a deadline but he'd be in touch in a week or so. She replied that it wasn't a problem, then forgot about him as Liesel arrived. The younger girl began boxing up jewellery for delivery while Bey herself worked on some pendants. But for the first time since starting her business, she wasn't thinking about her customers. She was totally taken over with thinking about her father and the rest of the Warrens.

She checked out their website but there had been no additions to the Adele collections since the Pansy, although the most recent range was now complete with earrings, necklaces, pendants and bracelets to go with the original ring. She didn't like the designs any better than she had before, and she thought again about Will's assertion that they weren't using the best stones any more. In fact, she thought, as she appraised the pictures critically, they weren't using the best of anything. She wondered how Adele felt about that.

At 5.30, she took off her apron, then changed out of the loose jeans and T-shirt she usually wore when working and into the tailored trousers and crisp white blouse she'd brought with her that morning. She replaited her hair and secured it with some jewelled clips she'd bought in Córdoba. She was wearing a simple silver ring and bracelet from her own range, but in her ears were the Adele Bluebell earrings, and around her neck was a Cascade pendant, which Gerritt Van Aelten had given her as a bonus. She'd been astonished when he'd handed her the beautiful box, and protested that she didn't deserve it. Afterwards, when she'd told Will, he'd snorted and berated her for wrapping herself in false modesty again. He'd told her that she absolutely did deserve it. That she was a great designer. That she was unique. Will had always known the right thing to say to her. He'd brought out the best in her. And she'd made a mess of it all.

No I haven't, she told herself as she pulled down the shutters of the workshop. I have Bijou by Bey. I'm going to make it a success. I'm already making it a success. Plus I'm doing it without anyone else's help, so that's a lot better than anything I achieved at Van Aelten and Schaap.

She strode along Stephen Street towards George's Street. She enjoyed walking through town, especially when – in typical Dublin fashion – it was dry and warm after the previous day's rain. The city was thronged with people and the hustle and bustle of life always invigorated her. But today she was conscious of a sense of anxious anticipation running through her, and her heart was beating faster than ever as she drew near the Westbury.

She was five minutes early arriving at the hotel, and she hurried up the stairs to the marble foyer, where she sidetracked into the ladies' so that she could check how she looked. Standing in front of the big mirrors, she adjusted her clips, applied some more lip gloss and sprayed herself with a floral scent she'd bought on her last trip to Birmingham. Then she took a deep breath and made her way to the extensive lounge area. Like the city, the hotel was busy and the low tables were occupied with people finishing afternoon tea. She looked around and immediately recognised her father sitting at a table near the window, reading the newspaper, a pot of tea and two china cups in front of him.

The years had been kind to him, she thought. His fair hair was now completely grey, but it was still thick and luxuriant. His blue eyes had lost none of their piercing quality, and he had maintained the physique of a younger man. For the first time, Bey saw him as a businessman instead of her father. And for the first time she didn't feel overwhelmed by his presence.

She walked over to him, oblivious to the fact that people glanced at her as she passed, their eyes drawn to her tall, slender figure and flaming red hair.

'Hello,' she said as she stood in front of him.

'Oh. Bey. I didn't see you arrive.' He stood up and extended his hand.

It was seriously weird being greeted by a handshake, thought Bey as she shrugged off her light coat before sitting down. But anything warmer would have been even weirder.

'I already ordered tea.' Philip picked up the silver teapot and began to pour. 'Would you like something to eat?'

She shook her head. 'Tea is fine.'

'So,' he said. 'I gather you've been back in Dublin for a while.'

She nodded.

'You didn't like London?'

'I liked it a lot,' she said. 'It just seemed the right time to come home.'

Philip frowned. 'You were chief designer at Van Aelten and Schaap,' he said. 'That was an amazing post for someone as young as you. And yet you gave it up. Why?'

'Have you seriously asked me to see you for the first time in seven years so that you can quiz me on my career choices?' She played with her earrings for a moment, then, realising what she was doing, dropped her hands to her lap.

'I'm just trying to understand why you left such a wonderful job,' said Philip.

'And I'm trying to understand why you think it's any of your business.'

'I'm interested,' he said.

'*Now* you're interested in my life?' She couldn't keep the scepticism out of her voice.

'I'd like to know why you decided that making cheap silver gewgaws was a better career choice than working with one of London's finest jewellers,' said Philip.

'Are you wondering if they fired me?' She looked at him enquiringly. 'Afraid that perhaps my light-fingered nature overcame me and I relieved them of a few polished stones?'

'Don't be silly,' said Philip. 'Of course I didn't think that.'

'You were happy enough to think of me as light fingered before.'

'Let it go,' he said. 'Honestly, you and your mum both live far too much in the past.'

Bey looked startled.

'She resents me,' said Philip. 'Though why she should feel that way is an eternal mystery to me. I tried to do the right thing by her. She was the one who kept secrets. Not me.'

'She thought it was for the best.'

'I would have given her everything,' said Philip. 'I loved her. But she lied to me. And she kept on lying. I can't forgive her for that.'

Bey said nothing, and Philip sighed.

'I didn't ask you here to rake over old coals,' he said. 'Sorry.'

'Why then?'

'I have a proposition for you.'

'I don't think—'

'Hear me out. Please.'

He leaned forward in the chair and started to speak.

407

Chapter 32

Baguette: a gemstone cut in a narrow rectangular shape

'It was your grandmother's birthday recently,' he said. 'We had a family dinner. And something came up.'

Philip hesitated and Bey waited in silence.

Her father scratched his head. They'd already got off to a prickly start and he was struggling to know how best to continue. From the moment he'd first met her, he'd never really known the right thing to say to his elder daughter. Initially it had been because he'd been unable to distance his relationship with her from the absolute fury he'd still felt with Lola; both for her refusal of his marriage proposal and her decision to keep Bey's existence a secret. Richard had told him about his accidental meeting with her when Bey was three and confessed that he'd persuaded her to maintain that secret because of the impact it could have had on Philip's marriage. Even though he'd been angry with his father too, Philip had agreed it had probably been the right thing to do at the time. Richard had also mentioned the sweetener he'd given Lola, although he hadn't said anything about the more substantial financial arrangement until after the fateful

Christmas. By then Philip was once again too angry with both his ex-girlfriend and his daughter to care. But as he looked at Bey sitting in front of him, her blue eyes steady and unwavering, he wished they'd all handled things differently.

'We talked about Warren's,' he began again as Bey remained silent. 'Your grandmother was concerned about our profitability.'

He grimaced as he recalled Adele's actions and her words that day. She'd taken a sip of champagne before turning her attention to both him and Peter.

'I was looking at the accounts,' she'd said. 'And I didn't like what I saw.'

They'd stared at her in astonishment, and Peter asked how on earth she'd got her hands on them.

'In Duke Lane,' replied Adele. 'A few weeks ago. When you were both off gallivanting in Basle. I wanted to see how the store looked after the most recent refit. In fairness to you all, it's lovely, but while I was in the office I checked the accounts, and even though it's all far more complicated than it was in my day, I'm not so senile that I couldn't see we've been making losses.'

Bey could practically hear her grandmother's clipped tones as her father repeated her words. So Will Murdoch had been right, she thought.

'The refits were certainly costly, but we expect to see the benefits,' Philip continued.

'That's capital expenditure, though, isn't it?' said Bey. 'What about your profit and loss?'

Philip was taken aback by her comment. Adele had said exactly the same thing. When Peter had tried to talk about the cyclical nature of business, their mother had fixed him with a steely glare and told him not to talk to her like a child. She'd reminded both of them that there had never been losses when Richard was alive and that the company was his heritage. And that they'd gone from being an iconic store to simply another jewellery shop. That there weren't waiting lists for their Adele collections any more. And that the last one, the Pansy, had been dull.

'It's been a difficult few years,' admitted Philip.

'I'm sorry if you're having problems,' said Bey. 'But I'm sure you'll overcome them.'

'So am I,' Philip said. 'Peter is too. But we're worried that they're a little more deep seated than we thought.'

Despite herself, Bey was interested.

'In what way?'

'We let Norman go when the recession started to bite,' he said. 'We were in the middle of the Hyacinth collection back then, so we already had a basic design. We kept David on as a consultant and he worked on the Pansy. But both the Hyacinth and the Pansy have done poorly. Peter and I think it's because people have moved on from the vintage styles that they associate with the Adele collections. So we asked another designer, Darren Daly, to come up with a new look for us.'

'I don't know him,' Bey said.

'He's based in Cork and we liked what he did,' said Philip. 'But . . .'

'But what?'

'But we don't think they're good enough for Warren's,' said Philip. 'We don't think they've got heart.'

It had been Peter who'd said that when Philip had shown

the designs to him, and Philip had to agree that he was right. They were technically excellent. They captured the essence of the Adeles. And yet they didn't grab you and make you long to own the jewellery. Which was a worry, Philip told Bey. Adeles were all about desirability.

She nodded in agreement. She remembered the first time she'd seen the advertisement for the Adele Tiger Lily in one of the many glossy magazines her aunt Gretta left at the farm-house, and being enchanted by the pictures of the beautiful set. That was why she'd copied it for the beaded bracelets she'd made for Donna and Astrid. She'd been proud that she'd captured the look but disappointed that they didn't have the same sheen of luxury. She remembered her grandfather talking about jewellery that Christmas Day, and her realisation that it made you want to be the person who could afford to wear it.

'I'm sorry you've lost your way,' she said. 'The Adeles were aspirational for a whole generation of women. But I honestly don't know why you needed to tell me all this.'

'Because I want you to design for us, of course,' he said.

'You've got to be joking.'

Bey was completely taken by surprise. She'd thought perhaps that he was going to ask her if she knew anyone who was suitable for Warren's. Or that he wanted her opinion on Darren Daly's designs. But she hadn't for a moment expected him to ask her to design for them herself.

It hadn't been the first thought that had come to Philip either when he and Peter had rejected Darren's work. As they'd sat together in the small office above the Duke Street shop, it was Peter who'd spoken first.

'We do have another option,' he'd said. 'The elephant in the room.'

'Huh?' Philip had looked around as though Peter was talking about an actual animal.

'Bey, you idiot,' said Peter. 'Your daughter. Who was the chief designer at Van Aelten and Schaap. A company that *does* have waiting lists for pieces. Particularly the Cascade pendant, which she designed.'

Philip had looked at Peter as though he'd lost his mind. He'd reminded him that he hadn't been in touch with Bey for years. That she was no longer with Van Aelten and Schaap and that she hadn't turned up at any other prestige jewellery company. That there had to have been a reason for her leaving. That they didn't know what it was.

'Are you suggesting she left under a cloud?' asked Peter.

'No. Not really. It's just . . . Bey. And Lola. And Warren's. It's a terrible mix.'

'Only because we let it be,' said Peter. 'I'm not saying that offering Bey a job would solve our personal issues, but it might very well solve our professional ones.'

'Like I said, though, we don't know what she's doing now.'

'Actually, we do.'

Peter had showed Philip the results of his internet search. Philip had looked at her streamlined website, with its pretty range of affordable jewellery, and then at the magazine pieces about his daughter when she'd worked at Van Aelten and Schaap. There were photographs of her as well as the jewellery she'd designed. In one she was standing beside the owners of the firm. In another beside a woman named Julia Ferranti, who, the caption writer said, was known as the Contessa. And there was a truly magnificent photograph of a tiara that had been worn by a Spanish duchess on her wedding day.

'All designed by Bey,' said Peter. 'All utterly fabulous. Not to mention the Cascade, which everyone knows is one of the most beautiful suites of the last decade.'

'But she's making trinkets now,' said Philip. 'And how do we know she actually designed those other pieces? She probably had an entire team working for her.'

'Even if she had a team for the haute joaillerie, the stuff she's doing now is really striking,' said Peter.

'She wouldn't want to work for us,' objected Philip.

'Why don't you ask her?' said Peter. 'What have you got to lose?'

My pride, thought Philip now as he watched his daughter process his request. Especially if she isn't as good as those photographs would have us believe.

'I don't want to work for you.' Bey's voice was firm.

'Why on earth not? It's a dream job.'

'I don't even know what sort of position you're offering,' she said.

'I've just told you. I want you to design the next Adele collection.'

'That isn't in my game plan at all.'

'What is? Fooling around in a run-down garage in a laneway?'

'It's not a run-down garage,' she protested. 'It's a proper converted business premises.'

'In comparison to Warren's, it's nothing special.'

'But you're coming to me because Warren's is nothing special now either.'

'We've stumbled,' said Philip. 'We thought . . . I thought you might be interested.'

He was beginning to wish he hadn't listened to Peter, no matter how good Bey might be. He hadn't followed her career with Van Aelten and Schaap in great detail, but he knew the Cascade was exceptional. Seeing it now, around her neck, was mesmerising. But who was to say that even if she did accept his offer she'd be able to come up with something equally exceptional for Warren's? Who was to say that she wouldn't try to damage the family firm? She wasn't part of it, after all.

'I don't think you really want me working for you,' she said when he remained silent. 'I don't think we'd be a good team.'

'Did you do it all yourself?' he asked. 'The Cascade? The Reed Flute Cave collection? That beautiful tiara? Or was it a team effort?'

'It's always a team effort,' she said.

It could be a monumental mistake, thought Philip. A bigger mistake even than the Hyacinth and Pansy collections had been. He'd been persuaded to ask her, though, because unlike Darren Daly's designs, Bey's were full of heart. The moment you saw a piece you wanted to touch it, to own it, to have it forever. But perhaps the magic didn't come from her at all. And yet, as he looked at her sitting in front of him, her expression serious, he knew that it did.

'There's no reason why we couldn't make it work.' He realised he didn't want her to turn them down. Not because he'd lose face, but because they'd lose someone who had the potential to bring them back to where they wanted to be.

'You, me and the Warren family? Make it work? We haven't managed it yet and that's only our personal lives. A business relationship would be impossible. Besides,' she added, 'I'm at a point where my own business is beginning to turn a profit. If I step away now, all my work over the last few months will be lost. Plus, I have orders to fill.'

'Many?' asked Philip.

'The Christmas ones are coming in now,' said Bey. 'And they're up significantly on last year. I know it's a clichéd name, but the Winter Wonderland set is very popular.'

It suddenly occurred to Philip that Bijou by Bey could be making more of a profit than the Warren's stores. She didn't have the overheads, for one thing. The thought made him shiver.

'Give it some consideration,' he said. 'Please?'

'What does Adele have to say about it?' she asked.

'I haven't said anything to Adele yet,' replied Philip.

Bey's laughter at his reply was genuine.

'That settles it. There's no way she'd want me working for you, even if I said yes.'

'It's not her decision to make,' said Philip.

'Oh please,' said Bey. 'She was always the power behind the throne and I'm quite sure she still is.'

'She's concerned about the company too,' said Philip. 'It's an emotional thing with her.'

'Emotional my arse.' The composure that Bey had been working so hard to maintain suddenly slipped. 'That woman doesn't have an emotional bone in her body.'

'You can't say that,' Philip told her.

'It's true,' said Bey. 'Although in fairness she'd probably be very emotional if you told her you'd offered me a job. Just not the way you think.'

'I agree that you and Adele aren't necessarily on the same

page,' said Philip. 'But she cares very much about the company.'

'And not so much about the people.'

'That's not true.'

'Of course it is,' said Bey.

'Please think about it,' said Philip. 'We could go with Darren's idea for the new Clematis range and it might work but it's not what we want. It's not what we need.'

'Did you bring the drawings?' Bey couldn't help asking.

Philip opened his briefcase and put them on the table in front of her. She studied them while she sipped her tea. Then she sat back in her chair.

'Well?' said Philip.

'They're very nice,' she told him.

'But they're not special, are they?'

'Even if I did come to work for you, it would be a nightmare.' Bey didn't see the need to answer his question. 'Most of you hate me.'

'We don't hate you,' said her father. '*I* don't hate you. I wouldn't offer you a job if I hated you. Peter doesn't hate you either. He thinks you're our only hope of salvation.'

'Adele loathes me,' said Bey. 'She has done from the start, although I never quite understood why. I'm not sure that Anthony or Astrid like me very much either. And they matter, don't they, because it's their business too.'

Philip looked at her in surprise. 'What d'you mean?'

'Isn't it true that Anthony will eventually be the one taking it over while Astrid swans around showcasing the jewellery? Adele said so, when I was with you for Christmas.' She kept her voice as even as possible.

'You remember her saying that?'

416

'Of course I do. I remember everything about that day. How could I possibly forget?'

'Anthony is currently our retail manager.' Philip ignored the tautness in her voice. 'But he has nothing to do with product development. And you're right, Astrid does wear a lot of the jewellery. In fact . . .' he shrugged, 'it was Astrid who made me see how poorly we were doing with the Adele range. She said at the birthday dinner that she preferred the Snowdrop and the Rose to the Hyacinth or the Pansy.'

'So do I,' said Bey. 'Actually, being honest, peak Adele was the Bouquet. That was magnificent and everyone loved it. But the Snowdrop is the collection everyone dreams of owning.'

'You're wearing Adele Bluebells yourself,' observed Philip.

'Because they were a gift from Mum.'

'From Lola?' Philip suddenly thought it would be better not to talk about the earrings. 'We should work together,' he said. 'It would be nice, don't you think? Another generation of Warrens.'

'I can't honestly believe you have the nerve to say that,' she told him.

'Why?'

'I'm a Fitzpatrick not a Warren.' She got up. 'I'll think about it, as you asked. But I wouldn't hold my breath if I were you.'

Chapter 33

Morganite: a transparent pink variety of beryl

'He did what?' When Lola heard about the job offer, she was as gobsmacked as Bey herself had been. 'And what did you say to him?'

'I'm supposed to be thinking about it,' said Bey.

'Are you?'

'I'm thinking it would be a total nightmare,' she said.

'It probably would,' agreed Lola. And then, when Bey said nothing, she added, 'But would you like to do it?'

'I don't know.' Bey was pensive. 'If it were anyone else, a different company, I'd be seriously considering it. I love Bijou by Bey, but I miss fine jewellery. Yet how on earth could I even think about working for them? Why would I put myself through it?'

'Because it's a challenge?' suggested Lola.

'I don't mind the professional challenge,' said Bey. 'But – oh, Mum – being part of their . . . their empire! Having to interact with them every day. Having to be nice to Adele! How on earth could I cope with it?'

'Are you looking for reasons to say no or reasons to say yes?' asked Lola.

'I honestly don't know,' confessed Bey.

'It's difficult to get your head around it,' admitted Lola. 'But it would be doing what you really want to do and I'd hate to think you'd cut off your nose to spite your face.'

Bey laughed.

'Seriously,' said Lola. 'I probably made more mistakes with that damn family than in anything else I did in my whole life. I don't want you to do the same.'

'You made decisions, not mistakes,' said Bey.

'Bad decisions,' Lola said. 'In the end, I messed up my relationship with all of them and I didn't need to. I could've done things better. I was weak when I should've been strong and I allowed myself to be swayed. And that's impacted on you, sweetheart, which was the last thing I wanted.'

'You had your reasons for not marrying Dad, and for not telling him about me, and they were perfectly good ones,' said Bey. 'You did it all on your own, Mum. You were – you still are – incredibly brave. I was the one who brought the Warrens back into your life by wanting to know about my father. You were doing fine on your own. *We* were doing fine on our own.'

'That's not strictly true.' Lola looked distressed. 'And I wasn't brave, just pig headed. I'd planned to tell you about him sooner but . . . I made another bad decision and . . .'

'Gran said something to me about that,' said Bey. 'But then you changed your mind.'

Lola nodded. 'I let myself be persuaded because I was an

absolute idiot. I told myself I was doing the right thing, but I knew I'd live to regret it. And I did. I still do.'

'What on earth are you talking about?' asked Bey. 'Who persuaded you? What happened?'

Lola took a deep breath and closed her eyes, then opened them again. Bey watched her intently.

'I met your grandfather when you were three,' said Lola. 'It was an accidental meeting. Then he came to see me . . .'

When her mother had finished speaking, Bey stared at her in shock.

'So . . . so Grandfather bought you off?' Her voice was just above a whisper. 'You could have sorted everything out with my father back then, but because Richard offered you money you decided not to?'

'That's not exactly how it was,' said Lola.

'You always said you didn't marry him because you didn't love him enough. I thought you didn't tell him about me because . . . well, when I was very small I had romantic ideas about it. Afterwards I thought that he sort of knew but wasn't in touch for a whole heap of different reasons. But never for a single moment did I think you were being paid to keep me away from him!' Bey's eyes glittered.

'It wasn't because of the money.' Every time she said this – to Philip, to Richard and now to Bey – Lola wondered if there was the slightest chance that she was lying to herself. She didn't think so, but she'd been asked so often she could never be a hundred per cent sure. 'I felt I'd caused your father enough grief and I didn't want to bring my problems to his marriage. Donna was pregnant with twins. I couldn't . . . I couldn't butt into his life when I'd made such a determined effort not to be part of it before.'

'I always thought I had a little bit of connection with Grandfather,' said Bey. 'He was nice to me that Christmas. Well, as nice as a Warren can be. And then after he died and I found out about Raymond Fenton, I felt closer to him than any of them. Yet I was completely wrong about him. He didn't want me close. He wanted to shut me out.'

'He thought he was doing the right thing,' said Lola.

'Spare me from people who think they're doing the right thing!' cried Bey. 'Because they very rarely are.' She said nothing more for a moment, then looked up at her mother again. 'When I asked and asked and you finally gave in and contacted Dad . . . what happened to your stupid agreement?'

'The money stopped, of course,' said Lola. 'Richard was a man of his word.'

Bey's eyes widened.

'But when they invited you for Christmas, I thought that perhaps he'd had a change of heart. Or that your dad wanted to take some responsibility for you.'

'So you sent me there for money too!' cried Bey. 'I didn't want to go but you thought it was a good deal?'

'Of course not!' Lola was close to tears. 'I never would've done that. I wanted what was right for you. I thought I'd been wrong before and so if your dad felt . . . if he wanted . . . I thought if they saw what a great person you were, they'd love you as much as I did and things might be different.'

'I don't understand you at all,' said Bey. 'All my life I thought you were as straight as a die. But now . . . now I can't help thinking that every choice you made was based around what the Warrens could do for you.'

'If I'd wanted that, I would've gone to your father as soon

421

as I found out about you,' Lola said. 'I would've begged him to marry me.'

Bey shook her head. 'I can't process this,' she said. 'All these things going on in the background of my life that I didn't know about. Secrets and deals and hiding away and . . . It's too hard. I have to . . .' She got to her feet and picked up her bag.

'Where are you going?' asked Lola.

Bey didn't reply.

'Bey, please!'

She walked out of the house and slammed the door behind her.

Lola sat on the two-seater sofa and stared unseeingly ahead of her. Somehow she'd known that one day it would all come crashing down around her. That her bad decisions would be seen as exactly that and not the justifiable ones she'd always imagined they were. What had given her the right to keep Philip in the dark about Bey for so long? And what had given her the right to keep Bey in the dark about Richard's involvement? The fact that he hadn't wanted her to say anything was totally irrelevant and had only stored up more trouble. Including the trouble with Adele, which had made the old battleaxe resent Bey even more.

Oh God, thought Lola. Her foolishness had hurt everyone who'd ever known her. Even her parents, who'd wanted nothing but the best for her but who'd had to put up with the gossip and innuendo when she'd turned up at the farm with a bump and no boyfriend.

Why was she such an idiot? Even now?

* * *

It was almost midnight and Bey had been working on the bracelet since she'd let herself into the workshop.

Now she was polishing it; first with fine sandpaper, then a series of silicone wheels to bring up the shine. As she attached the pink wheel to the flex shaft, her mobile rang. Lola's name came up on the screen. It was the fourth call since Bey had left the house. She ignored it like all the others.

Then the doorbell buzzed. She got up and peeped through the small window. Her mother was standing outside holding two takeaway coffees.

Bey hesitated for a moment, then opened the door and let her in.

'You weren't answering your phone,' said Lola. 'It's late and I was worried about you.'

'Oh for heaven's sake!' exclaimed Bey. 'Did you just ring from the street?'

'I'm sorry,' said Lola. 'I messed it all up. My life. Your life. Everyone's lives.'

'Y'know, that's something that Dad might be right about.' Bey moved aside to allow her mother in. 'He said you were a drama queen. That you were obsessed with the past. And you probably are. You didn't mess up anyone's life. We're all perfectly capable of doing that ourselves.'

Lola handed Bey a coffee then sat on the chair in the corner of the room. Bey returned to her seat at the workbench.

'I have to finish this,' she said as she placed the coffee to one side.

'I'll wait for you,' said Lola.

'Whatever.'

Lola watched as Bey put on her safety goggles and dust

423

mask before continuing to work on the bracelet. She didn't speak and Bey took no notice of her as she worked. Finally she switched off the flex shaft, pushed her goggles from her face, removed her mask and examined the bracelet.

'It's beautiful,' said Lola. 'It's a pity people don't realise how much work goes into each one.'

'All most of us care about is how things look on the surface,' said Bey. 'Same with families really, don't you think?'

'I should have told you everything,' said Lola. 'I'm sorry.'

'Everything?' Bey began to wash her hands at the sink. 'What more could there be? I'm really Aunt Gretta's daughter? Dad sold the farm to the Warrens? Adele is an alien?'

'Nothing quite so dramatic,' said Lola. 'But you need to know about your grandfather. He didn't want me to tell you about the money. Like I said, he stopped paying it after you met your dad. But . . .'

'Oh God, what?' demanded Bey.

'But he stayed in touch with me. He knew it wasn't working out with your dad but he wanted to know how you were getting on. When you left school, he was delighted when you decided on jewellery design. He thought that maybe one day you might end up with Warren's. He . . . I'd put the money he'd given me into a fund for your college fees. That's how we were able to pay them. But Richard started to give me money again. To pay for your accommodation.'

'You told me you'd got a tax break for that!' cried Bey.

'He still didn't want you to know.'

'What is *wrong* with you people?' demanded her daughter. 'Why shouldn't I have known? Anything else?'

'Well . . .'

Bey looked at her mother in complete exasperation.

'That first time, he also gave me something for myself,' Lola admitted. 'He called it a sweetener.'

'He was paying you separately?'

'No,' said Lola. 'He gave me the Bluebells.'

Bey's fingers went to her ears.

'These Bluebells?' she exclaimed.

Lola nodded. For the first time she explained about leaving Dublin not realising she was wearing them, and the Warrens' fear that she'd stolen them – and her belief that for a long time they still believed she'd tried.

Bey took the earrings from her ears and looked at them. 'So that's it,' she said slowly. 'That's why Adele thought . . .'

'Thought what?' asked Lola.

'I heard her say it was in my genes,' explained Bey. 'That Christmas. I was sitting on the stairs and they were talking about me and Astrid's ring and she said "like mother, like daughter" and I thought maybe you'd once taken something from them and they knew about it only nobody talked about it.'

'Oh!'

'I didn't actually believe you'd stolen anything,' Bey said. 'But I thought they'd decided you had . . . It was part of the reason I ran away. I wanted to get home to you before they started phoning up and saying that we were a family of jewel thieves and they were going to report us to the police.'

'Is that why you didn't want to go to the Garda station after your abduction?' Lola's eyes were wide.

Bey nodded.

'Oh God. I never realised. I didn't think . . .'

'I was worried they'd start investigating you and arrest

you even though deep down I knew you couldn't possibly have done anything wrong. I thought if that happened I'd be left in Dad's care. But they all hated me so it would've been awful. I didn't want you to go to prison either. And I knew Granny and Grandad would be really upset too. I was afraid they'd never ask us to Cloghdrom again.'

'Oh, Bey.' Lola was distressed. 'If only I'd said something before.'

'It sounds mad now and like I was keeping secrets of my own, but in my defence I *was* only twelve,' Bey added.

Lola's expression was stricken.

'I was going to ask you more about the Bluebells when you gave them to me,' Bey told her. 'You said you'd been given them too and I wondered about it. But you sort of avoided the issue and I didn't want to drag it up in case it was something you didn't want to talk about.' She rolled the sapphires around in her palm.

'Richard gave them to me in an enormous padded envelope,' said Lola. 'Naturally I thought it was cash. I felt wrong about opening it. So for months I didn't. But on the first day we moved into the house in Ringsend, the central heating boiler packed in. The guy who came around to fix it said he'd do a better deal for cash. So I thought of Richard's envelope. I got a shock when I opened it.'

She hadn't quite believed her eyes when she'd seen the earrings. And the note from Richard saying that they were hers to keep no matter what. *I gave my wife a piece of jewellery after the birth of both my children*, he'd written. *It seems only fair that I should do the same for the birth of a grandchild.*

'Oh.' Bey's hand closed around the earrings. 'I hate him and love him at the same time.'

426

'I offered to give them back after I got in touch with your father,' she said. 'But Richard pointed out that I might need them in the future. He said that a piece of Warren's jewellery was an heirloom. That perhaps one day I'd want to pass them on to you. And when you went to college, I did.'

'You said you sent me to Cleevaun because you thought Richard might be having a change of heart. Or that Dad might want to take responsibility for me. Did he? Financially, I mean. Do I owe him too? As well as Grandfather.'

'Obviously everything went a bit pear shaped after that Christmas,' said Lola. 'I didn't speak to your dad for ages. When he heard you were going to counselling, he offered to pay for it but I told him I was doing fine and didn't need anything. He didn't know back then that your grandfather had paid me anything at all. He didn't know about the earrings either.'

'What was Adele's role in all of this?' asked Bey. 'Was she part of the agreement?'

Lola pursed her lips.

'Was she?' demanded Bey.

'Not at first,' said Lola. 'But she found out some time later because she went through the accounts and saw the debit going out to me every month. She thought . . .' She took a deep breath before continuing. 'She thought Richard was having an affair with me.'

'That's absolutely gross!' cried Bey. She looked anxiously at her mother. 'You weren't, were you?'

'Exactly what sort of a woman d'you think I am?' demanded Lola. 'Of course I bloody wasn't. But Adele . . . well, her father had left her mother for a younger girl and ruined the family business. She thought Richard might be doing the same thing. It was one of the reasons she didn't want me involved with Philip in the first place. Apparently I reminded her of this Sophie person.'

'No!'

'I didn't know that, of course,' said Lola. 'Your grandfather and I didn't speak about Adele very much. But then I bumped into her at the hospital. Your grandfather had gone in for his bypass surgery and I was visiting him.'

'Was that not a crazy thing to do?' asked Bey. 'Wasn't there always the chance you'd cross paths with her?'

'I checked there was nobody with him. And he thought she wasn't coming in till later. But obviously she was furious when she saw me there and told me in no uncertain terms what to do with myself. After I left, she and Richard had a fight.'

'I'm not surprised.'

'The fight wasn't about me coming to visit him,' said Lola. 'It was because . . . because when Adele saw me at the hospital, she was convinced that one of her other suspicions was actually true. She was afraid you were his child.'

Bey looked at her mother in horror. 'I always wondered why she seemed so angry with me all the time. As though there was something she could never quite forgive me for. D'you think she still feels . . . Ugh, I don't even want to think about it!'

'I can't imagine she does,' said Lola. 'But she's the sort of person who would have hated to even have the thought.'

'I hate that she had it too!' cried Bey.

'She was crazy about Richard, you know. I don't think she seriously believed he'd betrayed her, but she couldn't understand why he wanted to help us if he didn't have an ulterior motive. Anyhow, I only spoke to Richard once more after that. He hoped he'd convinced her how silly she'd been. And now you're up to speed on all my past history and dodgy deals,' Lola ended. 'I understand if you're disappointed in me.'

'I'll never be disappointed in you,' said Bey. 'You're still the strongest, bravest woman I know. But . . . but I really do owe the Warrens.' Her expression was troubled. 'Grandfather's money meant I was able to do what I wanted to do. Without him – and without you saving it for me – I wouldn't have been able to go to Birmingham. I wouldn't have had the qualifications to get the job at Van Aelten. Or even to set up my business. And of course it was coming back for his funeral that helped me to find out about Raymond Fenton too. He's been there for me every step of the way, even though I didn't know it. And even though he's dead.'

'I didn't tell you this to make you feel as though you had to take the job with them,' said Lola. 'I told you because . . . because I should have told you before.'

'Yes,' said Bey. 'You really should.'

'Are you coming home tonight?' Lola looked at her anxiously.

'You know, I definitely have to get a place of my own,' said Bey. 'You were married with a kid at my age. I'm a grown-up and I've been sponging off you all my life.'

Lola said nothing.

'But for now . . .' Bey put her arm around her mother's shoulder and hugged her. 'For now, it's still you and me together – and where else would I go?'

Chapter 34

Pavé: stones set close together showing no metal between them

It was Terry, Lola's boyfriend, who said that the least Bey could do was see what kind of contract the Warrens planned on giving her before she made a final decision on whether to work for them.

'Go in with a game plan,' he said. 'Ask for a lot of money. Remember that your skills are valuable, that you're a professional person, and that they've come to you, not the other way around.'

'But they're a very important brand,' she pointed out. 'And the Adele range is a classic.'

'And floundering,' said Terry. 'You're in a strong position here, Bey. You've got to press home your advantage. If they're prepared to accept your terms, then you can think about it seriously. But there's no point in getting yourself into knots until you know.'

She'd been far too excited at the job offer from Van Aelten and Schaap to even consider the terms and conditions. She'd happily accepted their initial offer without question, just as she'd accepted the intern job with Jurado's before that, thinking that she was lucky to be working for such great companies in the first place. She wasn't used to having the advantage, she told Terry. She wasn't used to negotiating anything.

'Other than the lease on your workshop,' he reminded her. 'And a start-up loan from the bank.'

'A very small loan,' she pointed out.

'You negotiated it all the same,' he said.

But it would be totally different with her father. Even though she had the skills he wanted, she was sure he still thought of her as his troublesome daughter. Nevertheless, she listened to Terry's advice, and when she met Philip a few days later, once again in the Westbury Hotel, she did as he'd suggested and laid out her terms and conditions as clearly and concisely as she could.

'You can't possibly be earning that sort of money selling silver trinkets to the masses,' said Philip when he heard the salary she wanted. 'You're being totally unreasonable.'

'It's what I was paid as chief designer at Van Aelten and Schaap,' she told him.

'Why did you leave them if they were giving you such an outrageous amount?' demanded Philip when he recovered from the shock. 'What on earth made you come back here to faff about?'

'I'm not faffing about,' said Bey. 'I'm building up a business. I decided it was what I wanted to do. And as I told you, I'll need a certain amount of time made available so that I can continue to work on that too. I have an assistant, but she's not very experienced.'

'You want to be paid a full-time salary for a part-time position?'

Was this part of the negotiation? wondered Bey. What should she allow him to shave off her demand to make it worthwhile? She tried not to let her anxiety show as she told him that she'd be giving far more time to Warren's than Bijou for Bey, but that she still needed to oversee her own business.

'We have a deadline for the collection,' said Philip. 'We need your undivided attention.'

'I can multitask, you know.' Bey realised that she was now trying to persuade him. That perhaps she did want the job after all. 'I can give tons of undivided attention to the Warren collection while still allowing some time for my own stuff,' she added.

'I don't know if it'll work,' said Philip. 'It's not what I had in mind.'

'It doesn't matter to me if I work for you or not,' Bey told him. 'In fact, I have serious reservations about getting involved with Warren's at all.'

'This is a great opportunity for you,' said Philip. 'You should be pleased we even thought of you.'

'I don't need your opportunities.' Bey suddenly realised that she believed what she was saying. That she believed in herself. There was more determination in her voice as she continued. 'I've done a pretty good job of making my own. I haven't been waiting around for you to think of me. Which is fortunate,' she added, 'because if I'd done that all my life, I wouldn't have got very far.'

'This is business, not personal,' said her father.

'I know.' Bey fixed her clear blue eyes on him. 'And you should be having this discussion in a businesslike way instead of talking to me as though I'm still twelve and making beaded necklaces in my bedroom.'

432

'All I'm saying is that you're demanding the kind of money—'

'That a professional earns,' she interrupted him. 'Now either you're interested or you're not. I don't mind which, but I don't want to waste my time sitting here being lectured by you.'

'I'll have to talk to Peter before I agree to anything,' said Philip.

'I thought you already had,' said Bey. 'And what about Adele? Have you spoken to her yet?'

'No,' admitted her father. 'I wanted to get the package agreed first.'

'The package I want?' asked Bey.

'I'll recommend it to Peter, but I can't be sure he'll accept it. It's way more than we would have offered Darren Daly.'

'You had to pay him for the outlines he gave you, though, I presume?'

'Of course.'

'You should've come to me first,' she said. 'You would've saved money that way.'

She took a sip from her cup of tea. It was almost cold and she replaced it on the saucer without taking any more.

'Have you had any design ideas since I first made the suggestion?' asked Philip to break the silence that had descended on them. 'Or do you charge for those too?'

Bey still couldn't help thinking that she wouldn't be designing anything for them if Adele had her way, but she considered the question anyhow.

'You'll want some statement pieces for which we'll have to source stones,' she replied. 'And there'll be other—'

'We don't look for stones ourselves any more,' said Philip

before she could go any further. 'The people who make our jewellery know what we need already.'

'This is a new collection,' Bey reminded him. 'Completely different. We'll have to get the right stones for it. Yes, there'll be core pieces that'll just need bog-standard diamonds – if you can call any diamond bog standard. But you want bespoke pieces too, don't you? Or am I wrong? Is this just some kind of marketing exercise for you? Aren't you serious about it?'

'Of course we're serious,' said Philip.

'Yet you don't seem to have thought it through properly. Either in terms of what you can offer me or in terms of what you want me to design for you.'

Philip stared at her in astonishment. When he'd offered her the job he'd thought she'd be grateful and he'd also thought he'd be the one calling the shots. But he'd totally underestimated her. He was beginning to wonder if he'd bitten off more than he could chew.

'We've thought it through enough,' he said. 'And we'll have detailed conversations before you start.'

'*If* I start,' she amended.

Philip felt himself grow even more tense. This wasn't going anything like he imagined. And he didn't know whether to be pleased or not.

'*If* I start,' she repeated to Lola later when she was telling her about the meeting.

'You're like a different person all of a sudden,' said Lola. 'And I don't mean that in a bad way. It's like everything is crystal clear to you and you know exactly what you want. Were you like this in London?'

'I might have been.' Bey was feeling more relaxed than

earlier. 'But it's also thanks to Terry. He made me feel like I was worth something after all. He's amazing, Mum. You're lucky to have him. As for the rest – I guess I learned how things should be done when I was with Van Aelten and Schaap. I know I can do something great for the Warrens. What I don't know is if they'll ever allow me to try.'

Philip rang the following day to say that they'd like to have a family meeting with her at Adele's house in Rathgar. Bey replied by saying that it was a business meeting and she wasn't going to have it in anyone's house, but that they were welcome to come to her workshop. Philip said that Adele wouldn't dream of visiting a converted garage. Bey then compromised by saying that she'd be happy to come to the Duke Lane shop.

The following day she stood outside the building, looking at the windows with interest. They certainly knew how to show their jewellery to best advantage, she thought. But no amount of stylish displays would make her like the fussy Adele Pansy.

She pressed the bell on the door and was buzzed inside. It was the first time she'd been inside the shop, and she looked around, comparing it to Van Aelten and Schaap in Bond Street and thinking that even though the Warrens were stuck in the past with the Adele range, the store itself was stylish and welcoming. Her father's office was more utilitarian, and when she arrived there was only just enough space left for her at the desk, the other seats having already been taken by Adele, Peter and Anthony.

All of them looked at her intently as she greeted them.

'Well,' said Adele. 'This isn't a day I ever thought I'd see.'

'Me neither,' said Bey.

'I'm not convinced it's a good idea,' added Adele.

'But it's good to know you're open to it,' said Bey as calmly as she could. The last person she wanted to antagonise today was Adele, no matter how much Adele might annoy her. She realised, with some surprise, that she was suddenly feeling sorry for the older woman.

'Look, we're here to thrash out whether Bey is the right person to take Warren's forward,' said Philip. 'I know there are reservations on both sides. I want to assure Bey that if she comes on board, we'll fully support her.'

'And I want to be assured that she knows what she's doing and won't sabotage our family heritage,' said Adele.

'You think I'd do something like that?' Bey said. 'Really?'

'I don't know,' replied Adele. 'I'm aware that you have a certain unjustified level of resentment towards us.'

'I promise you I don't,' said Bey. 'If there's any unjustified resentment, or suspicion, it's not coming from me, Adele.'

There was a moment's silence during which Adele stared at her while Philip and Peter looked anxiously between them and Anthony tapped at the open iPad in front of him.

'Look,' said Bey, when none of them spoke. 'My father made a proposal to me and I gave him terms. I care very much about what I do and the last thing I'm thinking of is creating something that would impact negatively on my future career, which I can assure you will be far away from Warren's.'

'So you're looking on us as a springboard to catapult yourself back into the kind of job that you left for reasons that are unclear to us?' Adele's voice was like cut glass.

'Why I left is nothing to do with any of you,' said Bey. 'But if you're thinking that there was some sinister reason for my departure, then there's such a lack of trust between us that there isn't a hope of me ever working for you.' She pushed back her chair and stood up. 'I'm sorry,' she said as she turned to her father. 'But if Grandmother detests me so much that she wants to believe the worst of me, there's no point in even talking about this any more.'

She left the office and closed the door firmly behind her. She was walking out of the shop when he caught up with her.

'Please,' he said. 'Mum doesn't mean half of what she says. Come back. Let's talk about it.'

'Why?' asked Bey. 'Why should I sit there and be judged by you all when I don't need to be? Why should I watch her looking at me as if I were some kind of viper come to poison you all? She may have her personal grudges, but I don't have to put up with them.'

'I agree that my mother has a . . . an unreasonable amount of hostility towards you,' said Philip. 'I don't understand it myself. But you'll be working for me and reporting to me and she won't – can't – interfere.'

He didn't know that Adele had accused Richard of having an affair with Lola, thought Bey. He'd been kept in the dark too. In fact, she realised, more secrets had been kept from Philip than from anyone else.

'I understand there are fears and resentments and all sorts of things going on,' she said. 'But I shouldn't have to prove myself to all of you when I've already proved myself to other people, and when Anthony has a job that involves playing some stupid game on his iPad when he should be focusing on what's at stake.'

'You're really not the person I thought you were at all,'

said Philip. 'I've underestimated your professionalism. We all have. I'm sorry, Bey. Please come back.'

She stood undecided at the entrance to the shop, looking at the diamonds and rubies sparkling beneath the halogen lights. Leaving Van Aelten and Schaap had been a decision based on her personal, not her professional, life. Walking out on the Warrens would be exactly the same kind of decision. Professionally, working for them would be a wonderful opportunity. But on a personal level . . . on a personal level she wanted to run away.

And then she remembered running away from them before. Which had only made things worse.

'If I go back up there, you'll have to agree to my terms without question,' she told Philip in a voice that wasn't quite steady. 'I'm not sitting there listening to your mother argue for me to be paid less than I'm worth.'

'Done,' said Philip.

'And I'll want the time I need to ensure my own business maintains its clients,' she added more firmly. 'I'll need to help my assistant even though I know she's very capable. I find that most women are, despite what many men think.'

'Is this a woman versus man thing now?' asked Philip.

'Not really,' Bey said. 'It's personal versus professional. And professional has to win out.'

He nodded and held out his hand. She took a deep breath, then shook it and followed him upstairs again.

The low hum of conversation stopped when they walked into the office together. Philip told them that he'd agreed to Bey's terms, which, he said, were perfectly reasonable for someone with her skills and experience. Nobody, not even Adele, objected.

'Good,' said Bey. 'Now, let's get one or two things clear about where we want to go from here. From what Philip tells me, the Adele range has flatlined, the stores are losing money and you want new designs to lift things. The latest ones you were shown didn't do the trick—'

'Actually I thought they were very pretty,' Adele interrupted her. 'They probably only need to be tweaked a little.'

Bey turned to her. 'You want more than simply pretty,' she told her grandmother. 'You *need* something more than simply pretty if you want to be iconic again.'

'Well, I—'

'Mum.' Peter was the one who interrupted this time. 'Enough. We're paying for Bey's expertise. Let her give it to us.'

'Thank you.' Bey smiled at her uncle. 'Anyhow, what I was going to say is that new designs on their own won't necessarily help. You've got to see what else might not be working.'

'I've done that already,' said Peter. 'We've cut back in a lot of areas. We've closed the least profitable stores. We—'

'Peter, we're employing Bey as a designer, not a manager.' Adele's tone was sharp. 'She doesn't need to know anything about the business. All she has to do is come up with something saleable. If she can.'

'That's true, of course,' said Bey. 'But design takes time. Sourcing the stones takes time. It's important to know that the business isn't going to fold before we're ready. And that we have a plan for the future too.'

'That's for us to worry about,' said Adele. 'Your role is clear. And it seems to me that we've been forced into paying you exceptionally well for it.'

'You wanted the best,' said Bey. 'You're getting it.'

'You're very arrogant.' Anthony put his iPad on the desk.

'Van Aelten still have a waiting list for the Cascade,' said Peter. 'She has a right to be arrogant.'

'I don't want to be arrogant,' said Bey. 'But I do think I know a lot about this business. However, what I'd like from you now is any old brochures you have on the Adele collections. I want to get a feel for Warren's.'

'If you don't already have a feel for it, you never will!' cried Adele.

Bey stood up. 'My father and I have agreed terms, but unless you all want me here, this won't work.' She looked straight at her grandmother. 'Adele, you have to get over whatever your issues are about me. I've got over the ones I've had about you, after all. Make up your minds and let me know by this afternoon. Working for Warren's will be as much of a gamble for me as it is for you.'

Then she picked up her bag and left the room for a second time.

'Well, really,' said Adele. 'That girl is way too big for her boots. You'd think she was doing us a favour.'

'She is,' said Peter.

'Don't be stupid,' said Anthony. 'She has a hobby shop in a laneway, for heaven's sake. It's beneath us and what we stand for. So is she. I don't know why you even thought about her.'

'Anthony!' Philip's voice was grim. 'Shut the hell up. You don't know what you're talking about. And put that damn iPad away.'

'Are you trying to make it up to her somehow, Dad?'

asked Anthony. 'Is it guilt on your part for not being there for her? For what happened that Christmas? Even though none of it was your fault?'

'Not everything has to be about the fact that we have a rocky history!' cried Philip. 'It's good business, that's all. We have home-grown talent on our doorstep and we have the chance to use it.'

'Phil's right,' said Peter. 'And given everything that's gone before, I'm amazed she's even thinking about it.'

'I don't trust her,' said Adele. 'Or her mother.'

'Oh for crying out loud, Mum.' Philip tapped the keyboard in front of him and the screen lit up with an image of a diamond necklace that was gossamer-like in its delicacy. 'This is the Cascade necklace,' he said as he looked at Adele and Anthony in turn. 'It followed the successful Cascade pendant and was a massive seller the year it launched. We know it's still a massive seller. It was designed by my daughter, *your* granddaughter and *your* half-sister – Bey Fitzpatrick. It was worn by the Duquesa de Olvera y Montecalmón on her wedding day. It's been featured in luxury magazines around the world. The tiara that the Duquesa wore was also designed by Bey Fitzpatrick. And you think she'd be the lucky one to be working for us?'

'We still don't know why she left them,' said Adele.

'I spoke to Gerritt Van Aelten yesterday evening,' said Philip. 'They were devastated when she handed in her notice. He said it was for personal reasons and nothing to do with her job.'

'We all know that employers can't say anything bad about people these days,' said Adele. 'They can be sued.'

'God Almighty!' Peter was so annoyed he banged his fist

on the table, startling everybody. 'We have the chance to have someone skilled and talented to design a range we hope will get us back to where we were before, and we're arguing about her motivations. Are you crazy, Mum, or just senile?'

The atmosphere in the room crackled. Nobody spoke. Then Adele leaned forward and tapped at the keyboard again. More images of the Cascade range scrolled across the screen. Her face remained expressionless.

'All right,' she said eventually. 'I agree. But she has to keep us up to date all the time. And we get approval for the design.'

'Naturally we have to approve it,' said Philip. 'What d'you take me for?'

'And we don't make a big thing about her being here,' added his mother. 'I can imagine that the media would like to run with some story about the prodigal daughter working for us. But she's not the story. We are.'

'I don't think she cares about that,' said Philip.

'You've become very sympathetic towards her all of a sudden,' said Anthony.

'She can help us,' said his father. 'She's the one doing us the favour, not the other way around. It took me a while to realise that. You have to realise it too.'

Bey was in her workshop when her phone rang.

'I'm sorry about earlier,' said Philip. 'I should have ensured that the meeting was a briefing and not . . . well, whatever it ended up being.'

'Yes, you should,' said Bey.

'But we're all sorted now. Everyone's on board. So if you're still OK with it, we want you to work for us on the terms we already agreed. You'll have time to spend on your own lines too – although you have to realise that Warren's takes priority. And we have to approve your designs.'

'Of course,' said Bey.

'Welcome to the family firm,' said Philip.

Bey released a slow breath.

'Thanks,' was all she said.

Lola was both pleased and apprehensive about the situation. Pleased that Bey had been offered a great job again. Apprehensive that it was with Warren's. Pleased that Philip had thought of her. Apprehensive about Adele's reaction. Pleased that her daughter would be doing something she loved. Apprehensive that it wouldn't work and that the fallout would be catastrophic.

'If it works, it works; if it doesn't, it doesn't,' said Bey, in such an offhand tone that Lola could hardly believe it.

'Aren't you excited? And worried?'

'Both,' admitted Bey. 'But the worry is about Bijou by Bey and hoping Liesel will be able to cope.'

'But the design? A whole new collection? For a company like Warren's! Aren't you worried about that?' asked Lola.

Bey looked at her, her expression serene.

'No,' she replied. 'This is what I do. This is who I am. Of all the things I'm worried about, coming up with a design is at the bottom of the list.'

She didn't feel quite as blasé when she sat down to think seriously about it. She already had ideas rattling around in her head, but as she stared at the mood board in her workshop, she knew that nothing there was right for the new range. She looked through Warren's past sales brochures. She went for walks around the city and sat in St Stephen's Green people-watching. She thought about the past and the present and the future and about Warren's place in it. And then she thought about her grandmother, an octogenarian but as cool and as cutting as ever. Still icily elegant. Still convinced she was right about everything. Still steely. Outvoted at the meeting, but not keeping her opinions to herself. Strong. Determined. Intractable.

The Ice Dragon, Lola called her.

It was a good name.

Bey took out her notebook and began to draw.

The Ice Dragon
Now

Chapter 35

Topaz: a hard refractive gemstone of many colours

There weren't enough hours in the day. Bey was getting up at six in the morning and going to bed at midnight. She divided her time between her Ice Dragon designs and liaising with Liesel in the workshop, making sure that their orders were being filled on time. She lived and breathed jewellery. Lola worried that she was working too hard, and even more that she'd broken off her relationship with Lorcan because he was so far down her list of priorities, but Bey didn't care.

'It's not like work to me,' she told her mother. 'I love what I'm doing. And as for Lorcan – well, I didn't love him enough.'

Lola winced at the phrase. She could hardly criticise her daughter for getting back to the thing she liked doing most. And she had to admit that she hadn't seen her so happy since she'd returned from London.

When Bey was finally certain that she had a strong central theme and pieces to go with it, she asked Philip to come to the workshop. She wanted to present them to him in her own space, and not surrounded by the history of Warren's.

'Will I bring Peter and Mum too?' he asked. 'Anthony is in Cork, but I could get him here by tomorrow.'

'I thought Adele wouldn't lower herself to visit a run-down garage,' she said with a hint of humour.

'I can make her come,' said Philip.

'Actually I'd prefer if we started with you and me together,' said Bey. 'If you hate everything then I won't have to listen to her telling us both what a mistake this was.'

Philip laughed. 'OK,' he said. 'This afternoon?'

'See you then.'

She'd sounded relaxed talking to him, but her anxiety ratcheted up as she waited for him to arrive. She'd always been anxious when showing new designs at Van Aelten and Schaap, but this was different. It had never been so important to her to get something right. Every other design she'd shown had been personal to her, but the backdrop had been entirely professional. This time, no matter what she'd said before, it was impossible to separate the two. She wanted the Warrens to know that she'd done a good job. She wanted them to see her not as the twelve-year-old jewel thief they'd always considered her to be, but as someone who was totally committed to their success. But she was acutely aware that not everybody was convinced that she was the right person to entrust with the fate of the family firm.

She swallowed the lump that had suddenly appeared in her throat and scrolled through her drawings again. She'd had a long conversation with both her father and Peter about what they were trying to achieve, the budget they had to work with and the likely cost of the type of stones they might use. She was sure that what she'd come up with ticked all the boxes, both commercially and creatively. But they might have entirely different ideas. As for Adele . . . it didn't matter that she wasn't in charge any more. Bey was quite sure her grandmother's opinion carried more weight than anyone else's.

The bell rang and she went to answer it.

'Come in,' she said, as Philip crossed the threshold and followed her into the workshop.

He stopped to look at the silver and costume jewellery in her display cases, remarking that it was very pretty and that it was interesting how she managed to work on both high-end and affordable pieces at the same time.

'I told you I could multitask,' she reminded him. 'Would you like coffee?'

'Yes please,' said Philip.

She popped a capsule into the coffee machine her grandmother had sent her. Eilis had been intrigued by the new development in her granddaughter's career, and phoned every so often to find out how things were coming along. Bey's only complaint had been about the quality of the coffee she was practically mainlining, and she'd been both amused and delighted when the top-of-the-range machine was delivered a few days later.

'OK,' she said as she handed him the coffee. 'Let's talk about the collection.' She traced her finger over the trackpad beside her and the large display screen came to life. 'I've called it Ice Dragon.'

Philip looked startled. 'It's an Adele collection,' he said. 'You can't change the name.'

'The Adele collections are all based on flowers,' Bey reminded him. 'You already know they're dated. So why on earth would I do the same thing?'

'I thought . . .'

'You thought you'd hired me to come up with a range of pieces that were the same as before but with slight variations?' Bey said. 'Don't be silly, that's not what you wanted. What you wanted was something completely different, and that's what you're getting. But,' she added, 'still based on Adele's personality. Cold on the outside but with a heart of fire. Or maybe it's the other way around.'

'That's how you see her?'

'She has the personality of an iceberg,' said Bey. 'But that's not the cool I'm talking about. I'm talking about her sophistication, which, in fairness, is beyond question. And as for her strength – she can flay anyone with a single word from her mouth. So I think the name is perfect.'

'Maybe you have a point,' conceded Philip with a slight smile. 'But we can't call the collection Ice Dragon. It's not pretty, like Adele Rose or Adele Bouquet.'

'Let's move on from what it's called for a minute and look at the designs.' Bey tapped the trackpad. 'It's important to get the name right, but you need to look at the concept first.'

Philip shrugged and looked at the screen. Then his eyes widened.

'Oh!' he exclaimed as the first image appeared. 'That's . . . unbelievable.'

The diamonds and rubies of the necklace formed an exquisite off-centre drop, while the stones themselves seemed to float above the fine gold links. It was both cool and sophisticated while almost glowing with life.

'Here it is with sapphires.' She flicked to the next image. 'And with emeralds.'

'They're amazing,' said Philip. 'Utterly amazing. But they're completely unique and with those stones very expensive. We won't be able to sell many of them.'

'Obviously these are the statement pieces, the ones that will be for the very few. For the core of the collection, this is what I have in mind.'

She continued to scroll through images. This time the gems, a mixture of precious and semi-precious, were smaller, but every pendant, ring and bracelet seemed to radiate intensity, and had the same ethereal balance between form and function as the luxurious necklaces.

'How fabulous they look in the end will depend on getting the right stones, and that'll be extremely important for the signature pieces because they'll be made to order. But for the rest, the prices should start at around three thousand, which is what Peter wanted,' said Bey. 'Haute joaillerie is like haute couture – you might not be able to afford the evening gown but you can splash out on the branded lipstick. In this case you can't afford the necklace but you could treat yourself to the earrings. Anyway, as you can see, the other pieces follow the same theme but with fewer stones. Even though the reds, blues and greens are the most striking, I've also added some with pink tourmalines and topaz – not quite as dragony, mind you, but very pretty, I think.'

Philip was scrolling back through the images.

'They're unlike anything I've ever seen before,' he said.

'Well of course,' said Bey. 'You wanted something unique. That's what you're getting. If you go with them, I'll need to meet with the goldsmiths you have in mind and talk through the design with them. We used different ones at Van Aelten and Schaap depending on the pieces.'

Philip nodded absently as he continued to move between images.

'We'll sort all that out when we decide on these,' he said. Then he looked up at her again. 'They're so completely . . . well . . . not like the other Adeles.'

'That's the idea,' said Bey.

'It's just I didn't expect . . . Seeing these . . . imagining us putting them out there . . . thinking of what Mum will say . . .' Philip grimaced.

'You're afraid of her?' Bey looked at her father enquiringly.

'You know what she's like. And truthfully – yes, I'm afraid of telling her you've called her the Ice Dragon. But,' he added as he finally stopped scrolling, 'dammit, you're right – it's a perfect name for them.'

'If you hate them . . .' Bey sighed and clicked on the computer, 'I have more traditional designs for you to look at. I didn't refine them, they're just ideas. And I haven't come up with another name.'

The images that opened reminded Philip very much of the earliest Adele collections – Bey had gone with a more modern take on the Rose, Zinnia and Bluebell. They were very elegant and Philip knew that his mother would love them. He loved them too. But he also knew that they didn't have the wow factor of the Ice Dragon set.

'You're exceptional,' he said. 'I'm sorry I never realised it before.'

'Why would you? You don't even know me.'

'I'm sorry about that too. I'd like to say it wasn't entirely my fault, but even if Lola had told me about being pregnant, I was so angry with her for not wanting to marry me that I would've told her to sod off anyhow.'

'Would you?'

'Yes,' said Philip. 'Nobody had ever said no to me before, you see.'

'Not even Adele?'

'Well, yes, my mother was always saying no. But outside of that, I was a Warren. I was invincible. If I'd asked any of my previous girlfriends to marry me, they would have.'

'You were a babe magnet?' Bey couldn't help smiling.

'I thought so. But it was probably the money. I'm not that great a person really,' said Philip.

'I don't suppose you're any worse than the rest of us,' said Bey. 'We all want to believe that we do the right thing and behave the best way all the time, but faced with circumstances – we don't.'

She thought again of the way she'd behaved with Will Murdoch and felt a stab of pain and regret in her heart. But if she hadn't kissed him, she wouldn't have come home and wouldn't have had this opportunity. And it had helped her to get a bit closer to her father, which had to be a good thing. Maybe it was all for the best, she told herself.

'You've been brilliant.' Philip didn't notice that she'd lapsed into her own world for a moment. 'You've taken everything we've thrown at you on the chin and you've produced some really fine work. Thank you.'

'You're welcome,' she said.

'I suppose I only ever saw the differences between us before,' said Philip. 'I never looked for the similarities. And yet I can see the Warren side of you now.'

'I'm a Fitzpatrick,' she told him. 'I always will be. But I'm happy to have done these for you. It was an interesting challenge.'

'You're part of the team,' said Philip. 'And we'll still need you to be part of it when they're being made.'

'Adele has to approve them first.'

'She will,' said Philip.

Bey hoped he was right. If it were anyone else, she'd be confident. But with Adele she wasn't sure at all.

'Ice Dragon!' Adele looked at her two sons, her face tight with anger. 'After me! How dare she?'

'It's a perfect name,' said Peter. 'When you look at the pieces—'

'Everyone knows the Adele range is all about flowers and beauty and elegance!' cried Adele. 'Not . . . not . . . whatever it is that "Ice Dragon" conjures up.'

Peter and Philip exchanged glances.

'What?' demanded Adele. 'You think it describes me? It most certainly does not. And these necklaces, clever though they might be, are nothing, absolutely nothing, in comparison to the Snowdrop or the Rose.'

'They're for a different market, Mum,' said Philip. 'A market that's passing us by. People's tastes have moved on.'

'They've been buying Adele rings for over thirty years,' said Adele.

'The whole reason we asked Bey to design something for us was because people haven't been buying the Adele ranges the way they once did,' Philip pointed out. 'We've fallen behind. You know that already.'

'We wanted it revitalised,' said Adele. 'Not butchered.'

'She hasn't butchered it,' said Philip. 'She's reimagined it.'

'And within the parameters I gave her,' said Peter. 'She's

very clued in on the cost of stones and settings and how things are done. I was sure we'd have an argument about what she wanted to use, but even with the one-off pieces she's been very pragmatic. In fact she's startlingly businesslike about it.'

'We don't want pragmatism!' cried Adele. 'We don't want businesslike. We want beauty and perfection.'

'We've got that too.'

'But not prettiness.' Adele looked mutinous. 'I'm sorry, I just can't approve these.'

'You don't have a veto,' Peter reminded her.

Adele stared at them. 'You mean you'd give her the go-ahead even without my approval?'

'Mum, you're the backbone of this company,' said Philip. 'You've been part of it your whole life. But you can surely see that we need to make changes.'

'Of course I know that,' Adele snapped. 'But beauty never changes.'

'These *are* beautiful,' said Peter.

'I grant you there's a certain quality about them.' Adele looked at the images again. 'But they're not . . . they're not what your father would have commissioned.'

Her sons were silent for a moment, then Philip spoke.

'Dad started off as a watch repairer,' he reminded his mother. 'Then he bought in jewellery. Then he started to create his own. He continually changed things. Do you really think he'd want to be left behind in today's world? That he'd want to see his clients move to other stores? Because that's what's happening now.'

'You're telling me that Bey Fitzpatrick has better taste than me?' Adele glared at them.

'She's in touch with today's tastes,' said Peter. 'She's young and forward-thinking and she's the greatest talent we could possibly have in our corner right now.'

'I'm not denying she's talented.' Adele sniffed. 'I just don't like what she has a talent for.'

'But other people will,' said Philip.

'And they'll associate it with me,' said Adele. 'The Ice Dragon.'

'What would you like to call the collection?' asked Peter.

'The Adele Charm,' she said. 'Or the Adele Elegance. Or the Adele Perfection. Or . . .'

The two men said nothing. The silence in the room grew heavier as Adele flicked through the images from the start again.

'Oh, all right,' she said, throwing up her hands in surrender. 'Ice Dragon it is. But if the whole collection crashes and burns, don't blame me.'

'We won't,' promised Philip. 'We'll allow you to say you told us so.'

As they drove away from the house, Philip glanced across at his brother.

'It had better work,' he said. 'We'll be flayed alive by the Ice Dragon herself if doesn't.'

'It will,' said Peter. But he crossed his fingers as he spoke.

Bey was at home in Ringsend when her father phoned. She took a deep breath before picking up her mobile and answering it.

'She doesn't like Ice Dragon,' Philip said.

'The name or the collection?'

'Either, really,' said Philip.

Bey felt as though she'd been punched in the stomach.

'But Peter and I agree that it's exactly right.'

'You do?'

'Of course we do. I think I knew it straight away. I also knew Mum would hate it. But that we'd talk her round in the end.'

'So . . .'

'So we're going ahead,' said Philip. 'I've already been talking to our suppliers. I'll set up a meeting with the gold-smith. I've also talked to our event management company. The Ice Dragon launch will be a huge event. We'll be putting Warren's back on the map with a bang.'

'But what about Adele?'

'Of course she hankers after something more traditional. But in her heart she knows we're right. And we're a hundred per cent behind you.'

'That's a relief.' Bey's stomach was churning now. With excitement, happiness and apprehension. Just as it always did when a new project got the green light.

'Thank you,' said Philip.

'Don't thank me until you've sold something,' she said.

'That's beyond doubt,' said Philip.

And he meant it.

Lola, who'd listened to Bey's side of the conversation, gave her a tentative thumbs-up.

'White smoke,' confirmed Bey. 'Oh God, Mum, I hope it all works out. They're laying a lot on the line with this collection. What if it goes horribly wrong?'

'Why should it go wrong?' asked Lola. 'You've worked really hard.'

'Hard work doesn't necessarily mean success,' said Bey. 'And they still have to make the damn things. That could go horribly wrong too.'

'Weren't your Van Aelten and Schaap collections successful?' demanded Lola. 'Why should this be any different?'

Because it was about more than the jewellery, thought Bey as she lay in bed that evening. Because it was about everything that mattered in her life. Because it turned running away into facing up to things. Because the Warrens had come to her and she'd been able to give them something that nobody else could. Because it was a new version of herself.

It was exhilarating.

It was terrifying too.

Bey and Philip went to meet Bernard Stephenson, a goldsmith they thought would be ideal for the Ice Dragon collection, in his workshop off Clarendon Street. He was a tall, gangly man in his forties who, like many other goldsmiths, had taken over the business from his father.

'I'd love to work on these,' he said when she showed him the designs. 'I know I could make them live up to your drawings.'

'It's not intricate,' said Bey. 'But it's very fine work.'

'I can see that.'

'I want to give the impression that the stones are almost floating—'

'Of course you do,' he said before she finished. 'I know what you want. We can do it here. It would be a privilege.'

Bey smiled. 'I'll need to meet you every so often to see how they're coming along.'

'Naturally.' He looked at the images on her iPad again.

'It's really quite clever what you've done. And I love the name.'

Bey glanced at her father, who winked at her.

'I'll be back with my brother to talk through costs with you,' said Philip. 'But I'm confident we can work together.'

'So am I.' Bernard held out his hand.

Philip shook it. Then Bey did too.

'And that's that,' said Philip as they left the workshop. 'The Ice Dragon collection is out of the starting blocks.'

'We still have to get the stones,' Bey reminded him.

'I'm working on that,' said her father. 'You were good with those too. They're not so big or so unique that we won't be able to find them. I've got a really good contact in Germany who can do it for me. I trust him completely.'

Bey thought for a moment of Will Murdoch, criss-crossing the globe, looking for the best stones for Van Aelten and Schaap. She hoped he was happy. She hoped Callista was happy too. She was glad that she was happy herself. And she was. Despite the ridiculous ache in her heart that had never quite gone away.

Chapter 36

*Alexandrite: a rare gemstone that changes from green
to red depending on the light*

When she finally got a call to say that the first of the Ice
Dragon pieces was ready, Bey was almost sick with anticipation. She met her father at the Duke Lane store and then
walked with him to Clarendon Street, where Bernard was
waiting for them. The workshop was busy, with many of the
other goldsmiths also working on Ice Dragon jewellery, and
as always when she saw her designs being made, Bey felt a
surge of pride and excitement shoot through her. Then
Bernard led them into a room at the back of the building
where the necklace was waiting for them.

'What d'you think?' he asked.

Bey stared at it without speaking. Philip didn't say a word
either. Then the two of them looked at each other and Philip
put his arms around her and hugged her.

'You're squashing me,' she mumbled, her face pressed
against his chest.

'Congratulations.' Instead of releasing her, Philip held her
even tighter. 'It's the most beautiful thing I've ever seen.'

'Isn't it.' Bernard sounded pleased. 'Of course we had a few issues initially, as you already know, but everything worked out in the end.'

She'd expected there'd be problems – nothing ever went completely smoothly in the process – but Bernard was right, they'd managed to resolve all of them without too much trouble.

'Dad, if you could let me go, I could actually see it properly,' she said.

'Sorry.' He released his hold on her and Bey picked up the necklace. She examined it carefully, noting how the stones had been set into the metal, perfectly capturing the floating effect of her design.

'It's wonderful work, Bernard,' she said. 'Thank you.'

'We'll have the others ready shortly and the rest of the collection will follow. It's going to be fabulous,' he added. 'Really fabulous.'

'I'm glad you think so,' said Philip. 'I hope our customers do too.'

'It's a classic,' said Bernard. 'Definitely. And it truly has been a pleasure to work on it.'

Bey and Philip left the workshop and he steered her towards the Westbury again.

'This is becoming like a second office,' she remarked as he led her to an upstairs table.

'Celebration time,' he told her. He took his mobile from his pocket and phoned Peter. 'Meet us here,' he said.

When Peter arrived a few minutes later, the waiter had already brought a bottle of champagne.

'It's even better in real life than in the images,' Philip told his brother. 'It's going to be phenomenal.'

461

'Please stop bigging it up so much,' implored Bey. 'Of course I think it's lovely, but I would, wouldn't I? Maybe we're all deluding ourselves. Maybe nobody else will like it. Maybe—'

'Bey!' Peter's glass was halfway to his lips. 'Stop! You were super-confident when you talked to us before. Super-confident when you showed us the design. You even lectured Mum about your talent. Why are you getting cold feet now?'

'I always do,' she admitted. 'Once I see the finished product, no matter how gorgeous it is, I panic.'

'Don't panic,' said Peter. 'It's amazing.'

'. . . and the PR around it all is so intense.'

Bey was sitting in the kitchen with Lola, warming her hands on a cup of tea. Ireland had been hit by the early onset of winter, brought about by arctic air swirling down from the North Pole. Temperatures had plunged, and even indoors the chill in the air was noticeable.

'It'll be brilliant,' said Lola. 'And you'll be fine.'

'I've never been involved in anything quite like it before,' said Bey. 'We had plenty of events at Van Aelten and Schaap, but they were much lower key than this. And I didn't go to all of them. It's usually the retail people because they're the ones who know the customers. I really don't want them to make a big thing of it.'

'It's very important to them,' said Lola. 'Of course they're making a big thing of it. And coming up to Christmas too.'

'The timing is good,' agreed Bey. 'Hopefully the rich and happy haven't already splurged on their festive gifts.'

'The rich and happy?'

'Something we used to say at Van Aelten.' She gazed

462

unseeingly into the distance. 'That we only ever saw people when they were rich and happy. Which is true. Even when people were buying themselves divorce jewellery, they were celebrating.'

Lola grinned. 'We're all entitled to be happy,' she said. 'And if you can afford to celebrate it too – well, why not?'

'That's what I think,' agreed Bey. 'All the same, it's a make-believe world.'

'Sometimes we need the make-believe to get us through the day,' said Lola. 'Besides, a great piece of jewellery can be very meaningful.'

Bey's fingers went to the Bluebells in her ears.

'I know,' she said. 'I wish . . .'

'What?'

'You gave these to me,' she said. 'They mean a lot. I wish you had something meaningful of your own.'

'That's sweet of you,' said Lola. 'But I'm rich in other ways. And happy too.'

'I know money can't buy happiness,' agreed Bey. 'But, oh, it can ease the pain of misery sometimes.'

Lola laughed. 'You're spending too much time with the Warrens. Tell me, what does Adele think of it all?'

'It's hard to know,' admitted Bey. 'Dad and Peter are so enthusiastic, they kind of carry the whole thing along with them. Even Anthony has said nice things, though not directly to me. But Adele . . . Leaving aside how she feels about me, she doesn't like the name and she's not mad on the design. All the same, if they make money, I guess she'll get over it.'

'What she doesn't like is that you've done it for them,' said Lola.

'You're right about that,' said Bey. 'It's like having to eat her words.'

'No harm.' Lola sniffed. 'She was always an old battleaxe. Even when she was young.'

Bey smiled and then shivered.

'What?'

'I'm terrified,' she admitted. 'This time next week the launch will be over and judgement will have been passed, and if I've failed . . .' Her voice trailed off.

'You won't have failed,' said Lola. 'Regardless of what happens, I think you're one of the most talented people I know. And even though I can't afford those fabulously unique necklaces, I'm going to buy myself an Ice Dragon pendant.'

'Mum!' Bey was shocked. 'They're way too expensive.'

'I'll demand a discount,' Lola told her. 'It's the least they can do for the mother of the creative genius who's going to save their business.'

Bey was more nervous than ever on the morning of the launch. The continuing cold snap had brought a light dusting of snow to the city, and although it didn't last long on the main streets, the laneway outside her workshop was treacherously slippy when she arrived to open up.

Liesel, who was now on a part-time contract, arrived a few minutes later wearing a duffel coat and wrapped in a wool scarf and hat.

'Excited about tonight?' she asked as she hung up the scarf and swapped her coat for her green apron, but kept her hat on.

'Terrified is more like it,' replied Bey. 'The press will be there and if it's all too horribly over-the-top they'll probably do a piece about people with more money than sense and the perils of having a family business.'

'Or they'll write about the art that's to be found in the Ice Dragon collection and the fabulous talent that Warren's uncovered,' said Liesel.

'You're so sweet.' Bey gave her a grateful smile. 'I guess it's too late to worry now. How are you getting on with the latest Bijou pieces?'

'Polishing today,' said Liesel. 'We've a lot of orders to go out too. I was checking your spreadsheets yesterday; they're ninety per cent up on last year.'

'At least I'll always have my silverware.' Bey's smile was a little wider this time.

'Are you going to keep designing for the Warrens after this?' asked Liesel.

'They haven't asked me and I haven't thought about it,' said Bey. 'I guess we'll have to see how tonight goes first.'

She said goodbye to her assistant at lunchtime, leaving her to get on with things for the rest of the day while she went to the hairdresser's, where she had her hair styled and her nails done, before going back to Ringsend. The house was empty – Bey wasn't sure that Lola would even have left work before she herself headed out for the evening. But her mother surprised her by arriving home early.

'I wanted to make sure that you were OK,' she said.

'Why wouldn't I be?'

'The most important night of your life is ahead of you,' said Lola. 'I'm here to support you.'

'Thank you. But it's too late to change anything now. If it crashes and burns, it's all down to me.'

'You've lived and breathed Ice Dragon for months,' said

Lola. 'Now all your hard work is coming to fruition. And it'll be fantastic.'

'I'm trying to downplay it in my head,' admitted Bey. 'Because if I don't, I think I'll be sick with nerves.'

'Come here.' Lola held out her arms and folded Bey into them. 'No matter what happens tonight, I'm immensely proud of you,' she murmured. 'You're smart and you're talented and you're a good person and you'll always be that way.'

'Not always a good person,' said Bey. 'I've done things I'm not proud of . . .'

'Show me anyone in the whole world who hasn't!' cried Lola. 'You should know that people are like gemstones. The flawless ones are exceptional. Although,' she added, 'nobody in the world is flawless. It's impossible to be perfect. But you're a perfect daughter and you've brought me more happiness than I ever deserved.'

'I'm glad you think so,' said Bey. 'Even though I held you back.' She gave her mother a rueful look. 'You dreamed of having a career and going places and being successful and it all got messed up because of me.'

'If you hadn't been born, I would have missed out on the most wonderful thing in my life,' said Lola. 'You might have changed my plans, but it was definitely for the better. Besides, who knows how things would have turned out without you? Maybe I would've been a principal officer in the Civil Service, or maybe I'd never have got past the next grade. Maybe I would've ended up like my old staff officer, Irene, mean spirited and joyless. Or maybe I would've met someone I loved and had a great marriage with loads of kids. Who knows? That's the thing – we can't go back, we can't worry

466

about "what if". We can only hope that we've learned from the past and think about now and the future.'

'You said it to Aunt Gretta one day, though,' Bey told her. 'We were all up at High Pasture and you and she were walking ahead of us and you said that she'd robbed your life.'

Lola remembered the day too. Scorching hot, the grass dry and brittle underfoot. Gretta had just been promoted at the creamery and had been outlining her plans while saying that she could never have got as far as she had without Tony, and how great it was that he was happy to stay at home and be a house husband. 'The furniture stuff is more a hobby than a money-spinner,' she'd remarked. 'But it gives him a focus outside of the children.'

Lola had replied that being a single mother was all about compromise. 'I've compromised on having a career,' she said. 'It's always going to be just about making enough money for us to be a family together. But I know I sometimes compromise on being a mother too. It's bloody hard. And what's even harder is knowing that your sister, who wanted nothing more than to get married and have a houseful of kids, somehow managed to steal your life and become the career woman with the stay-at-home husband instead.'

And Bey, who hadn't meant to eavesdrop, had felt a knife twist in her gut.

'Has that bothered you forever?' Lola looked concerned. 'Because I wouldn't change things for anyone.'

'All the same, you could've been someone really important if it wasn't for me,' said Bey. 'More especially if it wasn't for how I behaved that Christmas. Because after that you never stopped worrying about me. You always put me ahead of you. And now, even though I'm a grown-up, you still do.'

'Hey, mothers never stop worrying about their children full stop!' cried Lola. 'I admit I worried a bit more after your abduction because it was such a traumatic thing, I still worry that you don't trust your own judgement when it comes to men because you got into a car with a very specific kind of man, who was horrible and evil. But not all men are, Bey. Most of them are lovely. I'm afraid that if you don't back yourself one day when it comes to a man, you'll lose out on true happiness. There's one other thing too,' she added. 'I'm delighted you've made such a great use of your talents, but you don't have to be a super-successful, ball-breaking career woman as compensation for the fact that I never was. You have to do what you want for you and you alone. And you have to do whatever makes you happy. Oh, I know we can't always have our ideal career or our ideal man, but follow the path that gets you closest to it. And be glad you did.'

Bey's eyes welled with tears. She and Lola rarely spoke about that night any more and even less did Lola say anything about the effect it had had on her. It was something of a surprise to Bey to realise that perhaps her mother knew her even better than she did herself.

'Now,' said Lola, 'you'd better go upstairs and change if you're to be ready when the car gets here. You're the star of the show and you can't leave them waiting.'

'The Ice Dragon is the star of the show.' Bey's voice trembled slightly but she smiled. 'Both the jewels and Adele – you don't think for a moment she isn't going to take centre stage, do you?'

'You couldn't be more right about that,' agreed Lola. 'But

468

tonight is about passing the mantle on to the next generation. Which, my sweet, is you.'

The car that Philip had booked to take her to the venue arrived ten minutes early, which threw Bey into a panic. She was still getting ready when the doorbell rang, and in her haste she dropped the butterfly back to one of her Bluebell earrings. She was on her knees looking for it when Lola came in to tell her that the driver was waiting outside.

'I know. I heard the bell,' said Bey. 'It's just my earring . . .'

Lola stretched out on the floor and looked sideways as she tried to spot the delicate piece of silver.

'It's always at the worst time . . .' Bey's voice was almost a sob. 'And I have to wear the Bluebells.'

'I thought you'd be wearing Ice Dragon,' said Lola from her prone position.

'They're being kept for the models,' said Bey as she patted the rug beside her bed in case the back of the earring had ended up there. 'The Bluebells are my talisman.'

'Here you go!' Lola's fingers closed around the butterfly. 'Found it.'

'Oh thank God,' said Bey. She stood up and dusted down her dress. It was full-length cobalt blue, with a beaded neckline. She'd bought it from TK Maxx in London for a Van Aelten and Schaap event years earlier, and it still fitted perfectly. It emphasised the blazing red of her hair and the subtle creaminess of her skin and it was ideal for the Ice Dragon launch.

She secured the Bluebell earrings and slipped into her high heels. Lola stared at her.

'What?' asked Bey. 'Why are you looking at me like that?'

'You look a total glamazon in that outfit. You tower over me with those heels and that hairdo; I can't believe you're my baby girl.'

Bey laughed. 'Less of the baby,' she said, taking her rain-coat out of the wardrobe.

'You're not wearing that over your beautiful dress!' exclaimed Lola.

'It's all I have.'

'Wait,' said her mother. She hurried out of the room and returned with an astrakhan fur coat.

'I can't wear fur!' cried Bey. 'I can't believe you do either.'

'Oh don't be so bloody silly.' Lola made a face at her. 'It isn't real. It's from Topshop. But it looks a lot better than that thing you were proposing to put on.'

Bey slipped it on. The silver-grey coat was stunning.

Lola handed her a pair of soft leather gloves.

'It's cold out there,' she said.

'I don't need . . .' Bey laughed and slipped the gloves on. 'All wrapped up.'

'Now go knock them dead,' said Lola.

The Warren's PR company had chosen Ketteridge House for the launch of the Ice Dragon collection. The listed building just outside the city had been an estate house for an English landowner, who'd sold it at the end of the eighteenth century to pay off his gambling debts. After that, it had passed through a number of owners before being bought by an Irish entre-preneur who'd built up a global telecommunications business. The businessman spent little time in his native country and rented the house out for private functions. It was a popular wedding venue because of its extensive gardens, and was also often used as a film set too.

The car crunched over the long gravel driveway and pulled up outside the front door. It was closed – the Warren family was arriving ahead of the guests so that they could be sure that everything was as it should be. Bey got out, thanked the driver and walked up the steps. She hoped she was at the right entrance. An image of herself banging on the door pleading for admittance popped into her head and she told herself not to be idiotic. Nevertheless, she was relieved to see a large buzzer for the bell and hear it ring loudly when she pressed it.

The door was opened immediately by a man from the PR company, who asked her name and ticked her off on his list. He took her coat and gloves and waved her towards the drawing room, where, he told her, the rest of the family were waiting.

The first person she saw was Adele, who was wearing a dusky-pink dress and the entire Snowdrop range. Donna, standing just behind her, wore red velvet and the Adele Bouquet. And Astrid, who somehow managed to look as dainty and pretty as ever despite her obvious pregnancy, had chosen a blue ballgown and the Adele Tiger Lily set.

The men – her father, Peter, Anthony, and Astrid's husband Jordan – stood beside them, groomed and suave in their tuxedos.

'Bey!' Philip came forward and hugged her. 'Welcome.'

'We said six thirty for family drinks,' said Adele. 'It's a quarter to seven now.'

'I'm so sorry.' Bey's tone was more confident than she felt. 'I didn't realise I was invited to the drinks.'

'Come here, sweetheart,' said Peter and gave her a hug. 'We're delighted to see you. And you look fabulous. Would you like some champagne?'

She nodded and accepted the glass he handed to her as another PR staffer, whose name badge identified him as Nikolai, asked them if they'd like to check the set-up. Bey moved with the rest of the family to the room where the display cabinets were arranged and where pre-dinner drinks would be served. Anthony stopped to check out the displays, then nodded at Nikolai and followed him to the dining room, where a dozen tables were beautifully laid with crisp white linen, Newbridge silver cutlery and elegant Waterford crystal glasses.

'Of course we've had to leave room for the centrepieces, which will be carried in later,' said Nikolai. 'It should be fantastic.'

'I hope so.' Adele sniffed. 'This is the most over-the-top event I've ever experienced. And I'm not at all sure it's what Warren's is about.'

'It'll be amazing, Mum,' said Philip. 'You're going to have a great time.'

'You will, Gran.' Astrid put her arm around her. 'It's nice that we're finally putting ourselves out there again after the last few years. We're all about glamour, but we haven't been for a while.'

'You certainly look glamorous,' conceded Adele. 'Back in my day, pregnant women didn't get dolled up to the nines and go out on the town.'

'Just as well we're not back in your day so.' Astrid grinned as she jangled the gold bracelets on her arm.

Bey knew that the Ice Dragon designs would be revealed

later in the evening, but she felt intimidated at being surrounded by so much Adele jewellery – and by being in the same room as the Ice Dragon herself, who was as cool and haughty as ever.

'This must all be very new for you, Bey,' Adele said. 'It's not often you'd get to spend time in surroundings like this.'

'I've been at quite a few launches in my day.' Bey reminded herself that there was no need to feel intimidated. That Van Aelten and Schaap had created jewels for the Imperial Russians and the crown princesses of Europe. 'And, of course, when I designed the tiara for the Duquesa de Olvera y Montecalmón, I visited her home in Cádiz.'

Peter stifled a grin while Adele fixed Bey with a flinty stare.

'What on earth is wrong with you, Mum?' asked Philip. 'You're being a real pain and you know Bey is the only reason we're here at all.'

'I didn't have a choice in any of it,' said Adele. 'You made it perfectly clear to me that I'm old fashioned and out of date. And,' she added as her hands went to her Snowdrop necklace, 'gimmicky jewellery is all very well, but style, real style, never goes out of date.'

'D'you really think the Ice Dragon is gimmicky?' asked Bey.

'It's interesting, I'll give you that,' said Adele. 'But it'll never be Adele style. It'll never truly be a Warren piece. It doesn't have that class.'

'You're talking about me really, aren't you?' Bey put her glass on the table. 'For the first time in my life I can completely understand why my wonderful mother never wanted to be part of this ridiculous family. And I don't care what worries might be eating at you, or what traumas you think you've suffered, because the problem is simply you. You're not an ice dragon at all. You're just a full-blown bitch.'

She strode back to the reception room, her high heels tapping on the wooden floor.

'Bey!' It was Philip who followed her and caught her by the arm. 'Come back. Mum didn't mean it.'

'Of course she did!' said Bey. 'She has all sorts of issues about me – you should ask her about them sometime. The fact that she still thinks I'm a jewel thief is the least of it. She hates the Ice Dragon collection and she hates me. She hates everything about tonight too – and you know what, so do I. I should've had more sense than to come.'

'Bey, please . . .'

'I hope it's a huge success,' said Bey. 'But count me out, now and forever.'

'We can—'

Philip's words were lost in a sudden burst of laughter and chatter as the first of the invited guests walked in and a woman in a gold dress embraced him.

'What a lovely event,' she gushed. 'So delighted you asked us.'

Bey took the opportunity to slip away. She didn't need to be here. She didn't need to spend another second with any of the Warrens. She didn't care if the Ice Dragon was a success or not.

All she wanted was to go home and be her own version of herself again.

Chapter 37

*Garnet: a purplish-red stone popular for its hardness
and brilliance*

She walked swiftly through the reception room and into the
entrance hall, which was already full of people handing over
their coats and receiving tickets in return. She realised that
the PR guy hadn't given her a ticket for Lola's fake fur, and
she couldn't see it on the rack in the hallway. He was too
busy to ask, but she presumed it had been put somewhere
nearby. She saw a door marked 'Ladies', and although she
knew it was unlikely her coat was there, she decided to check
it out anyway. There were no coats, but an attractive woman
wearing a yellow and gold cocktail dress was fixing her
make-up in front of an ornate mirror. Bey gave her a small
smile and then went into one of the cubicles. She didn't
actually need to use the loo, but nor did she want to engage
in conversation with any of the guests.

'Oh, Noelle, hi!'

Someone else had come in. Bey felt trapped as she listened
to her talking to the woman who'd been doing her face.

'Tanya. How are you?' Noelle greeted her. 'Haven't they

really gone to town tonight? It's just like the old days! Myra McCarthy said that they've a new designer and the new collection is amazing.'

'It'd want to be,' observed Tanya. 'I haven't bothered with Warren's in years.'

'Me neither,' said Noelle. 'Which is a shame because Byron bought my engagement ring there.'

'Oh, I got mine there too,' said her friend. 'It was specially made. It's the original Adele Rose design.'

'Mine's the Snowdrop,' said Noelle. 'It's the only one of the early Adeles they still make. There's no question that the quality is great, but the last collections simply haven't done it for me. And I don't like buying something I don't feel passionate about.'

'I know what you mean,' said Tanya. 'When Jack asked me what I'd like for my birthday this year, I thought about the Pansy but in the end I went with a diamond from Boodles.'

'In fairness, they do good diamonds.' Noelle laughed.

'And yet I would've loved something from Warren's. I'm sentimental about them.'

'Maybe tonight,' said Noelle.

'Maybe,' said her friend, 'but I doubt it.'

Then the two women left and Bey was alone.

Tanya and Noelle were exactly the sort of people she was targeting with the Ice Dragon range, she thought as she opened the cubicle door. Women who could afford beautiful pieces but who also connected to them emotionally. Women who'd loved the Adeles in the past but who were looking for something more contemporary now. She wanted to run after them and see their reaction to her designs, but she couldn't do that. Besides, she reminded herself, she wasn't staying.

A chill breeze suddenly whistled through a narrow window that had somehow become unlatched. Bey began to close it but stopped abruptly when she saw the garden of Ketteridge House. The faint dusting of snow glittered beneath the yellow glow of the garden lights, while the occasional flake drifted from the leaden sky and landed on the windowsill. Suddenly she was transported back to that Christmas twenty years ago, sneaking out in the middle of the night, walking lightly over the frosted grass before letting herself out of the gates and hurrying along the slippery pavement beyond.

She'd never expected it to be the night that changed her life, but it had. It had turned her from being open hearted and trusting to someone who doubted her judgement about everything. And it had made her question who she really was. Was she Bey Fitzpatrick, who was loved by everyone, or a different Bey, who was regarded with suspicion and disapproval? The thing was, she thought, the Warrens had been right not to trust her, because that night she'd behaved badly, even if she'd ended up being brave and resourceful when it mattered. The police, her mother and Paige Pentony had all said how brave she'd been. But that wasn't how she'd seen herself. Her weakness in taking Astrid's ring far outweighed any strength she'd shown in escaping from Raymond Fenton. And yet he was the only person she'd ever truly needed to run away from. Every other time – leaving Cleevaun House, leaving Van Aelten and Schaap, even leaving the party tonight – she could have chosen to stay. She could have faced up to the consequences of her actions. But she hadn't trusted herself to be able to do it. Which meant she wasn't brave at all.

She pushed open the door to the corridor. The hallway was deserted. Most people had drifted off to the reception room, which was where she was supposed to be too. Stay or go? she asked herself. Run away or face up to things?

Oh hell, she thought, taking a deep breath and turning towards the reception room, I'm done with running. This is the most important collection in my life. I have to see the reaction, no matter what it is.

She secreted herself close to the stage and to the long mullioned windows overlooking the garden, where she could observe without being seen herself. The hum of conversation was eager and excited. She felt her own heart beat faster with excitement too.

She turned and looked outside again. The gently falling snow was landing on a spider's web, stretched taut across the cold pane of glass.

Although she'd wanted to close the door on the past, the spider's web made her think of the other web. The one that came to her in her dreams. The one that wrapped itself around the knives and forks and spoons in the cutlery tray. The one that she had to clean off so that she could stretch it in front of her to protect her. So that nobody could reach her. Nobody could touch her. So that she was safe

She shivered as the images flashed through her mind. Then she felt the hand on her shoulder and the lights went out.

She whirled around, ready to lash out, but even as she raised her arm, she realised that it was her father's hand, and that it was Philip, not her abductor, who was standing in front of her, a troubled expression in his eyes.

'I've been looking for you everywhere,' he said. 'I was afraid you'd left. I'm really sorry about Adele's attitude. She's wrong, Bey. Very wrong. I've told her so. Quite forcefully. Are you all right?' he added, seeing the anxiety in her face. 'Has she really upset you?'

'No,' Bey croaked. 'I'm fine. Honestly.'

'I have to go on stage and get ready for my speech,' said Philip. 'I should've been practising but I had to find you first. I hope—'

His words were lost as a spotlight pierced the darkness and music filled the air. At the entrance to the room a colourful Chinese dragon appeared. It danced and gyrated its way through the crowd, followed by a dozen glistening dragon-shaped ice sculptures each carried by two waiters. It was an amazing sight and Bey had to admit that – crazy as she'd thought it was going to be – it was enthralling. The guests gasped and applauded as the dragon and the ice sculptures made their way towards the dining room.

'We'll talk afterwards,' Philip said. 'But I want you to know that I'm eternally grateful to you for everything you've done.'

'It was my job,' she said.

'You didn't have to do it,' said Philip. 'I'm honoured that you did. And I couldn't be prouder that you're my daughter. I wish I'd known to be proud long before now. I wish I hadn't let my anger with Lola stop me.'

He dropped the briefest of kisses on her cheek and walked towards the stage. As the spotlights illuminated him standing at a small lectern, the guests began to applaud again and he held up his hand for silence.

'Thank you,' he said. 'Thank you, friends of Warren's, for coming along tonight for the launch of our new and truly exceptional collection of jewellery.'

Bey listened to him talk about the Ice Dragon collection, and then held her breath as a dozen stunning models strode onto the stage wearing the collection, which sparkled and dazzled beneath the lights.

'The Ice Dragon range!' cried Philip. 'New heirlooms for a new age. Bespoke necklaces with the highest-quality gems. A collection of earrings, pendants, bracelets and rings that you'll want to own. We're extremely proud of these pieces and we hope you'll love them as much as we do. Now I want to introduce someone very special to you. My mother, Adele Warren.'

Adele, who had taken off her Snowdrop jewellery and replaced it with Ice Dragon, stepped onto the stage and stood beside Philip, who whispered quietly in her ear. She looked at him silently for a moment, then nodded and stood behind the microphone.

'I also want to thank you,' she said when the applause had died down. 'Many of you have been customers of Warren's for a long, long time. As my son said, we consider you our friends. And this is a night for friends, old and new.'

She was a good speaker, thought Bey. Everyone was listening to her, nodding at her words and smiling at each other as she talked about some of the more iconic Adele pieces and what they meant to her.

'But now I'm in my eighties and it's time for me and the Adeles to be put out to pasture,' she said.

'Never!' cried a voice from the crowd.

Adele smiled. 'Well, we'd all like to think we can go on

480

and on, but the truth is that only diamonds are forever.'

This time people laughed, and even Bey allowed herself the faintest of smiles.

'My husband used to say that we were only passing through, and that the legacy of beautiful gemstones would stay long after we'd gone. I like to think he was right about that.'

I wish I'd known him better, thought Bey. Even though Richard had been manipulative and wrong, he'd looked after her and Lola. Her fingers touched the Bluebells in her ears. They would always be a tangible connection with her grandfather, and she was glad about that.

'I hope very much that Warren's has left some beautiful jewellery as our legacy,' continued Adele. 'And I hope that you'll think the Ice Dragon range continues our commitment to quality and style. Our stunning models will be walking among you shortly so you'll have the opportunity to see the pieces at close quarters for yourselves. And of course if you want to try any of them, please ask one of our people for help. We're the ones with the badges, although I hope that many of you know us already. I'm not wearing a badge because as the oldest person here I'm hoping I don't need one.'

There was more good-natured laughter.

'There's someone else not wearing a badge either, and I'd like you to give her a warm welcome. She's the creator of the Ice Dragon range and, in the Warren spirit of being a family company, she's also my very, very talented grand-daughter. Bey Fitzpatrick.' Adele looked towards where Bey was standing and, even though she couldn't see her, held out her arm.

Bey stared at her in shock. Nobody had said anything

481

about her going on stage. Nobody had said anything about her standing side by side with the Ice Dragon herself.

Her grandmother's arm remained outstretched. Bey didn't move. She didn't have to do this. She didn't have to make nice. Especially to Adele. She could simply walk away and leave her there. She could humiliate her grandmother the way her grandmother seemed to like humiliating her.

But I'm a professional person, she reminded herself. This is my job. And I'm not running away.

She walked up the steps and stood beside her grandmother on the stage.

'I have to admit,' said Adele when the applause died down. 'I wasn't sure about the direction the collection would take when Bey came to us. But she was very clear in her ideas and very clear about how the pieces would fit together. Old fogey that I am, I made some suggestions. Thankfully she ignored every one of them.'

The crowd laughed again.

'I'm truly delighted that another generation of the Warren family has taken on the mantle of our heritage,' she continued. 'And I want to thank Bey for working so hard for us and with us. We didn't ask her to prepare a speech, but it would be nice if she could say a few words.'

I could say that you didn't want to know me, thought Bey. That you were mean to my mother. That you called me a thief and an ungrateful wretch. I could say that you thought – maybe even still think – I was your husband's daughter and because of that you couldn't hide your resentment of me. I could say that I've never been a member of this family and that I have nothing to do with its heritage. I could say that it means nothing to me. That *you* mean nothing to me.

482

And that your legacy means nothing to me either. Although that wouldn't be strictly true, she thought, because Ice Dragon meant everything to her and she wanted it to be part of Warren's heritage as much as the Adele Rose or the Snowdrop or even the Bluebells.

She took a deep breath and smiled out at the people watching her. Rich and happy. Waiting for her to speak. Waiting for her to be the Bey they wanted her to be. The Bey she knew she was.

'Thank you, Adele,' she said. 'I'm delighted to be here tonight. I'm thrilled at the opportunity to have created what I too hope will be part of Warren's for a long time to come. The collection was a joy to work on and I'm honoured to have been part of its creation. I know I'm biased but I hope everyone here will love the pieces as much as I do.'

She stepped back and Adele hugged her. She couldn't remember ever having been hugged by her grandmother before, and she was surprised at how thin and fragile the older woman was.

'Thank you,' murmured Adele. 'I meant what I said. I was wrong: you knew exactly what you were doing, and I know your grandfather would be very, very proud.'

'You're welcome.' Bey was more touched than she'd expected by Adele's words. 'It was a pleasure to work on the collection.'

'And it's a great name.' There was the merest hint of a smile on Adele's lips. 'Richard would have loved it.'

Philip returned to his position behind the mic.

'I just wanted to add that Bey is my daughter, and I couldn't be prouder of what she's achieved tonight.'

Bey smiled. I don't think we'll ever be close, she thought

as Philip put his arm around her, but maybe things will be better in the future. Not perfect. Not wonderful. But better.

The guests continued to applaud as the models began to leave the stage and mingle among them. Philip and Adele were also applauding. And so were the other Warrens, standing close by, smiling broadly.

Bey wished Lola was here. She wished there was someone close to her who could share the triumph of the moment, no matter how bizarre it felt. Someone who really knew her.

And then she saw him, standing in the crowd, looking up at her. She stared in absolute bewilderment, quite unable to believe her eyes and completely astonished as to why he should be here at all. She turned to her father, but Philip was already leading them off the stage to where the rest of the family were waiting.

'When we didn't see you earlier, I thought you'd run out on us, Bey,' said Adele as they walked. 'I'm very glad you didn't.'

'I wouldn't walk out on the biggest night of my professional career.' Bey tried to forget that she almost had.

'It's a big night for us as a family too,' said Adele. 'I don't know if closeness will ever be possible between us. But I hope we can be friendly. And I hope you and your father have a better relationship than I had with mine. I'm afraid that might have clouded my judgement about you a little, and for that I apologise.'

'That's OK.' For the first time in her life, Bey smiled at her grandmother.

There was no time to say anything else, because Peter was patting her on the back and telling her that all he'd been able to hear while the models were on stage were the gasps of appreciation and desire from the guests.

'One woman told her husband she wanted every single piece,' he said. 'I really do think we've got a success on our hands. And you're the reason for it, Bey. Whoever would've believed it?'

'Yeah.' It was Anthony who spoke next. 'We're totally geared up for big sales in retail. Fingers crossed.'

Astrid looked at Bey without speaking for a moment and then sighed.

'I never really liked you,' she said. 'I don't know why. You were always sort of exotic, you know? The mystery sister. I think I might have resented that. And then there was the ring, of course. I was a bit of a bitch about that, wasn't I? Especially after Grandad died and you brought it back. Gran found it and your locket and she gave them to me. The locket is still yours, you know.'

'If your baby's a girl perhaps she'd like it,' said Bey. 'It can be my way of apologising to you for taking the ring in the first place.'

Astrid smiled. 'We're very different people for all that you're my half-sister,' she said. 'But I can tell you here and now that if I don't get at least one piece of that Ice Dragon set for Christmas, I'll be very, very disappointed. They're the most gorgeous pieces of jewellery I've ever seen.'

'Thank you.' Bey was overwhelmed by the Warren love-bombing, but she was desperate to get away. 'There's someone I wanted to see. Would you mind if I leave you for a moment?'

And she broke away from them even as a woman came over to Anthony and asked to try on an entire Ice Dragon set.

* * *

Bey had no idea what she was going to say to Will Murdoch. But she knew that she needed to say goodbye at least. Because she hadn't before.

Her heart was pounding when she eventually found him at one of the display cases, where he was studying the tourmaline and diamond pendant.

'It's not my favourite,' she said as she stood beside him. 'The sapphires will always be my favourites. But it's very pretty and I bet it's the best seller.'

'I bet it is too.' He turned to her. 'Hello, Bey. Congratulations on yet another stunning collection.'

'Thank you.'

The memories suddenly flooded into her head. Will at the office, emptying beautiful diamonds onto her desk. Smiling at her as she showed him her ideas. Laughing at the impossible demands of some of their most demanding clients. And Will in Cádiz, warm and caring when her bag had been snatched. Handing her a glass of wine. Letting her lean on his shoulder. Letting her kiss him. Kissing her in return.

She could never forget the kiss.

'I believe one of the bespoke necklaces has been sold already.' He was smiling at her as though they were still working together. As though she hadn't made a fool of herself with him.

'It has?'

'Not only sold but being worn by the owner,' he told her. 'Apparently she's the wife of a movie producer. Or director. Or something.'

'Warren's have a better client list than they admitted,' she said. 'I had to persuade them that it was worth making those pieces. That they were an investment.'

486

'Of course they were an investment,' said Will. 'And you were right to persuade them. You were right to design for them too,' he added. 'You couldn't have done work like this at Van Aelten and Schaap. It's not their style.'

'I know,' said Bey. 'Although to be honest, I didn't leave to work for Warren's. I was making silver jewellery myself when my father asked me to design for them.'

'You left without saying goodbye.' Will's eyes darkened. 'While I was away on a buying trip. You simply disappeared. I couldn't believe it. I tried to get in touch, but you'd changed your phone and everything.'

'I had to get a new one when I came here,' she said.

'It would have been nice to talk before you went.'

'I was busy. And there was nothing to say.'

'Oh, Bey . . .'

'I should've spoken to you.' She kept her voice calm and measured even though she seemed to have a positive swarm of butterflies in her stomach. 'It was very unprofessional of me.'

'I'm not talking about professional,' said Will.

'Oh, look, all of that is in the past,' said Bey. 'I've forgotten about it completely. I'm sure you have too. Anyway . . .' she smiled brightly at him, 'I really wanted to ask how come you were invited tonight. You work for a rival firm.'

'Not any more,' he said. His tone was as suddenly bright as hers, but his expression was still serious. 'I've moved on too.'

'Oh?' She looked at him in surprise. 'I didn't know that. I thought you loved Van Aelten.'

'I've gone back to dealing in gemstones,' said Will. 'It was always more of my thing really. I'm in partnership with a guy called Harvey Kramer. I've known him for years. We sourced some of the stones for your collection. That's why I'm here.'

'You did?' She was astonished.

'I could've contacted you when Warren's came to us, but I didn't want to . . . to upset you when you were in the middle of a new collection.'

'I asked Dad about the stones,' said Bey. 'He said he went to his usual guy in Germany. He's always liked to pick them up himself rather than have a supplier come to the store. He didn't mention your name.'

'He dealt with Harvey but I sourced most of the diamonds,' said Will. 'We work out of Hamburg. I asked Philip for the invite. I wanted to see how the collection turned out. And I have to say that it's the best thing you've ever done.'

'Thank you.'

'We should get out of the way,' said Will. 'In fact it would be nice to go somewhere quieter.'

'I should hang around.' She gave him an apologetic smile. 'In case I'm needed for anything. Listen, it was great to see you again and I'm delighted everything is going so well for you, but I'm sort of busy right now so I have to say goodbye.'

'Could we—'

'Honestly. You know how it is at a launch. I need to schmooze.'

She smiled again, and then eased her way back into the throng of people. Her heart was beating so fast she thought it would explode, but, she told herself, only because his presence had been so unexpected. Nevertheless, it had been good to see him. He'd always been unfinished business in her mind exactly because she'd never said goodbye. But now she had. She'd moved on. In fact, she thought, she'd moved on from a lot of things tonight.

And moving on, being able to leave the trickier parts of her past behind, was surely just as important as making a success of the Ice Dragon collection.

Chapter 38

Turquoise: a greenish-blue variety of lapis lazuli

The guests were clustered around the tables in the dining room, eating buffet food in the reflected light of the ice sculptures. As Bey walked by, some of them stopped her and asked her about the collection, and told her how beautiful the pieces were. She recognised the voice of one of the women who'd been in the ladies' earlier; she was going to buy earrings tonight, she told Bey, but she hoped her husband would buy her the bracelet for Christmas.

Bey thanked them all as she looked out for her father. She wanted to leave. She wasn't running away this time, she told herself, but she'd done what she was here to do and she didn't want to stay any longer. Not while Will was here. But she couldn't see Philip anywhere. Adele, however, was holding court in the centre of the room, chatting to a group of guests, her jewellery flashing and sparkling in the light. She looked as elegant as ever, thought Bey, but for once the term Ice Dragon didn't truly suit her, because she was laughing as she spoke, and the happiness on her face seemed genuine. Maybe she'd put the past behind her too. Maybe one day she might even speak to Lola again. Although that might be a bridge too far.

She didn't want to interrupt her grandmother, and the only other Warren she spotted was Anthony, who was fastening one of the bracelets around a potential customer's wrist.

'As you can see, the clasp is very secure,' he said, smiling at the woman. 'It was specially designed for this collection.'

She decided there was no need to say goodbye. They were all doing what they needed to do. But her work was done.

She made her way to the entrance hall and asked about her coat and gloves, which were brought to her at once despite her lack of a ticket. Then she took out her phone and looked for the number of the driver who'd brought her to Ketteridge House. He'd said to call when she was ready to leave. But as she scrolled through her contacts, she frowned. She was certain she'd saved it, absolutely certain.

Maybe he was waiting outside anyway, she thought. She opened the door, shivering as an icy blast of air hit her. There was only one car on the gravel circle in front of the house – a black Mercedes limousine, which she supposed was for the rest of the family. The car Philip had organised for her had been a Mercedes too, but an ordinary saloon car in silver-grey.

'Stood up?'

She turned at his voice behind her.

'Looking for my car,' she said.

'Didn't you call it from inside?' asked Will.

'Lost the number,' she told him.

He laughed.

'It's not funny,' she said. 'It's bloody freezing out here. I'm going to Hailo a cab.'

'I already have,' said Will. 'It's less than a minute away. 'I'll drop you home.'

'There's no need.' She took her phone out of her bag again. 'I'm sure there are plenty.'

'Don't be silly,' he said. 'Look, it's pulling up now. You might as well get in. You'll freeze out here.'

She shrugged.

'Where to?' he asked.

'Ringsend. Where are you staying?'

'The Westbury.'

She laughed.

'What's so funny?'

'It's where Dad offered me the job,' she told him. 'It's where we often meet. But going to Ringsend will take you out of your way. Much better to go to the Westbury first.'

'You're always worried about taking me out of my way,' remarked Will. 'However, if it makes you happy . . .' He gave the driver instructions.

The snow had stopped falling now, and although the side road from Ketteridge House was still covered, the main roads were clear. Bey sat upright in the back seat, making sure there was some distance between herself and Will. She felt she should keep talking but she didn't know what to say. Until Cádiz, she'd always known what to say. But afterwards, she didn't have the words.

'It's a long time since I was in Ireland,' said Will. 'It's nice to be back.'

'Didn't you ever visit my dad here?' asked Bey. 'I wish he'd mentioned you were buying the stones. I did think,' she added, 'that the diamonds were exceptionally good.'

'Thank you,' he said.

492

'Are you based full time in Germany now?'

'I divide my time between there and Scotland,' he told her. 'It suits me.'

Bey frowned at his reply, but he'd moved on to talking about his business. By the time the car pulled up outside the hotel, he'd turned to reminiscing about their time together at Van Aelten and Schaap, remembering the pink diamond set she'd created for the Contessa.

'It was gorgeous,' he said. 'Pretty and feminine without being too girlie. It was one of my favourites of all your designs. I so liked working with you,' he added. 'I really did.'

'I liked working with you too,' said Bey.

He looked at his watch and then at her.

'D'you have time for a drink?' he asked. 'For old times' sake.'

'I'm not really a believer in old times any more,' said Bey. 'In fact, tonight was all about moving on for me.'

'Please? We might not see each other again and I'd really like to . . . Well, you disappeared, Bey. One day you were there and the next you weren't, and it would be lovely to talk.'

She didn't need to talk to him. And yet she wanted to.

She opened the cab door and got out. The hem of her long blue dress skimmed the damp pavement as she followed him into the hotel and to the upstairs bar.

'We're closed, sir,' said one of the bar staff.

'I'm a resident,' said Will. 'Could you get me some coffee, please?'

'Of course,' said the staff member. He turned to Bey. 'Madam?'

'Coffee is good for me too,' she said.

As they settled into two of the comfortable armchairs, Bey's phone buzzed with a text message from Philip, asking where on earth she was and saying that the family was going back to Adele's house to celebrate among themselves a little later and that they'd love her to be there too.

She replied that she'd already left but that perhaps she could celebrate with them another time. She realised, with a sense of surprise, that she wanted to.

Tonight was a great success, Philip added. *We've sold the four statement necklaces. I can hardly believe it. Thank you so much.* He even included a beaming emoji at the end. Bey smiled at it and sent back her own hand-clapping emoji, after which she put her phone back in her bag.

'So,' she said, as a waiter arrived with a silver pot of coffee. 'What will we talk about?'

Will took his time pouring the coffee, then adding milk and an oblong of sugar to his own. He stirred it slowly before he spoke.

'I wanted to tell you that Callista and I are divorced.'

Bey set the cup she'd picked up back on its saucer. She said nothing for a moment. Eventually she looked at him.

'Since when?' She was finding it hard to sound casual when she'd just been shaken to the core.

'Last year.'

'Oh God,' she said. 'Was this because of . . . because of Cádiz?'

'Of course not,' said Will. 'Cádiz was a moment. My marriage was much more than that.'

'What happened?' she asked.

'Everything I say will sound like self-justification,' he

494

told her. 'But the truth was that I was dazzled by Cally when I first met. She was so vibrant and lovely and so . . . so unlike anyone else I'd ever known that I wanted her for myself. I didn't care that she was a city girl and loved the buzz and the socialising and everything to do with being out and about and seen in all the right places, while at heart . . . well, I do those things when I have to, but it's not who I am. I thought it could be me. I wanted it to be me. For her. Because I wanted to be the person she chose.'

'I always thought you were happy together,' said Bey.

'I wanted to be happy. I wanted her to be happy. That's what you're aiming for when you get married.'

'And it went wrong? After Cádiz?' Her voice trembled.

'It was going wrong before,' said Will. 'But I swear to you I had no intention of . . . That kiss shook me as much as it shook you, Bey, but it *was* only a kiss. It would never have been more than that, I promise you. Because of all the people I wanted to be, I very definitely didn't want to be the man who cheated on his wife.'

'I never wanted to be the woman who helped him cheat,' said Bey.

'I tried doubly hard after Cádiz,' said Will. 'But it wasn't enough, and we both knew it. Somehow things had changed. She was the one who said it first. She was always braver than me.'

'I'm really sorry,' said Bey.

'So am I,' said Will. 'Nobody gets married thinking it's not going to work out. You want it to, you really do. But sometimes you have to learn to admit you were wrong. I couldn't change enough for her and she couldn't change

495

enough for me. We tried to keep it amicable.' He made a face. 'But we move in completely different circles now.'

'Do you have children?'

'Thankfully no,' said Will. 'I would've felt an even worse failure if there'd been kids.'

'It's always a shame when things don't work out.' Bey picked up Lola's coat. 'But I hope you're doing well now.'

'You're going?'

'It's late. Tonight was a difficult night for me, and meeting you . . . having this conversation . . . There's only so much I can process in one go.' She pulled on the coat in one fluid movement. 'I hope . . . well . . . good luck, Will,' was all she could say.

She headed for the stairs, blinking tears from her eyes.

Tonight had been her triumph, her glorious success in the eyes of the Warren family. Tonight she'd been the Bey she'd always wanted to be. As she'd stood on the stage beside her grandmother, doing the right thing, she'd really and truly felt as though she'd left the past behind.

But the past wasn't only about the Warrens. It was about Will Murdoch too. Listening to him talk about the breakdown of his marriage had made her realise that she'd allowed herself to have feelings for him precisely because he wasn't available. Being in love with him had meant she didn't have to try with anybody else. That she didn't have to let anyone else in. That she wouldn't be hurt.

But she'd been hurt anyway. And no matter what Will said, Callista had been hurt too. Maybe it had nothing to do with Bey. Maybe their marriage would have failed anyway. But she hadn't helped.

She stepped outside the hotel and shivered. The snow had

started to fall in big lazy flakes that were getting faster and faster. There were no taxis at the stand, and when she tapped the app on her phone to hail one, it said that they were currently experiencing heavy demand and no cars were available.

'Dammit,' she muttered. 'Not again.'

The doorman told her that there was about a thirty-minute wait for cabs and that there were a number of guests ahead of her. She thought about walking to College Green to see if she could hail one directly, but when she said this out loud, he shook his head.

'Busy night,' he said. 'Lots of events on in the city. Better wait here. It's warmer, for a start.'

She sighed and sat on the bottom step of the staircase. She wouldn't have been able to walk anyhow; her feet were killing her in her high heels. She undid the buckles on the pretty blue sandals and wriggled her toes.

'Cinderella?'

It was Will again, standing on the stair behind her.

'Apparently there's heavy demand for coaches tonight,' she told him. 'But don't worry, I'm sure there'll be one soon.'

'They're not glass slippers, but you left these behind.' He held out Lola's gloves.

'Oh, thank you,' she said as she took them from him. 'They're my mum's. She'd be really mad at me if I lost them.'

A taxi pulled up outside the hotel. She looked at it hopefully, but the doorman shook his head and ushered a couple who'd been standing out of sight towards it.

'Still a few people ahead of you,' he told her.

'Are you sure you want to wait here on the stairs?' asked Will.

'If I leave, I'll never get a cab,' she said.

'How long?' He raised his voice to the doorman.

'Half an hour,' he replied. 'Maybe more. It's the Christmas rush, you see.'

'Bloody hell, it's only November,' objected Will.

'Earlier and earlier every year,' said the doorman. 'We start Christmas before Halloween these days.'

'Which I shouldn't complain about,' Bey said to Will. 'After all, I need people to buy my stuff.'

'Your own stuff or the Ice Dragon collection?' he asked.

'The Ice Dragon belongs to the Warrens,' she told him. 'There have always been two Beys. Haute Joaillerie Bey and Bijou Bey.'

'There aren't many people who can be both,' said Will.

'Versions of me.' She smiled. 'I was thinking about it earlier. But sometimes it's hard to know which the right one is.'

'In both versions, you're the most beautiful, wonderful girl in the world,' he told her. 'And I've thought that for a very long time.'

She stared at him.

'I always loved working with you,' he said. 'But after you'd left . . . I thought I missed your brilliance as a designer, but it was more than that. And I kept thinking that if Cally and I had truly been right for each other, I'd never for one second have thought of you as anything other than the most talented designer I'd ever worked with. All the same,' he added, 'you were gone. I tried to make my marriage work. I did my best.'

'Don't make excuses.'

'Cally's engaged to someone else. The guy she was going out with before me. After the divorce, I made a different life for myself. I felt I needed to atone somehow. We all have parts of ourselves that we're proud of and parts that we're not. We all do great things and make terrible mistakes. We want to get it right but we get it wrong.'

Bey thought of Adele and Richard, Lola and Philip. All making mistakes. All with triumphs and disasters in their lives. Just like her. And just like Will. Nobody got it right all the time, she realised. Most people just stumbled their way through life hoping for the best. Hoping to be rich and happy. Or happy at least.

'It's taken me a while to figure out my own mistakes,' said Will when she didn't speak. 'For a long time I moped over them. But you can't do that forever.'

'My grandmother – Eilis, not Adele – said something similar to me once,' said Bey. 'She was right.'

'So . . . where does that leave you?' he asked.

Another taxi pulled up. The doorman went in search of the guests who'd ordered it.

'Not feeling guilty about getting some things wrong,' she said. 'Happy that there's more than one side to my character. And not running away any more when things get tough.'

'And yet you're running away from me,' he said.

She shook her head. 'I'm not. I've made my peace with our . . . moment. I'm truly sorry if it might have triggered the beginning of the end of your marriage, but I'm not going to blame myself for it. Same as I'm not going to blame myself for . . . oh, so many things I've done and not done.'

'You really have changed,' he said. 'I'm happy for you, Bey.'

'Thank you.'

The doorman returned. He told Bey he couldn't find the

guests who'd ordered the taxi and it was hers if she wanted it.

'Great,' she said as she fastened her sandals again.

'I guess it's goodbye once more,' Will said. 'And good luck for the future, Bey. I don't think you'll need it, because the Ice Dragon is going to be a roaring success. It already is. Maybe you'll buy more stones from me one day.'

'Maybe.'

There was nothing else to say. She walked outside. The snow was settling now, and muffling the sound of the taxi's engine as it idled in front of the hotel. She opened the door and slid into the back seat. She was thinking about love and loss. Mistakes and atonement. About getting it wrong and getting it right. Wanting the things she couldn't have. And the things she could. She looked through the misty window of the cab. The doorman was rubbing his hands in the cold night air. The cab driver waited for her to give him directions.

She opened the door again.

Will was sitting halfway up the stairs when she walked back into the hotel.

'Forget something else?' He stood up.

'No,' she said. 'But I do need to find something out before I can properly make my peace with all the Beys I seem to be.'

'What?' he asked.

'How much of a mistake I made in Cádiz,' she said.

'How are you going to do that?' His eyes were fixed firmly on hers.

'How d'you think?'

She walked up the stairs and stopped on the step below him. He looked back at her, not blinking.

500

She put her hands on his shoulders.

And then she kissed him.

Behind them, the doorman cleared his throat.

'Are you taking that taxi, madam?' he asked.

She pulled away from Will. Her hands were still on his shoulders. As she turned towards the doorman, Will spoke.

'It's up to you,' he told her. 'It always was. It always will be.'

She smiled at the doorman. 'I think we're OK for the moment,' she said. 'In fact, maybe for a bit longer than that.'

Will pulled her closer.

'Really?' he asked.

'Yes,' she said.

Their lips met again.

And all the versions of herself finally, happily and gloriously clicked into place.

Acknowledgements

There are lots of stages in turning the germ of an idea in to a published book and I'm lucky that so many people had my back for this one.

A big thank you to my editor, Marion Donaldson, without whose long conversations and batches of editorial notes I certainly would have finished writing Lola and Bey's story a lot more quickly, but a lot less effectively.

Thanks also to Jane Selley whose thoughtful copyediting saved me from myself on more than one occasion.

Thank you to the entire team at Headline for their continued friendship, support and professional expertise. I'm proud to work with all of you.

Big thanks too, to everyone in the Hachette family around the world. It's good to know that my books are in your very capable hands.

Researching the world of jewellery was one of the nicest jobs I've ever had to do. It was made all the more rewarding thanks to the generous help of Madeline Hanlon and her staff at Boodles in Dublin, along with equally generous advice from Rebecca Hawkins, their talented head designer in Liverpool. I was also given a wealth of information on looking for the perfect gemstone from Jody Wainwright, the original Stone Man. Any mistakes I've made are, of course, entirely my own!

Advice and expertise on design and silversmithing were given to me by the fabulous Jill O'Malley in Dublin, who answered my stupid questions with a sunny smile and a large amount of patience.

As always my extended family are the best supporters I have, and a million thanks to them for being there no matter what. Special love to Colm who has to put up with me in my demented author mode, and Hugh who rescued me from demented author mode after I seemed to have lost the entire book and the backup when I accidentally hit 'New' on my laptop.

I've dedicated this book to my late and very wonderful agent Carole Blake, who died just before I got to finish it. Carole was a unique, generous person and the world is a duller place without her in it. A big thank you must go to all of the staff at Blake Friedmann who, in the middle of their own grief, were so lovely and supportive at a very difficult time.